Books by Jacquelyn Frank

JACOB * GIDEON * ELIJAH * DAMIEN * NOAH
ECSTASY * RAPTURE * PLEASURE
HUNTING JULIAN * STEALING KATHRYN
DRINK OF ME

Books by Kate Douglas

WOLF TALES * WOLF TALES II * WOLF TALES III
WOLF TALES IV * WOLF TALES V * WOLF TALES VI
WOLF TALES VII * WOLF TALES VIII
WOLF TALES 9 * WOLF TALES 10
DEMONFIRE * HELLFIRE

Books by Jess Haines

HUNTED BY THE OTHERS * TAKEN BY THE OTHERS

Books by Clare Willis

ONCE BITTEN * BITING THE BRIDE

Published by Kensington Publishing Corporation

NOCTURNAL

JACQUELYN FRANK
KATE DOUGLAS
JESS HAINES
CLARE WILLIS

ZEBRA BOOKS
KENSINGTON PUBLISHING CORP.
http://www.kensingtonbooks.com

ZEBRA BOOKS are published by

Kensington Publishing Corp.
119 West 40th Street
New York, NY 10018

All Kensington titles, imprints, and distributed lines are available at special quantity discounts for bulk purchases for sales
promotion, premiums, fund-raising, educational, or institutional
use.

Special book excerpts or customized printings can also be created to fit specific needs. For details, write or phone the office of
the Kensington Special Sales Manager: Attn. Special Sales Department. Kensington Publishing Corp., 119 West 40th Street,
New York, NY 10018. Phone: 1-800-221-2647.

Zebra and the Z logo Reg. U.S. Pat. & TM Off.

ISBN-13: 978-1-4201-0987-0
ISBN-10: 1-4201-0987-1

First Printing: September 2010
10 9 8 7 6 5 4 3 2 1

Printed in the United States of America

Contents

THE PHOENIX PROJECT

By Jacquelyn Frank

Chapter 1

Amara couldn't even count the places she ached in.

As usual.

She opened her eyes and for those two instants between waking and awareness, she hoped for the miracle of opening them to her gloriously dismal little room in the county workhouse. She never would have thought she would long for the days when she had worked hard labor just to have a dim little windowless cell to live in. The small gray mattress on the canvas and coiled struts had been big enough for only one person, and the cell itself had been long enough only to tightly fit the bed, and wide enough to fit a nightstand and a small dresser besides. The lights and digital readout clock alarm had been automatically shut off at sleep hour and had awakened her with a blare an hour before she was to report for her shift. It had been a tedious, cramped way to live, but it was better than the alternative of starving or being raped at night in the streets by local gangs because you had no safe roof over your head.

It was better than *this*.

She opened her eyes to the bright glare of overhead lights

and shock-white walls. It gave her an instant headache, all that brilliant brightness, and she groaned as she tried to blink her stinging eyes into adjustment.

As always, within seconds of her first opening her eyes, the door opened and Raul stepped into the room.

"Good morning," he greeted her with his usual efficiency and lack of sincerity as he went about his morning routine, which consisted of taking several tubes of blood from the permanent port imbedded in her arm. He checked other vital statistics pertaining to her body just as he always did, and she lay there stiffly acquiescent.

It wasn't as though Amara had much of a choice.

Not anymore.

"How do you feel, Amara?"

"Sore. Tired. Bitchy." She affected a sweet smile that was glaringly false. "And I have a headache."

Raul made his usual "hmm" of comprehension. He never pretended to give a damn, and it was obvious that he didn't. There was no use being nice to her, she supposed. From what she knew, she was one of many, many lab rats and it wouldn't pay to get too attached.

Especially when the so-called Phoenix Project had a rumored mortality rate of 90 percent.

"So tell me, Raul," she said conversationally, scooting herself up in bed and trying to avoid the tangle of leads they stuck in her hair, against her scalp, every night. Most of the women had shorn off their hair, keeping it peach-fuzz short or completely bald, the stickiness of the glue from the leads just making it easier to deal with, but Amara refused. They'd taken enough away; she wasn't going to let them have her long, platinum blond hair too. Besides, what else did she have to do all day? She could afford the time it took to wash and work free the adhesive. So what if her hair was thinner than it had been from being pulled out in the process? It was still long and it was still hers. "What's on the agenda for today? Drug testing? Narcos? I admit, I dig the narcos so long as they don't give me hallucinations. Those last ones were a bitch. Or are we gene splicing? Maybe . . . ooo, don't tell me! Radiation therapy? No? C'mon, not even a teensy clue?"

"Do you have your period?" Raul asked, ever efficient and bored, even in the face of the questions they both knew he would never answer.

"Nope. I might be PMSing, though. Bitchy, remember?"

"And all of your implants are comfortable?"

He meant had any broken through her skin. She was very delicate skinned, and her body liked to push out their implants at various intervals, spitting them out in defiance as if to say, *"Take that, fuckers!"*

Amara loved her body.

Knowing Raul would check for himself despite his courtesy of asking, she showed him both forearms and calves where she had been implanted with tracking and disciplinary devices. They promised to keep her confined to the grounds or kill her if she dared try to escape. They could inject a reservoir of tranquilizers on command if she got rowdy. They could give her a bitchin' case of heaving nausea for punishment if she copped an attitude and didn't comply with the medical personnel and their constant testing and assessments.

Luckily, they didn't count being a smart-ass as having an attitude. Otherwise, she'd have been puking for the entire three months she'd been there.

"Big day today."

Raul turned and left after that rare parting remark and she gaped after him.

Big day today? What the hell did that mean? A cold feeling of dread infused her every cell as she wrapped her arms around herself against the chill and hurried into the small cubicle shower off her room. It was the only amenity this place had over the workhouse. A private bathroom. But that was probably because it made it easier to control other bodily samples and monitoring of private behavior. She had figured out there were cameras in her room and bath pretty quickly. She might have to put on a show every time she went to the damn toilet, but at least she'd caught on before they'd caught her masturbating or something. Perverted jerks. What in hell did science need to know about that required them to watch a woman pee?

Big day today.

Ninety percent mortality rate.

She doubted it was going to be a good day.

Then again, it never was.

Chapter 2

"He's new," Mina said with an affected meow and growl as she leaned forward in her chair to peer with her usual obviousness at the man in question. He was dressed in the same heather gray sweats and T-shirt as everyone else, but even Amara had to admit he stood out from the others around him. But that was probably because he was at least a head taller than the others around him. "Wow. Look at the shoulders on him. No wonder they nabbed him. Talk about a physical specimen."

Okay, Amara grudgingly agreed, *she has a point there as well.* The guy was built like a brick institution. That would probably change, the boring days of playing cards in the sanitarium or the walks around the drab perimeter hardly made for an active lifestyle. The broad shoulders wouldn't stay so thickly muscled, and the tight six-pack abs would no doubt fade. It would be a shame to lose those thighs made like the trunks of two trees and the cut of his fine ass, though, because he was all kinds of juicy at the moment.

Amara indulged in a smile and watched as the dark-haired male turned again in the agitated circuit he was pacing in. The beauty of sweats, she mused, was that they clung very nicely to certain male body parts. She could definitely make out the hefty line of his cock beneath the snug fabric. Realizing where she was staring, Amara chuckled to herself and looked for neutral territory.

"He seems a bit tense," she noted to her companions as she took in his clenched jaw and fists. He looked like he would really like to punch someone.

"I bet I could relax him," Mina chuckled. "All that tension all knotted up inside him. I bet he'd come after just a few deep sucks."

"Mina!" Amara scolded. Still, she squirmed in her seat and laughed at her friend's blunt audacity, trying to quickly push away the imagery Mina's words drew up. "Don't you ever think about anything but sex and blow jobs?"

"Oh, please, like you aren't thinking about sex and blow jobs just looking at him? You know you are. He's oozing testosterone. He's out in the common room, so he's been here long enough to have learned the score, obviously, but he's not happy about it and is fresh enough from the outside that he hasn't grown apathetic yet. He's full of piss and vinegar. Look at him. He's prowling that corner of the room like a caged jaguar." Mina smiled. "He's all male animal."

"For now. He'll be like the rest of them soon enough." Amara sighed, nibbling her lip nervously as her attention left the new male and returned to Raul. *Big day today.* Why? God, what did they have planned this time? Which of them would never come back? Mina, Rachael, and Devona were the closest things she had to friends, despite her efforts not to get attached to anyone else around her. She had made fast friends in fear early on when they all had been new and in the dark, but when Julie had dropped suddenly dead right at her feet from the new drug they were testing on her, she had realized she would never survive if she continued to give parts of herself away to anyone else. Despite those intentions, the three tough women who had survived just as long as she had had begun as a coffee clatch, progressed to a breakfast clatch, and now they pretty much spent the entire day clutched together.

It had been necessary to gain friends, actually. There was no social or mental discrimination in the common population the experimenters had gathered together, so there were quite a few sickos, psychos, and weirdos. Despite all of the cameras watching just about everywhere, staff wasn't in all that much of a hurry to intervene when one of their lab rats was being accosted or, sometimes, raped. They often let the men work themselves up in acts of aggression and observed. Amara thought it was a cross between morbid fascination and the results of some sick drug testing. She had come to that conclusion after watching Spencer Holbrook, the sweetest, shyest guy on the planet, go totally ape-shit savage on some poor girl right on the recreation room floor. He'd torn into her like a rutting animal and he literally screwed himself to death. He'd had a heart attack or stroke or something after his sixth orgasm in about six minutes' time.

Then the security staff had strolled in on the scene and cleaned it all up, bodies and victims never to be seen or heard from again. Amara didn't know what was worse—that it had happened like that, or that six minutes had gone by without a single one of them moving to help any more than security had. But after three months of something awful happening every single day, all the fury and indignation and fight was dying in them as fear for when it was their turn to snap or die stole over them.

Amara had considered warning her friends of what Raul had said, but she never knew what was a psychological tactic and what wasn't. *She* might have to stress out over it, but she wasn't going to force her friends into the same thing. Whatever was going to happen was going to happen whether they knew about it or not. Avoiding the drink or food was a waste of time because they would just find another way if your time was up. In the end, they were just one big animal supply to the labs in the compound. Like rabbits, monkeys, and rats, they were kept in a clean, sterile environment until an order came up for their specifications. Then they would be tested, injected, and either released back into the captive populace . . . or they were never heard from again.

Amara had a feeling her specifications had just come up.

Sure enough, she'd just put down her empty cup of coffee when Raul and two beefy orderlies came up to stand behind her meaningfully. Mina's eyes narrowed angrily, her hands fisting furiously on the table. There was nothing she could have done, and Amara was glad when the women didn't start any trouble. She didn't want them to suffer over her. They would suffer for themselves soon enough, given the current trends.

She stood up and obediently walked between the orderlies as Raul led the way. She noticed a scuffle of temper when the new male was also chosen and led from the common room. The man was pushed roughly forward, his orderlies readily armed with the remotes that activated his internal disciplinary measures. She couldn't help but look down at his forearms to see just how old the surgical scarring appeared to be. His incisions were almost completely invisible, which told her he had been putting up a long, long fight against his captivity. Amara was glad he had finally acquiesced, however unhappy it made him, because she knew they would have killed him and written off the expense eventually.

He was pushed again, the orderlies clearly getting off on having the upper hand over someone of his obvious strength and build. Some of them were like that. Some were nice. Most were just Raul.

The shove sent that wall of muscle slamming awkwardly

into Amara. She stumbled and hit the heavily waxed floor with a face-planting sprawl. Before she could even feel the stinging of her skinned knees, elbows and the bruise on her chin, however, large hands were sliding around her body, gingerly turning her over into strong arms and the amazing warmth of intense body heat. She hadn't been so warm since she'd been kidnapped from her bed at the workhouse and dragged into this icebox environment that discouraged the growth of any germs.

"Are you all right? I'm sorry, the Asshole Twins here knocked me right into you."

Amara looked up into sea-green eyes full of honest concern and she had a ridiculous urge to cry. It would be so very sad the day those eyes stopped giving a damn just like everyone else's had. They were so very pretty when they were being kind. He even smiled a little, making them warm softly for her, and he reached to pull away some of the long tendrils of hair that had wrapped over her face.

"You've kept your hair," he remarked, almost as if he hadn't meant to say it aloud. "It's nice to see a pretty woman with long hair. Been awhile."

"Thank you," she said softly, not knowing what else to say. "It falls out a lot."

His smile faded and he gave her a jerky little nod. Then they both felt the prodding feet of the orderlies against them.

"Are you okay? Think you can stand?" he asked.

"Sure," she agreed.

In a single surge of confident movement, they were both back on their feet. He held her in the circle of his arms, close enough that her nipples brushed his chest through the cotton of their matching T-shirts. Since she had never been allotted any underwear, just like everyone else, it felt strangely exposing. Probably because she hadn't been touched by someone who wasn't medically examining her in a long time. As sea-green eyes wandered slowly down her length, she was quite sure there was nothing scientific about his examination.

"Move it!" the orderlies barked at them.

They moved. Some were known to be trigger happy, and neither of them felt like puking their guts up for the next three days or riding an electrical current of punishment. Amara felt his arm fall around her waist.

"Hope you don't mind," he said softly. "Figure maybe I'll spare myself a few shoves if you're close by. They are starting to piss me off and I'm two seconds away from buying myself a puke festival. Be worth it to crack a couple of jaws, though."

"Be careful," she whispered back to him. "They won't hesitate to kill you if you're too much trouble."

"Yeah," he grimaced. "I figured that out. So, I'll just be occasional trouble." He gave her a flashing grin at that. The lines of his slightly longer than military haircut and the strength of his rugged jaw and cheeks made him seem tough, but that disarming smile that reached deep into his jade eyes made him seem almost as mischievous and guileless as a boy. "So where'd they get you from?"

Amara frowned, not wanting to exchange captivity stories, but as they were herded down the imposing white corridor, she needed anything to calm her racing nerves.

"The Reeceville Workhouse. They took a bunch of us in our sleep. You?"

"I'm a cop. A Federated States cop. Something tells me I got a little too close to this operation," he said drolly. He grimaced as he looked at her. "I am sorry."

"For?" she asked in surprise.

"For not doing my job right. All I can do is hope my coworkers can figure out what I was doing when I disappeared. I was working alone and got in too far too fast. Before I could make the right reports, I got made. I guess I should be glad I'm not dead."

"I wouldn't be too sure about that," Amara whispered sadly.

She felt his grip around her waist tighten in what she could only deem as a brief hug of comfort. He was a total stranger, and she had no reason to trust a thing he said or did, but the gesture of kindness was difficult to resist in such a vacuum of feeling humanity. She rubbed at one of her skinned elbows as she snuggled up to his warmth some more.

"You're cold," he noted with a frown.

"Always. I'm used to it." She shrugged.

"Well, I tend to generate a lot of heat, so anytime you need warming up, you can come by me."

She shot him a look, and he instantly groaned as he realized how that had sounded. She couldn't help but laugh at his woebegone expression.

"I meant . . ." he said quickly.

"I know what you meant. And thanks. It's a kind offer."

"What's your name?"

"Amara," she said softly. When she saw the lab doors looming before them, she couldn't help but lean against the strength and protectiveness of the male who held her. "Yours?" She tried not to sound as panicked as she was becoming, and she knew she failed miserably.

"Nick. Nick Gregory."

"Nick," she repeated. She stopped long enough to look up into his eyes directly, her hand reaching to cover the one at her waist. "Nick," she said with gentle sincerity, "I'm sorry I ever met you."

Nick understood what she meant instantly.

"Yeah," he agreed as he glanced at the lab doors when they opened with a pneumatic hiss. "I'm sorry I met you, too, Amara."

Chapter 3

Nick woke up as if he were dredging himself out of a mire of crude oil and molasses. It was almost impossible to move, or even to breathe. His every muscle hurt as though he'd overdone his circuit training six times, and everything screamed angrily inside of him when he tried to move.

The last thing he remembered was a pretty little blonde with copper-penny eyes and a lost expression etched behind them. It was clear she had given up all hope, but she had still felt fear and resistance those last instants before they had been torn apart and dragged in to be strapped down onto waiting tables. For the millionth time, Nick cursed himself for being an irresponsible idiot. He should have been more careful. He should have reported in. His manager was always bitching at him for his "cowboy" cop work, warning him it would bite him in his ass one day. Well, one day was here. Now. And it hurt like a fucking implosion.

Nick tried to open his eyes, feeling ten tons of grit scraping under his lids. He had a savage case of cotton mouth, too. He wondered what they'd done to him. Since he felt like he'd gone a few nasty rounds with the Jinko world champion, it hadn't been anything fun. Bad enough he'd been bound down and helpless when one of the Asshole Twins had purposely baited him by copping a feel of Amara's breast. It had all but killed him when she'd simply turned her head aside, bit her lip, and closed her eyes as if she could send herself away from her situation just by the will of her mind.

It was just one other thing that he could add to his tally of screwups. He should have known not to show any favoritism to her. Not while they were still in the process of teaching him exactly who was in charge. He'd fought them like crazy from the outset, causing mayhem and tearing furrows of havoc for about a month before they'd delivered their ultimatum: Comply or die.

Realizing more than his own life would be at stake if he let them kill him without examining all possibilities of escape, he had complied. Nick was beginning to wonder if that had been such a good idea.

The department shrink said he had a "hero complex" and that it was going to get him killed one day, or worse.

This was definitely bordering on worse.

His eyes opened the tiniest fraction, and he closed them instantly. Damn. This place was so white it hurt. Everything was white. Monitors, computers, bottles, and tubes. All of it. The only things not in white were the little lab rats in heather gray tees and sweats running around like whipped dogs.

Except for Amara. She had kept her long blond hair, and whether she knew it or not, it was an act of sheer defiance. He had instantly liked that about her. Of course, in the "not dead yet" category, he'd thought she also had a killer body. He wondered if he could still be considered a "hero" if he had spent a good amount of time thinking the damsel in distress had nice tits. Really nice tits.

Then he remembered he hadn't been the only one to notice and a rush of fury balked through him. Oh, he was going to get that miserable fucker who'd touched her if it was the last damn thing he ever did.

Nothing "complex" about that.

Well, best to get on with this mess, he thought wryly. He was starting to get hungry, to add to a roaring case of thirst, and the sooner he dealt with the business of getting to his feet, the more likely it would be that they'd feed him. Nick opened his eyes and bore the glaring shock of white as it pounded into his head. He realized immediately that he was back in his room, dumped in his bed facedown and totally naked.

"Ah, shit."

He hated waking up naked without knowing how he'd gotten that way or what'd happened since then. It made him paranoid. Especially when he hurt so bad he couldn't figure out what kind of damage had been done and where. He felt like they'd taken him out and beaten him with clubs. He rolled over and tried to see if any bruises accompanied the way he felt. That was when he heard the locks on his door snap open. It slid free with a hiss and then, with a shout, the pretty little blonde Amara was shoved into his room and the door was locked after her.

"Shit!" Nick jolted upright, reaching for his blanket to cover up, but then realized Amara was just as stripped as he was. "You fucking prick bastards!" he shouted out to the powers-that-be he knew watched everything he did.

They did.

Despite the agony he was in, Nick forced himself to his feet and reached to wrap the shivering girl in the blanket. She flinched away at first, until she realized he was helping her cover up. Then she was clutching at the thin excuse for a blanket like she would a life preserver after being dumped in rough seas.

"Did they hurt you?" he asked gently, momentarily ignoring her efforts at resisting and pulling her close after the blanket was snug around her. He immediately began to rub warmth into her, hoping he could at least ease the chattering of her teeth.

"I don't know. I just woke up and they grabbed me and threw me in here," she said in a shivery voice. "I'm sorry."

"For what? You didn't do anything."

"But I will. Or you will. Why else would they force us into the same room like this? They are expecting something to happen. They are going to watch while something happens."

"Something? Like what kind of something?" he demanded, not liking the things that began to filter into his guessing mind.

"Maybe you'll rape me," she whispered.

"The hell I will!" he exploded.

"You won't be able to help it. They do that. They give drugs that do that. I've seen it. God, I am so scared."

She was. He realized the chill of the room was nothing compared to the way she was shaking in terror. Frankly, if he was her and had been locked up with a man of his size and strength thinking what she was thinking was going to happen, he'd have probably pissed himself in fear.

"Hey. Listen to me. If I start getting nasty or anything, you just feel free to bash me in the balls as hard as you can, okay? Consider it a personal favor to me. I would hate myself if I did anything to hurt you." He drew her over to the bed and sat down with her. He grabbed his pillow and dragged it over his lap. It was the only other cover left in the room, and a quick glance had shown him that the towels in the small bath had been removed. It made him sick to his stomach to think of what it was they must have planned for by throwing them together like this, purposely eliminating all sources of cover except for the single blanket. "How are you feeling?"

"Like death chilled over," she sniffed. "And I can't get warm."

Nick immediately moved as close as he could, insanely grateful for his hyper body heat for a change. Apparently he processed energy really well. She could benefit from that. Despite her curves, she was pretty small. Generous breasts, nice round hips, and a killer ass didn't serve as a large enough percentage of overall body fat. It might attract the hell out of a man like him, but it wouldn't keep her warm in these conditions.

He drew her in tight, and after a moment she threw caution to the wind and snuggled up hard against him. She leaned in to burrow a cold nose against his neck, and after a moment he heard her sniff. It was different than the upset, chilly sniffling she had done. It was slow and soft, accompanied with a little rub of her nose.

"You smell nice," she said, actually seeming surprised. It surprised him, too. Usually these tests not only made him feel like hell, but he would smell like it as well. Truth be told, she smelled kind of nice herself. He couldn't place it as a particular fragrance, but maybe it was her shampoo. Whatever it was, it was rather delicious. He turned his nose into her hair so he could breathe deeply of the aroma.

"So do you. Are you warming up?" he asked.

"Actually, I think I am," she said, rubbing up even closer to him, if that was even possible. Now, not only did she smell good, but he was realizing just how good she felt as well. The abrupt understanding that he was feeling *aroused* just by the nearness of her made him suddenly jerk away from her. He abandoned her to slide the length of the bed away from her, his fist clutching the pillow tightly against his stirring cock as it began to harden with its interest.

"Shit," he hissed, running his free hand through his hair as he looked wildly around the tiny room for some way to put more distance between them.

"What's wrong?" she asked, those coppery eyes studying his agitation curiously as her grip on the blanket became negligent, allowing it to slide off one of her pale shoulders.

"Nothing," he lied quickly. "Just trying to think what I can put on."

"I know. They only give you one set of clean clothes every morning. Once you lose them, that's it until the next day. God, I'm so thirsty right now. And I'm getting really hungry." She stood up and paced the confined space a little. Every time she came close to him, Nick was overwhelmed with the scent of her and how amazingly sexy he found it to be. It was almost like the lusty smell of sex, only far sweeter and even more alluring, if such a thing were actually possible. His heart began to beat a rapid and worried tattoo. Lately, he hadn't noticed anything but the aroma of the institutional shampoo they were given; the astringent stuff smelling slightly like coconuts. But this wasn't anything like that.

Amara went into the small cubed bathroom and he heard the water running. She made hungry little slurping sounds as she drank water from her hands and, in an instant, Nick was hard as rock.

Fuck. He was in trouble. They both were. He knew himself well enough to know when something was normal for him and when it wasn't, and Nick Gregory, the man with the hero complex, would never get off on a situation as fucked up as this one was.

Was it some kind of aphrodisiacal drug? Had they given them something designed to make them easily aroused? It sure as hell felt that way, Nick acknowledged grimly as he felt the awesome straining of his cock. Regardless, he told himself firmly, so long as he kept control over his mind, he would keep Amara perfectly safe from himself. There was no way he would voluntarily push himself on a woman so long as the moral centers of his brain weren't chemically screwed with.

He just had to pray he stayed in control of his mind.

At the moment, though, the idea of a drink of water was very appealing. His mouth felt glued together and he was very thirsty. He got up cautiously and peered into the bath. He froze in place when he was presented with the complete rear nude of Amara's shape, the blanket pooled in neglect on the floor as she used both hands to shovel water into her mouth. Bent at the waist as she was, he was given a fine view of those lush hips and the sleek crease of her buttocks that led to the unbelievable sight of her pussy and the brush of golden hairs that guarded it. The ultimate tease, Nick could see the tiniest hints of pure pink and all she would have to do is step out to the side in order to give him a full-spectrum view.

And he could smell her again. She was steps away in the cramped room and he could smell the sugary, sultry allure of her. . . . What was more, he could swear he was catching the deeper, sharper tang of womanly arousal.

Nick moved forward and reached down to retrieve her blanket, meaning to cover her back up. The mistake was in bringing himself so close to her that his cheek brushed her ass and the incredible smell of her sex rocked his senses back hard.

"Hard" was the key word. He'd never been so hard. He was so agonizingly aroused that he could feel his own pulse working its way down his shaft with every heartbeat.

Amara felt him make contact with her, and she turned around as he straightened up, giving him a slow tour of her lovely thighs, golden bush, and coral pink nipples at the tips of her outstanding breasts. Her nipples were rigid little points, probably from the cold, but they stuck out at him like tempting little tongues of impertinence.

"Cover up," he croaked as he shoved the blanket at her. "Go inside and sit and don't come in here."

Amara looked at him, her appraisal a cross between sly

and perplexed. Part of his instincts cried out to him that she was luring him, tempting him on purpose and matching his state of arousal perfectly, but he also knew he couldn't trust any of his instincts any longer.

He couldn't trust anything in this hell he found himself in.

Amara took her blanket back and, without wrapping up in it, she turned and did exactly as he had asked. As soon as she was gone, he began to think he could breathe just a little easier. He dropped his ridiculous pillow and checked to see if he was ten times his usual size or if it just felt that way.

"Holy hell."

Not ten times, but not normal either. *What the hell . . . ?* Nick hefted himself in his hand, his heart racing. He had to admit, on the whole he was a good-sized man, but not like *this*. And while in joking conversation or in fantasy it was nice to imagine what it would be like to have a super-sized cock, it was godawfully unnerving when it actually happened right before your eyes. As a rule, men didn't like for anything weird to happen to their penis—good, bad, or otherwise.

"Great. They got me testing out some kind of enhancement drug."

Fine. He could play this game. All he needed was a little lotion or soap and he'd take care of this straight away. Taking the edge off would make Amara safer just in case there were any other surprises in store. Of course, he had a pretty decent recovery rate, but he'd worry about that when the time came. Maybe he could figure out a way to stuff up his nose so he couldn't smell that delightful smell of hers.

"Nick."

Nick jumped in his own skin, a combination of feeling highly strung and more than a little guilty for not having better control of himself. Getting caught with his hand on his dick wasn't his idea of heroic or even gentlemanly behavior.

"Damn it, Amara, I asked you to stay inside," he snapped at her, his nerves starting to run a little raw as he braced himself against the white porcelain sink.

"I can't."

Can't?

Nick looked over his shoulder at her and instantly regretted it.

Sort of.

Something was happening to her, too. He could see it in the glow of her skin, where she looked like some kind of angel in iridescent perfection. Her hair gleamed in gold and white coils that were almost blinding. But what he really saw was the way she held her body as she leaned back against the wall, her incredible figure shifting restlessly as she ran desperate hands over her smooth, bare skin as if she couldn't help herself.

"Oh, God," Nick groaned as he tore his eyes off of her and tried to force himself not to sniff after her as if she were some kind of bitch in heat. He wasn't going to do this. He wasn't going to let them do this to him. They'd taken away his freedom, his rights to his own body, and every other damn thing that was important to him, but he wouldn't let them make a rapist out of him. She might seem willing and even eager, but he knew damn well that it was an effect of a drug of some kind, and when she came down from it, she was going to feel violated. Plain and simple.

"Nick."

Nick stiffened when he felt her warm breath speaking against his back. Then he felt the heat of her body, the radiant temperature of it increasing in leaps and bounds. With that came the wild smell of a woman's sensually aroused scent. He may as well have his face buried between her legs.

"Goddamn it, Amara! Go inside!"

"I can't. Nick, I'm so hungry." Her hands touched against his sides and then slid around him. Her fingers drew across his chest, up over his nipples briefly enough to torture him, and then began to slide down over his belly. He felt her breasts against his back, the nipples prodding him tauntingly as she rubbed the rest of herself against him wherever she could reach.

"Hungry?" he asked hoarsely.

"For you, Nick. For you."

Nick was in numb shock, his heart thundering hard as she pushed his hands out of her way and wrapped her fingers around his monstrously over-developed erection. He felt the embrace all the way to his toes, and he jumped in savage pulses between her fingers. His head tipped back as he groaned out from the depths of his soul. Nick knew what she meant by hunger. He ached with appetite. Not only in his empty belly, but everywhere else, too. Even his teeth ached as he thought about all that creamy soft skin he'd seen and how good she promised to taste. As she caressed him rhythmically along his shaft, exploring his amazing girth and length so very thoroughly, he began to ooze pre-cum down over her fingers. The slick wetness made for torturous improvements to the fit and feel of her stroke, and it was all completely out of his control from that moment on.

Nick turned around to face her, reaching for her face with both hands and cradling her tightly between them as he swooped to seize her mouth in a kiss. He barely tasted her lips before he was probing for the taste of her tongue. Nick knew he could be as aggressive as the next guy, maybe more than average when he got familiar with a certain kind of lady, but it wasn't at all like him to ravage a woman, a total stranger, with blunt need like he was doing just then. His fingers were clutching her scalp and hair, holding her fast so he could devour her deliciousness and heat. Like the addictive rave of a perfect gastronomical experience, she tasted amazingly appetizing. Better yet, she moaned into his mouth and met him just as eagerly in response.

A part of Nick wanted to howl in frustration, to cry out how sorry he was for what he was going to do, but as her hands came back to their stroking discovery, he lost even that last little bit of regret as animal need rode over him hard.

"Oh, God, that feels amazing," he ground out against her lips as he bit and gnawed at her mouth. His hands raced from her hair down to her lush breasts in all of an instant. "I need to fuck," he groaned as he palmed her and plucked at her nipples. His hips surged mindlessly into her grip as every fiber of his being agreed with that directive. He needed to fuck.

"Me, too," she said breathlessly. "I need that too."

"Yeah? Say it. Say it to me, Amara," he demanded roughly as he began to back her into the next room. He was going to need room for this. A lot of room. And a lot of time. He had never been so famished for a woman, and his entire body was on fire with the need of her. He shoved her down onto the bed, watching her bounce and shimmy in fabulous places from the perspective of standing over her. Now that she was sitting on the edge of his bed, it put her mouth level with his cock, and she surely knew it. She was on him like a babe to a mother's breast in a heartbeat, her mouth sliding wetly around the bulging head and sucking him in like a lollipop. She let him go just as abruptly, and his legs actually began to tremble as she licked and flicked her tongue against him.

"I need to fuck," she told him quite obediently, reminding him he'd made the request of her. "I want to fuck you. And suck you." She was back around him, teeth scraping dangerously over screamingly sensitive skin. She slid her mouth and hand down and around his rock-hard flesh, her sly little tongue flickering around him and scooping up every drop of pre-cum he oozed. She began to show an almost ferocious appetite for the taste of him, her enthusiasm for sucking him too much to bear with any sanity. Nick's hands were in her hair, his thumbs stroking her cheeks as they drew concave with her powerful, drawing efforts. Watching himself slide deeper and deeper into her mouth made his balls burn with the need to come. He wanted so badly to flood her mouth with his essence, needed to see her gulp him down.

No. No. He needed something else. Something more powerful. Something wild. He didn't know what it was, not all of it, but he wouldn't get it like this.

"Enough!" Nick roared out the command as he gripped hold of her working head and forced himself to pull free of her sweetly torturous lips. Then, his brain seared with need, he threw her back on the bed, turned her over, and hauled her up onto her knees until her curvy ass was held between his hands and was drawn back against him. Nick made low, grunting sounds of satisfaction as he came into contact with the slick valley of her pussy. Her labial lips rubbed wetly against his shaft, her juices spreading up over him as he fumbled to aim the tip of his swollen cock into the opening of the passage he so craved.

Nick was so eager, so in need, that he couldn't see straight or even think coherently. *It will get better once we're connected,* he tried to tell himself. *Just need to connect.* He certainly wasn't thinking of whether she was prepared well enough to take him, or that he'd barely done anything for her in the way of foreplay. He didn't even consider how the monstrosity of a cock he was wielding might need something in the way of a careful introduction.

Instead, the instant he felt himself notch into place on her, he began to shove and thrust for entrance. Nick ground his teeth together as her body resisted his efforts, although the woman herself was another story.

"Please! Please," she begged him as she worked herself back against him. Her desperation to have him may have been part of the problem, but Nick wasn't thinking like a rational man who could use logic to problem-solve any more than she was behaving as a rational woman. She began to keen in frustration, and her eager body started to drown his probing cock head with viscous drippings of need. Her scent was raw musk and primal need, and he lost all patience with a howl.

All remaining gentility or consideration was shoved to the wayside as he rammed himself into her. Finally his bulbous tip popped past that ring of resistance that had thwarted him. She cried out and he took it as encouragement, whether it was or not. He pushed and thrust until he began to sink into her inches at a time. The instant he slammed himself balls deep inside of her, Nick growled with satisfaction and dug fierce fingers into her hips to hold her right where he wanted her. The hunger inside of him suddenly spiked in powerful ways, his empty belly crying with cravings even as his cock throbbed for a wild fucking. His teeth hurt like a bitch, his whole jaw aching so terribly it snapped across his eardrums. And then he could feel the awkward realignment and pain of shifting teeth, as if his mouth were reshaping itself right in that very instant.

When upper fangs, needle sharp and a good half inch in length, descended to meet the matching lower ones, he was growling and snarling like the beast he had become. If anything else about himself had changed, he took no note of it. All he knew was the need to fuck . . .

. . . and the need to feed.

He started with wild, rutting surges into his bitch's body, her muscular heat like a glove around him; so tight and so right. The pleasure of it was, of course, amazing, but he wasn't out for that alone. What he wanted was to mate. He wanted to fuck her and fill her with his seed. He wanted to force his get onto her, make his bitch the mother of his progeny. He would own her after this. Forever. One lifetime, one true mate. Just the understanding of it made him burn with the need to pour his come and scent into her. His thighs and balls were on fire as his thrusts grew wild and harsh, each deep slam into her lifting her knees from the bed. He felt as though he were swelling inside of her and it was making it harder and harder to plow through her even though she was so very slick. His jaw ached, his hunger burning, his cock near to bursting. Nick never realized he was clawing into her, his nails curved down now into wicked, sharp talons that pierced and scraped her delicate skin.

But he did smell the blood.

Fresh-spilled blood, sticky between his fingers and then on his tongue as he shoved his fingers into his mouth. Sharply sweet and tangy like the sourness of metal, the taste of it sent him over the edge. With a primal shout he began to come in burning jolts, his hips slamming hard in time to the bursts of ejaculate into her channel.

Deep! Deep inside! Yes. Oh, God, he could smell the mix of their scents already, his mark on her now. His. She was his. His bitch. His mate. His woman. Nick continued to come, the force of it staggering even as his balls strained to load even more into her. She dripped with him, her thighs running wet with his seed.

Yes. Oh, yes.

She was his now.

Chapter 4

Amara mewled and snarled into the bedding as Nick came in hard, jerking thrusts. She was aching with the need to come, so close yet somehow completely locked away from it. Her talons shredded the mattress unthinkingly, and her fangs gnashed together ineffectively. The only satisfaction she had was in accepting the mark of this potent male. Regardless of being locked in with him alone or locked in a whole room of them, this was the male she would have wanted. He was the most powerful; the most potent. He was what she needed. Her match. Her mate.

Amara heard him grunting as the spasms of his orgasm subsided. But she knew, and maybe he did as well, that he hadn't done what he had needed to do. That was evidenced by how hard he remained inside of her. She was glad he had come, though, because it made her so slick even as the scent of it pervaded her every cell. She didn't mind the mark at all, because she would do the same in return. He was now hers, and woe to any bitch who thought to approach him.

She could feel him fucking her relentlessly, realizing he had somehow forgotten something so his release had no true satisfaction to it. She had no more of an idea than he did as to what it was they both needed, but neither would stop until they figured it out. Amara suspected, though, it had something to do with the aching, empty feel of her belly. The hollow starvation screaming for fulfillment. Just as her body screamed for fulfillment.

Pushing away from their connection, bearing his resistant, clawing attempt to hold her into his dominant positioning, Amara turned over on the bed and faced the beast who was her lover head on. The moment she saw his descended fangs, the gleam sharp and primitive, her body's response was just as primal. Nick seemed to feel a similar reaction when he saw her toothy grin, and he fell on her eagerly. Tongues and teeth clashed in biting kisses, both of their lips paying the price in blood. Their tangy flavors combined and they both moaned and moved in restless need.

"Give me your cock again," she begged him, her sharp nails clawing down his back until he howled in the pleasurable agony of it. He shoved into her in a single, gliding thrust and she immediately felt the difference. Oh, he was as brutish and big as before, despite his having come so recently, but what was different was the way she felt in reaction to his invasion. With the tartness of their blood on her tongue, she suddenly felt like she could burst in just a few strokes. To that effect, she dug her nails into his buttocks in encouragement. The pain made him surge deep, and then retaliation for that pain made him brutal. He banged into her in hard, wicked thrusts, the sound of wet, slapping flesh filling the small room as he drilled deep with grinding surges of his hips.

Amara felt it all, and her body coiled in pleasure. So close! She was coming so close! But it seemed the closer she came to the crest of pleasure, the more cruel her distracting starvation became. Crying out in frustration, she dragged her male down to her breasts in hopes he could do something to help her. The lave of his flat tongue scraping across her sensitive nipples was a damn good start. Then he was biting at them, chewing on the points in voracious little nibbles and she felt her vagina drench him in a flash flood of hot juices in response. Her whole body burned with need and she keened for release. Then, without knowing why, she sank a hand into his hair and jerked him up to her so she could burrow her face into his neck right where it met his shoulder. She sniffed him, could smell the testosterone pumping thickly through him on its adrenaline piggyback ride. She wanted to just taste him. To take a bite. The craving of it was overwhelming.

Amara's fangs sank deep into his thick neck.

Several things happened all at once. His blood burst onto her palate, and it was by far the most erotically delicious flavor her tongue had ever encountered. He was full of so many male hormones, to match the irresistible reek of his pheromones which had made it impossible to stay away from him despite his requests, earlier. Her mouth filled and she swallowed him down. Finally the agony in her belly eased.

And instantly, her body released.

Amara came, her orgasm hitting her so hard and so fast that her head whipped back in such a violent way that she tore through the flesh of her lover's neck. Heedless of the blood pouring from his wound, she writhed as wild spasms of pleasure shook and rode through her like an electrical current. She was squeezing the rigid flesh inside her body, her back arching up hard as her bloodstained breasts thrust up at him.

When he suddenly sank his teeth into her breast, his fangs piercing deeply above and below her nipple, she came again. She cried out, her vagina wrenching around him as he, too, began to climax once more. He suckled at her greedily, and she felt her blood pouring into his throat with each hungry draw. He humped hard into her, their pelvises smashing together as he spent himself to the utmost.

They collapsed together on the bed, a panting tangle of sweaty limbs covered in sticky blood and come. Amara sniffed at the aroma of freshly flowing blood and turned to lick and suck at the damage she'd done to his neck. She licked the area clean and slowly continued to do so until the bleeding eased and finally stopped altogether. She realized it soothed him, what she was doing, because he kind of purred in approval, and then thought to imitate her kindness against her bitten breast. Tingles of blissfulness radiated out from the swipes of his rough tongue, and need rekindled when he found himself constantly attracted by the thrust of her nipple. He sucked at her again and again, and she sighed and moaned in encouragement. When she stopped bleeding from where he had fed from her, he switched to the other side.

Amara took note that his fangs had retracted quite a bit, and so had her own. Her famished belly was not so keen any longer, but neither was she fully sated. Certainly not as sated as her male clearly was. All of his desperation and dominance had subsided into lazy contentment. He had, she realized, taken far more from her than she had taken from him.

Taken blood.

Reality suddenly rushed in on Amara with horrifying coldness and she shoved hard against the man lying heavily on top of her, his penis still half hard and deep inside of her. He rose up at her urging, his hands braced by her shoulders, and the minute he saw the look on her face, the chill of knowing rode over him just as fast and hard. His sea-green eyes widened as they raked down over their naked, blood-stained bodies.

Nick surged off of her and the bed in a single violent movement, hurtling himself away until his back hit the opposite wall of the small cell.

"Oh, my God," he rasped. "What—What have I done? What did they do to us?"

Amara sat up and together they looked at the evidence before them. Her nails had grown long and curved, as sharply pointed as a cat's with a visible quick under the opaque white. Yet, even as she watched with her heart racing, they began to retract and re-form until they eventually became a set of beautifully long, feminine nails that were armor hard and brightly healthy. She had always had such weak, flimsy nails that the difference made quite an impact on her. Nick was watching the same thing happen for himself. His talons had been thicker, a little bit darker, and visibly stronger than her own. When they fully retracted, though, they were a tiny bit long for a man, but not as hers were.

Almost simultaneously, they both reached to touch their protruding teeth. All the rest were quite normal, just as squared off and blunt as always, perfect for gripping and holding prey while the newer teeth did the job of puncturing. Again, even as they examined themselves, the changed attribute began to withdraw from their ready positions, making Amara's jaw ache as everything seemed to shift. The fangs, she realized, were not a part of the front row of natural teeth, but were instead extraneous to them, set flush in front of them. They were also at a distance of about an inch apart from one another. Once they were fully retracted, they were no more than white pointed nubs hidden beneath her lips even when she smiled her widest.

Amara watched as Nick looked down at his resting cock, examining himself a little tentatively. She recalled how enormous he had been and realized why he was curious. Even without being erect, he was still of impressive size, but she had no idea if this was normal for him or not. Her slightly sore vaginal walls were ready to guess *not*.

"Fuck," Nick hissed. "I never lacked for size, but this is ridiculous."

Well, Amara thought, *that answers that question.* What was strange, however, was that she took note of each physical difference almost clinically. She saw the benefits to having stronger nails, teeth that could tear, and a lover with a gorgeously huge cock.

And *that* made her really realize what they'd done to each other. Not only had they thrown away all inhibitions and had mad, animalistic sex together in spite of being absolute strangers, *but they had drunk each other's blood.*

Sick. She was going to be sick. Amara was sure of it. Covering her mouth, she raced to the bathroom sink. Her body heaved, wanting to throw up what her human mind needed to reject as an act of horror, but nothing came. Nick, who had followed her in, was looking gray and distraught beside her.

"What have they done to us?" She echoed his earlier query, her voice strained as her body hunched over the sink and tried again to reject the meal she'd made of him. But even as this happened, another part of her brain warred with her over it, arguing that the warmth and spicy flavor of him had been the best meal of her entire life. She'd never known such satisfaction or such pleasure.

"Amara, I'm so sorry. God, look at what I did to you," he choked out, reaching to touch her bloodied, wounded hips where he'd clawed into her.

"It doesn't hurt," she said quite honestly. "Just stings a little." She splashed water over her face and drank the coolness from her fingers. She wiped her face against her arm and stood up straight to examine him. "Turn around."

Nick hesitated, the avoidance of his usually direct eyes confirming what she already knew. She reached for him and, after a look of admonition, turned him gently between her hands. She saw the raw slices of her nails down his back, and even deep into his buttocks, which she didn't as easily recall doing as she did the other.

"Does it hurt?" she had to ask, her fingertips ghosting over the wounds. Then she reached up to touch his neck, where she could see the savage bite of her very own teeth torn into his flesh. But she could also see he was already healing from the damage. She had ripped him up unthinkingly, but despite the ugly look of the melded wound, it was clearly sewing itself together again. "You're healing," she marveled.

Nick turned and reached for the breast he had bitten, gentle fingers cupping her warmly even as he stroked his thumb over the deep punctures and surrounding bruises. "So are you," he noted. "Amara, I never wanted . . ." He swallowed loudly, remorse and distress resonating deep into his intense green gaze.

"Neither did I. You aren't to blame any more than I am. I knew the minute they threw me in here we were in trouble no matter what we did. I've seen too many things here."

She squeezed past him and tapped the water temp panel for the shower. The cube was quite small, but she reached for him regardless and drew him under the spray with her. Amara figured there was no need to be shy anymore, and she wasn't quite ready to be left alone just yet. She hoped he didn't balk, and she smiled when he obeyed the silent request to join her. She felt the sting of the hot water in the many pricks and cuts on her body, and when he winced ever so slightly she could imagine it was quite a lot worse for him since she'd tracked up his back pretty fiercely.

"Let's avoid soap," she advised as she ran her hands down over his chest and helped the water run red with his blood. "Are you dizzy or anything? You lost a lot of . . ." Amara frowned. Nick reached up quickly to cradle her cheek against his palm, his thumb rubbing away the lines of distress between her brows.

"No. Not at all. I feel fine. Strangely, better than fine. Don't worry. I did my share of damage, too."

"There are no towels," she noted.

"We'll have to settle for the heat dryer. I hate the damn things, but there isn't much of a choice."

Nick gently rubbed his free hand down over her chest, rinsing away places where blood had dried on her skin. A mixture of his and of hers. Suddenly, Amara wanted more of his gentility. There was something very compelling about his animalistic mastery, and she wouldn't kid herself about how it had felt despite how it had come about, but she also craved this human kindness from him. It was almost as if she yearned for the balance of it.

He turned off the water and hit the drying switch. Bright heat lights flared on over them and warm air blasted against their bodies. Nick turned her, lifting her hair, her breasts, and skimming down her body again and again until she was mostly dry. He even made her step her feet wide apart to dry her between her legs, his fingers stroking through tight pubic curls and beyond. He turned her and very familiarly cupped her backside, parting her cheeks and very intimately made certain she was dry there as well. Amara flushed as his touch ran over her. There had been a time when she would never have allowed such familiarity. Now, she had no more secret or sanctified places on her body after three months at the whim of medics, doctors, and others who couldn't care less about her modesty. But at least with Nick it felt welcome. Like a choice. Odd, since it was clear choice had been manipulated in both of them. But at this moment, it was voluntary.

They stepped out of the shower and the instant she was away from the warmth of his body and the dryer, she began to shiver, wrapping herself up in her own arms.

Nick reacted immediately, drawing her against his own warmth and leading her out of the chilled bathroom to find the blanket she'd abandoned earlier. He wrapped them up together and, after flipping over the bloody mattress, drew her down onto the bed. "Seems cuddling is the least I can do after all else I've done to you," he joked a bit grimly. Amara appreciated the humor, black as it was.

"I wonder what will happen now. I'm afraid of what will happen next. I know they are watching us. They know we're done doing what they wanted us to do." She had no more caution, no more reason to be shy or withdrawn, so it allowed her a new freedom. She exercised it as she touched him over his chest, rubbing a thumb over a Land Corps tattoo on his biceps. He had served in the military. He was a cop. Everything about him evidenced that he was a man who wanted to do good, but he had to do it in rough and tough ways. The beast he had become under the duress of the experimenters' drugs had probably already existed in part inside of him. She had easily seen his aggressive tendencies the moment she'd first seen him in the common room. She imagined he would have been a dominant lover even under normal circumstances. But she also sensed he would have been far more attentive, and much more caring of his partner's needs. His actions in the shower had made that clear to her.

For herself, after having grown up destitute and living half her life on streets far too dangerous for a child, she knew there was an animal inside of her as well. She had repressed it and every other emotional reaction she'd ever had as she had turned herself into a labor machine. Work, eat, sleep. Work, eat, sleep. There had been comfort in that. It kept her isolated and insulated. She didn't have to fight for food, for her body, or for her life. Until this very moment, she had continued to react numbly to what had happened to her, perhaps having given up even before she had gotten there. But in the end, she had been herself, numb or not. What they had done these past three months had altered all of that. Taken her all away.

Made her into what they had wanted her to be.

Now, Amara felt as though she had just wakened from a

long, paralyzing coma. Perhaps it was seeing what had happened to Nick while looking into sea-green eyes turned savage and outrageously wild. Or she was more inclined to believe it had been that moment of reckoning striking with guilt and horror across his face when he'd seen the blood on their bodies. It surprised her to realize that what happened to someone else really did matter to her. She had spent a very long time convincing herself otherwise, figuring it was just easier that way.

But it was different suddenly. She felt energized and revitalized and . . .

Powerful.

Whole. That was it. She suddenly felt like missing parts of herself had been retrieved and connected to her soul where they belonged. It was such an elemental sensation and so very raw at heart. And she knew, somehow, that it was because fate had thrown her into Nick's path.

"I don't want them to take me away," she blurted out suddenly.

"They can't take you away," he said, his voice suddenly low and rough. There was such a deep-seated level of threat and, seeing how his eyes flashed virulent green wildfire, she believed him. He dragged her up closer, rubbing his face against her hair and locking a leg around both of hers as if that would keep them from taking her when the time came. But the truth was they weren't the ones with the ultimate power in the end.

They were. The experimenters.

Except now, their experiments had suddenly developed very interesting new strengths.

"Do you think what they have done is permanent?" she whispered.

"Feels like," he said just as softly, not knowing if it helped them speak privately or not. "Drugs don't grow body parts. I think they fucked with our genetics."

"Maybe we're the end result of all the trial and error they've been doing. They culled out all the weakest of us. You are the first new person we've seen in ages, and like you said, you were chosen deliberately because you were snooping around where they didn't want you."

"From what I learned," Nick replied, his frown hidden in her hair, "the Phoenix Project is supposed to be some kind of anti-aging protocol."

"Great, so they make vampires out of us?" Amara couldn't believe she'd had the temerity to say it aloud. It seemed so ridiculous, but at the same time it was the best description. "I wonder what else it does to us. Did. Did to us. Are we immortal? Will we go 'poof' in sunlight?"

"I'm sure they are testing those theories on some poor assholes as we speak. But they must have known about the animalistic need to mate and feed, otherwise why pair us up so fast?"

"You think we can eat regular food still?"

"We can drink water. You proved that."

"Oh, hey. I did, didn't I?" She sighed. "I have to admit, I am scared to find out the answers to all of this. Worse, it scares me to think of this savagery being let loose inside of some of the nasty weirdos we have around here. They brought in a really large group with us, and we probably weren't the only ones. Raul, the medic on my floor, said it was a 'big day today.' Maybe they culminated this part of the project? Maybe everyone was changed?"

"We won't know until and if they let us back into the general populace. But here's the part that freezes my soul, Amara. My investigation, the one that led me here? It was in pursuit of a rash of kidnappings."

"I know. That's how they get us."

"No, honey. I mean kidnappings. As in *kids*. They've got children here, too."

Chapter 5

Nick dozed off in spite of himself. Considering all he'd been through that day (though he doubted it was the same day), it was to be expected. There was also the factor of the warm, very sweetly curved woman who had turned her back to his chest and was spooned up against him, her bottom snuggled tightly into the lee of his hips and her ankles clinging around his.

It had been a long time since he had lain like this with a woman. He'd been so damned busy lately; he had hardly had time to catch the quick, occasional screw with Lydia in the apartment three doors down from his. She was fun, casual, and had nice tits, and didn't expect anything more than a good orgasm from him. That had suited him just fine. Overtime and undercover work had made everything else unfeasible. Far be it from him to start something he couldn't invest the proper time to. It wouldn't have been fair to a woman if he had.

But everything was so different now. Not just being torn out of his life so harshly, either. As far as he was concerned, this was just a temporary glitch. He'd had undercover work go deadly wrong before and was alive to tell the tales, and while this was obviously much, much worse than the worst-case scenario, he still believed there had to be a way out.

He was beginning to think his captors had handed it to him on a silver platter. What if he could figure out how to call up all this new natural weaponry on command? What else was involved in this anyway? Strength? Was he stronger than before? He certainly felt physically more powerful. However, he also felt he had traded it for some mental stability. Every so often a surge of primal instinct would overrun him. He was finding it was usually somehow connected to thoughts associated with the female lying asleep beside him.

Whatever logic or reasonable social norms his brain was used to, he knew it had all been thrust aside and there was now a single irrefutable fact. Amara was his mate. For now, forever. Instinct drove the knowledge into him. It didn't care that he knew next to nothing about her. It didn't feel fazed in the least by her status as a stranger. There could be a thousand things wrong with her to make her incompatible with the man Nick was.

But she was the perfect mate for the beast he had become. She smelled like divinity to him, the aroma of her a constant depth of allure. Now it was deeply imbedded with his, and that pleased his new beast to no end. He smelled their sex on them, as well as the blood they had both shed, but more crucial than that was the understanding that they had both changed on some kind of chemical pheromone level. This essential alteration was what marked her as his, just as it marked him as hers. Somehow, he realized, the rest would have to follow this forcefully laid path.

He expected to feel a bit panicked by the noose this created around him, and by the implications that made him suddenly responsible for someone other than himself for the first time in a long time. However, it just wouldn't come. In fact, he was feeling quite the opposite. He felt eager to keep her close and protected, even relishing the idea of fending off others who might try to take her from him. He would prove himself worthy of his choice. He had no doubt about that.

Nick felt a streak of possessive need rushing dizzily through him, and before he realized it, he was stroking a proprietary hand along the length of her body until he was clutching her full breast in the seat of his palm and leaving bruising fingerprints in his wake. It wasn't until he smelled fresh blood that he realized his talons had extended back out, pricking her delicate flesh.

He would remember that. These possessive thoughts seemed to trigger their appearance. Meanwhile, he felt badly for scratching her again, so he turned her gently onto her back and bent to lick a tender tongue over the wounds. The flavor of her blood was intensely narcotic, not to mention how it felt to nuzzle himself all around her breast. He began to grow hard again, but he warned himself that this time nothing would come of it. She was exhausted, her pale skin showing dark circles beneath her eyes. He wanted to lick her there as well, all of a sudden, so he did. The instinct was quite strong, as if he believed he could heal her with the action of his stroking tongue. The truth was, the wounds at his neck and on her breast had healed far more rapidly than the shallower ones elsewhere on their bodies. He suspected their saliva might now carry some kind of healing salve that helped to close the wounds they created. Perhaps all wounds. This, he realized, could be extremely useful to know.

Nick would never have admitted it to Amara, but these drastic changes terrified him. It was clear the scientists of the Phoenix Project had no sense of ethics or moral rectitude, their practices shoddy and even bordering on demented. That people like that were behind what was happening to their bodies made him fear for the stability of it all. It was already very obvious they had unleashed something within both of them that had probably been bred out of their species through hundreds of thousands of years of evolution, lending a hand to becoming a so-called civilized species.

Were they really purposely trying to make vampires? If so, to what end? Immortality? And it was also clear that these savages inside of them could be put aside. Could be hidden away. Perhaps even controlled. Maybe the intensity and violence of need they'd experienced was because they were "new" or because of the trauma of the changes in their bodies. . . .

They would never know enough, he supposed. He hadn't said anything to Amara, but he realized that if they weren't exactly what these people were looking for, the odds were frighteningly in favor of them being discarded and destroyed in favor of the next batch of guinea pigs. He hoped to God they were at least close to what they were looking for. It could buy him the time he needed to get them out of this place. At the very least, he had to try. In the final analysis, all roads led to a bad end for them.

And it wasn't just Amara he was worried about. He had seen the children's center. When he'd first been captured, he'd been given a mocking, gloating tour by some maniac in a white coat named Dr. Paulson who'd shown him the building housing what had to easily be five hundred children.

"Orphanages. Gangs. You'd be surprised how often our society discards its young like trash," Paulson said, tsking his tongue and shaking his head. "We are hoping to improve these types of human flaws by bringing out the best in our instincts."

"Mrs. Rockwell's third-grade class wasn't full of orphans," Nick spat at the other man. *Paulson was tall, elegant, and pretty much everything a handsome, brilliant middle-age doctor should appear to be, but Nick could see the feverish*

existence of a damaged, fanatical mind behind those decep-
tive blue eyes.

"Well, they are now. Their parents gave up looking for
them."

"Because their bus was found at the bottom of the fastest
running river in the States! With only ten miles to the ocean
outlet, they knew there was no hope of recovering their bod-
ies!"

"But you didn't give up, now did you, Agent Gregory?
Seems you cared more about them than those who spawned
them. I think that will make you an excellent volunteer for
our Project."

Nick closed his eyes and found himself squeezing hold of
the warm female. She made a responsive sound and it was
almost enough to make him put aside worrying about how
much trouble they were really in. When she wriggled a bit
against his awakening cock, he squeezed his eyes shut
tighter and tried to think of something other than how tight
and how eagerly hot she had felt as she had surrounded him
earlier. He was amazed he remembered any of the details. At
the time, he had just been about the possession, the thrust,
and the climax. Just the same, it had also all been about the
woman. The smell of her, the glorious flavor of her . . . both
with and without the depth of her blood.

God, he still craved that depth, he realized. Not with the
reviling hunger that had forced him to take from her, just as
it had forced her to take from him, but there was no denying
the desire and appeal of it that still lived within him. However, it was no more powerful than the desire he had just then
to know the flavor of her pussy. Now, in the stillness of his
human self, he realized just how much he desired to know
her in normal physical ways. Was it even possible? Would
that savage inside overtake him once he became heavily
aroused by her?

He was going to find out soon enough, he realized grimly.

The more he thought of having her, the more his body demanded follow-through. Letting her sleep was no longer an option, though he cursed himself for the inconsiderate selfishness this beating need forced on him, and would now force on her.

Oh yes, the beast was rousing, he understood. The question was, would Nick be able to exert any control? At the moment, despite the demand pounding insistently through him, he didn't feel blinded or overrun in any way. He was pulsing fully hard along her hip, his erection rubbing against her already in absent request, but he was determined to maintain his civilization this time.

There had to be a "this time." He should have asked. He shouldn't just take. However, this was the one thing he knew he couldn't gainsay at the moment.

Pounding, relentless need for her.

Nick decided to stop wasting time trying to fight what was inevitable. Just in case he completely lost his mind, he wanted to at least have made a preliminary show of being attentive to her needs. Rising up on an elbow, he dipped his head and caught her lips in a gentle, wakening kiss. His free hand was still at her breast, still sporting curved claws, but he scraped them gently across her nipple without breaking her skin.

Amara sighed into his mouth, her lips parting as her eyelashes fluttered in place. She squirmed when he stimulated her, making a sound of protest as she was drawn from sleep, and one of pleasure when she found her mouth full of his probing kiss. She moaned softly, then louder as he tugged on her nipple sharply. Her hand curled into his hair at the back of his head, holding him to her return kisses.

It was several minutes before she pulled back and asked, "Aren't you afraid of how we'll be with each other?"

He realized he wasn't. Not afraid. He knew, just like he seemed to just "know" so much so suddenly, that he would never cause her permanent harm. She was his to protect, even from himself.

"I'm more afraid of how we will be if we keep away from each other," he remarked baldly. Her eyes widened in surprise.

"You feel that too?" she asked.

"Yeah. Very much. It's pretty brutal, actually." As he spoke, Nick trailed sharply tipped fingertips down over her ribs and belly. He raked claws through curls and dipped between her legs as gently as he could. Amara helped him out by parting her legs wide for him, not showing even an instant's trepidation. What made her so brave? he wondered. How could she so willingly turn herself up to him after the way he had been with her?

"I'm not afraid of you," she whispered softly as she reached to kiss his cheek. She nuzzled him and ejected a contented sound from her throat as she so obviously took in his scent down the length of his neck. She licked over his pulse again and again, her teeth nipping at him with sharp points that told him her fangs were now in play. As yet, his were not.

Not knowing how long he would have that advantage, Nick surged over her and began to devour the delectable tastes of her body. Neck first, then nipples and breasts. At the same time, his fingers drifted between her labia, searching for her clit in the sea of ready wetness that greeted him.

Amara gasped when a talon found it first, pricking her sharply. But before he could curse himself for it, he heard her moan and felt her purposely writhe against his fingertips until it happened a second time.

"Oh, God," she groaned, "why do I like that?"

Damned if he knew, but Nick wasn't the type to waste information. Promising himself to get back to the rest of her body later, he slid down between her thighs, pressing against the back of one to push her wider open. Her pubic hair was

so fair that it was almost translucent. This left him with a
slash of pretty flesh in a surprisingly deep pink. Or maybe it
just seemed that way against the paleness of her skin and
hair. The dark claws tipping his fingers looked obscene
among all of that delicacy, but there was no denying the flow
of aroused juices dripping from her.

To say nothing of the smell of her.

Now he felt the aching presence of his rousing fangs as
they began to push from their retraction. Not knowing if they
would interfere with what he wanted, he quickly lowered his
mouth to her heated sex. He lapped at her slowly, ignoring
everything else just to savor the way she tasted across his
tongue. He realized in that moment that his sense of taste
had mutated into something wildly sensitive and sharp. Oh,
women had always tasted good, and always so different from
one another, but he knew immediately that there were depths
and nuances to her he was sensing and tasting that he simply
should not be able to.

Like . . . he knew she wasn't ovulating. How he knew that
was beyond him, but it was like the other mating instincts.
He just knew. Without a doubt. He also knew that it would
change within a matter of days. She would come into heat
then, and then he could put his babies into her.

This was a thought that would normally have terrified
Nick Gregory, since he'd had no fast desires to father a child.
Yet, in that moment, all it did was make his cock stretch out
thicker and stiffer than ever, as if just the thought alone were
the ultimate aphrodisiac.

Nick could also taste the edginess of her arousal. He
could sense how close she was to orgasm, just by her flavor.
Now that, he thought, *could be very useful.* Certainly a theory worth examining. By now his newborn fangs were level
with his regular teeth, and they seemed to be holding off
from full extension at his desire. It was enough, though, that

when he suckled her clit, then drew his lips back just right, they would prick at her sensitive flesh until she was crying out, thrashing under him. She shuddered and quaked with the wild pleasure it roused in her. Her legs had seized him over his shoulders. Her heels were digging into his back desperately. Amara's fingers were deep against his scalp; her talons nipped him again and again as she held him to herself in demand for more.

He gave her all of that, and beyond. He dared to work a lethally tipped finger into her vaginal tunnel, not drawing back yet, but keeping sunk into her as he danced his tongue over the sweetly flooded tissues of her sex. He nibbled and bit at her, licked along her perineum, tasting the tangy rise in her arousal with each passing second. He could smell it on her, especially when he pushed up her hips and tongued her flatly over the tight sphincter of her ass.

She was going to come any moment now if he let her. He probed that pretty pink circle just long enough to feel her flooding his fingers and hands with hot, needy liquid. Nick surged up along her wet flesh with a single, encompassing sweep of his tongue, from rear to clit as if he were playing connect the dots. Then he sucked her clitoris into his mouth hard and tickled the tip of his tongue against her.

She came with a scream. Her whole body locked up into an arch of pleasure, and he looked up to see the undulation of her torso and the shimmy of her breasts as she rode wave after wave of bliss. Relentlessly, he began to probe with the finger inside of her. He knew every single time the sharp end of his talon caught against her because it sent her right back up to a new, writhing crest. He greedily drank the resulting ambrosia as she came all over him.

Nick suddenly jerked free of her, the scratching of his withdrawal sending her over again so she was hardly aware of him surging up between her legs, taking his too-thick member in hand and shaking with the need to feel her while she came like that. He needed to be balls deep inside of her while she screamed and writhed around him.

His fully distended fangs pricked against his lips as he slid himself into place at her liquid-drenched portal. Just feeling the fierce heat difference between himself and her blood-pulsing flesh made him throb with the urge to find release. His mouth ached, hunger stirred. She had gained pleasure without taking blood. Could he?

"God. Relax, baby, please," he begged her in a wild rasp. She was so excited, so clenched with pleasure, that he couldn't find entrance into her. Not a gentle one at least, and his patience was fading really damn fast. That resurrected animal within him was starting to kick up a fuss, snarling for release.

"Nick. I can't help it!"

He knew she couldn't. She was so aroused, even the slightest eroticism was setting her off into low little spasms of joy. Cursing on a monstrous growl, he forwent gentility and started to force himself into her, pushing hard past the rippling, convulsing muscle in his way. His invasion seemed to only make her all the more mindless. She came. Hard. Her claws were biting into his shoulders and sending a spear of stimulation right down his spine, across the seat of his scrotum, and down his steel-hard cock.

Oh. He was ready now.

Now.

He hilted into her in the next thrust, the smack of his sac against her ass so damn satisfying he had to growl roughly with his approval. He scooped up her knees into the crooks of his elbows, pushed forward nice and deep, thumping against her cervix quite securely. Now he was deep enough. Now she was going to come for him harder than she ever had before.

Chapter 6

Amara was in a daze of pleasure that wouldn't seem to end. The only thing cutting through it all was the painfully persistent intrusion of Nick's shockingly huge cock. It seemed even thicker and longer than last time. Either that or she was just swollen. Regardless, he only made it halfway into her before pain became ecstasy, and she went flying into an endless night sky full of stars, fresh air, and freedom. She hadn't seen the night sky in so long. *So very long.* It was so beautiful, and her whole spirit soared outward to try and touch all those glittering stars.

Her eyes were still dazzled by it all when she tried to blink into focus. In all that light there came the imposing shadow of Nick's darkness. Just as his body was a glorious intrusion into hers, his dark presence above her shaded her stinging vision, looming over her as both a force of protection, satisfaction, and domination. Her climaxes had made her slick and ready, and he was able to sink deep as he caught up her legs. Her belly clenched, the need to come yet again so tight inside of her that tears sprang into her eyes. She had never been this responsive, this sensitive. Her body was completely alien, half of her feeling ethereal and free, the other half demanding more of him. More of *them*. Somewhere deep within she understood they were a combined entity. They would no longer be just Nick, or just Amara. They were Nick and Amara. Nick and Amara. NickandAmara.

"I'm so hungry for you," she breathed on a sob when his head dipped low near hers. "I need you, Nick."

He bent to kiss her mouth, drenching her in her own scent and taste as his tongue dove deep against hers. She licked him voraciously, pricking her tongue on both their fangs as she suckled the flavor of herself off of him.

"You'll always need me," he rumbled deeply against her lips as he thrust hard against her womb. "You'll always want me."

"Yes," she gasped.

"You are mine now," he growled roughly, driving harder and faster into her with every word. "No one else, Amara. Never." He groaned in his pleasure, his big body shuddering hard under her gripping hands.

"Why would I want anyone or anything else? Nick . . . Nick, please."

"Okay, sweet. Let me feel you come around me."

"Bite me, Nick." Amara turned her head, exposing her throat and the line of her shoulder to him. "God, I'm going to come!"

"Damn right you are," he hissed as he bent to lick her where she had beckoned him to go. She felt him hesitate, knew there was still a part of him resisting his desire to taste her. He turned his head, focusing on the driving force of his hips as his cock plowed through her dense, clutching sheath faster and faster.

Amara burst into little brilliant bits of light, her whole body shuddering and quaking with the powerful impact of her climax. She could hear herself crying out in a lusty, cresting cadence that blended with Nick's.

"Fucking hell! Amara! *Amara!*"

She felt him unravel, the harsh slams of his pelvis punctuating the violent rush of his orgasm. She felt the burn of his seed flooding into her like superheated magma, the heat of his body so extreme compared to hers in that moment. He shuddered hard, gasping for breath and balance as he tried to keep from crushing her.

"I didn't bite you," he said in heavy panting rasps. "I wanted to—God, you made it so hard to resist—but I didn't do it."

Nick dropped hard onto his elbows, his sweaty forehead falling against the bared length of her neck where she had invited him to taste her. Amara wasn't certain what he was trying to say, or why it was so important to him that he didn't even wait to catch his breath to explain.

Then she understood. He wanted to know he could control himself. He wanted to know he could master his beast even at the most extreme of moments. She envied him that, because now that she had her breath, she couldn't control what happened next.

She sank her teeth deeply into his shoulder.

Nick jolted against her lips, and she instinctively wrapped him up in her arms and legs to hold him in place. She wished she could explain why she needed to drink from him, but she wasn't exactly certain for herself. All she could assume was that she had not taken enough last time, because she had been increasingly in need of it the more energy she had burned in their lovemaking.

This time she was much more careful. Amara kept her lips sealed to his skin and did not wrench against him in any way that would tear his flesh or break her seal. Her mouth filled with the heavenly flavor of warm, vital male. He shuddered in her grasp, his body otherwise trapped within hers. He grew hard inside of her again, and she heard him moan low and rough as he bent his head and helped her to himself.

By the third swallow, he was moving inside of her again, clearly unable to help himself. Her feeding aroused him. So much so that by her sixth gulp, he was reaching crisis again.

"Don't stop," he commanded her gruffly, his thrusts not even necessarily deep or hard. They didn't need to be. He could have stayed completely still and the effect on him would have been exactly the same. "Oh, yes . . . oh, shit . . . don't . . . *don't stop!*"

Nick climaxed again, his body straining to meet the demand of his new nature. She felt herself overflowing with him, both vaginally and orally. She carefully opened her jaw, and swiftly swept her tongue over the four punctures. Nick was shaking with his exertions and the remnants of the incredible ecstasy he'd experienced. He gasped for breath, his open mouth against her neck. When she was satisfied his wounds were closed, she finally relaxed into the mattress.

They spent several long minutes recuperating, and then Nick lifted up and looked them both over. "You didn't spill a single drop," he noted, looking rather impressed.

"Waste not," she said with a shrug she hoped looked blasé. Then she grinned. "It was rather cool. I just needed to focus and be more careful. It didn't hurt?"

"Babe, it hurt so good I'm still reeling. You needed that?"

"Yeah," she admitted. "Does that make me weaker than you? You could resist."

"No. I doubt it. You didn't take as much as I did the first time. Frankly, I don't care why you did it. You can do it again right now if you like." The grin he shot her was positively lascivious.

"Can't. Look. No fangs." She opened her mouth and sure enough, they had fully retracted. He examined the little white enamel nubs under her lips for a moment.

"Guess you got your fill this time."

"Yeah. But you didn't." She nodded toward his as-yet heavily fanged state.

"I wanted to know if I could control it. I needed to know," he corrected himself. "I need to know what all my limits and limitations are. I don't want to ever hurt you, Amara."

"Yes but, that's just it." She bit her lip. "I don't think I process pain the same anymore. It's like you said. It hurts so good. Every time you did something that should have . . . *would* have hurt under normal circumstances, I interpreted it inside myself as pleasure. Weird, huh? Like a natural sadist or something."

"Perhaps. Perhaps it's just because it is me."

"Maybe so. Do you feel hunger?" She reached up to touch the deadly sharp tip of a tooth.

"No. Not at all. This time it was more like . . . well, eroticism. The desire was like the desire to suck on your sweet little clit. I was dying to do it, but could have resisted and still survived. I wouldn't be happy, and part of me isn't, as you can see." He touched his tongue to a fang. "But I can certainly survive. Last time, it was a matter of survival. No bones about it. I had to feed. So did you. I'm not certain how long we can continue to do this off each other, but I hope we can." He frowned darkly down at her. "If your bite causes that kind of reaction in me, I'm not sure I want to see some other guy getting off on you doing that to him."

"One step at a time. Now that we've both 'fed,' let's see how long we are able to go before we have to do it again no matter how hard we resist."

"I'm all for science," he noted with a chuckle, "but do we hafta?" He affected a little whine, and then gave her a growling little nibble against her neck. "I bet I could make you come if I just bit you and did nothing else at all. That's exactly what you did to me."

"Mmm. I bet you could," she agreed breathily. "I'm beginning to think you could make me come just looking at me the wrong way. Or the right way. Whichever."

"Well, there's a theory I'm willing to—"

Nick halted midsentence when the sharp sound of releasing locks came from the doorway. He was off of her body in an instant, jerking the blanket over her for cover as he sat up on the edge of the bed, keeping her behind his body as he faced the opening door.

Raul and the Asshole Twins entered the room.

Chapter 7

Nick found he was really quite glad to find himself with ready fangs and talons that quickly began to ache for tender human flesh to mark. He made a low sound of threat, like an animal protecting its den. He supposed that was exactly what he was doing. His den *and* his mate.

He wasn't going to let them touch her. He'd rip them apart first.

"We'll be taking blood and the usual vital statistics," Raul announced. "I'm to ask if you wish to remain together or to be separated."

"Together," they chorused.

"Hmm," was all Raul had to say about that. "Behave, or you will be heavily tranquilized." On cue, Asshole #1, the one who had fondled Amara in the lab, produced the remote to the implanted behavior modification devices.

Nick's hands clenched into fists as Raul cautiously approached, and Amara gently covered one of his hands with one of hers, knowing he was puncturing his own palms with his nails. The medic began to prepare the tubes on his tray, and his sharp eyes spied the fresh wound on Nick's neck.

"Would you say the climax you experienced with her bite was any different than the others? Stronger, perhaps?"

"Why, you miserable little fuck!"

Nick launched off the bed and grabbed Raul around his throat, slamming him hard against the wall even as he tore his nails across the throat of the twin with the remote and wrenched his head off his spine with a single-handed snap. The remote went skidding under the bed as Nick let the body of the first twin fall. Then he snarled viciously at the second one, who was fumbling for his own remote and all of a sudden looked ready to piss his pants.

"Leave it or he's dead," Nick spat in warning to the other man, making certain he could see the rivulets of blood oozing down Raul's throat. "I owed him for touching her," he noted, pointing to the dead orderly. "I'll let you both walk out of here with the blood and vitals you want, but you're not going to ask any more questions. Got it? You want answers, you just keep spying on us like the slimy little pervert bastards you are. If you don't figure it out that way, then you can fuck with your own genes and find out for yourselves. We're done with answering your stupid surveys. Oh"—Nick flashed fierce fangs for a smile—"and we'd like some fresh bedding and clothes so we don't freeze our asses off anymore. We clear?"

Raul nodded and so did the other orderly. Nick wasn't certain they would comply once he let go, but he didn't have much choice. He was certain reinforcements were already on their way. It probably hadn't been wise to react as he had, but he hadn't been able to help himself. He'd seen red at what he had perceived as an insult to Amara, not to mention the bald fury at Raul's blasé admission that they had been watching everything they did. He had suspected, of course, but to know for certain was intrusive and painful.

Especially for Amara, he figured.

He looked back at her as he let go of Raul, suddenly wor-

ried about how she would react to the way he had so easily
and coldly dispatched another human being. Even he was a
little shaken by it. It was true, the crimes being committed
against them warranted severity of punishment, but death?

For touching Amara, death was too good for him.

"Agent Gregory."

Nick turned sharply at the familiar voice near the door.
There stood that same smooth doctor with the very same air
of superiority he'd seen on him nearly a month ago. Of
course he could afford to feel superior. He stood with three
rather beefy-looking orderlies at his back. At the clear
threat, Nick felt his entire being bristle in defense. Every
hair on his body seemed to stand on end and he didn't check
the low warning growl rolling out of his throat.

"Relax, Agent. No one is here to harm you. You are much
more valuable to us alive. I thought you might like to know
that." Paulson glanced over at Amara, his eyes lingering on
her much too long for Nick's peace of mind. "I see we've
made you an excellent match," he noted with a leering sort
of self-satisfied smile. "It doesn't always work out so well.
Some resist and sulk. Others just savagely feed and then
pick separate corners. Too often, the male kills his intended
mate. Haven't figured out why. You might like to know you
are the exception and not the rule. This compatibility is what
fascinates me. You don't even know each other, yet suddenly
you are as familiar as old lovers. Now, I can observe from
now until doomsday, as you well know, but I can't learn what
I want to know without asking you some questions."

"Then you're fucked, because we aren't answering."

"You will answer, or you will be separated. If you continue to be disagreeable, Agent Gregory, I will force you to
watch while I lock her in another room with a newly turned
male."

"You can't do that!" Amara cried. "Another male would
kill me!"

"Why?" the doctor demanded. "How are you so certain of that?"

"Because she is mine!" Nick roared with fury, everything inside of him screaming to attack this threat before him. But before that imperative was the demand to protect his mate at all costs. He could do nothing that would risk what Paulson was threatening him with. Amara was right. Now that she was marked as Nick's mate, she would be in danger with any other males. Oh, another male would certainly want her . . . but he wouldn't take her unless he could kill the male who had marked her first. Until he killed Nick.

How did he know this?

He just did. Just as Amara did. Instinctually. To the bone. It was an imperative written deeply into their altered DNA.

"She is mine," Nick repeated, trying to keep his head clear of rage so he could focus and protect them both. "Another male would know that. Resent it."

"Hmm. No man likes another man's leavings," Dr. Paulson sniffed. "But I sense more. Instinct. Scent marking? Dominance? We've never had so large a group turned before. In a day or two, we are going to turn you all loose in the common areas. Morphates and regular humans all together. It will be quite a show, I imagine."

"Morphates?" Amara asked hoarsely, her knuckles white as she clenched the blanket around her.

"You aren't vampires, my dear. We call your breed Morphates. Humans, or rather, primates, morphed into a better breed. Everything about you is enhanced. Senses, strength, sexuality, reflexes, and, obviously, animal instinct. We revived what has been so deeply repressed. Think of it, Agent Gregory. You have undergone a dramatic physical change on a cellular level that allows you to heal and regenerate at a phenomenal rate of speed. This means you will be forever young and always perfectly healthy. The savagery you exhibit, granted, is a poor side effect, but we will perfect this one day. Watching how you have maintained and regained control over yourself tells us how close we are coming to exactly that. Now we will turn you loose on each other and see what happens."

Paulson glanced over Nick's naked form.

"Clothe them. Fresh bedding. Bring them some food."

The doctor exited and kept his head attached only because Amara reached for Nick's hand and drew him back toward her.

"Please. I'm frightened."

Nick understood she meant to ask him not to do anything that would separate them. He wouldn't. He *couldn't*. God, what would have happened to Amara had he not desired her? Nick wondered. What would he have done to her? Clearly, these men of medicine didn't want to intervene, preferring instead to observe as their creations ripped each other to shreds. The very idea of it made Nick sick to his stomach. He turned and wrapped his arms around Amara, holding her tightly against himself as they watched the orderlies carry out their orders in the cramped room. With shaking hands, Raul took the blood he needed, beating a hasty retreat when Nick curled an aggressive lip back from his distended fangs.

As soon as the door hissed closed on its pneumatics, Nick grabbed for the pile of smaller clothing and quickly helped her into the sweats and tee. He snagged sweats for himself and then sat down on the new mattress. He drew Amara down onto his lap and into the protective circle of his embrace. She hooked an arm around his neck and he could feel the burn of her cheek against his and knew she was struggling with emotion.

"Morphates," she rasped. "Well, at least it wasn't random. At least they were looking to produce something specific."

"Yeah," he agreed stiffly.

"What is it?" she asked, immediately picking up on his tension.

Nick's gut feeling, again, was to protect her, but he was also aware that she had a right to know everything since it was her fate as well as his.

"He told us too much," he whispered softly against the curve of her ear. "It means they are never going to let us go, Amara. They are never going to allow us to tell anyone what happened to us. They're going to kill us when they're done with us. Obviously we aren't the first generation of these Morphates. We're just the latest and the greatest. Once they develop a better batch . . ."

"We'll be obsolete."

"Yes," he sighed softly, squeezing her in comfort when she shuddered with fear and revulsion toward their captors.

"Nick. Nick, I'm afraid of how I feel. I watched you kill that man and I was so satisfied, so proud of you for it. I can manage that. I can understand what made me feel that way. But when that doctor was in here . . . I wanted to sink my teeth in his throat and rip it out. Half of me wanted to feast on his blood, the other just wanted to rip him to shreds. If he hadn't left just then, I would have. I haven't killed anyone . . ."

"I know, honey." He tried to soothe her softly.

". . . since I was sixteen."

That made Nick go really quite still in shock. Strange. He had seen just about everything from killer grannies to drug-pusher babies. Why would it so surprise him to realize the quiet woman in his lap was a murderer?

"Excuse me?" he said, figuring he'd heard her wrong in spite of his acutely improved hearing.

"I grew up on the streets of Dark Chicago, Nick. My mother was a junkie selling herself from fix to fix. I used dirty old syringes to play darts, learned to run fast and hide in small unreachable places, and stole everything I ate for years. The first person I killed was a gang boy when I was thirteen. He tried to steal from me."

She meant he had tried to rape her. Nick could see it from the way she turned her eyes down and away. Her clenched fists told him she didn't regret what she had done, that she would do it again in the same circumstances. But Nick couldn't hold that against her. She'd been all alone, fending for herself in the worst Dark City there was . . . tied only with Dark Manhattan. The so-called Dark Cities were the abandoned sections of the cities where gangs had overrun even the police forces. They'd been walled away, fenced up high, and ignored as best they could be by ignorant people who hoped they would stay put. The Dark Cities grew larger with every passing year, though. Some of them, like Chicago and Manhattan, were completely infested. Los Angeles was third runner-up.

"You don't have to account to me for how you survived that kind of life," he told her quietly.

"But don't you see? I got out of it. As soon as I was able to work legitimately I left the city and worked my way into a workhouse. It was always cold and always dismal, but it was safe. I could sleep at night without being afraid. I could put away those bestial instincts I'd become grown with. I have no idea how I even knew how to be anything other than a savage. TV, I think. But . . ."

Nick watched with an ache in his breast as tears stung wetly into her tough copper eyes. She swallowed them back, though, clearly too proud or too stubborn to show the weakness of them.

"They've turned me back into one," she whispered. "Don't you see how easily I am adjusting to this? God, I think I am even enjoying it. Relishing it!"

"Hey, no more or less than I am," he said sharply. "I had the good life compared to you, but it wasn't easy from my perspective. I was always angry. Always violent. My mother swore I had been born mad at the world. Thing is, I hate injustice, and this world is so full of it, it makes me choke. When I was young I was impotent. Our society doesn't give kids ways of helping make things better. When I was seventeen, my father bought me a low-level commission in the Corps. He knew if I wasn't tempered, I'd be in jail before I was twenty because my rage would have gotten me into trouble." He reached to brush gentle lips against her temple. "Thank God he did. I learned control there. I learned empowerment."

"You learned how to make a difference. I've never made a difference. I've just survived."

"That isn't anything to be ashamed of. Right now, that's all I want. I want us to survive. We have to figure out how to do that, and frankly I am glad you have all that killer survival instinct in you. When the time comes, it's going to be really handy."

"I never wanted to be like that again," she said sadly, resting her cheek on his shoulder.

"Let's just be glad we finally have a choice."

Chapter 8

"Are you awake? I hear someone coming."

"Yeah, I'm up. Been listening to you bite your claws."

"I was not," Amara hissed. "Besides, they aren't bitable. They are like titanium."

"And how would you know that?" he teased her softly as he sat them up to face whoever was coming to the door.

Amara didn't dignify that with a response. Okay, so maybe she had been nervously nibbling a little. It had been two days since Dr. Paulson's visit and his ominous threats of releasing them into the general populace. Since then they had discovered they could, indeed, eat. They had not needed to drink blood, although it was tempting when they were having sex to indulge in the act.

Which made for a lot of temptation, because closed up in such a small space there was nothing else to really entertain them. Not that they wanted any other entertainment. Nick and Amara couldn't seem to get enough of each other.

Amara's worrying was doubled, however. Not only did she dread what would happen next, feeling the ponderous wait of the forward-ticking time as if it were set on an explosive device, but Nick had warned her of another danger she hadn't even considered.

"You're going to begin ovulating soon," he had said softly as they caught their breath from their latest sensual attacks on each other's bodies. She had jolted in surprise at that at first, and then realized that once she thought about it, she knew it was true. "I can smell the change on you. I can feel the imperative inside of me that's eager for it. I'm terrified to think that's exactly what they want. I'll be damned if I will breed my children for them."

"Me, too," she agreed with a little shiver.

Now Nick pulled on a fresh T-shirt and they both got to their feet as the door slid open. Amara knew he wanted to step in front of her, but she stubbornly kept to his side and ignored his dark frown. He might be feeling all kinds of butch and manly because of his alterations, but she wasn't in a very submissive space herself any longer.

The orderly was armed.

It was the first thing she noticed. Granted, it was with tasers, obviously a little added security after what Nick had done the last time. Also, there was a significant change in uniforms. While they remained the same annoying white, they were now boasting armored vests, padded sleeves no doubt meant to protect from sharp claws, gloves, and helmets. They looked like a contingent of guards, which in actuality they had always been. They just had not looked so much the part before.

Taser guns and nightsticks at the ready, they made way for Nick and Amara to move out of the room. Their sharp gestures said there was to be no argument, and Amara couldn't see any point in doing so. They eased out of the cubicle room side by side, Nick's arm tight around her shoulders. As if everything were the same and it was just another normal day as involuntary lab rats, they were marched into the common area.

Only there had been significant changes.

The common room had all been caged in. Steel bars disrupted the perfection of white everywhere there was a section of glass or an opening leading out of the common area. The exterior access had been cut off and was now guarded heavily, but not from inside the room. The guards all remained outside the caging.

They came from four compass points, small groups of them being hustled and even shoved into the common rooms all at the same time. Nick and Amara were the last to step inside from their section and the steel gate rang with finality at their backs as it slammed shut.

For a moment, everyone was quite still. Hesitant. Amara gripped at Nick, feeling the tension in his muscular body. She automatically looked for the familiar faces of her friends, having been worried about them since this had started.

That was when she first noticed the smell.

Then came the sensation.

Her skin felt as though it were vibrating in a supersonic dance, the hairs at the back of her neck pricking up even as her nose began to sniff out all the signals it received.

"I can sense them," she breathed. "I can tell which are still human and which are Morphates."

"You're not the only one," Nick whispered grimly as he drew her back against a wall where no one could come up behind them. He nodded toward a human male who had approached someone else as if he recognized him, greeting him. He now suddenly found himself the focus of two and then three Morphate males who began to actively sniff him. "I have a feeling this isn't going to be pretty," he warned her softly.

Amara was in agreement with that. She watched as the three males started to shove at the human, batting him between them like cats toying with a ball. Claws appeared, and

then fangs. The human male screeched in fear when he saw
it alter them into feral-looking beasts. Amara sniffed,
smelling how the keenness of his fear called like a sweetly
baking treat in an oven beckoned one's hunger.

Then it was ending in a sudden flash of violence as the
first Morphate male sank his fangs deep in the human's
shoulder. The second chose the opposite bicep, and the third,
heedless of how it nearly ripped him apart, grabbed up a leg
and tore into his thigh.

Once the feed was on, the rest of the room erupted into a
frenzy of reaction. Other hungry Morphates tried to find their
way into the feast, only to be viciously rebuffed. Humans
began to scream and clamor for release at the exits, terrified
they would be the next meal for these inhuman beasts. Then
there were other Morphates who seemed to have no appetite
or simply no care for the tableau that played out.

Amara felt Nick's awful tension and sensed how badly he
wanted to do something. But there was an entire pack of
feeding Morphates now, other humans being picked off to
satiate those who either had not been fed properly or enjoyed
satiating themselves on the bloodlust and power of their new
forms. They could clearly see a good deal of both.

There was blood and human death everywhere by the time
the furor for feeding had died down and the worst of the pack
had grown too full to continue to drink or they were just
growing bored of the easy prey. The remaining humans were
huddled and sobbing or simply sitting in traumatic shock.

Amara scented something familiar and turned her attention to the approach of a beautiful female Morphate. It was
Mina, she realized with no little shock. Mina had always
been a confident and sexually attractive female, but now
with her Morphate enhancements she positively reeked alluring femininity. Readiness. Sex. She was not marked by a
male, not like Amara at all. It was obvious, though, that she
had been with more than one male in the last block of hours.

And she was in search of another.

Mina practically slithered up to Nick, the slink in her spine and the sway in her hips so suggestive. Her nipples stood out under her tee attentively, and Amara could smell her ready excitement as she approached her desired target. She saw Nick's nose twitch as he took in her scent as well and felt the knee-jerk male response of interest. Mina was in a full-blown heat, and that was designed to attract any viable mate.

Even *her* mate.

Amara reached out and smacked away the hand Mina reached out toward Nick's chest hard enough to get her message across. She even backed it up with a growl of threat.

"Back off," she hissed, placing herself between Nick and the trashy little Morphate seeking to usurp her place at Nick's side.

"Come on, Amara," Mina scoffed at her. "There's no way you'll ever keep all that to yourself." Amara's friend sniffed at her in disdain. "Why he ever picked you is beyond me."

"Because I ride his cock like it's an Olympic event," Amara retorted smartly. "Just the feel of my teeth in his skin makes him come as hard and fast as lightning. He knows a good thing when he finds it."

"Holy shit," Nick whispered just behind Amara. She was standing right in front of him, her back brushing his front, so she was immediately aware of his bodily reaction to her words even before his hands clamped onto her waist to cuddle her backside back against his jutting erection.

"Mmm, perhaps. But maybe he wants a little changeup. Some variety." Mina's tongue appeared between her lips to lick them with appetite as her eyes dropped to where Nick's hips were flush with Amara's rear. She could smell his arousal and it made her willing to risk the threat Amara might pose. Mina hardly even saw the other female as an obstacle. She'd been a weak, apathetic little thing for the entire time they'd known each other. So Mina doubted she'd put up much of a challenge when push and shove might come into the picture. "What do you say, stud? You seem more than a little ready to have some fun with an energetic woman. The girl is nice in a pinch, I'm sure, but you need something a little more hot-blooded."

Mina ignored Amara's presence and sidled up to Nick's side, rubbing her eager tits against his arm as she fondled the shape of his muscular shoulder.

Amara hardly knew what happened next. She could only recall the feel of her mate tensing in response against her back, and then a blinding wall of possessive fury. She literally saw red, *that* was how hot her temper was as it bolted through her. She was all fangs and fearsome talons in a heartbeat and she tackled her competition with a wild snarl of rage. She did not take their former friendship into consideration for even a second. On the most primitive level of instinct she had, she was realizing that Nick could be stolen away from her. All it would take was a woman who wanted her mate badly enough to be willing to kill her for him. They would all want him, of course. He was the most beautiful male specimen in the entire room. Biological imperative demanded they try to mate with the strongest and most powerful genetics available, and Nick was 100 percent prime DNA real estate.

Unless she set an example, one that was brutal and definitive, she would find herself fighting challengers to her position all the time. They weren't playing by human rules any longer and she couldn't afford to be nice. She would end up dead, and Nick would belong to someone else, if she did.

It took only two rolls across the floor for her to gain the upper position. She hissed down at the other woman in warning, giving her the opportunity to put up her hands and slink away alive but smacked down in defeat. Mina was all about sex and getting what she wanted. She had been that way even when she'd been human. She wasn't about to give up her target and she delivered that message with a swipe of deadly claws that raked Amara from her right ear to her jaw and throat.

It was just enough to really piss Amara off. The blonde reached out and caught Mina's head between her hands just as she had seen Nick do to the orderly, and with all of her inhuman power, she wrenched it completely around.

Amara let go of Mina, her face dropping against the floor in grotesque opposition to the faceup position of her body. She ripped wild eyes completely around the room as she surged to her feet. The fight had drawn bloodthirsty attention and she could smell the sexual interest from the women who could see Nick was the point of contention. But the moment Amara barked out a savage warning to all other females nearby, there was an immediate exodus of women stepping back so she wouldn't mistake their presence as a challenge. In a matter of seconds she had proven herself capable of defending her position as an Alpha mate.

She turned to look at Nick, furious with him for how he had reacted to the stimulus of another female. Logically, she realized he had little control over his urges and interests at the outset. She also knew that he would never take another woman so long as she was alive. Still, jealousy and hurt made her belly ache as though it were filled with weighty lead. He quickly crossed over to her and took her into his embrace. He held her tight and secure, drawing her up to the powerful body she had inspired to feel amazing pleasure just as she had claimed. With comforting strokes of his hands, he reassured her that there was no other for him. Nick hugged her warmly, her back to his chest, and drew her head aside so he could touch his tongue to the gashes Mina's claws had left behind. He licked away the blood until the wounds closed and she was relaxed and all but purring her forgiveness in his arms.

Chapter 9

When Nick looked up from his maintenance of his mate's wounds, he met a half dozen aggressive gazes. The six males reeked of challenge and, most important, sexual desire. A sweeping glance told him each and every one had a massive erection and a yen for his woman. They had watched her dispatch her competition in a matter of heartbeats, her viciousness and strength arousing their interest in her . . . as well as their cocks. Nick felt the way their eyes fastened onto her ripe breasts, the rigid nipples he knew were so easily seen through her snug tee. They sniffed for her pussy, seeking her scent as they edged closer. The pack had no loyalty to one another, but they would use the others to weaken him so they might gain advantage and the victory prize.

They all could smell how close to season she was. She was almost ready to be bred and they all wanted to mate with a female who could fight with such dominance.

Nick realized then that the challenges weren't likely to ever stop. He could discourage them, but others would always want Amara. She was a worthy and breathtaking mate. He had known it from the very start. She would whelp amazing children of strength and equal beauty. She would fight for all that was hers to her very last breath. If she had ever been apathetic, it had been forever discarded. It was no longer in her makeup.

Nick gave her scratches one last lap, savoring the flavor of her blood. That, too, had attracted them. Her blood-scent. He knew because it attracted *him*. He was rock-hard with need just from watching her defend her place and desperate to be inside of her now that her flavor washed against his tongue.

But first things first.

Nick ran a proprietary hand over Amara's breast, palming the full weight of her and even catching her nipple in teasing pinches between his fingers. She had borne his bite there, her orgasms and his own quite arousing. His touch certainly aroused her. He could smell the tangy change in her scent as her pussy went wet in anticipation of him. Soft growls of challenge began to erupt from the other males as they began to crave her just as he did.

Good. Let them. Let them build themselves into a fever of need for what they would never have. The frustration would make them stupid and sloppy. His own need was empowering. It made him steady and quite clear on what was his to protect if he wanted to find himself back inside her sweet heat once again. He slid his hand down his bitch's belly, his fingers gathering up fabric until he touched the bare skin of her tummy. All the while, he remained alert, his eyes trained on the restless six watching what he was doing. His hand glided under the waistband of her sweats and his fingertips combed through tight curls he knew were the color of fine golden filament. He sought for and found her clit quite easily. It was moist and a little swollen already, anticipating the pleasures of the cock pressed to the crease between her bottom cheeks.

Nick's fangs slid into place, his claws curving and pricking her until she gasped and moaned in response.

All hell broke loose.

Nick spun Amara back behind him as the first two males lunged at him. Natural weaponry aside, before he'd been forced to become a Morphate, Nick had been a federal agent trained in the deadly art of hand-to-hand combat. Facing down such powerful odds simply didn't faze him. He never once worried about the fact that these were Morphates, not men; that any one of them could have the power to defeat him alone. He never believed it.

Luckily for Nick, he really was the most powerful male there. The others had been slack and lazy with defeat for months. Nick had still been powerful and fit with rebellion at the time of his transformation. His strength and skill combined to make him a deadly force of nature—even if that nature in and of itself had been forced.

He mimicked his mate's kill with his first, snapping the Morphate's neck like a twig and already attacking the next before the first hit the ground. This one he took out with a strike across the bridge of his nose. He went down howling, blood spraying everywhere. The third and fourth were the first to actually lay hands on him. Or rather, claws. They shredded through his shirt in front and back, flaying his skin in deep furrows he didn't even bother to feel. The idea that Amara would heal him with the stroke of her erotic little tongue was all he needed to swing him swiftly around, hooking the third male by the throat with his arm and ripping him off his feet with his momentum until he sent him slamming into the fourth. They landed in a tangled sprawl of arms and legs and at least one of them was still alive. Nick didn't much care.

Number five was smart. After seeing how quickly he had dispatched the others, he abruptly threw up his hands and backed off at a speedy pace. Number six . . . well, now, there had to be at least one real challenger. Number six was definitely it. He was a big, blond bastard, but in a ponderous way. He was like a tank.

"Keep that snatch warm, baby," he called crudely to Nick's Amara. "I'm going to want it just as soon as he's dead."

Nick saw Amara flip him off, and it was the only thing that kept him from going totally ape-shit on the guy for daring to speak to his mate in such a way. Just that single flash of humorous defiance helped him keep his head and probably his neck.

The two titanic males clashed and tables and chairs were crushed or sent flying in their wake. Morphates and humans alike plastered themselves to the walls to keep out of their way. Once Nick threw off the other man, his eyes sought Amara to make sure no others were coming near her. She was leaning back so casually against the wall she nearly looked bored. Then Nick realized it was because she had no doubts he would prevail and she was impatient for him to finish what his teasing touches had started. Her matter-of-fact attitude inspired the same in him. Suddenly he saw exactly how to dive past those meaty, hammering fists and he took his shot, using his claws to rend through the cotton crotch of his opponent's sweats and the flesh of his scrotum and penis as he tore up and away.

Had Nick still been human, it would have been considered a low, dirty tactic. As a Morphate protecting his rights to his mate, it was poetic justice. The man fell in a screaming, writhing mess of blood and agony. Nick stood there catching his breath for a minute, his glare challenging the room to incite him further; warning that he could do much, much worse. All eyes turned away or down submissively, whether they were human or Morphate.

And, without ever meaning to, Nick and Amara became the Alpha Morphates of the room. They didn't realize it just then, but it would change everything for them all over again.

Nick flung the blood of his enemy off of his claws with a sharp snap of his hand, then he turned to look at his woman. He lifted his chin, his nose seeking her aroma through the heavy rusted stench of spilled blood. Still, he found it easily and in an instant. Sweet ambrosia and eagerly awaiting him, it called him back to her in rapid-fire strides. He grabbed hold of her as she crashed her chest against his, her arms wrapping around his neck and her legs climbing up around his waist as their mouths melded and dueled in hot, wild kisses of need and victory.

He couldn't wait.

The knowledge pounded through him with an animalistic roar. He had to reclaim her, right now, right there.

"I have to take you," he gasped into her mouth as her back hit the cold cinderblock wall. *"Right now!"*

"Yes. Yes, yes, yes!"

"Watch my back, babe," he said roughly. It was the only thought he gave to the rest of the room. He grabbed the waistband of her sweats and pulled them off her bottom. He bared her just far enough and then withdrew his aching cock from his sweats. Nick was aiming and thrusting in the very same movement, his instincts for fucking her like second nature now. They both understood this was a reclaiming. It would be hard and fast and as crude as could be, but it would stain them with each other all over again and everyone would know she was his. He was hers.

He enjoyed the hard counterforce of the wall, the immovable object allowing him to thrust deepest, hardest, and fastest. She oozed juicy and slick around him, her walls burning hot as his aggressiveness and dominance excited her beyond reason. She stopped watching behind him when her head fell back so she could eject lusty moans in cadence with his every thrust. He struck her pleasure spot with ease, his huge cock and the erotic circumstances speeding her swiftly beyond her tolerances. She began to come, squeezing around him so tightly it was like plunging up through a clutching fist.

"Bite me," he hissed at her as his body burned violently for release. He wished he could lose himself in her, in the moment, but there was too much danger around them. Still, in spite of that threat, he could no more have resisted taking her than he could have talked reason into the Morphates who had wanted to take her from him. Like so many things now, it was a demand he couldn't ignore.

Amara didn't argue. She didn't even hesitate. She tore aside his shredded tee and latched onto his neck with a primal little growl of ownership. Nick felt his blood bursting into her mouth and his cock simultaneously bursting inside her core. He roared out in pleasure, in warning, in ultimate domination. He came as hard and fast as lightning, just as she had claimed, the electric charge of it scrambling his brain until it was fried with ecstasy. Amara was struggling to drink even as orgasm after orgasm rolled through her writhing body. Nick shuddered with his sense of ultimate privilege, content in knowing that this time he had not just been given her at random. This time, he had earned her. He had fought for her, defended her, and earned his entitlement inside of her.

He was catching his breath and trying to coordinate the strength in his legs as she licked his wounds closed. She dropped off of him and he straightened their clothing.

Now that all Morphate urges had been satisfied, Nick turned around and was suddenly struck with the very human understanding of what he had just done. The entire room was staring at them, having watched his every thrust into her, heard every cry he'd wrenched out of her. The intimacy between them that had no privacy as it was, had just been displayed in public with the heedlessness of two dogs fucking without a care of who watched or who was embarrassed by it. He had behaved utterly like an animal from the moment he'd first caught Mina's open and admittedly provocative scent. He wouldn't have touched her, but he'd still been stirred by her, the beast inside reacting purely by instinct. But it was also instinct that cleaved him to Amara alone. Mina would only have pissed him off eventually if Amara hadn't intervened. When he had responded to the scent of an available female, it had been Amara's body that he'd craved to be his only solace. His only relief.

Now everyone in the room knew it.

Nick backed up against Amara's warm, lush body, pressing her between his back and the wall he'd so artfully used to wring deep pleasure from her.

"God, I can't believe I just did that to you," he said in a voice strangled with a confusion of human emotion and satisfied Morphate instinct. "In front of everyone. Like some kind of savage."

His heart was racing so hard and his chest hurt with shame for his behavior and anxiety for Amara's sensibilities. Fucked-up DNA or not, they had been raised with a lifetime of humanity. She had to care. She had to care that he had just taken her like a common street whore against the nearest convenient wall. Remembering the type of woman her mother had been and how hard she had struggled to avoid that fate, he felt lower than dirt.

Nick felt her hands slide around his waist, hugging him with possessive warmth. Her cheek pressed against his back as one palm crept up to lay flat over his thundering heart.

"It isn't the same world anymore," she reminded him with a whisper. "None of the old rules apply. I know you already understand that, but I want you to know I understand it, too. Nick . . . I'd fuck you like that in Times Square if you asked me to."

"I think this is as far as my public displays will go," he said grimly. "I will not share you with the rest of the world, damn it. Not if I can help it! I just . . . I couldn't stop," he said quietly, his tone dropping in defeat.

"I know. Be easy on yourself. We've only been altered for a few days. It's clearly going to take time to gain control. Look at them all. Every last one is responding like animals. Just as we are."

Nick did as she asked, looking at the others in the room. Only, it wasn't the submissive turn of gaze after gaze as they tried to keep from accidentally challenging him that caught his attention.

No.

It was movement.

From the dead woman Amara had killed. Only she wasn't entirely dead. She should have been, considering the vicious twist in her neck, but she moaned and stirred and he felt Amara stiffen at his back, so he knew he wasn't imagining it.

"I'll kill the bitch again!" she hissed, suddenly surging to move around him. But he reached out to grab hold of her, drawing her back to his side and pressing a soft, shushing kiss to her temple.

"Easy, baby," he soothed her. "Let's just see what happens. I don't think she's a threat to you."

"Said the man who got a hard-on when she walked up to him," she scoffed.

"Hey, what happened to realizing it was going to take time to control this?" he demanded with irritability even though he knew she was right and, if the tables had been turned, he would have likely blown a gasket. But she hadn't responded to the aggressive approach of the other males in the least. Not that he'd given them the opportunity to get that close to her. That and he'd been touching her for himself and wouldn't have known otherwise if she had. "I'm sorry. I want to promise it won't happen again," he said with soft re-gret, "but I don't know what I am anymore."

It was all too true. He kept vacillating between the man he had been and the powerful beast he had become. As he watched a dead girl slowly right herself on what had obvi-ously been a broken neck, he realized it went far beyond being a bigger, badder sort of animal.

The entire room was watching with rapt interest as, over the next half hour, Mina recuperated from her "death" enough to draw herself up onto her knees. She frowned, her wary eyes looking at the woman she had once called a friend in friendless circumstances.

"Well, hell, Amara," she pouted, her voice rasping as if her vocal chords might still be twisted around a bit. "You didn't have to get so bitchy about it."

"That wasn't bitchy," Amara said darkly. "Come near him again and you'll see bitchy. Next time, you stay dead. Got it?"

"I wasn't dead," she argued. Mina bit her lip. "I saw the whole thing. Saw him fighting." She pointed to Nick, then thought better of it and snatched her hand back against her chest and looked down.

That was when Nick's first victim stirred.

Eventually, all the Morphates fully recovered their lives and, with a bit of rapid healing, their total health. Not a one had the least desire to try his luck a second time, although there were a few permanent enemies made. Nick was deter-mined to keep his eye on the big blond who sulked and glared from across the room. It was still an attitude of ag-gression and very near a challenge and Nick wasn't going to turn his back on him until he started to respect the way things were going to be.

Mina departed for the farthest corner from Amara her-self, but other than irritably shooing away any males who came sniffing after her, interested in perhaps licking her wounded pride, she didn't show any obvious resentment for what had happened. Yet.

However, Amara was satisfied enough to relax in Nick's grip.

It took only fifteen minutes before the next approach took place. Since it was a woman closing the distance, Amara's relaxed state, such as it was, flew away instantly. She sniffed the air warily, but Nick didn't scent any threat of sexual challenge from the beautiful brunette. She was tall and, like Amara, generously curved in all the right places. She had intriguing and intelligent eyes and was clearly a Morphate by the scent and sensation she gave off in strong waves as she came cautiously close.

"Devona," Amara greeted her warily, making Nick realize they knew each other.

"Don't concern yourself," Devona said with a hand held out in calming encouragement. "I am not here to poach your territory, Amara. I don't think Mina even meant to, really. You know what she's like. She was a bitch in heat before she even became . . . well, a bitch in heat."

Nick chuckled at that, and he saw Amara's eyes narrow on him. He disarmed her threat by swatting her hard on the backside. "Come on," he scolded her. "They aren't all after our bodies."

"I'll believe it when I don't see it," she muttered, moving to cut him off when he went to extend his hand to Devona. She stood stubbornly in front of him, her arms folded tautly beneath her breasts. "What do you want, Devona?"

"To get out of here alive," she said softly.

Chapter 10

"Well, by the look of it, it's going to be hard for them to make us dead," Nick observed.

"And don't think they won't try," Devona retorted, her jade eyes sliding over all of the exits and the cameras. "Don't you see how the guards are running about all freaked out? I think they expected us to kill each other, but not to come back to life. This is our only advantage, far as I see it. But not for long. We have to figure how to get out of this mess before they figure out how to kill us."

No sooner were the words out of her mouth than the gates at all four compass points burst open and large contingents of guards poured into the room.

"Move! Back to your rooms."

"No!"

Nick shouted the countermand before he could think about it. To his never-ending shock, every Morphate in the room halted.

"It's like a pack mentality," Devona whispered to him quickly. "Even I feel it. You made yourselves our Alphas today. That means unless you are challenged and succeeded, you are our commanders. It's intuitive. It tells everyone where they are as a pecking order is formed."

"How do you know this?" Nick demanded as guards began to approach them in force.

"Devona was a zoological veterinarian," Amara said. "She's one of the 'brainies,' as we call them. Most of us were taken off streets and out of workhouses, but some like Devona and you are the 'brainies,' intelligent, employed people who mattered, who for whatever reason were taken out of their lives for this. For you it was because you got too close with your investigation. Nick's a Federation cop," she informed Devona.

"And for me it was because they tried to recruit me to be a scientist on the team for this nightmare, my zoological expertise clearly needed. When I turned them down I found out there was a 'no is not an option' clause. They needed a multi-breed vet because, as you can see, they are messing around with some dangerous primal instincts. I don't know what they did to us, but this isn't all human DNA, I promise you that."

"You! One more word out of you and you're toast! You hear me?" the nearest human guard threatened Nick, waving the remote he held.

"Don't back down," Devona hissed. "Fight 'til you drop, Nick, but if you back down, you lose face. You lose Alpha. You'll have to fight challengers off all over again. They'll try and take Amara from you."

"The fuck they will," Nick snarled, turning on the human guard sharply. "Point that thing at me again and I'll make lunch out of you."

The guard went completely gray, and his hand with the remote in it shook as several more men flanked him and withdrew tasers. Nick felt the hairs on the back of his neck stir to attention as Morphates came up behind him. Great. Just what he needed. Trouble from the front and the back.

Devona moved to his right side, flanking him while Amara stood on the left.

"They are backing you up," Devona whispered. "Challenges only come when the pack isn't being threatened and only if you show weakness. Of course, they'll be happy to take your place if you die. . . ."

"Fuck all," Nick spat.

"But not for lack of their help. They want to live too and their instincts tell them you're the one who will make it happen."

"Nick . . . ," Amara said anxiously.

He knew she could feel the tension of building aggression in his body. But it wasn't as though he had much choice in the matter. Fangs were already descending into place and talons curved with deadly intent, and Nick didn't even need to create the need in his thoughts. His body knew even before his mind did what was needed of it.

"Take him out!"

The lead guard fired first. He pressed the remote, sending a painful electroshock through Nick's body. Amara yelped as her contact with him bridged the gap between nervous systems and she took part of the charge. Hearing her hurt was all it took for whatever was human in Nick to utterly vaporize.

Nick didn't remember much of what happened after the third external taser dart plunged into his body. He reached for the barb and yanked it out just as he had the others and kept marching forward. Suddenly there was a wall of Morphates and guards clashing. It didn't take long for the humans to realize they were in trouble and their weapons were insignificant against this new breed of animals. The Morphates took pain and injury without flinching. Tranquilizers flooded their systems, staggering them, weakening them, and just as quickly leaving them.

Nick was the first to grab a human and make a meal of

him, as promised. His fangs sank true and he tasted his first human blood. It was nothing compared to what his luscious Amara was on his tongue, but it was enough to push back the pain of electricity and shed the nibbling lethargy of tranquilizers. Revitalized, he drew back and growled a command to the others.

"Feed. Do not kill. Despite how they've treated us, we aren't the animals they would make us." He turned back to his appetizer and made certain the rest of his feast saw the intent in his eyes. The scent of fear and aggression flooded the room. Nick halfheartedly licked the guard's wounds closed and then discarded him for the next.

When he became sated, he bit and clawed, punched and kicked. Every so often he would swing around to spy Amara.

"Keycard!"

She held up the prize and he watched her run for the south door.

"Amara!"

Nick was knee deep in human discard and Morphate fighters. He struggled to race after her. He knew all she wanted to do was open up a path they could fight through, but he also knew it would never be that easy. When he suddenly caught Paulson's scent, then saw the bastard step into the frame of the south doorway, he knew she was in trouble.

That was when he caught a smell he had known perfectly well even as a human.

Gun oil.

Paulson drew the heavy-caliber handgun, and aimed through the bars at Amara even as she tried too late to skid to a stop in her bare, tractionless feet. With one arm held casually behind his back, Dr. Paulson pulled the trigger and shot Amara right between her eyes. The bullet's enormous caliber blew a hole out of the back of her skull and sent blood and gray matter spraying everywhere.

Nick didn't realize the roaring scream of denial echoing into the large room was his own.

He was shoving and lurching through the crowd around him, his horrified eyes never once leaving the sight of Amara's slowly crumpling body. She hit the floor on her back with a hard smack and her copper-penny eyes stared up straight and cold at the ceiling. The keycard in her hand dropped uselessly to the floor.

Nick finally broke free and ran to her, dropping to his knees and skidding to a stop at the same time as he reached her body. He was a cop. He knew . . . he knew what that bullet had done to her. He knew what the next one was going to do to him as Paulson took aim at him.

"Stop them, Agent Gregory, or you will be next. Not even a Morphate can survive a .44-caliber bullet at point-blank range. I think I just proved that."

Nick didn't hear any of it. He didn't care. He was too busy struggling with the screaming urge running through him to throw back his head and howl out with his pain and loss. He grabbed hold of her hand, shoving her limp knuckles against his lips as he stared in disbelief at her blankly fixed gaze. Nothing else penetrated his awareness, just that unnaturally still expression and the perfectly neat little hole in the left center of her forehead.

Blood was beginning to pool beneath her head now, the circle of it widening and seeping into her golden hair.

"Oh, honey. Oh, God . . . baby . . . ," he choked out, his chest on fire with things he had never felt in all of his life. A level of rage like no other. Grief so deep and so wide it couldn't be crossed. Love.

Love.

Beyond lust. Beyond mating. The utmost and absolute purity of the only instinct that truly mattered, the only one he'd never experienced as a human male, but instead had needed to become an animal to know the depth of it.

"I don't know anything about you," he rasped as he gripped her too tightly between his hands. "It's not enough." It wasn't enough. They couldn't do this. Paulson had given her to him, but he couldn't take her away!

Yet he had.

Nick flicked cold, deadly eyes up to meet the superiorly smug gaze of Dr. Paulson.

"I'm going to suck the blood straight from your heart." The threat came out with the cold dispassion of wrath beyond visible expression. Paulson found it amusing and laughed.

"You're going to die with your brains blown out all over her, you idiotic Neanderthal. You might be the best breed I've ever created, but I am still the god that created you and I can just as easily destroy you. If you had realized that sooner, you wouldn't have gotten her killed." Paulson shrugged and pulled the trigger. The bullet blew into Nick from the side of his chest wall.

He could almost feel it rattling around inside of him like a vicious little pinball. The hollowness inside of him was confirmed by the painless sensation.

Paulson had blown out his heart long before he'd even aimed the gun at him.

Chapter 11

"Nicky, you'll get yourself killed if you keep up this cowboy bullshit of yours," Jamie Mulloy said with a resigned sigh. "Then I'll have to lie my way through a eulogy at your funeral so people will think you weren't an asshole."

"Anyone who comes to my funeral will know perfectly well I was an asshole. Don't lie on my account," Nick chuckled.

"Your brother will hunt me into the tomb beside you if I let anything happen to you. I'm begging you. Kincaid Gregory scares the piss out of me. You know that."

Nick smiled slow and wide. His big brother was a bit intimidating at that. "Kin won't kill you. He'll just bat you around a little. Then he'll dig my ass up and kick the shit out of it for getting myself dead."

"Nick! You wake up right now, or so help me I am going to kick your ass!"

Nick opened his eyes and drew a breath, not realizing it was his first in nearly two hours. Previous to that, his lungs had contained too many holes to hold air. His chest hurt like hell, and he had the weirdest sensation that his heart wasn't beating quite right.

Or at all.

"Am I dead, or what?"

"Or what."

Nick sat up sharply, ignoring the savage backlash of pain it caused as he turned to stare into copper eyes that were filled with tears. They spilled over onto her cheeks and it was the most amazing thing Nick had seen in all of his convoluted life. Tears. Crystal-clear drips of emotion so normal, so common, and so *alive*. Tears falling from beautiful, blinking eyes completely unmarred by an off-center bullet wound.

Yet . . . her hair was stained red and crusted with the heavy remnants of her own blood. Possibly even his as well as he had bled out on top of her body.

"Amara?" he said dumbly, reaching out to touch her and see if she was real. His wrist snagged on the zipper teeth of the plastic surrounding him. That was when he looked down at himself and realized he was stripped naked.

Again.

And he was in a damn body bag.

"Holy hell!"

Nick jolted so clumsily to get out of the creepy plastic covering that he fell off of the autopsy table and onto white, sanitized floor tile. Amara, just as naked as he was, bent to put her hands on her knees, and peered at him with a sniffle.

"I did the exact same thing," she noted with a shrug as she held out a hand to him. Nick took it automatically and she helped him coordinate getting to his feet. When he was up, he immediately saw the second metal table and the empty body bag. *God. She had woken up alone zipped up in that thing!*

"Honey, are you okay?" he demanded, using their clasped hands to drag her up against himself. She was warm. She was pliant and soft, her heart beating against his chest beneath her breast. He couldn't bring himself to make a visual check, so he cautiously reached up to slide his fingertips into the hair at the back of her head. It crackled with dried blood and she tried to shy away.

"Nick, I'm icky and crusted . . . and I have weird goo in my hair," she complained, trying to draw back.

"That goo is probably half of your damned brain, Amara! What in hell were you thinking! You got yourself killed!"

"Only for a little while!"

They stared at each other when they realized the absurdity of the argument.

"My God, I think we're zombies," she said with a shudder.

"Mara," he chided her, finally chuckling with the peculiarity of it all, "we aren't zombies. Just . . . remarkable healers. Man, even your hair is growing back," he marveled as he stroked his fingers over the very solid bone of her skull under her scalp. Finally he turned her around and looked for himself. No hole. No gore—discounting what was stuck in her hair. He looked around the autopsy room and saw an empty table with the handheld spray nozzle they used to wash cadavers before beginning the postmortem. "Come here."

Nick drew her to the welled metal table and gave it a pat.

"Nick, we don't have time for this," she said, eyeing the table skeptically.

"If there was a reflective surface in here, you'd disagree with that. Get up."

Sighing, she did as he asked. He arranged her so she was leaned back on her elbows with her head closest to the drain. He didn't think she needed to see what he was about to clean off of her.

"Close your eyes. Let me take care of you," he said softly. He grabbed the nozzle and squeezed. It took him a minute to figure out how to adjust the temperature so he wouldn't freeze or scald her. He started at her feet and with the pressure of the spray and the thorough stroke of his free hand, he cleaned her of all the evidence of her violent "death." He didn't stop until her hair ran crystal clean and both sides of her body had been tended to. The room was very cold, and she was shivering even before he turned the nozzle loose and stopped the water. He spied piles of fresh towels and crossed to grab some. Better still, he saw freshly packaged scrubs, each set conveniently marked for size. He held up both in triumph and she smiled as she eagerly reached for the towels. He helped her to dry off, buffing her skin to a warm, rosy glow.

It wasn't the time or the place for it, but Nick couldn't help the way his whole body seemed to grow tight with need for her as he dried her under her breasts, across her chill-hardened nipples, and up the elegant curve of her throat. Her pulse beat sluggishly there, making him realize that despite her recuperation, she had lost a great deal of blood and probably needed to replenish her energy and regenerative resources with a supply of blood.

Blood *he* could not provide because he was just as starved for it as she was. His heart had yet to find a regular beat, though he had felt it fit and stutter, especially when he had become stimulated by touching her.

He left her to the act of dressing and hopped up onto the table himself. As he washed away his blood he examined his healing body. He found the entrance wound from memory and saw it was almost invisible already. The exit wound low in his gut was a little more noticeable, but it wouldn't be for very long, he was certain.

Growing impatient with details, Nick finished washing up and dried himself in quick passes before getting dressed in the scrubs. He quickly moved to examine the exits as discreetly as he could. Nothing was locked. Why would it be?

Everyone was supposed to be dead. But if this morgue was anything like the morgues he had seen, it had a door leading directly outside for easier body disposal.

To freedom.

He saw it instantly, the view of green vegetation through the small window visible even from where he was. He walked over to it almost as if in a daze.

"Amara," he said softly as he pressed a palm to the door and looked outside in wonder. It had been an entire month since he'd been beyond the cold walls of this place. A month since he'd been outside. When he saw a parking lot and a roadway, his heart finally began to beat in hard, steady thumps. He saw cars. Cars he knew how to break into and start. He held out a hand to her without taking his eyes off of the outdoors, trying to judge which car would be best for them and provide the least risk of getting caught.

"Nick."

He could hear the protest in her use of his name and it drew his full attention. "What's wrong, honey?" he asked a little impatiently. "We need to get going before someone comes in here."

"Nick, we can't leave them. They'll kill them. The children, too. If they find we've escaped, they'll burn this place to the ground and they'll run. Turned or unturned, human or Morphate, they will find a way to permanently destroy them all."

Nick felt his heart sink with the realization that she was right. He desperately looked back toward freedom. "I can get us help in a matter of hours. All I need is a phone."

"And you don't think they won't have planned for a cleanup in less than a couple of hours? Nick, we're probably sitting on a radical bomb as we speak. Something that will blow our atoms into such tiny bits they will never be able to heal."

"And what's to say they aren't already planning to do just

that?" he snapped at her, running an agitated hand through his damp hair. "You saw what a cluster-fuck that was for them! We don't know what happened, Amara. They could all be gone, this place already written off! If we don't go, there's no hope for any of us. We have to get help."

"We can't abandon our pack!"

"They aren't a fucking pack!" he exploded, even though everything inside him hissed in contention. "They are people who need help!"

Amara's hands balled into fists at her sides, her bronze eyes flashing with fury. "You are a liar! If they aren't a pack then I am not your mate!"

"Mara," he warned icily.

"You can't pick and choose what you are going to believe and what instincts you are going to follow! Don't stand there and tell me your whole psyche isn't screeching to go back and lead them to safety." She stuffed a clenched fist against her belly. "It's writhing in my guts like a virus I can't choose to ignore, Nick. We did things that made us responsible for leading those people. If we leave without them and Paulson destroys them, we'll have hundreds of deaths on our hands."

"Thousands," he corrected her softly. "Look."

He nodded out of the little window. She bit her lip but obeyed him and came up to look. What he saw froze his soul, and he knew she felt the same. Identical buildings. Six others besides their own. One, he knew, housed all of the children. The others, he imagined, held any number of experiments just like theirs.

"Even if we go back to our pack, baby," he said gently against her ear, "nothing we do from inside here will ever free them from inside their prisons."

"But—"

Nick held a finger to her lips suddenly and ducked away from the glass as two employees entered the lot, chose their vehicles, and left down the long roadway.

"God . . . I think I just had a very cold-blooded idea," he said grimly. "All we need is a few hours, right? A few hours where they won't know we're gone?"

"Long enough to get a phone and for you to do your . . . cop things." She waved a hand at him in summary, making him laugh softly.

"Okay. What if we fill those body bags with bodies? All we have to do is hope the autopsy isn't until tomorrow. It's late. Shift is changing, looks like."

"We're going to kill two people?" she asked, shivering.

"Not my first plan, no," he said with a head shake. "But you need blood and so do I. We drink deep enough and they'll be out a good long time. If they die in the interim . . . well, two lives for thousands—I can live with that if it's two pricks from the workforce here."

"That doesn't sound very coplike, Agent Gregory," she scolded quietly. But she was looking out of the window and judging distances and shadows for herself. "The black Honda Envy?"

"I was thinking the gray Mitsubishi Heron. Gray has a way of being unnoticeable. Besides, it's out of sight lines from almost everywhere but the south." Nick reached for the door but she grabbed his arm.

"Wait."

She hurried away and he impatiently watched a few others go to their cars. He didn't want it to get too busy out there. They'd get caught.

Amara returned and he realized she had a knife in her hand. A scalpel actually. He was wondering why she felt she had to arm herself when she suddenly stabbed herself in the arm with the thing.

"Shit! What the hell are you doing?!"

She was bending over a sink, her blood pooling thick and slow, the precious drops doing everything they could to remain in her body. She stuck a finger inside of herself and there was a clang in the bottom of the sink.

The implants.

"They don't work on us anymore," he reminded her fiercely.

"Maybe. There's a perimeter device. One of these four implants triggers it. It's incendiary. Raul said anyone who tries to escape gets ashed. I don't know about you, but I'm not willing to test my new genes that far."

"Right. Give me that thing."

Chapter 12

"Nick!"

Jamie Mulloy almost fell flat on his back in his tipped-back chair when Nick Gregory suddenly appeared in his office doorway. The bastard had gone missing months ago, and suddenly he strolls in looking like . . .

Nick was a big, fit man. Pretty impressive overall. He was handsome as a devil with his black hair and ocean-green eyes and had the track record with women to confirm it. In fact, he had one in tow right that very second. A blonde. But while Jamie was certain it was Nick Gregory standing before him, this was a very different-looking version of him. Gone was the easy, almost blasé humor around his eyes. Now there was more of the predatory Nick, the one Jamie saw on the coldest, darkest assignments he'd managed him on. Usually the ones where little kids were at stake. Nick always took on the brutal stuff involving victimized kids.

Overall, there was something dangerous and harsh about Nick that hadn't been so readily apparent before. He also looked like he'd been through hell a few times.

Now the cute little blonde he was holding hands with like

a teenager with a crush . . . she was something else. She had mouthwatering curves and held herself in that sex-kitten way some women just seemed to be born with. However, her reddish-brown eyes held that same lethal glint he could see in Nick's.

"Nick, where the fuck have you been?"

"Long story. Glad to tell you if you get the team together ASAP. I should have called this in but . . ." Nick hesitated and ran a hand through his hair in agitation. His blonde drew up against his side, comforting and supporting him with the warm press of her body and the soothing stroke of her fingers over his Land Corps tattoo. "Where's Kincaid?"

Jamie startled and Nick instantly caught the reaction. Was he out of his mind, or had Nick just sniffed at him? *Weird*.

"Nick, Kin went looking for you. We haven't heard from him in two weeks."

Jamie had never seen Nick settle so still and quiet before. Nick wasn't the still type. He was an agitator. He had to move or pace the more upset he got.

Still was fucking scary on Nick Gregory.

"Team. Conference room. Now."

Nick bit out each word in command. Jamie knew it wasn't the time to get touchy about who was ordering whom. Something bad had happened to Nick, and apparently time was wasting.

Jamie picked up the phone.

Chapter 13

Amara did not envy Nick's position in the least.

He was sitting at the head of the conference room table, his hands gripping tightly to the arms of his chair with the tension that had been locked into his big body ever since he'd heard that a man named Kincaid was missing. *His partner?* she wondered. He'd implied he worked rogue. A close friend? It disturbed Amara that she didn't know. She frowned, wondering why it should matter so much to her. He was upset and that was enough; it was all she needed to know . . . wasn't it?

Nick had also just told all of his closest friends and coworkers that he had been turned into a genetically mutated being, by a mad scientist, and that there was a secret compound full of others just like him.

Silence reigned, and Amara tried to will Nick's eyes to hers. She wanted to be there for him, but he wouldn't allow it. He was sitting stark and alone, as if she could do nothing for him. As if no one could. All of his fire and determination had evaporated when he'd heard about Kincaid. Now he was on autopilot.

It made his story unconvincing.

So Amara wasn't surprised when one of the men busted out laughing.

"Oh, man. Nicky! You've told some hot shit in your time, but that has to take the cake. Why can't you just admit that you ran off with your little chickie here and fucked like bunnies for a month and lost track of time?" His laughter spread around the table in masculine chuckles. Amara wondered why there were no women there, and then shrugged it off as unimportant at the moment. Male, female, or otherwise, they needed to make these men act quickly, and that meant convincing them fast. Since Nick seemed to be paralyzed in his own mind at the moment, that meant she had to do something.

Amara used every new reflex she had to grab the sidearm Nick's manager had holstered onto his hip, and even as the whole table was reacting in surprise, she disengaged the safety and shot herself through her palm.

"Amara!"

Nick exploded out of his chair.

"Jesus fucking Christ!" Jamie exclaimed.

"Shit!" the laughing man cried, no longer laughing. Amara slammed the gun down on the tabletop and held out her dripping, bloody hand even as Nick rounded the table and went to grab hold of her. She warned him off with a look and a primitive sound, which he responded to just as savagely— his way of telling her she wasn't to boss him around.

"Jeez, Mara," Nick complained, "you could have just flashed some fang."

"I don't know how to do it on command like you do," she said with a shrug.

"I'm getting a medic," Jamie said urgently.

"No! Wait. Watch," she commanded them all, her tone brooking no argument. The room was full of tough, lethal men who didn't take orders from much of anybody, but at her bidding they all sat back in their seats and watched her bleed.

Clearly, Nick couldn't bear to see her injured. Certainly not after seeing her shot to death before his very eyes. He could also help her show what she was trying to show a little faster. He touched her shoulder and slowly, with the tenderest of caresses, he ran his fingers down her arm and cupped her injured hand into his. He brought her palm to his lips and, his eyes fixed only onto hers, he slowly lapped at the raw, ugly gunshot wound. Someone at the table made a sound of revulsion, but they both ignored that. Nick turned her hand and licked the exit wound closed, sealing it with a sweetly romantic kiss. Then he turned to his gaping peers and showed them her rapidly healing hand.

"No friggin' way."

"It's a trick!"

"You think I carry dummy bullets in my sidearm, Agent?" Jamie snapped irritably. He pointed to the carpeting where the slug had punctured it. "See?"

"You're a fucking ghoul," the no-longer-laughing man spat as he surged out of his seat and drew his sidearm.

"Carl!"

"Carl, no!"

"Agent Jackson, put that weapon down," Jamie barked.

"Don't you get it?" Carl hissed. "They're vampires or something! They are unnatural . . . *things!* He lapped up her blood like it was flavored body oil, for fuck's sake! Look at him. He's got a goddamn erection. He got off on it!"

Amara glanced down Nick's body. The surgical scrubs left no mystery to the state of Nick's arousal. She met his wry gaze and smiled.

"Men," she sighed with an amused roll of her eyes. "Were you thinking of flashing *that* for proof?"

Nick's boss choked on a laugh; so did a couple of other

men. Carl Jackson, however, grew furious and thumbed off the safety of his weapon.

Ten seconds later, the handgun lay next to Jamie's on the tabletop and Amara was giving Carl a fanged grin as she held the burly man a foot off the floor by his throat with a single clawed hand.

"There are easily over two thousand people in that compound," she informed on a deceptive little purr. "They might be human, and they might be Morphate. Whoever or whatever they are, none of them asked to be illegally kidnapped and turned into guinea pigs. Your job is to uphold the law and protect the citizens of this country. Nowhere in our constitution does it say 'these rights apply to everyone except Morphates.' "

"That's because there weren't freaks when it was signed!" Carl gurgled.

"Babe, let go," Nick said calmly from behind her, that always gentle touch stroking softly into the small of her back. She frowned, frustrated by the time this was taking, but she let Carl drop like a stone. Amara crossed her arms defensively under her breasts and faced the stares of the other agents.

"I've grown up in gangland, been sold by my mother for her daily fix, and nearly starved to death waiting for a spot in the workhouse to open up for me. Never, in all of that *human* existence, did I ever ask a cop for anything because I always thought cops wouldn't give a shit about the likes of me," Amara said quietly, slowly meeting the eyes of every man in the room, including Carl's hostile glare. "Don't you dare prove me right."

Amara urgently needed to leave the room. If she had to listen to them waste time debating whether her fellow captives deserved saving, she would completely lose her cool. Since that wouldn't help any of them, she left them to Nick and hurried into the corridor.

She hadn't even realized they'd drawn a crowd of others, the gunshot and shouting having attracted everyone in hearing range. At some point the conference room doors had been opened and any possibility of secreting this situation with a sweep under the rug had been completely dissolved. *Good*, she thought angrily.

Amara didn't even care how everyone jerked back away from her and made a wide path for her to pass through. She was used to being treated like one of the many untouchables of their society. Still . . .

As horrible as their captivity had been, it had been incredibly equalizing. She'd never formed friendships with intelligent, normal women like Mina, Rachael, and Devona before. Not with anyone, really. They'd always been a cut above someone like her, or just incomprehensible. It wasn't until she'd had nothing to do all day but talk with them that she'd slowed down to realize station in life didn't make all that much difference in how damn difficult things could be. Without them, she'd never have been able to appreciate the trust, companionship, and loyalty of friendship. If it hadn't been for that pathway being built first, the encounter between her and Nick could have turned into something dreadfully different. Amara repressed a shudder when she realized she actually had to be grateful to Paulson for that. For Nick.

What of Nick? When this was all over and they were free, what would happen to them? Could this damage to their genetics be reversed? Would Nick eagerly seek a cure and a way out of this forced bond between them?

Amara found herself running, rushing until she was bursting out into the cool, open air outside. She found a cut of the building to hide herself behind and slowly sank down against the rough, scraping brick until her knees were under her chin, her arms squeezing around her shins as she hugged her thighs against her chest. She closed her eyes tight.

They were freaks and monsters. Everyone would know.

Most, she knew, would react just like Carl had. People had no tolerance for differences, especially horrifying ones like blood drinking, fangs, and claws. The immortality part would scare the living piss out of some, and attract all the wrong kinds of others. This was a society that, instead of solving the violence of gangs, had simply walled them all up and hoped they'd all kill one another eventually as they fought over what little territory there was. They hadn't cared that not everyone they'd walled up with them had anything to do with gangs. They'd written it off and waited for it to get better.

Just how were they going to respond to thousands of immortal killers, most of whom had been sucked out of the lost populaces of the Dark Cities or the impoverished areas that surrounded it? How should they respond? She'd been in captivity with some of these maniacs for months. The idea of a rapist or serial killer who couldn't be stopped or killed, set free to run loose in the world was sickening. And would the general public be able to see the difference between a Morphate like that and ones like her and Nick?

She knew with rock-solid dread of surety that they would not. She realized that, perhaps, they should not. Morphates, by the looks of things, were the only ones who would ever be able to police their own.

By the time Nick came to find her over an hour later, she only needed to look into his face to see that she wasn't the only one beginning to come to these conclusions.

"Oh, Nick," she whispered as dread sank into her every cell, "we have to do something."

Chapter 14

Nick nodded in a short, jerky movement.

He'd been so sure. So fucking cocksure. He'd actually thought he could stroll into the agency that he'd dedicated his entire postmilitary life to, put out a call for help, and they'd all come running to help him just as he'd always run to help them.

He was a naive idiot.

Maybe if Kin had been there it would have been different. Kin would have backed him no matter what he'd become, and would have forced their companions to see it the same way, at least for the short term. Just long enough to free about five hundred kids and who knew how many hundreds of adults. But Kin was missing in the action of searching for *him*. The idea of what could have happened to his brother had kept his stomach churning endlessly since Jamie had first dropped the bomb on him.

If Paulson had gotten ahold of Kin Gregory, wouldn't he have been eager to gloat and taunt Nick with the knowledge?

No. He would save it and savor it. He had been waiting

for a chance to play Kin in a hand that would trump him. But, if that were the case, why hadn't he used that card instead of putting a bullet into him?

After all, he'd become more trouble than he was worth much more quickly than Paulson had anticipated. And how could he continue to apply logic to a man who clearly had gone way off the logic tracks?

Besides, there were much more dreadful things to worry about. Realizing abruptly that he knew the government he worked for just a little too well, he knew they had just bet everything on a losing hand and they were in incredibly deep shit.

They had a debt to pay and the proverbial leg-breakers were breathing down their necks.

"Come on," Nick demanded of Amara, holding a hand down to her. She had understood long before he had, so he knew there was no need to explain much. "They're calling higher-ups for direction. When this agency has to look higher for permission to do something, it's never a good thing."

She took his hand and they hurried across to the car they'd taken.

"What are we going to do, Nick?"

"The only advantage we have, babe, is that it always takes a bureaucracy fucking forever to get their shit together. Jamie will stall for me as long as he can, but we need to get back there first and solve this before the government can swoop in and step in exactly where Paulson is. They'll probably even keep the sick prick on as a consulting source of information. None of those people will ever see a moment of freedom again in their lives. They'll become permanent lab rats or military weapons . . . trained killer K9s." Nick slammed the car door shut, taking a moment to breathe in so he could see past the fury he hadn't felt so overrun with since he had been a kid. "You were right. We should have stayed. The government will get hold of us and the first thing they will want to know is how to kill us. If they can't kill us, then they'll vaporize the whole thing."

"Maybe they should. I mean, we're all animals and monsters, right?" she said softly.

Nick jerked around to look at her, for the first time seeing that meek, defeated girl he'd been shoved into only a few days earlier. He wanted to explode in rage at her, but he realized that it would be hypocritical if he did. He had just had to try defending human deaths and explain the uncontrolled nature of things civilized humans could not or would not be able to accept. Some, he knew, they shouldn't accept. And when Jamie had asked him if there was a way to control the Morphates, he'd rushed to say yes . . . *he* could control them. But it wasn't true. He could control only that one building. That single pack. He didn't know for sure if there were others, but he suspected there were. Each pack would have its own leader and, he knew, would feel threatened by any other it came across. There was no such thing as two Alpha males. Even a grunt like him knew that. They would figure out how to kill or dominate each other, or they would choose territory just like the gangs, and humans would get caught in the crossfire.

"Amara," he said quietly, "my brother came looking for me. He's twice the cop I ever was. He found me. I know it. He's either dead or . . ."

"Paulson has him."

"Yeah."

"You think he's been turned?"

"If Paulson had him, he turned him. You know he did. Just for shits and giggles. Or just because Kin wouldn't have ever given in." Not like he had. He should have known Kin would come after him. No matter how scarce his reports, Kincaid wouldn't have stopped until he was looking at Nick's body, dead or alive.

"Nick, there's only one thing we can do."

Nick turned to look at her again, staring into coppery eyes and trying to figure out how in hell he could keep her safe and help his brother and uncounted others at the same time. "Babe, I am completely open to suggestions," he said roughly. "And it better be a fast one. We're out of time."

"Drive. I will explain on the way."

"Back to the labs?"

"No. Not yet. We need to pick up some things first."

Chapter 15

Miranda Alvarez had never lost her cool in all of her ten years in the field, and she'd seen some godawful stuff. Stepping behind the van to vomit up lunch had never, ever happened to her before, but she had to admit she did it with aplomb. She straightened, took the towel Joey handed her and patted away all evidence without messing up her makeup, and then reached for a breath mint in her pocket as she turned back to the million-dollar moment of a lifetime.

"Mira, we're live in three . . . two . . ."

"Good evening. This is Miranda Alvarez with the Investigative News Force. What you are seeing is a live broadcast of what we have been told is a secret facility of labs. . . ."

"I always liked her," Nick remarked as he and Amara walked up to the labs amid an army of news companies and, by the sound of the military helicopters on approach, their unwitting backup. It was actually a simple sort of plan. All they had to do was broadcast everything live before the government could shut them down and try to hide it. Nick and Amara had already given Alvarez a detailed private interview, played show-and-tell and everything, only with less shock value than what Amara had done for the Federated cops.

Nick knew he was intimidating as all hell, so he had let Amara make her public proposal. It was dangerous and probably insanity, but it was a solution that just might work in this society of short-term thinkers. They liked to close away trouble? Well, this time trouble would volunteer to help build the walls.

With a madman at the helm of the labs, thousands of things could have gone wrong. They could have all been vaporized instantly by some hidden bomb the minute security cameras caught sight of them. However, Nick knew a man who liked to play God wouldn't blow himself up just when he was on the verge of perfecting how to become one. Nick had seen it in the doctor's face just before he'd shot him. Paulson wanted immortality. Invincibility. When he perfected it, he would make himself in his own image.

Dying would rather be contrary to that.

So would getting caught. So Nick and Amara had gambled that Paulson would run before he'd make a stand. He'd abandon the whole of them in a heartbeat and run away so he could play Frankenstein another day. Without his direction, Nick hoped the rest of the place would simply unravel. Losing Paulson was a heavy price they might pay if he did indeed get away, but there really had been no better choice in so little time.

Nick just prayed there were still people left to save. The press van had hardwired into the security systems and they could see far more than was able to be processed.

Nick knew everyone had finally been separated, and realized this was a good thing. It had prevented others from becoming Alpha and the resultant need for another challenge for Nick and Amara to reassert themselves. At least in their building. Now he had to pray that Paulson had not repeated his lunacy six times over. None of the other common rooms were in use. There were signs of life here and there and guards clearly ignorant of what was coming. It wasn't the same in every building.

If there were Alphas in every building, it was going to be a hell of a mess.

Nick wished he could leave Amara behind, but instinct said differently. It said they needed to make a show together. By the time Jamie and the Federation forces touched down, the news crews had been live for twenty minutes and they had been taping the interior activities for over an hour. It was enough evidence to ensure very little about any of what happened next could ever be covered up.

His boss strolled up to him, armored and armed to the teeth. Nick wondered if it would do them any good if things went to shit.

"You disappeared on us, Agent Gregory," he greeted.

"Who are the geeks, Agent Mulloy?" Nick countered, nodding to the men in suits and lab coats who were coming out of vans of their own.

"Just doctors who want to see everyone come out safe and healthy, just like we do." Jamie flashed his "press smile" and Nick slid a glance to Miranda Alvarez. "Nick, back at the briefing you said you could lead the first group out safely?"

"Yeah."

Nick prayed it was just that easy.

Chapter 16

It actually was. Once the staff and guards had been neutralized in the building, it was as easy as keying one door at a time, greeting the shocked individual or couple inside with a few sniffs and words of reassurance. They brought out their Packmates one and two at a time, gently and calmly, and they all remained docile for the most part as each tried to get over the amazement of seeing their Alphas very much alive.

Amara and Nick had practiced, together, exactly what they would say to each male and female. It was actually quite simplistic.

You are not to harm any human being. You are not to make any public display of your Morphate traits and nature. You will wait patiently during this transition for this Pack to reassemble. Watch the news. Exercise every human right you have within the letter of the law.

But that was only building one.

Nick chose the children's labs next. The building bore six separate floors and this was the first warning they had that they were going to encounter six different protocols in each building. Paulson had batched the children to match their adult guinea pig counterparts. Nick and Amara could display dominance over at least one floor, the one that matched their protocol. Once that floor was evacuated, the officials puzzled over what to do next.

"We would have to recruit the Alphas from each protocol," Devona advised them from Amara's side. "Unfortunately, two Alphas in a room together will be a death match."

"Maybe not all of them," Jamie spoke up as he held out a clipboard one of the doctors had handed him. "Look who is Alpha in building four."

"Fuck me." Nick laughed. "Kincaid Gregory! God, I bet that pissed Paulson off." Despite his relishing the joke, Nick's reaction was harsh and obvious with relief. Amara felt her throat closing in sympathy when she saw him turn his head to hide the emotion in his eyes from his boss.

"Yeah, well, now he knows how I felt trying to manage the two of you on a daily basis," Mulloy retorted.

"Nick," Devona interrupted with a soft warning, "pack mentality doesn't account for brotherly bonds. Wolves dominate their siblings all the time. Siblings will war for Alpha just as any others might."

"The difference is," Nick retorted sharply, "we're not a bunch of goddamn wolves. We're human beings. Or at the very least that's the way we were raised." He frowned and Amara instinctively reached to touch him on his arm. The simple contact seemed to relax him a bit, clearing his thoughts. "I'm just worried about what made the difference in each protocol. What did they do to him that they didn't do to me?"

"They won't figure that out from the medical notes for a very long time," Devona informed. "Only way to find out . . ."

"I figured as much," he said grimly.

"But if you can do this, get two Alpha males to coordinate, you can tag team the rest and control their evacuations. It might still get hairy, but it's better than the alternatives."

"Well, then, better go get this brotherly reunion started. Amara," Nick said, "you better stay here."

"Excuse me?"

Nick frowned at the attitude in those two words and took in the aggressive hand on her curvy hip. "I don't want you in the middle of this, Mara. He could be seriously altered. If I can't control what he has become, you could get hurt."

"I see. You can control me, right? Keep me in line right here?"

Nick hesitated when she snapped the words off at him very sharply. He glanced at the assortment of cops and scientists surrounding him. He saw Jamie grinning smugly as he waited to see what he would do next.

"I didn't mean it like that," he said uneasily. "I just don't want you hurt."

"And I'm supposed to sit here and watch you potentially get killed by your own brother? Watch you get hurt? That's different somehow?"

"Lordy, Amara," Devona sighed, "preaching sexism to an Alpha male is like climbing Everest on roller skates. You aren't going to get anywhere you want to go."

"Stop it!" she cried, slamming a fist on the table near her and making the entire room of on-edge people jump in their shoes. She pointed sharply at Nick. "You're a human being, too, damn you! You have a responsibility to act like one and to treat me like one!"

"I thought I was!" he shouted back at her. "One that I care about and want to keep safe! I won't get you killed twice in one day. Not when neither of us knows just what might end up being permanent!"

"Get me killed?" she echoed. "You didn't get me killed."

"Yeah, man, she looks pretty much alive to me."

"Shut up, Jamie," Nick snapped. He turned on her again.

"Paulson blew your brains out because he was trying to control *me*. Do you have any idea how that felt?"

She wasn't the only one who looked at him like he'd lost his mind.

"I mean emotionally! I know you know how it felt physic—God! You drive me insane! You have since the moment I met you. I've been on an emotional bender for days now and it's all connected to you. I just need twenty minutes so I can talk with my brother without being afraid someone is going to take you away from me!"

Amara stood there with her arms wrapped defensively around her lower ribs, her expression troubled but unreadable otherwise.

"Fine," was her only response. Then she turned and left the room, pushing her way past the thick ring of people.

As soon as she left, Jamie said, "Nick, that girl is *not* 'fine.' "

"Yeah. I can see that," he responded, pushing away to go after her.

"Hey, what's the wolf term for being pussy-whipped?" Carl asked snidely. "Bitch-whipped?"

"How about I show you the wolf term for what my fist down your throat feels like?" Nick snarled, turning on his former compatriot so nastily that nearly the entire room gasped to see the as-yet reasonable human male shift into a fanged, clawed creature.

"How about it, freak?" Carl egged him on.

"Nicky! Whoa!" Jamie stepped between the two men, eliciting another indrawn breath from those around them. Nick realized the balls it had to take to step in front of such a frightening unknown as he had become. Then he realized that to Jamie he'd never become an unknown. Fangs, claws, or otherwise, Jamie had still seen him as the same man he'd managed for years. It was why he'd looked away and given him a head start with news services. It made Nick feel instantly human.

It reminded him he hadn't exactly remembered that Amara was a human female at heart. With very human needs. "I'll be right back," he sighed.

Jamie didn't realize Nick could still hear him when he turned to Devona and asked, "Think it's in bad taste to make a crack about him being 'in the doghouse'?"

Chapter 17

Amara could smell her mate approaching long before he reached to stop her progress. He knew it as well as she did, and she was not going to make it easy for him. She'd already been plenty easy. The minute he made contact with her, she pivoted and rounded on him angrily.

"I drive you insane?" she demanded hotly. "You think you've been some kind of picnic for me? I never asked for any of this! I was happy just worrying about myself! I was happy having no expectations, no needs!"

"You weren't happy," he shot back, "you were existing. Surviving."

"Well, thank God you came along and gave my life meaning. It sounds like it was wretched without you."

"Wasn't it?" he asked, his sea-green gaze troubled rather than arrogant. "I'm thinking, all things considered, mine's definitely taken a turn for the better these past few days."

Amara was so genuinely surprised by that remark that she gaped at him a full ten seconds before she snorted in disbelieving laughter. "That's a joke, right? You were a cop with a career, friends, family, and a human life. Now you've been through horrible physical changes against your will, have to face a potential threat from your own brother, and your friends are calling you a ghoulish freak!"

"If Carl was my friend, then he'd never call me that, even if I was one. Kin isn't the one I'm worried about. You are. And this isn't some damn biological imperative I'm operating under either. It's a very human, very emotional one." He reached for her, taking her face against his hand even when she tried to move away. His touch always disturbed her so deeply. Be it physical response or just the way he had of portraying the sense that she was somehow worthy of special treatment, it shook her to the core.

"Don't," she said, trying not to feel the hurt her thoughts sent spearing through her even as she voiced them. "Don't act like you chose me. Don't act like you wouldn't have looked right through me if you'd seen me in the street when we were human. You made me your mate because you had no choice. No choice. Not in what you became and not in what you had to do because of it. I don't blame you for any of it, but don't expect me to believe you'd want anything to do with me if you got your humanity returned to you right this very second."

"That isn't fair," he returned sharply. "There's no way for me to prove otherwise to you. You and I both know we're never going to be fully human again. And if staying a Morphate means I get to keep you for the rest of my life, then I don't want to be fully human again."

"And there's no way you can prove that either! You just said you and I both know it isn't going to be an option. And frankly, I don't think you've considered what 'the rest of' your life really means. Your life has just become significantly extended, Nick. Hundreds, maybe even thousands of years!"

"Thank God, because it's going to take me that long to figure you out!" he shot back furiously.

"There's nothing to figure out! Don't you get it? I'm just some girl from the wrong side of the wall. You said it yourself; the only thing I am good at is surviving. Apparently I'm good at fucking, too, or you wouldn't even be here."

"Amara!" Nick grabbed hold of her suddenly by both arms and shook her so violently her teeth clacked together. "Don't you fucking ever say anything like that to me again! Do you hear me? Despite what you think, I have feelings, too! You're the one who keeps saying I'm still human, damn it. Well, I can be hurt, too, you know. Part of me died today when I thought Paulson killed you. I've never known such a totality of grief and regret. You think I didn't choose you? Paulson shot me while I was kneeling over your body, baby, not while I was immediately sniffing after Mina to replace you! No choice? Oh, I chose. Mina chose to fuck a half dozen males before she tried for me. They must have tossed her room to room when they saw she had an appetite for it. But you heard Paulson. You and I were an exception, not a rule. We didn't have to choose to mate for life, Amara, but we did. Are you saying you had no choice? That you regret giving that to me?"

"No!"

"Then what the hell makes you think it's any different for me?" he challenged.

"Because you're better than I am," she whispered painfully. "You treat me like I'm special, but I'm not. You are."

"Baby, baby," he groaned as he jerked her hard into his embrace and hugged her so tightly she squeaked. "You and I are going to wish we weren't special soon enough. I can promise you that. But there has never been anyone in my life as special to me as you are. I think I've loved you from the moment you told me you wished you'd never met me. I think that's why when they put you in with me I couldn't resist but take you for my own as thoroughly as I could." He took her head between his hands and tipped it back so he could see deeply down into her tearing eyes. He blurred until she couldn't see him, but she heard him even over the painful sob she could no longer contain. "Morphates don't have to mate for life, honey. We just know immediately when we are supposed to. If we were human, our human hang-ups and bullshit would have made it take forever to figure out. Damn it, are you going to make me admit I'm glad Paulson did what he did just because it got me you?"

"That's a lie," she sobbed softly.

"I don't think so," he said honestly, his thumbs brushing tears off her lashes. "I can't be glad he hurt so many of us, Amara, but I have to give credit where it's due. If Paulson hadn't been so cocksure and megalomaniacal, he wouldn't have made the mistake of keeping me alive and then compounding it by giving me something as powerful as you are. Honey, just accept that I love you. When we're done here, I'll spend this long lifetime of ours convincing you of it."

"Will it take that long for me to convince you I love you, too?"

"I'm going to say yes," he said with a sudden grin, "just because it will be fun to watch you try."

Epilogue

"This is Miranda Alvarez reporting from the White House, where today Nick and Amara Gregory watched the president sign the now infamously named Morphate Land Bill. The bill declares the six so-called Dark Cities as now belonging exclusively to the Morphate packs, or clans as they now prefer to be called, making them Morphate territories. These territories will act much in the way of Native American territories, establishing a subculture within a culture, while at the same time providing a solution to the rampant gang violence that spreads out from these Dark Cities more and more every year. As the president said earlier, 'I wouldn't want to be the one to cause trouble behind those walls once the Morphates move in to take possession.' Morphates will be responsible for policing their own peoples and territories; however, federal jurisdiction will still apply. They have pretty much already proven that under their current leadership they are far more capable of controlling themselves than the gangs have proven to be. Of course, opponents to the signing of this bill say this is an act of insanity on the part of the government. 'A case of letting the lunatics run the asylum,' said Congresswoman Fiona Huron. She and others like her believe that within only a few years, the clans will not be satisfied with their territories and will only grow stronger and stronger over time. 'If they decided to take over the world, who could stop them?' one aide was heard to say, referring to the apparent immortality of this new species among us. This begs the question: Can we only trust those whom we have the power to kill?

"Considering all they have suffered, I think this is one concession that is long, long overdue. Barren, walled-in cities polluted with drugs, violence, and worse are our idea of a gift to compensate them for their suffering, and in return they offer to repair and rebuild those cities and their infrastructures, ridding them of the influences this government could not. Some have publicly called the Gregorys and their clans monsters, but this reporter has been with this story since it began to unfold a year ago, and I have seen the Morphates treat us with far more patience and respect than we have ever given them."

Nick shut off the television and dropped the remote onto the night table.

"They make it sound like we haven't already been living in the Dark Cities for the past eight months. We went from four months continued lab analysis, poking and prodding by the damned government, and straight into here." Amara pressed her cheek to the glass of the Dark Manhattan highrise apartment. The clan was currently spread out over the entire territory, a precautionary tactic to keep them from being lumped all together where they'd make an easy target, should anyone ever figure out how to kill them without using a radical bomb that would destroy human populations as well. It was also why they had chosen to send each protocol to a different city: Dark Chicago, Dark Phoenix, Dark L.A.,

Dark Manhattan, Dark Houston, and Dark Philadelphia. "They make it sound as if we had a choice of living among the rest of the world. We'd have been as welcome as a leper colony."

"Hey," Nick said gently as he slid off the bed and came up behind her. He rubbed large, warm hands over her hips, drawing her backside flush against him. "You were the one who came up with this idea."

"Because I knew it was going to be like this."

"It won't always be. And even if it is, we'll make better places and live in better ways. It's our choice."

"I don't know," she sighed softly. "We're still so animalistic, Nick. And some of those other Alphas . . . I don't trust them. Ambrose gives me the creeps."

"Yeah, me too. But he's in line for now and keeping his clan in line. The Alpha Council is working out pretty well so far. Better than I expected."

"You and Devona. She was sure it would never work. But I think part of its success is because you and Kincaid act more like brothers than Alphas, and because you had the very smart idea that it had to be male *and* female Alphas. It provides a certain balance."

"I'm glad Kin took Philly. Kept close."

"Mmm. He's on his third Alpha mate, though. He needs to find a good, strong female to mate with permanently or the constant power plays will cause a lot of trouble."

"He will," Nick assured her.

She snorted in disbelief. "More likely one will have to kick ass, become Alpha, and force him to fall stupidly in love with her. Your brother is a very stubborn man. If he wasn't so nice to me, he'd probably scare the hell out of me. He's rather intense."

"Don't ever say that to him. You'd hurt his feelings if he thought you were afraid of him. He really likes you. Sometimes I think he likes you too much." Nick frowned against the back of her head. "He stares at you a lot."

"I think he's trying to figure out what I see in you," she teased him, her grin reflected back at him from the window.

"Maybe." Nick pushed aside her hair to rub his lips and nose against her warm neck. He took in several long breaths, which he exhaled hotly against her skin in rolling sounds of male intrigue. "God, you smell incredible." His hands circled her waist, stroking across the low plane of her belly. His fangs made their appearance and he scraped the wicked tips down the length of her pulse until her nipples were painfully hard with the chilling stimulation and making a prominent show under the silk of her blouse. Amara reached down to close her hands around his at her waist when she knew they were about to move on to new and exciting adventures across her skin.

"You know we can't," she said breathlessly as he nudged his awesome erection against her soft bottom cheeks. "Not for two more days."

He growled and nipped her neck in frustration, crowding her against the cold glass window. "I don't want to wait. I smell you everywhere and I can't get a damn thing done all day because of it. The president was signing that bill and all I was thinking about was how much I needed you. God," he groaned with agonized reflection as he rode his hips into her, "I'm so hard it hurts."

"I can feel that," she said in a hitched gasp as her sensual chemistry began to clamor for what he was offering. "L—let me turn around. You'll love me on my knees, baby."

"No!" He barked at her as he pressed her roughly to the glass, his body, and his persistent phallus all at once. "No," he whispered much more softly against her sensitive skin. "As much as I love your mouth, honey, it simply will not do."

"But . . ." Her protest faded away jerkily when his hand dipped below the waistband of her skirt and crept into the warmth and moisture beneath the fabric of her panties. His large fingertips skated over her in an instant, the slick readiness of her excited body making it so easy. Of course she wanted him. She always wanted him, and now more than usual. They'd long since discovered it was designed this way in their new natures. "Nick, you can't . . . we said we wouldn't. You made me promise not to let you do this. Oh, God," she groaned, her head falling back against his shoulder as his touch glided around and around her hypersensitive clit.

"I've been suffering for two days," he rasped, his words scratching fangs into her skin until she creamed a flood of juices over his buried hand. "You've been very attentive with this mouth of yours," he said, kissing the corner of her mouth. "You have the tongue of an angel gone so very bad, and your hands are divinity. However," he stipulated, using his deep hold in her pussy to push her rhythmically back into the steady rock of his hips, "heaven only exists for me when I am buried balls deep inside of your hot body. I want my heaven now. It calls to me with heat, liquid need, and incredible scent. God, you're drenched in it."

"Nick!" she cried as his touch and bodily movements worked her into a blind frenzy of desire. It wasn't hard to do. She had been walking the edge of need ever since she'd gone into heat two days ago. But . . .

But they had agreed now was not the time for children. And since human methods of birth control for females didn't seem to work for Morphates, it meant abstaining or the use of condoms. Nick's extraordinary size made the latter a very uncomfortable choice for him. Amara's irresistible body chemistry made the former uncomfortable for them both.

"You have to . . . wear a condom . . . ," she panted as he drew up her skirt over her backside and reached to shuck off her underpants. His reply was an irritated grunt that sounded too much like a negation to her.

"I'll pull out," he said hotly, struggling with a single hand to release his belt and the zipper to his pants.

"You won't!"

Amara didn't know how she managed it, but she ripped herself free of him, gasping for breath as she stumbled back into the room away from him. He turned on her with a very intimidating sound of displeasure and immediately began to stalk her even as he stripped himself of his shirt and then his pants. Amara swallowed hard when his gorgeous body was in full, glorious display, his arousal absolutely mouthwatering to her starving and ramped-up libido.

"Nick . . . ," she half warned and half begged him. "Nick, you won't. You can't control it like that. You know that. Don't put this all on me. It isn't fair."

Nick reached for her and she leapt out of his grasp with only threads to spare. She backed up even farther, nervously glancing at the shut door of the bedroom.

"Come here," he beckoned, his grin absolutely wolfish. "Let's make a baby, then. Let's make lots of babies."

That stopped her retreat cold, and her eyes flashed with sudden fury. "In this hellish place? With killers and rapists at our gates and dirty needles and broken vials the landscaping for their playground? No!" She reached out and slapped him so hard it echoed through the large room and sent his head snapping sharply to the side. "Damn you, Nick! Knowing the way I was raised, you ask me to be that careless? You selfish prick!"

Trying not to burst into tears, Amara turned to grab the door. It was barely open an inch before the slam of his hand above her head sent it crashing shut. Then he was against her back again, the impact of his body flattening her to the wall near the door. He grabbed her wrist, pinning it high above her head, and she felt him dragging up her skirt once again. She cried out, and the tears burst free as her heart raced with dread and panic.

"Shh," he hushed her softly against her ear. "Don't you

trust me, baby love?" he demanded fiercely. "Hmm? Don't you trust the man who loves you to know what would hurt you?"

"I trust the man . . . but not the beast," she sobbed as he wedged his thigh between hers and made her step out wider. He eased her hips away from the wall and toward him, bending her slightly at the waist and opening her sex to the intrusive glide of his rigid cock from behind her. "No! Please, Nick," she wept.

"The man and the beast are the same," he whispered roughly, biting her ear briefly as he wetted himself with the slickness coating her heated pussy. "You love and trust us either completely, or not at all, Amara."

Nick slid himself into place at the entrance of her body, merely a single thrust from sinking into her ripe sheath. The smell of her pheromones called to his every male instinct, her ovulating body begging for impregnation from her mate. Amara wanted to trust the man she loved, but after a year of these awful four-day cycles every month, she knew how crazy this chemistry made him. It made her just as desperate to have him as it made him to take her.

"I . . ." Amara's heart was pounding with the terror of becoming pregnant before she was ready, before Dark Manhattan was ready to safely contain their offspring. "I love you, Nick," was all she could say. She closed her eyes tightly, her hands balling into fists.

Amara felt his head drop slightly, his mouth lowering to her shoulder line, edging up to her neck beneath her hair. His mouth opened on her, fangs pricking and holding her still without breaking her skin. He thrust in a slow, shallow series of increments, entering her and teasing her at the same time, backing completely free of her before returning in prodding touches.

"You say you love me," he breathed against her, nipping her as if in punishment, "but you mean you don't trust me.

You don't trust me to protect you. To care for you and your feelings. To know how much pain it would cause you to watch your child grow in a place without safety, love, or even green grass."

This time he rushed deep inside of her, the pleasure of feeling him filling her warring with her other volatile emotions for control of her. She hadn't felt him for two days. Two days. For them, it was so long. Too long. Longer still while they were tormented by the natural cravings a madman had forced onto their biological makeup. Nick surged up into her once more, finally burying himself completely into her. He was so heavily aroused, so thick and hard with it, that she felt impaled straight to her pounding heart. Her body ignored the distress of her emotions, the need of it overriding her mind with anything and everything it needed to do to coax what it wanted from her mate.

She couldn't resist the need to thrust herself back against him, to squeeze his cock tightly within her. She knew all it would take was just a little more movement and she would come hard around him, her body ready to milk him for his seed.

"Oh, God!" she gasped when he began to glide into her in a slow, steady rhythm. Three strokes, then four, and she pitched over the edge. She ejected a cry that combined pleasure with dismay as her entire body locked in rich, wrenching spasms.

Nick's fangs punctured her deeply and she screamed as it jacked her ecstasy up beyond reason, if not completely beyond caring. She could feel him drinking deeply of her, each swallow punctuating the increasing speed of his thrusts, like a car shifting gears with her blood acting as the clutch. Her feet lifted completely off the floor with each impact between them, and she felt the vibrations of his moans shimmering over her skin. She closed her eyes, tears staining the wall where her cheek rested even as she climbed a second peak just listening to his crisis approach. She would be ready for him, suckling him of everything he had, ensuring his genes were secured to her own as her body demanded.

He released her shoulder to throw back his head and shout a cadence of onrushing climax. He surged deep and hard, slammed to a hard stop as his body locked . . .

. . . and was gone.

He left her so fast she nearly fell to her knees, but suddenly his arm was around her and crushing her with thoughtless strength as he shuddered hard against her. He was groaning as if in terrible pain, and then suddenly she felt the full lean of his weight against her as he gasped for breath.

Stunned that he had been able to pull out of her at such a moment of ultimate need and pleasure, Amara tried to turn around, but he kept her forcefully facing the wall as he tried to get a hold of himself. After a minute or two, she felt him pull her hair back from the sticky side of her neck, making her realize she was bleeding actually quite heavily. He returned to the wound, licking her until the bleeding stopped. Then he touched his forehead to her temple.

"Never, ever doubt me again," he whispered.

Then he was turning and leaving her to walk wordlessly to the bathroom. Amara turned around and watched his back as he went, the amazing flex of his taut muscles along his thighs and buttocks and spine not helping her to clear the dizzy fog in her brain. She heard him enter the shower and then she got really, really . . .

Mad.

"You son of a bitch!" she hissed.

Amara quickly stomped after him, shedding her stained blouse and skirt so she was naked by the time she opened the shower door and stepped in to confront him.

"What the hell was that?" she demanded. "Some kind of test? Is that your version of figuring out how much I really love you?"

"I hope not," he retorted, "because you would have failed it miserably." He turned his back on her and picked up some soap as steam clouded between them. The neo-angle shower was very large and had multiple showerheads, something she had insisted on during the remodeling. She recalled how much effort it had taken just to get the supplies delivered to the gates of Dark Manhattan. Now she dodged under one of the sprays to get face to face with him again.

"You asked me to stop you from making love to me! You and I discussed this entire issue like two rational, mature adults. You admitted to me that you didn't know if you could keep your head on straight in the heat of the moment. Then suddenly you think it's an issue of loving you and trusting you?"

"It became one when you took a joke so seriously you belted me across the face for it! I don't give a flying fuck how hot I am for you, Amara, I would never force a child on you . . . on us . . . under these circumstances! I wanted to make that perfectly clear to you. To both of us."

"And what if you had been wrong? What if you couldn't control it? What if you hadn't been able to pull out of me in time? Do you realize what that would have done to us? To me? You would risk everything we have just to prove a point?"

"Yes! Because if we don't have that much trust and control over ourselves, then we don't have anything going for us at all, Amara. If you think I could stand there watching you cry and in that much pain and not do the right thing for you, then this is all wrong, babe. I had a choice . . . walk away and let you think the worst of me, or I could prove what I knew I could do. I knew I could love you right. Not just physically, but knowingly and sympathetically. I've always known it, even if you haven't. What it comes down to is you don't trust me any more than I trusted myself, and we can't lead all these people if we work under that kind of doubt, never mind expect us to last long enough to see the day when kids actually become possible." He reached to hook the back of her neck with a palm and drew her up close, staring hard into her eyes. "All I did was show you I could do what needs to be done. I pushed myself to the utmost, baby. I was inside you, surrounded with the conditions of your heat, and I was drowning in the aphrodisiac of your blood *and I still protected you.* I will always protect you. No matter what. I need you to believe that. It hurts to think you don't believe that."

Nick cursed when his voice broke and he cleared his throat of the betraying emotion. But Amara was grateful she had heard it because it sent home to her how truly hurt he felt. That it wasn't just words or even about posturing and one-upmanship, which seemed to plague the instincts of their new breed. She slowly began to understand his perspective, though she still didn't agree with his high-handed methods.

"You could have just asked me," she said quietly.

"You would have thought I was affected by your heat and trying to get around you. I had to do it right then and exactly that way. Tell me now that you don't believe we can always control this. Think about it. I'm going to make you trust me, Mara. I won't have babies with you until I believe you trust me implicitly to provide, protect, and help raise them well. Besides, we can't spend forty-eight days out of every year screaming with lust for each other and denying it. Do I like climaxing outside of your body? No. I don't. And in a way it kind of hurts. But I'll pay that price any day to feel you come around me like you did." His voice dropped an erotic octave and he closed his eyes briefly as the memory rode over him. "In the future, I'll plan a little better and pick one of so many other, safer places on your body to come in." He reached to wrap her up tight to his body, his tongue darting out to lick the water from her lips. "Mmm, shall I count the ways?"

"Nick," she scolded, suddenly breathless for him all over

again. "I swear, you turn me inside out. What am I supposed to do with you?" She rolled her eyes at his lascivious grin. "Never mind." Then she grinned in return. "Just how do we go about conditioning me to trust you, do you suppose?"

"Hmm," he hummed speculatively. "Now there's an intriguing proposal. Conditioning. Isn't that where you do something over and over and over and over again to elicit a desired response?"

"Oooh, Agent Gregory. You took a psychology course!"

"Yeah. I got an A, too. Wanna see?"

"I don't know . . . not sure if I trust you . . . ," she goaded softly.

"Okay, now you're just begging for it," he growled gruffly.

"About time you noticed. Thought I was going to have to drop to my knees for a minute there."

"Don't rule that out just yet."

CRYSTAL DREAMS

By Kate Douglas

*My sincere thanks to Ann Jacobs, Sheri Ross Fogarty,
Jan Takane, Amanda Haffery, and Rose Toubbeh for their
wonderfully critical eyes*

Chapter 1

Mari Schwartz glared at the red and blue lights flashing on the highway patrol cruiser as it pulled in behind her. Cursing softly but steadily, she dug out her registration papers. She was just reaching for her purse when the California Highway Patrol officer leaned over and gazed at her through the window.

Rolling it down, she plastered a bright smile on her face. "Hello, Officer."

He nodded. "Ma'am. Did you realize you were doing eighty-five miles per hour in a fifty-five zone, one that's zoned for construction?"

Innocent smile. She could do this. "I was? But I couldn't possibly have . . ."

Stern glare. Obviously he wasn't falling for the innocent-maiden shtick.

He nodded and held out his hand. "Yes, ma'am. We got you on radar. Your driver's license, proof of insurance, and auto registration, please?"

She sighed. For a day that had started out so shitty, she honestly hadn't thought it could get any worse. Obviously she'd been wrong. Mari handed over the requested paper-work and stared straight ahead, just waiting.

It didn't take long. She could tell he was trying to maintain, but his snort didn't disguise his laugh. "Marigold *Moonbeam* Schwartz?"

She glared at him out of the corner of her eye. One of these days, she really was going to change her name. Raising one eyebrow she said, very drily, "Conceived during an exceptionally good acid trip, according to my parents."

This time he laughed out loud. "You or the name?"

Sighing deeply, she shook her head. "Both, I imagine." This time she looked him straight in the eye. He was definitely cute and appeared to be about her age. His blue eyes twinkled as he held out his hand. "I'm Officer Phoenix Rising Friday. Believe me, you have my utmost sympathy. I go by Nic, and daily I thank the good Lord I'm not a sergeant."

She shook his hand, laughing. "I don't blame you. I'm Mari."

He released her hand and stepped back, but he was still grinning. "I'm not going to write you up, Ms. Schwartz. I can't do that to a kindred spirit—bad karma, as my mother would say. Just a warning this time, but please slow down and drive safely. I'd hate to see a name as unique as yours in the obits."

"Thank you." He was cute and nice and . . . she glanced at the simple gold band on his left hand. *Married.* Definitely married. "I really do appreciate it, Nic. Not getting a ticket, I mean. I'm in a hurry to get home. My father's had some emergency surgery and . . ."

"Then get going, but drive safely. You won't help your parents any if you're in the hospital, too. Construction ends in another mile and you can legally go seventy." He shook his head. "But not eighty-five." He stepped back.

"I'll remember that. And thank you." Mari carefully pulled the used Miata she'd recently purchased back into traffic. Thank goodness she'd dodged that bullet. A ticket in a construction zone would have cost her double, and for an unemployed investment banker with a very thin savings account, it could wipe her out financially.

Which was another reason she'd agreed to come home to Evergreen to run her mom's shop until her dad recovered. Well, that and the fact she couldn't afford to keep her apartment in San Francisco, not to mention the beautiful leased Mercedes she'd had to surrender now that she didn't have a job.

Damn, she'd surrendered way too much. Her 401(k) was long gone. As of today, so was the gorgeous little studio apartment with the view of the Golden Gate Bridge, and even the boyfriend she'd thought she loved, who'd once talked of marriage.

Of course, if she was totally honest, losing Brad was the only positive thing that had happened lately. What a jerk! Telling her he loved her, that she could count on him. Then when he'd been among the first laid off when the bank downsized, he'd blamed Mari, like it was entirely her fault.

The bastard. How could she possibly have been so stupid?

It was bad enough when her own pink slip had arrived a couple days ago. Worse when she checked her savings account and discovered that Brad had burned through most of her ready cash impressing a new girlfriend she'd somehow not noticed.

Thank goodness she'd already turned in the Mercedes and given notice on her apartment. It hadn't taken long to put her belongings in storage, spend way too much of her cashed-out 401(k) on a used car, and get the hell out of Dodge.

So here she was, Stanford grad with MBA and pride in hand, headed home to Evergreen, California, to run what was nothing more than a tourist trap. Without a job or anything waiting, she hadn't had an excuse when her mom asked her to manage Crystal Dreams, the successful little business she'd had in Evergreen since before Mari was born.

Spirit Schwartz, who claimed to be a witch for crying out loud, would be busy caring for her beloved husband during Freedom's recuperation from back surgery, while Mari, with all her amazing business background, sold magic crystals and potions to gullible tourists and serious New Age nuts.

"Aaarrgghh!" Mari huffed out a big breath along with her primal scream. "Damn, that felt good." She blew out another breath and passed through the last of the orange construction cones, hit the open road, and pressed down on the accelerator.

She carefully kept it just under seventy, as per the officer's instructions, but as foothills and farmland disappeared behind her, she wondered again for at least the millionth time—why couldn't she have had normal parents instead of a couple of sixties throwbacks who'd never quite come down from the last acid trip? What could she possibly have done to deserve parents who'd stuck her with a name and a legacy she'd never live down, no matter how long she survived?

And how in the hell was she going to stand living so close to Freedom and Spirit? She loved them both dearly, but even their phone calls made her nuts. Living in the same town within hailing distance of her parents and running Crystal Dreams was going to turn her into a raving lunatic.

An unwelcome shiver raced along his spine. Darius of Kronus grasped his crystal sword with both hands and studied the wall opposite his position. He'd been guarding the portal to his home world of Lemuria for almost a week without any sign of trouble. Even now, all was well with the Lemurian gate, but the once sealed gateway to the hell that was Abyss and home to demonkind suddenly glowed with a most unsavory pulse of life.

After a quick glance over his shoulder, Darius stepped across the silent cavern and stood directly before the same portal the now exiled Alton of Artigos, son of Lemuria's leader, had so bravely closed with his crystal sword not quite two weeks ago.

Darius glanced at his own sword and wished once again that it would gain sentience and speak to him. He hadn't been raised to carry crystal. He had no idea what the gods-be-damned thing could do, though he'd observed how crystal killed demons.

He'd never seen one close a portal before, and it appeared the gateway to Abyss was about to reopen. "Nine hells." He held the blade up and frowned. "If you would speak, you could at least tell me what I'm supposed to do next!"

The sword remained silent, but new light ebbed and flowed at the center of the portal, pulsing with the cadence of life. Heat surrounded the entire area and the dark stone began to change, spinning faster and faster. Colors flowed and spread—shades from white to orange and then blood red.

Darius leaped back as the center spun too fast for the eye to follow. The pulse took on sound, a sense of life that expanded with each breath he took. He glanced over his shoulder again. Should he notify his comrades? But he couldn't move. Something held him in thrall, some sense of portent—a power that drew him close even as it repelled.

Mesmerized by the swirling colors, the thrumming pulse, and the harsh intake of his own suddenly labored breathing, Darius stared into the very center of the awakening portal.

Like the lens of an eye expanding in darkness, it opened.

A black mist seeped through the deepest, reddest part of the reawakened gateway. Demonic mist, thick and oily and entirely formless, flowed out through the center. Like purulence from a festering wound, it slid down the wall to the ground. Another wraith followed, and then another.

Faster now, boiling up and out of the portal, flowing along the wall, filling the chamber within the vortex, the demon wraiths oozed out. They bled away from the Abyssian portal and merged into a black, foul-smelling cloud that ebbed and flowed across the floor.

There was no sense of purpose to their movement. Not yet. They spread across the floor toward the portal to Earth's dimension—an Earth Darius knew was already reeling under demon attack. Then they doubled back and oozed up a wall, down the way they'd come, and across the floor toward the Lemurian gateway.

Snapping out of his rapt fascination with the hypnotic demons' *danse macabre,* Darius held his breath and slashed his crystal sword through the black cloud.

He prayed to his gods—*Let this blade be death to demonkind.*

It had never been tested before, but then, neither had he.

Sparks flew. It worked! A banshee cry deafened him as the demon mist morphed into a single entity and faced him. He'd seen demons only once before, in a battle inside this same vortex when Alton and his mate had battled demonkind. Then he, a lowly guardsman, had carried a steel sword, useless against demons.

That day had been a turning point in his ordinary life—he'd been gifted with crystal. Empowered now, armed with a demon-killing blade, Darius slashed through the wraiths once again and the screams and cries, the sparks flaring and then dying in a sulfuric stench, told him that his blade cut true.

Again and again he attacked the dark mist.

Demons died, yet more came, spilling out of the portal, one after the next, dark and ugly and stinking of sulfur. More than Darius could fight alone. More than any single man— even a man wielding crystal—could hope to stop.

He raced to the Lemurian portal and stepped through the

dimensional gate into his world. Down a short tunnel, through the energy veil that protected his unsuspecting people from the threat their ruling council refused to admit even existed.

He sent out a telepathic call to the sergeant of the Lemurian guard, his cousin Roland. Waited a brief second for Roland's reply.

Stop them. At any cost. Do not let any of the demons survive. I'm on my way. I'll bring the others.

The others. Only four of the guard—and that included himself and Roland—carried crystal blades. Four swords to protect an entire world. Darius turned and ran back to the vortex, back to stop the demons from invading Lemuria.

Except, when he arrived, the demons weren't coming toward the Lemurian portal. No. They'd changed course once again. As he watched, the seething mass of demonkind reached the gateway to Earth's dimension. Between one heartbeat and the next, they hit the portal and disappeared.

Only their stench remained.

Darius stared at the blue and green gateway that led into a world he'd only imagined. He glanced toward the portal to Abyss. It was quiet now, glowing softly red, and though it practically screamed its own malevolence, it was, in reality, silent.

Lemurians had long been forbidden entry into Earth's dimension. It was how they'd remained hidden for thousands of years, and yet, Darius had met citizens of Earth. In fact, two of them, both women, carried sentient crystal swords, an honor given to very few Lemurians and never before to a human.

He gazed at his own sword. He'd been honored to receive crystal, but his was not sentient. No, until he proved himself in battle, his sword would remain silent. He glanced toward the portal, the one the demon wraiths had passed through to Earth. That way led to the true threat. For now, anyway, demonkind appeared more intent on invading Earth than Lemuria.

He had his orders, directly from Roland of Kronus, sergeant of the Guard. *Stop them. At any cost.*

The alarm had been raised. Maybe Roland would know how to close the reopened portal from Abyss. Darius didn't have a clue how to do it. He was useless here. The real battle lay on the other side of the gateway—in Earth's dimension.

Earth. He'd dreamed all his long life of one day setting foot on the world Lemurians had once called home.

He glanced once more at his silent sword, raised his head, and stared at the doorway to Lemuria. Then, before he had time to talk himself out of such a precipitous move, Darius of Kronus threw caution to the wind and stepped through the blue and green portal, away from everything he knew.

Yet in many ways, he was actually going home.

Long before his birth, Lemurians had lived on Earth until their continent had disappeared beneath the sea. His ancestors had escaped the destruction of their home, but stories of the lost continent had filled Darius with dreams of one day setting foot on the world his people had once known.

He couldn't believe he'd actually done it, when, a few short steps later, he stood on the solid reality of Earth—more precisely, on the upper flank of Mount Shasta—just above the tiny community he'd heard of, called Evergreen.

The sun—the sun he'd never seen in his almost ten thousand years of life within the Lemurian dimension—was sinking beneath the broad curve of the earth, disappearing behind the silent mountains that stretched to the west. The sky above glowed in shades of violet and dark blue, edging to pale peach and yellow where the brilliant slice of sunlight hovered for one brief second longer before finally winking out beneath the horizon.

Caught in the awesome beauty of the mountain on which he stood, in the vast world around him unlimited by cavern walls and painted frescoes, Darius paused in total amazement.

Nine hells. So this was the world they'd been denied, this huge, limitless expanse of greens and golds, of blue sky and tall trees and vast mountain ranges. This was the world where Lemuria had once prospered, where her children had enjoyed the glory of sunlit days and star-filled nights—glory that was now merely legend and the stuff of dreams.

This was the world demonkind had chosen to attack, a world so filled with beauty Darius fought a powerful yet exceedingly unmanly urge to weep.

Instead of giving over to tears, he sheathed his sword, put a glamour upon it to hide it from unsuspecting eyes, and tightened the belt around his long, blue robe—the uniform of the Lemurian Guard. He shivered, suddenly aware of the chill air and the crystals of frost already forming on the ground around him. When he exhaled, a soft cloud of steam formed before his lips and nose.

Then he caught a hint of demon stench fouling the pristine air. His duty was clear as he headed down the mountain, following the sulfuric stench toward the tiny lights twinkling in the distance.

Humans would be there.

So would demons, and hadn't he been told to stop them at all cost? Darius tossed his many long braids over his shoulders and placed one sandaled foot in front of the other, following the narrow trail that led down the flank of the mountain. He might be here to hunt demons, but by the nine hells, he was finally going to see Earth.

Chapter 2

Mari glanced up from the book she'd been killing time with and realized it was almost dark outside. The shop glowed with artificial candles and crystals of every shape and size, and she'd lost track of the time since the last customer had wandered into—and out of—Crystal Dreams around three hours ago.

Yawning, she glanced at the clock. Almost six, which meant she could start the process of shutting down and closing up for the night. Damn. She'd spent an entire week here already, which was at least six days longer than she usually hung out in Evergreen, but Dad was still unable to get around without help and her mom was definitely needed at home by his side.

Thank goodness those two had found each other. Mari figured no one else would ever have been able to stand either one. Not that she didn't love her parents, but there were days . . .

The phone rang. She checked caller ID, sighed, and took her mom's call. A few minutes later, she hung up the phone, relieved to have gotten out of a dinner invitation. Not tonight. Tonight she wanted the peace and quiet of her own company. No one else, and certainly not her mother's nonstop advice on how Mari really should be living her life.

In Spirit's world, it was all about staying in tune with the spirits, cultivating good karma, and existing within a sphere of positive energy.

Mari glanced at her book—an old one of her mother's filled with personal notes and comments about casting magic spells, of all things—and then at the door leading to the stairs that would take her up to the little apartment she'd cleared out on the second floor. That's where she planned to find some positive energy—once she got upstairs, crawled into her jammies, and opened a bottle of wine.

She'd found enough old furniture stored in the attic from the years her parents had lived over the shop to turn the small apartment into a fairly comfortable place to stay. Thank goodness, because there was no way on God's green earth she'd ever want to stay with Spirit and Freedom. No, then she wouldn't be worried about going nuts, she'd be worried about ending up charged with the murder of one and maybe both of her parents.

At least this whole situation was only temporary. Her father was on the slow road to recovery, the economy had to turn around, she'd find another job, and another boyfriend—hopefully not one like Brad—and she'd get her life back. For now, though, she had a clean and quiet place to sleep, enough leftovers to fix for dinner, her mother's book to put her to sleep, and the anticipation of a quiet night all by herself.

Mari walked around the shop, turning off the fake candles and covering the locked counters displaying semiprecious stones. It really was a cute little shop. For all her flakiness, her mom had still managed to create a successful business.

Spirit had held on to her spot here on Lassen Boulevard

for close to forty years, ever since she'd fallen for the tall, skinny hippy who was her beloved life mate. And she'd maintained a lot higher profit margin than the bank where Mari'd worked.

Mari would never figure out how Spirit had managed to tap into the collective weirdness of an entire generation and actually make a profit. How her unconventional mother could succeed while so many Fortune 500 businesses had rolled over and died made absolutely no sense at all. When she'd asked her mom the secret, Spirit had smiled that Earth Mother smile of hers and blamed it all on good karma, the positive energy of the Mount Shasta vortex and the blessings of the Goddess—along with a magic spell or two.

Go figure. Chuckling softly, Mari opened the front door. It was always quiet here this time of year, now that the summer crowds were long gone. Halloween was still a couple weeks away. It wasn't yet time for Thanksgiving and the holiday season to get rolling. Most of the neighboring shops had closed early and the street was empty, so it wasn't like she was missing any customers by shutting down a few minutes ahead of schedule. She dumped some kibble in the little dish where the stray cats ate, and pulled the display cart inside.

It was loaded now with candles and books and a few little carved wood items, though she vaguely recalled some cute little ceramic figurines that had sat on the bottom shelf for years. Her mom had said something about vandals coming through town just a few days before Mari'd arrived. No one had caught them, but they'd destroyed the rock and ceramic statues in front of all the stores and businesses along Lassen Boulevard, and even in some of the other parts of town.

Weird. Why would anyone do such a stupid thing? Mari flipped over the OPEN sign and reached for the door to pull it closed. A low growl caught her attention. She stared into the gloom, didn't see anything, and again reached for the door.

She heard it once more, closer this time. Tiny little hairs on the back of her neck rose to attention. A yellow cat slunk across the road in front of the shop, one of her mom's strays that Mari'd been feeding all week. The big tom's ears lay flat against his head, his tail stuck straight out behind his long, lean body, and all his hair was standing on end.

"Hey, kitty. What's the matter? You look like something really has you spooked."

The cat paused with one front leg lifted in midstep. Blinking, Mari stared at the cat. He growled again and stared right back at her out of eyes glowing incandescent red. Then he snarled and his lips peeled back. Mari gasped.

She was staring at row after row of shining, triangular teeth. Set into blood-red gums, they looked razor sharp, like something out of a cheap horror film or *Jaws*.

Before Mari could slam the door, the cat let out a banshee wail and launched itself through the opening. It took a swipe at Mari as it flew past, but she twisted out of the way of the extended claws—claws that looked more like talons and much too long and sharp to belong to any normal cat. The screaming creature hit the wooden floor and skidded all the way to the back counter, turned, and scrabbled for purchase on the floorboards. He left claw marks in the oak as he rushed Mari.

"Holy shit!" She dodged to the left and raced for the back door. The cat blocked the way, yowling and snarling like a creature possessed. Mari ducked behind a counter that displayed books on everything from local legends to witchcraft. The cat howled louder. Stiff-legged, it stalked her.

"Get back, you stupid cat." Except Mari was the one backing quickly across the small store until she came up against a wall lined with shelves of carved stone figurines and sparkling, gem-filled geodes.

Trapped, her back to the wall, Mari grabbed a handful of polished stones and threw them at the cat. It skipped out of

the way and howled even louder. Frantic, she reached for
something else to throw. Instead, as if she'd been drawn to
the thing, her fingers wrapped around a geode. Over a foot
long, it was shaped like a club with gray stone along the
back and faceted rubies filling the inside and glistening
through the cutaway front.

It was heavy but balanced and fit her hand perfectly. It felt
like she thought a weapon should feel. She curled her fingers
around the thing and hoped like hell she wouldn't have to
use it—that would mean the cat had gotten way too close.

It yowled again and crouched low, ready to spring. Terrified and trembling from head to foot, Mari clutched her
makeshift club. The cat shifted and flexed his rear legs—and
Mari did something she'd never done in her life.

She opened her mouth and screamed bloody murder.

It took Darius longer than expected to reach the town that
sprawled haphazardly on the western slope of the mountain.
It was almost completely dark by the time he walked
brazenly along the main thoroughfare. No one was out and
about. The occasional vehicle passed by, but for some reason, no one seemed to notice a man almost seven feet tall,
dressed in a dark blue robe with his waist-length hair hanging in many braids down his back.

The few humans he'd seen had either nodded politely or
looked away, but no one appeared all that surprised by his
presence. Of course, he'd seen one man dressed in a similar
robe with his long white hair unbound and his beard flowing,
but he'd been standing on a corner, carrying a large placard.

The sign said something about repenting, that the end
was coming, though Darius wasn't sure what it was the end
of. At least he'd been able to read the crude printing, which
meant his Lemurian ability to understand most languages
and writing worked even in Earth's dimension.

There was no sign of demonkind about, though Darius was almost certain he'd followed their sulfuric stench to the right place. Now, though, the smells were not of sulfur but of foods. Wonderful smells that had his stomach growling with hunger and his nose twitching to follow the scents to their source.

He had no currency for use in this place, though he did carry a few gems in his pocket. He wondered if a diamond would be enough to purchase whatever it was that seemed to draw him like filings to a magnet. Pausing in front of a small café, he stared at the lighted window and inhaled the savory aromas.

A scream sliced through the night. Loud, terrifying, and not far away. Putting aside all thought of food, Darius spun away from the building and raced down the dark street toward the bloodcurdling scream for help.

Mari screamed again. The cat stalked closer, snarling and yowling. Saliva dripped from its jaws and she was sure it was rabid. It had to be rabid. What else could cause something so horrible, so totally unbelievable?

She clutched the geode and wondered if she could knock the cat out if she threw it just right, or at least distract the animal's attention so she could make a mad dash for the door and get the hell out before . . .

The front door to the shop burst open and slammed against the wall with a deafening crash. The glass in the upper half cracked from top to bottom. A man rushed in—a huge man wearing what looked like a dark blue monk's robe and sandals, with his coal-black hair in dozens of braids flying behind him like so many snakes. He raised a huge sword in both hands, screamed something in a language Mari'd never heard, and raced directly toward her.

Ten years of living in the city and regular classes in self-

protection and martial arts kicked Mari's survival instincts
into overdrive. Ignoring the cat, she flew at the new threat
and kicked high, connecting with his very flat stomach with
the sole of her boot. When he doubled over, gasping for air,
she chopped down hard on the back of his neck with the side
of her hand, exactly the way her karate instructor had taught
her. Then she followed through with an upraised knee between his legs, connecting solidly with his unprotected
crotch.

She noticed, when his eyes crossed, that he had the most
beautiful emerald-green eyes she'd ever seen on a man. Then
he dropped like a rock and hit the floor hard, groaning, gasping for air, and drawing his long legs up to his chest. Still, he
managed to twist to one side and strike out with his sword.

Only then did Mari realize it wasn't a metal blade—his
sword appeared to be made of glass. And it glowed!

Ignoring Mari entirely, the man touched the glowing blade
to the screeching cat. Mari jumped back as a thick, oily mist
seemed to ooze up and out of the cat's back. It hovered for a
brief moment above the animal, long enough for the man to
twist his blade and slash weakly through the mist.

Mari screamed when the mist burst into sparks, flamed
brightly, and disappeared in a sulfurous stink. Then the
man's eyes rolled back in his head, his sword fell to the floor,
and he collapsed on his side. His knees were still drawn up
to his middle, but now he clutched between his legs with
both hands.

The cat shook himself, hissed once, and then walked
around the fallen stranger. He batted at a couple of the long
braids, lost interest, and wandered out the open door, where
he stopped to eat some of the kibble Mari had tossed in the
dish.

She stood as if she'd been turned to stone, and stared at
the comatose man on the floor. Dear Lord, he hadn't been attacking her. He'd rushed to her rescue, and she'd . . . she'd . . .

Oh, crap. She'd kneed him in the balls.

He was no longer groaning. He'd passed out. Still clutching the geode like a ruby-faceted club, Mari knelt beside him and stared at his throat. The big artery running down his neck pulsed in a slow, steady beat—proof she hadn't killed him.

"I am so sorry," she whispered. "I didn't know you were trying to help me. Oh, crap." She sat back on her heels, glanced at the front door, and realized the street had grown totally quiet. All the other shops on either side had shut down for the night and she was here all alone with a man she'd just flattened. Trembling like a leaf, Mari stood up, and looked out the door and down at the cat.

It stared up at her. "Meow?"

The damned thing was purring. What in the hell had just happened? Mari slowly shut the door and locked it. The quarter-inch-wide crack ran from the bottom of the window to the top, but at least the glass hadn't fallen out of the frame. She'd have to call for repair in the morning.

But what to do about her rescuer? She couldn't very well call the sheriff's department. The poor guy hadn't done anything but try to help and she'd assaulted him. She thought about calling for an ambulance, but he didn't look too badly hurt.

Just unconscious.

"Just unconscious! Sheesh." And gorgeous. Now that she actually had time to look at him, she could tell he was absolutely the best-looking man she'd ever seen, once you got past the sheer size of him. Of course, it wasn't as if she were petite. Far from it. At almost six feet, she was unusually tall for a woman, but this guy made her feel like a shrimp.

She'd never seen hair so black. And long. As tall as he was, his braids looked as if they went all the way to his waist, which meant his hair would reach his butt, unbound. Damn but she'd love to see that. His eyebrows arched like dark wings over his eyes, and his lashes were black crescent moons curving against his fair skin.

She wasn't even going to look at his mouth. His broad mouth and full lips were absolutely sinful, and she'd been without for too long. *Way too long.*

Oh, crap. Mari couldn't believe she was standing over the poor guy with a ruby geode in her hand like a damned club, fantasizing! How could she possibly be thinking about seduction when she'd just knocked him out? Blushing, she curled her legs under herself and sat on the floor beside him. She thought of putting the geode aside, but it was heavy and solid and fit her hand perfectly. She wasn't ready to give up her only weapon.

Except she'd flattened this big bruiser with her bare hands. She glanced again at the geode. Thank goodness she hadn't hit him with that heavy thing, but still . . . Mari covered her mouth so she wouldn't giggle out loud. Sensei Tanaka would be proud of her!

But her sensei had never once mentioned what to do with an assailant once you had him knocked out flat on the floor. In class, your opponent always stood up and bowed politely. This guy wasn't going to be feeling very polite toward Mari at all.

She glanced nervously at the dark front window. When it got dark in Evergreen, it was like they just rolled up the streets and put the town away until morning, and here she was, alone in her mother's crystal shop with a total stranger—a guy armed with a glass sword, no less—out cold on the floor.

Mari scooted closer to the sword. It wasn't glowing now, and it wasn't glass, either. Up close, she could see it was made of some kind of crystal. The blade was long—at least five feet in length. It had a silver pommel with what looked like a jewel set in the handle. In fact, it looked like the sort of thing her mother would sell at Crystal Dreams—if her mother sold swords.

Which she didn't, thank goodness. Mari ran her finger along the blade. The crystal pulsed with a blue light. She yanked her hand away and bit back a scream. After a minute, she touched it again, and again the glow pulsed. Mari slowly pulled her hand away, swallowed, and turned her attention to the unconscious man.

Only he wasn't unconscious anymore. His eyes were open, and they were every bit as green as she'd thought. He groaned, and Mari blushed.

What else was a blonde with really fair skin going to do? Especially after kneeing her rescuer in the balls? She flashed a guilty smile at him. "Are you okay? I am so sorry!"

He blinked, frowned, and tried to sit up, but that brought his thighs together. He groaned and grabbed for his crotch, glanced at Mari, and pulled his hand away. He looked confused as he pushed himself up to one elbow and shook his head.

"Why did you attack me?" His voice was deep, his accent unfamiliar, and his frown grew deeper. "Did you not scream? Were you not threatened? I came to your aid only because you cried for help."

Oh Lordy . . . he was so right. She felt her blush go darker, hotter. "I know, and I am so sorry, but you came through the door with that sword in your hand and scared the crap out of me, and the cat was snarling and I looked up when I heard the door slam open and the glass cracked and I thought you were attacking me, and I freaked. I'm so horribly sorry, but really, I totally freaked out and all I could think was foot, hand, knee. Please forgive me. I just . . ." Her rapid-fire explanation trailed off and Mari took a deep breath.

He cocked his head. "Foot, hand, knee?" Groaning, he

slowly rolled to a sitting position. Even sitting cross-legged on the floor he was huge.

Embarrassed, Mari shrugged. "Attack with the foot, follow up with the hand, and finish with the knee." She spread her hands wide. "That's what Sensei Tanaka taught us."

He slowly rubbed the back of his neck. "He taught you well. Your approach obviously works. I believe we could use your Sensei Tanaka as part of our training program." He ran his hand over his flat belly, touching carefully.

Mari was almost positive he was tracing the shape of her boot on his stomach. She glanced down at her size eleven black leather ropers. She'd put her entire weight behind her kick and she knew it had to hurt. The guy probably had a huge bruise, right in the middle of his stomach. When she raised her head, he was shaking his and smiling at her.

"Where I come from, women do not fight, but you are proof that women make truly capable warriors." Slowly, carefully, he reached for his crystal sword. Then he stood up, standing so tall he towered over her.

Mari scrambled to her feet, yet she still had to tilt her head back to look into those unbelievable green eyes of his.

He dipped his head, as if he bowed to her. "I am Darius of Kronus." His deep, formal-sounding words sent shivers racing across her arms. "It is my honor to meet you." Then he slowly pressed the flat of the blade across his heart and bowed from the waist before Mari as if he were acknowledging royalty.

Chapter 3

Darius's head felt as if someone had used it to pound rocks, his gut ached from the force of her kick, and he wouldn't be surprised if he were no longer capable of fathering children, but it mattered little right now. This woman was absolutely magnificent! He'd never seen another like her.

Tall and lean with long blond hair tied in a simple tail at the back of her neck, she had eyes the color of sapphires and lips that would put rubies to shame. And she was proof—living proof—of the strength and power of a woman.

How could his people deny the legends of the women warriors of Lemuria? How could they teach that women, as the weaker sex, should remain in the background, subservient to the men of their society? This woman of Earth was a warrior. She'd brought him to his knees and then some. In fact, there was a period of time where he recalled nothing at all, but Darius wasn't certain he wanted to pass that information on to his brother guardsmen.

He straightened up and smiled at her. She looked a bit overwhelmed, but he could understand that. According to

Alton of Artigos, the people of Earth had no idea there were demons invading their world. In fact, he'd said that very few of them believed his world of Lemuria actually existed.

Of course, humans also thought Atlantis was nothing more than myth, which left Darius in a rather uncomfortable position. Did he tell her who he was and where he was from, or did he wipe clean the memory of this attack by demonkind and slip away before his existence was too firmly lodged in her mind to erase?

She offered him a shy, almost embarrassed smile, and Darius knew he couldn't leave. He'd watched as dozens of demon wraiths entered Earth's dimension. For some reason, this woman was their target, or at least the target of one of them. He couldn't leave her unprotected. What if more found their way to her tiny shop?

What if they threatened her life?

Unacceptable. He could not leave her unprotected. His honor as a Lemurian guardsman was at stake. Besides, he had his orders, straight from his sergeant, Roland of Kronus.

And with that thought, he made his decision to stay.

Mari glanced once more at the thick darkness outside the store and then back at her unusual savior. The events of the past few minutes flashed through her mind until none of what she'd witnessed made any sense at all. He watched her carefully, but she didn't feel a threat from him. "Are you okay?" she asked. When he nodded, she added, "Come, sit down."

She pointed to the comfortable old couch set against the far wall for customers looking through her mom's library of books on everything from witchcraft to gemstones to the history of Mount Shasta. The eclectic library was all that kept Mari from losing her mind through the long, slow afternoons watching the shop.

She glanced at the huge man standing politely beside her. Check that. Maybe she'd already lost it.

Darius stepped aside and waited for her to proceed. Mari led him to the couch and sat at one end. He went to the opposite end and carefully sheathed his sword in a beautifully tooled leather scabbard she just now noticed across his very broad back.

The sword disappeared as he slipped it into the sheath.

So did the scabbard.

Mari gasped. "Where did your sword just go?"

"Ah . . . I'm sorry." Smiling, he swept his hand over his shoulder and the sword and scabbard reappeared.

Mari felt a little light-headed. There was a strange buzzing in her ears.

"I forgot to remove the glamour," he said as he sat down. "It's the way I hide my blade from curious eyes."

"That's impossible." But then, so was a cat with demon teeth and red eyes, and a glowing sword made of crystal, and . . .

But he was shaking his head, still smiling. "How can it be impossible if you've just seen it happen? Don't you believe your own eyes?"

"Generally, yes." In fact, Mari thought of herself as pragmatic beyond belief, probably as a defensive measure to having been raised by parents as offbeat as hers. "But you have to admit, the events of the past few minutes haven't been entirely normal or believable."

"True." He sent a most devastating smile in her direction. "You have no reason to understand what's happening in your community. From what I've been told, the demon invasion has been kept out of your media, though it hasn't been easy. Demonkind have become much bolder over the past couple of weeks."

He wasn't smiling anymore. "We've never seen an incursion outside of Abyss quite like this one."

Blinking, Mari sat back against the thick arm of the sofa. "Say again? Demonkind? What's Abyss? What do you mean by . . . ?"

"Abyss is the place you call hell. It's home to demonkind. The cat that was attacking you? The poor creature had been possessed by a demon, hence the rows of teeth, the glowing red eyes, and the long talons instead of typical cat's claws. When I tapped the cat with my sword, the demon spirit was forced out. Demons are difficult to kill, but crystal works."

He reached over his shoulder and smoothly withdrew that amazing sword once again. Mari leaned close and stared at the blade, which made a lot more sense than trying to understand all that garbage about a demon possessing a stray tomcat. "It looks like it's made of diamond. What is it?"

"A form of diamond, actually. I am one of only four Lemurian guards who carry crystal." He shook his head and smiled at the blade as if it were his best friend. Mari's thought of *men and their toys* disappeared when he added, "And while it has not yet found its voice, I fully expect my sword to finally speak to me before the war against demonkind has ended."

Mari opened her mouth. Nothing came out. She tried again. "Did you say Lemurian? Like from Lemuria?" She glanced at the book sitting on the shelf just over his shoulder—the one with the words "Lemuria" and "Mythological" in the title. "A place that isn't real?"

He smiled. "I did. And Lemuria is quite real, actually. At least to those of us who call it home."

Okay. So she was sitting here alone in her mother's store after dark in an empty downtown with a certifiable nutcase. An absolutely gorgeous nutcase, but just the same . . . Mari plastered a smile on her face. "Lemuria's a myth. A fable. A legend like Atlantis. It's not real."

"Actually, you're right."

Thank goodness!

"Lemuria is very much like Atlantis. Both our continents slipped beneath the sea at about the same time, when the earth was undergoing a period of great geologic upheaval. Atlanteans chose to protect their world with a force field that allows them to live in total obscurity beneath the sea. Lemurians simply switched dimension and location. Our home now is inside the dormant volcano you call Mount Shasta, in a separate dimension sharing the volcano's space."

He said it all so matter-of-factly, like it was no big deal that he couldn't possibly exist and there was no such thing as moving a whole civilization from one dimension to another. Mari blinked owlishly. How could he look so sane, so absolutely gorgeous, sitting there smiling at her as if she were some kind of idiot?

Then he raised his head and focused beyond her, toward the front of the shop. His smile slipped. He put a finger to his lips for silence and slowly withdrew his sword. The blade glowed with a soft blue aura.

Mari stared at the sword and then spun in her seat to look in the same direction as Darius. At first, everything seemed perfectly normal. Then she noticed the crack in the glass on the front door. A shadow hovered midway along the crack, a dark, oily-looking substance that slowly spilled through the crack, flowed to the floor, and formed into a solid black cloud.

It looked exactly like the thing that had burst out of the stray cat, only larger. Much larger, and getting bigger by the second. Another black shadow slipped through the cracked glass, followed by another. They joined the first and formed into a single thick, black cloud of oily-looking mist.

"Stay here," Darius whispered close to her ear. Then he slowly moved through the cluttered shop, slipping easily between the shelves and display racks with more grace than she'd expect a man his size would have.

He reached the roiling cloud of mist and swung his sword

through the center. The thing burst into sparks with an ear-splitting shriek. Mari covered her ears and cowered down into the cushions on the couch.

Darius struck the next wave of black mist, and then the next. He spun carefully as he wielded his sword with obvious skill, easily avoiding the cluttered shelves and display cases. Inhuman shrieks and earsplitting wails echoed off the walls, and the air reeked with the stench of sulfur as more of the silent wraiths oozed through the crack in the glass, directly into the deadly path of Darius's flashing blade.

Mari clutched the geode in one hand and a pillow to her chest with the other. She stared at the battle taking place in her mother's little shop and wondered just what in the hell she'd gotten herself into now.

Darius stepped back from the door after destroying the last of the wraiths. No more seeped through the crack in the glass. He turned to Mari just as she stood up from the couch. She was obviously trembling, but in spite of her fear, she came closer.

Sniffing the air she tilted her head and looked up at him. He felt as if he were falling into the deep sapphire pools of her eyes.

"What is that horrible smell?" she asked. Her voice shook. "What were those things?"

She still clutched that odd stone in her hand as if it were a weapon of some sort. Darius thought it merely looked like a geode. They were common in Lemuria when crystals formed within cavities in volcanic rock, though he'd never seen one filled with rubies before. Never seen anything held by such a breathtakingly beautiful woman.

Blinking, he caught himself. Time to end such an unprofessional perusal of the one he'd just sworn to protect.

Darius straightened and then nodded toward the door. "Those were demons, still in their mist form."

She shook her head. Taking a defensive stance, she folded her arms across her chest. "Demons? I don't think so. They don't exist. They're like fairy tales, aren't they?"

He cocked one eyebrow. "Like Lemuria and Atlantis? Demons are every bit as real as I am."

She looked at him as though she still wasn't sure she believed he was real, either. How could he possibly convince her she might be in danger?

"Mari, demons have reopened the portal—a gateway— from Abyss to Earth. I didn't know how to close it but I contacted my sergeant before I left my post. Hopefully he's sealed it by now, but dozens of the creatures—maybe even hundreds—had already slipped through. More might have followed me. From what I know, demonkind can only exist as mist in Earth's dimension, unless they take on an avatar. That's usually something of the earth—ceramic or stone statues, carvings, that sort of thing."

Her head jerked up and her eyes went wide. "There was a rash of vandalism here a little over a week ago. All the little stone statues in front of the stores were destroyed." She shook her head. "No, it can't be."

"It can and it is, and it's getting worse. We've had reports of demons taking over animals in a place called Arizona. There's been quite a problem down there in the town of Sedona. Also north of here, in Oregon. And now your cat."

Shaking her head, she laughed. "You know what's really weird? I'm starting to believe you."

"Good. You need to, for your own safety. Now I want to try and repair that crack in the glass. I didn't think it was wide enough for demons to get through, but obviously I was wrong." He raised his sword and hoped like the nine hells he was doing this right. Roland had tried to explain how to call on the power within the blade. Darius had been afraid to try it on the portal to Abyss, but there was no one else he could ask to repair Mari's broken window. Nine hells, but he hoped this worked!

He concentrated on the blade and imagined it as a conduit for pure energy. The blade started glowing, exactly as he'd hoped. Slowly he ran the tip along the crack in the glass. Blinding light shot from the crystal—light and power. The glass melted and flowed until the edges sealed together. Darius carefully ran the sword from one end to the other, leaving a smooth, unmarked window behind.

Silently, he thanked the blade. It wasn't sentient yet so he didn't expect an answer, but he hoped the spirit within realized how much he appreciated the power of crystal.

Mari stared at the once broken glass. Then she looked up, shaking her head in obvious disbelief. "If I hadn't just seen that with my own eyes . . ."

He grinned. He couldn't help himself. He hadn't once thought of using the sword's power to impress a woman, but it was certainly an added benefit. "Then you finally believe me?"

She shook her head. "I don't know. This is way too weird for me." Then she looked at him and laughed. "Not for my mother and father. You're right up their alley, but I don't usually . . ."

Her voice trailed off and she blinked warily. "What now?"

Good question. He gazed around the store. "I would like to walk you to your home. I don't think it's going to be safe for you to go out alone right now. For some reason, the demons are drawn to either you or your shop. Until we know for sure what's happening, I don't think you should go out by yourself."

"But I live here, at least for now. Above the shop. And there's absolutely no way in hell I'm going to stay at my parents' house." Her laugh sounded nervous. "My sanity's at stake here. I think I'll take demons anytime over a night with Mom and Dad."

Perfect. He nodded in agreement. "Then I will stay here with you. You have my protection for as long as you need it."

Wide-eyed, she stared at him. "You? Here? But . . . where?"

He shrugged. "Wherever you go."

"I don't think that's really necessary, do you?"

He felt his sword pulse within his grasp and quickly turned. A black wraith hovered against the glass, just outside the door. It appeared to be testing the area he'd just repaired. Now how would it know there'd been a crack in the glass?

Unless the demons were somehow communicating.

Mari's voice had a decided quaver to it. "Is that another of those things?"

Darius nodded. "It is. Stand back." He opened the door and slashed his blade through the mist. It burst into sparks and the disgusting stench drifted into the shop before he had time to shut the door.

He couldn't help the small flare of satisfaction he felt when he sheathed his sword and smiled at Mari. "Okay. What now?"

She stood as if shell-shocked for a moment, staring at the closed door. Then she shook her head, a short, sharp jerk. "I need to close out the register and make the deposit. It'll only take a minute, but I have to walk to the bank. It's at the end of the block." She stared at the closed door, as if finally accepting the existence of the evil that waited outside.

"I'll go with you. You'll be safe." He crossed his arms and leaned against the door, guarding it. Protecting her.

Mari nodded her head and spun around. She set her geode on the counter, opened the cash register, and counted out the money. She pushed a few buttons, printed out a strip of paper, compared her numbers, and shoved everything inside a small pouch.

Next she slipped the register drawer into a closet behind the counter and locked the door, picked up her geode, a leather bag, and the small pouch, and raised her chin. "Okay. I really would appreciate it if you went with me."

"I would not even consider allowing you to go alone." He opened the door and stepped aside.

Mari walked out, waited until he closed the door, and then locked it. The key stuck in the lock. She jiggled it for a moment, before finally pulling it free. Her soft yet very unladylike curse made him smile.

"This way." She started out at a brisk pace toward a lighted parking lot at the end of the block.

"You walk this alone at night? With currency?" Darius glanced from side to side, looking for danger. There were lights along the street, but the shadows were dark and the night very still.

"Evergreen's such a small town. We all know each other. I've always felt pretty safe here." She glanced over her shoulder and gave Darius a halfhearted shrug and a small, uncomfortable smile. "At least I have in the past."

Darius nodded. He'd always felt safe in Lemuria. Before. Now, though, things were changing, and not in a good way. Just as they were changing here in Evergreen.

Chapter 4

Mari hated to admit how comforting it was to walk the short block to the bank with a big man like Darius following close behind. Her mother always made the deposit from the safety of her car on the drive home. Mari had been making this walk every night since she'd arrived in Evergreen, and while she hadn't been particularly afraid, she hadn't felt all that comfortable carrying money alone on a dark street, either.

With a bodyguard the size of Darius, she actually enjoyed the chance to stretch her legs. The night was fairly mild for October, and she'd not bothered with a jacket. Her plaid flannel shirt tucked into jeans was enough. She glanced at the big man beside her and wondered how he fared in his robe and sandals.

Any other man would look ridiculous in an outfit like his. Somehow, even though it looked like something a monk would wear, it was just right on Darius.

There was certainly nothing at all monkish about the man.

When they reached the bank, Darius stood off to one side

with his powerful arms folded across that broad chest, carefully watching the parking lot and all the area around. Mari slipped the bag into the overnight deposit slot. "That's it," she said. "We can go back now."

Darius nodded, but again he scanned the surrounding area. When they headed down the street toward Crystal Dreams, he walked close beside her. His sword and scabbard were hidden once again, but there was no disguising an almost seven-foot-tall man in a flowing blue robe. She doubted anyone was out tonight who might notice him, but if he was going to hang around, she'd have to find something else for him to wear.

Her feet suddenly lost connection with her brain and Mari stumbled. Darius's strong hand wrapped around her arm as he steadied her. "Are you okay?"

"I'm fine," she said, pausing to catch both her breath and her balance. *Well, crap.* He wasn't a figment of her imagination. He really was staying. Not only was he staying, she obviously wanted him to stay or she wouldn't be wondering how to find clothes big enough to fit him.

Her mind was still spinning when they reached the front of the shop. Mari dug the key out of her purse and stuck it in the lock. She jiggled the key, searching for the sweet spot. After a couple of aborted attempts to unlock the door, she flashed an apologetic grin at Darius. "One of these days, my mother really needs to get this fixed," she said, bending to the task again.

An eerie screech, a blast of ice-cold air, and the sense that she'd better duck fast had Mari hitting the deck as Darius spun around with his sword already in his hand.

Demons! From her crouch on the ground, Mari grabbed the geode out of her bag and swung it at the black wraith streaking through the air toward her. Her makeshift club passed right through the mist, but for just a split second, she thought she saw an actual demon. The mist seemed to take on the appearance of something hideous, with a gaping mouth, too many teeth, and long, sharp talons, as it wrapped around the geode for a mere heartbeat during the course of Mari's swing.

Shrieking, the wraith shot straight up, hovered overhead, and then zeroed in on Mari again as she lunged to her feet. Her fingers slipped on the key. A blast of icy air streaked by and she raised the club to protect her face. The demon evaded Darius's swing and headed straight at Mari again. She spun out of the way, but it howled in defiance and left a burning slash along her forearm.

Thick, swirling black mist surrounded Darius, but the darkness was alight with flashes of sparks and bursts of blue flame. The stench of sulfur made Mari's eyes water, but she finally got the key turned and the door unlocked.

"Darius. It's open. Get inside! Hurry!" She slipped through the doorway and Darius followed close behind. Only a couple of demons made it through before Mari slammed the door shut.

Darius took care of them with a few quick slashes of his crystal blade, until all that remained was the eye-watering stench of dead demon. Blowing hard, he turned and leaned against the door, holding it closed against the threat outside.

"I thought you said they were just mist. That they needed an avatar to function." Mari set the geode down on a rack near the door and tilted her left arm up to the light. The long sleeve of her flannel shirt was shredded. Blood dripped from a nasty slash that ran from her wrist to her elbow.

Darius gaped at the wound. "Where did that come from?"

She shrugged and walked across the shop to the register, reached under the counter, and found a roll of paper towels. "From one of the demons. The damned thing came right at my face. When I raised my arm to protect my eyes, it felt like he slashed me with a razor."

Darius shook his head and gently steadied her arm by

holding her hand and elbow. "This should not happen. They can't take corporeal form in this dimension. They are mist. Merely mist."

"Well, it was mist with really sharp claws, if you ask me." Mari dabbed at the cut with the towel. It wasn't deep but it hurt like the blazes.

"This is impossible." Darius kept shaking his head.

If her arm hadn't hurt so badly, Mari might have laughed. Nothing quite like a big guy in complete denial.

"Never," he said. "This can't be. My sergeant needs to know about this."

"How do you intend to tell him?" Mari wiped at the blood that continued to flow sluggishly down her arm.

"Telepathy, but first he has to be outside the portal. We can't cross dimensions with our thoughts. I've kept my mind open to him, but so far I haven't felt him."

She wasn't sure if it was the pain from the slash on her arm or just the evening in general, but a lot of what Darius said made absolutely no sense at all. "What, exactly, is this portal you're talking about? Where is it?"

"They're the gateways between your world and mine, between all worlds and Abyss. There's one that leads into Mount Shasta, powered by the energy vortex that . . ."

Oh shit. Mari pressed the towel to her arm and raised her head. He looked at her with such guileless honesty, there was no disbelieving him. "You're saying the vortex is real, too?"

He frowned. "Is that a problem?"

For a brief moment, she wondered if he'd totally freak out if she started laughing hysterically. Instead, she slowly shook her head. "No. Not a problem. Not at all, if confirming every tall tale told by every nutcase in the area is actually true isn't a problem."

Darius grinned at her. "Maybe they're not such nutcases after all?"

"I'm not ready for this, Darius. I feel like I'm getting a

major info overload here. Too much, too fast." Mari grabbed her geode, her purse, and the book she'd been reading earlier. "C'mon. I need to clean this cut and see how deep it is." She reached for the door to the stairs leading to her apartment.

"And then," she muttered, "I may have to call my mother and father and apologize."

Darius followed Mari up the dark, narrow staircase to her small apartment above the shop. He was sorry there were so few stairs and not very much light, as he quickly discovered there was something quite pleasant about following a woman with such a beautiful body.

She glanced over her shoulder, opened the door at the top of the stairs, and stepped into the dark room.

"I'll get the light." She flipped a switch and a soft glow illuminated the stairwell and the apartment. Darius stepped into the single room and glanced about. There was a tiny kitchen to his left, with a small table barely large enough for two. A couple of mismatched chairs—one wood, one metal— were shoved beneath the wooden table.

A faded couch that appeared to have been some shade of brown at one time stretched along the wall to his right. Above it, a large window partially covered in dark curtains looked out on the main street below. Beside the window was an open closet with a few items of clothing hanging inside. Straight ahead, a mattress sat on the floor with pillows and blankets neatly folded on top. A door beside the bed opened to a small bathroom.

Mari stood in the middle of the room holding the blood-soaked paper towel to her arm. "It's just temporary," she said. "Only while I'm here to help my parents."

It was obvious she didn't want him to think she lived in such squalor all the time. This place might have seen better days, but they hadn't been recent. "It's good of you to come and help them. You're a good daughter." He stepped close to her and touched her shoulder. She didn't flinch. Didn't pull away. Instead, she stared up at him out of those glorious blue eyes.

He lifted her hand and cradled her injured arm. "Let's see to this. It should be cleaned."

Mari let out a big breath. He wished he knew what she was thinking. She seemed amazingly calm, considering he'd totally upended her life this evening, though she would have been in even more danger had he not arrived. Still, she was being forced to accept things she really didn't want to believe.

Of course, if Darius had his choice, he'd choose not to believe in demons, either. Unfortunately, whether one believed or not, they were here, they were dangerous, and they weren't going away on their own.

"I've got a first-aid kit." She carefully freed herself from his grasp and turned toward the kitchen sink.

Darius followed her and watched while she turned on the water and let it run for a moment. She unbuttoned her sleeve and tried to roll it back. The fabric stuck to the blood on her arm.

"Crap. That hurts."

"Let me help you take it off. It will make it easier to clean the wound."

She flashed him a cheeky grin. "I bet you'd like that, wouldn't you?"

"It really would be easier to treat if you . . ." *Nine hells.* He swallowed. Maybe she wasn't wearing anything underneath. He'd assumed . . . He dipped his head. "My apologies. I thought you wore another shirt beneath this one."

She laughed. "Actually, I'm wearing a sports bra. It's like a shirt. Help me get this off, will you?"

He was suddenly all thumbs, trying to help her lift the shirt off her shoulders once she'd unbuttoned the front.

When he finally slipped it over her arms, he realized a sports bra was nothing like another shirt.

Nothing at all. It bared her back and her flat belly and showed the curve of her breasts and the dark cleavage between. Darius forced himself to look away as he carefully worked the shredded sleeve over her injured arm. The fabric stuck where blood had dried. More blood seeped slowly from the wound.

Once Mari's shirt was off, he tossed it on the counter and opened the first-aid kit while Mari rinsed her arm clean under the faucet.

"Let me dry it first," she said. "Then you can use that spray. It's an antibiotic and should take away the sting, too." She dried her arm carefully with another paper towel.

Darius did as she directed. Once her skin was dry, he sprayed the length of the wound. Then he carefully wrapped her arm with soft, sterile gauze and closed the ends off with tape.

She looked up at him and smiled brightly. "Thank you. It feels better already."

Darius merely nodded. There was a strange tightness in his chest, an unexpected reaction to touching her, to standing so close to her with all that beautiful fair skin uncovered.

As if she might be aware of his reaction, Mari walked across the room and grabbed a soft-looking shirt out of the closet. Favoring her injured arm, she slipped it over her head.

Nine hells. He almost sighed when she covered up the smooth expanse of skin he'd hardly had time to admire. Almost, until he realized he enjoyed watching just as much as she pulled her hair out of the back of the shirt and smoothed the hem down over her slim hips. Those subtle, graceful movements as she covered herself held his attention every bit as much as her bare skin.

So many strange feelings swirled through him—feelings he wasn't certain how to interpret. Confused and unusually off balance, he walked over to the big window and pulled the curtain aside so he could get a better look at the street. "It appears quiet for now."

"That's good. Wow . . . black, misty demons aren't going to be easy to spot on a dark and cloudy night. Not from up here."

Her soft words in his ear shocked him. She'd followed and stood beside him. For a moment she was much too close, but then she glided away and headed toward the kitchen area. "I'm going to fix something for dinner. Are you hungry?"

He was starving, but he didn't want to impose. "You go ahead," he said, thinking of how she was injured and that he should probably offer to cook for her. Then his stomach growled.

Mari laughed, and the change in her was amazing. Her smile lit up her face. He could have sworn it made the room brighter.

"Sit down," she said. "Your brain might be telling you to be a polite guest, but your stomach knows better."

She opened the door of a tall white cabinet filled with packages and bowls. It took him a moment to realize it was her cold storage. Earth was really not so different from Lemuria, but then he figured that all civilizations probably needed the same things to run efficiently.

"Oh, look! I forgot about the soup." Mari turned and smiled at him. "We've got a feast in here. Lots of really yummy leftovers." She pulled out white boxes and colored bowls and within a few minutes the tiny apartment smelled wonderful.

After the boring food prepared for guardsmen in the barracks, the different scents coming from the stove and the machine Mari called a microwave drew Darius away from the window and close enough to lift lids and sniff appreciatively.

"That's my mom's minestrone. It's the best soup you'll

ever eat." She checked the microwave. "I nuked some lasagna from the deli next door and there's leftover chicken and some potato salad." Then she looked in the oven beneath the pot of soup. "When the garlic bread's warm, we can eat. The bathroom's in there if you want to wash up."

The sheer variety of foods had his head spinning. Taking another deep breath, he decided to do as Mari suggested, rather than drool all over himself and look like a complete idiot.

He went into the small bathroom and washed his hands. This facility wasn't all that different, either, from what they had in Lemuria—except for Mari's personal items. There was a sink, a commode, a stall for showering . . . but a hairbrush sat beside the sink with a few long, blond hairs caught in the bristles. Next to it, a toothbrush and assorted tubes and bottles.

All very personal things of Mari's.

A couple of pairs of tiny pink panties hung from the shower rod. More of Mari's belongings. The thought of her wearing those small, feminine items beneath her tight-fitting pants made his mouth go dry. He quickly dried his hands on a towel next to the sink and reached for the door.

This little bathroom had suddenly become much too intimate, too personal. Too indicative of the private side of the woman currently preparing his meal in the room beyond.

That was another thing. No woman other than his mother had ever cooked for him before, and that had been so long ago he'd forgotten the tastes, the feelings of eating food prepared especially for him. Prepared with a woman's touch.

Why was the thought of Mari cooking for him so unsettling?

Darius turned back and took one last look at himself in the mirror. His hair was still neatly braided. His robe appeared clean, without stain or tear. He was the same man as always. Nothing had changed, and yet all was different.

He stared at the closed door and panic seized him.

What in the nine hells did he think he was doing? He didn't belong here. He had no business intruding on this woman's life. He should leave, now. Go back to Lemuria and leave demon hunting in Earth's dimension to Alton and the others who belonged here.

"Darius? Dinner's ready."

He glanced once more at his reflection and knew there was only one truth, only one path he could follow. The die was cast. There was no way he could go back to Lemuria. Not now. He had tasted the freedom that was Earth. Had seen beauty in one very special woman. Though he could never claim her, he couldn't leave her unprotected. Demons had found Mari. Either they wanted her, or they were after something in her small shop, and that put Mari at risk. She'd already been injured. He could not abandon her, not with danger so close.

"Who the nine hells am I kidding?" He glowered at himself. "I couldn't leave her even if she weren't in danger."

In just a few short hours in her presence, she'd left an indelible mark on his soul. He had to stay, if only to see where this would lead.

Knowing, deep in his heart, it couldn't lead anywhere good. Knowing himself just as well—that he wasn't going to let that stop him.

His life might be immortal, but Mari's was so short by Lemurian standards he couldn't afford to waste even a moment of time. She was a rare treasure, one he had to experience even knowing he'd eventually have to let her go. With those depressing thoughts clouding his mind, Darius joined Mari at the kitchen table.

Chapter 5

Mari wasn't going to allow herself to think about anything, especially about sharing her tiny apartment with that great big, absolutely breathtakingly gorgeous man.

She bit back a laugh. *Yes, proof that size does matter . . . especially when there's something weird and threatening just outside the door.*

Darius was huge, and the flowing blue robe made him seem even bigger, but big was good—at least until she figured out what that black mist really was that had slashed her arm. Even if she wasn't quite ready to accept that they were actually demons, she realized she was a lot closer to accepting Darius.

Lemuria? It was not easy to wrap her mind around *that* one even though every kid in Evergreen grew up with tales of the Lemurians, and the powerful energy vortex and sense of magic that surrounded Mount Shasta. They were bedtime stories, though. Legends for the tourists. Make-believe.

Darius was definitely not make-believe.

He was much too real—so real he seemed to suck the air out of the room. It had to be something like that, because she felt light-headed when she looked at him—really looked at him—and she couldn't blame the feeling on that stupid cut on her arm.

If Darius was telling the truth, he wasn't even human, yet he was the most perfect man she'd ever met. Everything about him turned her on. She wasn't sure how much longer she could keep up this disinterested, independent woman façade.

He certainly wasn't making it easy!

She'd sworn she'd never need another man, not after all the crap Brad had pulled. So why did Darius make her feel so needy? She had to quit making comparisons between the two men. There was nothing at all about Darius—other than his gender—that was anything at all like Brad.

She almost giggled, imagining her ex-boyfriend protecting her from demons. Too bad she hadn't kneed Brad in the balls when she'd had the chance.

Darius took the seat she pointed to and his massive size made the tiny table look even smaller. Mari poured a glass of red wine for each of them and set a bowl of soup in front of Darius. At least she had two of everything in the cupboards—exactly two.

Plates, forks, knives, wineglasses. This tiny apartment was the first home her parents had shared, and it was still stocked with their old stuff. She tried to imagine her mom and dad sitting here like she was with Darius, but she wasn't sure she wanted the visual of her parents as two young adults.

They'd launched their relationship in the late sixties in a haze of marijuana smoke and regular acid trips. Over forty years later, they still hadn't entirely moved past their hippie roots.

It was just weird, thinking of her mom and dad living here when they had been so much younger than Mari was now. They hadn't been married then. In fact, they hadn't married until years later, right before she was born. Her mom had told her they'd only known each other a couple of weeks before the two of them actually shared an apartment for the night.

Mari had known Darius for only a couple of hours.

No. Don't even try to make sense of this. She took a sip of her wine and decided she'd just take it one step at a time.

She filled a plate at the stove, glanced over her shoulder at the man, back at the plate, and added more food. Darius's eyes lit up when she put it on the table beside his bowl of soup.

She served a small plate for herself and sat down.

Darius sat perfectly still and stared at his meal.

"Go ahead." She grabbed her spoon, inordinately pleased that he'd waited for her. Chalk up another plus in Darius's column, another minus for Brad. She really should quit comparing them. "Don't let it get cold."

He smiled at her, nodded, picked up a spoon, and tasted her mother's soup. If there was one thing she couldn't fault dear old Mom on, it was her minestrone soup. Darius seemed to agree. He closed his eyes with a look of pure bliss.

"Amazing. This is wonderful. We have nothing like this."

"There's plenty more." She smiled at him, but he wasn't even looking at her. No, he focused entirely on the meal she'd set in front of him. It gave her the warm fuzzies, knowing the simple leftovers she'd prepared pleased him so much.

They ate quietly, but there was nothing uncomfortable about the silence. Mari took the time to observe and wonder. For a woman who had forever relished the ordinary, she felt as if she hovered on the cusp of something amazing, as if her life was about to change.

But hadn't it already? She'd thought she would never leave San Francisco, yet here she was, back in Evergreen. When she'd lost her job, she was certain she'd never be happy again, not until she was firmly established at another bank or brokerage house. Yet she sat here smiling, pigging out on her mom's homemade soup, happier than she'd been in years.

She'd never had a fanciful nature, yet she was sharing

dinner with a man who claimed he wasn't even human, that he'd come from the mythological world of Lemuria for the sole purpose of protecting her from demons.

In fact, he didn't just say it—he did it. If those black misty things weren't demons, she knew they weren't anything good. She was certain of that. If it weren't for the stinging cut on her arm, she might have trouble believing, but something had slashed through her flannel shirt. Something had shot out of the darkness, screamed like a banshee, and left her bleeding.

The image of fangs and scales, of strangely shaped limbs and a twisted body flashed through her mind. No, she couldn't possibly have seen that, but whatever it was had died in a burst of blue sparks and flames and stinking black smoke. It had died because Darius of Kronus had killed it, and he'd killed it to protect Mari.

He glanced up at her and smiled, and something inside her—something long unraveled—knit together. She couldn't explain it, couldn't describe it, but in that brief glance, that single moment, everything tumbled into place. Like puzzle pieces once scattered, all the separate parts of her life that had never before seemed to fit, found their match, slid into their proper position, clicked, and became whole.

She blinked, carefully wiped her lips with her napkin, and realized she couldn't have looked away from his emerald-green gaze if her life had depended on it.

But she didn't want to look away, because her life did depend on it. Her life, her future, her soul, all caught up, somehow, in the man sharing her little kitchen table in this dinky, dingy little apartment over her mother's store.

Premonitions weren't her thing. Her mother was convinced she had psychic abilities but Mari had always feared her flashes of foresight and weird hunches. She'd learned to block them—Mom made the predictions, not Mari, but this one was so clear, so powerful, she didn't even try to fight it.

Her future opened in front of her like a tapestry woven in light. The glowing strands were tied to this man, this place, and this time. Instead of shying away from it or trying to block it, Mari let the vision take her.

And, as with all her premonitions, not a lick of it made any sense at all.

"Are you okay?"

She blinked and the vision snapped out of existence as if it had never been. Darius stared at her with a frown marring that otherwise smooth forehead, his black brows twisted and his green eyes narrowed.

Mari nodded. "I'm fine. Just tired." She pushed herself away from the table. "You go ahead and finish eating. I'm going to take a shower." She glanced at the gauze covering the slash on her arm. "Do you mind helping me rewrap this when I get out?"

Darius nodded. "Of course I will. Anything you want."

Mari almost laughed. Almost. No way was she going to tell him what she really wanted. What she'd seen in that brief premonition: the two of them, naked and aroused, together.

Very close together.

With that visual planted firmly in her mind, Mari headed for the shower.

"There's no sign of him, Sergeant Kronus."

"Thank you, Leland. Stand down." With worry eating a hole in his gut, Roland of Kronus checked the small tunnel leading to one of the lesser portals. He'd sealed the reopened gateway to Abyss, but damn the nine hells, it appeared he'd lost Darius.

All he had was his cousin's frantic call for help, a warning that demonkind was pouring through a newly opened portal and headed for either Lemuria or Earth. Darius hadn't been sure.

Since then, there'd been no word. Nothing at all.

Roland stared at the portal leading to Earth's dimension while his two crystal-bearing soldiers waited beside him. He went over that last conversation, when he'd given Darius orders to kill the demons.

Darius wouldn't have followed demonkind to Earth, would he? Roland groaned. *Nine hells.* Earth was forbidden territory. Could Darius have decided to take that risk, hunting demons on Earth when they were no longer a threat to Lemuria?

Knowing Darius, it was entirely possible. And, if what Alton of Artigos said was true, demons invading Earth *were* a threat to Lemuria. They were a threat to all worlds in all dimensions.

Darius would have understood that. He wouldn't have ignored the threat. Besides, like all young men, Darius craved adventure.

Roland tightened his grasp on his crystal sword and glanced at his men. Both were armed with crystal—the only weapons known to work against the demon threat. While the aristocrats of Lemuria possessed crystal blades, they'd long ago lost the will to fight, which meant that with Darius missing, only three armed soldiers stood between Lemuria and the scourge of demonkind.

He or one of his men must stay behind while the other two attempted to rescue Darius.

Roland gazed at the portal to Earth and sighed. "Let us return to Lemuria and make our report. We've pulled a long night's duty. We will rest first, and then we must launch a search in Earth's dimension for Darius of Kronus."

Both young men snapped to attention. Roland hid a tired grin. Lemurian curiosity about Earth appeared as powerful as ever and he was offering a rare opportunity.

"Leland of Arctus, you will remain on guard at this portal

while Matthias of Strachus will accompany me to the other side. For now, though, we all need to rest and recharge."

He ignored the elbow jab Matthias gave to Leland. With thoughts of Darius heavy on his heart but a visit to Earth raising his sense of anticipation, Roland led his men back through the portal to Lemuria.

With the sound of Darius's shower running in the background, Mari put away the dishes he'd washed and dried while she'd taken her shower earlier. Knowing he'd cleaned up the kitchen without being asked gave her even more warm fuzzies than preparing his meal had. She really needed to find something wrong with him.

Anything. He couldn't possibly be this perfect.

She hoped the pair of her father's old cut-off sweatpants she'd found would fit him. First thing tomorrow she'd make a run to the feed store and see what she could buy for him to wear. There were a lot of good-sized ranchers and cowboys in the area. With luck she'd find clothing large enough.

She tried to picture Darius in blue jeans and a shirt, but she couldn't get past the image of him without the robe. Period.

Damn it, girl. Focus! Boots. Boots were good. She'd shop for boots, too. He couldn't very well continue running around Evergreen in a monk's robe and sandals.

She tried not to pay attention, but the sound of the shower running gave her an explicit visual of that huge man, naked in her shower with all that long dark hair streaming beneath the spray. When the shower shut off, she pictured him drying off, rubbing the soft white towel across his chest, over his long legs, drying his hair.

Then she giggled. Damn. Did she have a previously unknown hair fetish? What was it about all that long, black hair of his?

By the time the bathroom door opened, Mari was trembling like a leaf . . . and it wasn't from fear.

Damn it! Where was her focus! Forcing a calm she was far from feeling, Mari turned around and almost dropped the pan she was holding.

He stood in the doorway, his big body framed in a cloud of steam. Without that flowing robe, he was even more impressive than she'd imagined. Sexier, bigger, more commanding. He'd taken out the braids. Now all that wet hair was combed straight back from his face. Slicked back this way, it emphasized the slight widow's peak, his high cheekbones, the harsh cut of his square chin, and his long, straight nose. His hair fell like a curtain of black silk shimmering over his shoulders, caressing his powerful arms, hanging all the way to his butt.

Her dad's old sweats clung to his body, riding low on his narrow hips, fitting closely around the most perfectly muscled thighs she'd ever seen on any man. The cut-offs had probably hung below her dad's knees. On Darius they barely covered his thighs.

He had it all, from the dusting of black hair running across his broad chest and trailing down his middle to disappear beneath the waistband of the sweats, to the rippling six-pack of muscle defining his taut belly. There was more of the same dark hair on his thighs—not a lot, but enough to scream out his masculinity and beg her fingers to travel through it. There was even more on his muscular calves and a bit on the tops of his long, narrow feet. She'd never seen such sexy feet on a man before, but it was more than obvious there wasn't anything about Darius that wasn't sexy.

His hands, his face, his body . . . his broad smile. *Damn.*

"Are you laughing at me?" Suddenly defensive, she folded her arms across her chest, well aware of the fact she wasn't wearing a bra beneath her camisole top. She tried her best to glare at him, but it was hard to keep her lips from twitching.

He'd studied her the same way when she'd stepped out of the bathroom after bathing.

It seemed only fair.

"I am," he said, laughing. He leaned against the door frame and folded his arms across his chest, mimicking her stance. "You're looking at me the same way I looked at you when you walked out of this little room, all warm and damp from your shower. With interest."

Well. Okay. She hadn't expected him to actually say it out loud, but . . . "I see. Well, I guess fair's fair."

He nodded, but he still had that big, sexy grin on his face. "I left my robe hanging on the hook behind the door, if that's okay."

"That's fine." She rubbed suddenly sweaty palms along her thighs. "I need to get you something else to wear so you won't stand out so much if you go into town."

"Will there be clothing large enough to fit me? Humans are not quite as big as Lemurians."

He walked across the room, all long legs and strong arms and bare, sexy feet . . . and long, long black hair.

Brazenly she looked him slowly up and then down. "I hope so," she said, reluctantly parking her gaze on his smile. "A few are. You can't run around town dressed like a monk."

He laughed. "Or naked. I don't think that would work, either."

Oh, Lordy . . . The images that conjured up made her mouth go dry. "So . . ." Frantically she searched for subject matter.

"So?" He raised one perfect black eyebrow.

"Tell me about Lemuria."

He chuckled. "I can do that," he said, grinning broadly. "It's probably a safer discussion than talk of running around your town naked."

She wondered if he heard her squeak. He certainly didn't mince words, but she wasn't sure if he was flirting or if this was just the way he was. She didn't know him. Not at all, and yet she'd allowed him into her home, into her life.

How the hell had this happened so quickly?

Demons. Oh. Yeah.

Somehow she had to get the image of his gloriously naked body out of her head. Maybe then her brain would work the way she expected it to—as if she were still an intelligent, thinking human being.

Darius solved her problem when he walked away from her, sat on the couch, rested his elbows on his knees, and in that deep, rolling voice of his with the slightest accent—one she couldn't describe if she'd tried—proceeded to spin a tale of a world Mari knew only as legend.

He described Lemuria's history, how an entire continent had sunk beneath the sea over twelve thousand years ago. He told her about a civilization with technology advanced enough to move everyone to safety within another dimension. His people now lived deep within the confines of the dormant volcano of Mount Shasta—yet in a dimension parallel to Earth's.

His were people who never saw the sun, who had forgotten what a real blue sky looked like, who ate manufactured foods, and, when the need for trade existed, bought goods with diamonds mined from deep within the earth.

They'd once been warriors but now were philosophers. An entire race that had forgotten how to fight, who had lost the voices within their sentient crystal swords. A people who had lost their courage at a time when they faced their biggest threat in millennia—an invasion by demonkind that could end everything as all worlds knew it.

It was not an uplifting tale, at least not as Darius told it, and his story left her feeling chilled and frightened. Unsure of a world she'd thought of as safe and whole.

"But you carry a crystal sword, right? You're a warrior, aren't you?"

He smiled and nodded his head. "I do and I am, but I am one of very few and my sword is not yet sentient. Until I prove myself in battle, it will remain silent. Now it is merely a weapon. A powerful weapon, but still just a sword. Once it achieves sentience, it will become my partner."

He slipped the sword from the tooled-leather sheath. The blade glowed but remained silent. "I know it's alive, but until I'm considered worthy, I'll not hear its voice. I'll not know its story." His hands swept lovingly along the blade.

Mari imagined those same strong hands sweeping over her body and her nipples puckered in response. She couldn't very well cover her breasts without drawing attention, but there was no way he could miss the visible sign of her arousal.

In fact, he seemed aware even before Mari'd figured it out. Darius raised his head and his gaze focused on her chest, and that made her nipples pucker and ache even more. For the first time, an uncomfortable silence fell between them. Then Darius cleared his throat. He leaned over and picked up the book she'd brought with her from the shop.

He looked at the cover. Then he opened it, glanced over the pages and raised his head. "Is this a diary? Much of it is handwritten. I expected to see only printed pages."

Thankful for a new topic—even this topic—Mari shook her head. "Part of it's a published book, but the notes are my mother's. It's her book of spells. She's a witch."

Darius's head shot up and he blinked. "A witch? Really?"

Mari laughed. At least here she was on safe ground. Sort of. "If you ask my mother she'll say yes, she's a real witch. My father will agree. Me? I'm not so sure I believe in witch-craft. Or witches."

Grinning, Darius tapped the pages of the book. "You don't believe in Lemurians, either. Or demons."

Mari leaned back against the kitchen counter and folded her arms across her chest. Finally, a chance to cover up her damned nipples without looking obvious. "True," she said. "But now that I've got you sitting in my apartment, I'm willing to be a bit more open-minded about the whole Lemurian thing. Witches? The jury's still out on witches."

He flipped the pages, stopped, and flipped back. Raised his head and frowned. "There are spells in here to counteract demonkind. Have you looked at them?"

Mari pushed herself away from the counter and joined him on the couch. She looked over his shoulder at the page he'd found. Her mother's precise handwriting covered both pages. "Where? No. I didn't see those." She tapped the word "demon" about halfway down. "Wow. Looks like a bunch of spells. I had no idea demons were something in my mother's repertoire. I was looking for a spell that would help me get my job back."

"I thought you didn't believe in witchcraft?"

Laughing, she shrugged. "Hey, I'm unemployed and desperate. I can't stay in Evergreen forever. I'd go nuts! If witchcraft will help, I'm there."

"Did you find a spell? One to help you find a job?"

"No." She shook her head. "Plenty of spells for finding your heart's desire or making your enemy break out in boils, but nothing that'll help me find a job with a good, healthy Fortune 500 company."

He tapped the page again with his forefinger. Right over the word "demon," spelled out in block letters. "Well, until you find that job spell, why don't we take a look at some of these?"

She glanced at the page, at her mother's familiar writing, and then shot Darius a flirtatious look. "What? You're not interested in finding your heart's desire? Making your enemy break out in boils?"

He tilted his head and studied her, but she didn't notice a bit of laughter in his eyes. None at all.

"I doubt demons, who already suffer the life of the

damned, would notice a boil or two." He shrugged, but his gaze never left her face. "As far as the other? I may be a fool damned forever, but I think I've already found my heart's desire."

Mari had no idea where the conversation might have gone from there if her phone hadn't suddenly blasted the first bars of "Jailhouse Rock." She jumped, scurried across the room, and dug the cell phone out of her purse.

She'd never been so happy for her mother's interruption in her entire life, though as she briefly updated Spirit on the day's business, Mari realized she was keeping the most important part of the day to herself.

She didn't mention demons or the broken window or the fact she'd been injured by a creature that shouldn't exist. Nor did she mention the man sitting just across the room from her—the one who'd be spending the night with her in this tiny apartment.

No. There were some things a girl didn't share with her mother, no matter how grown-up the girl was. At thirty-three, Mari was plenty old enough to make her own choices and follow her own path, but even Spirit, for all her open-minded, free-spirit, and free-love philosophy might have a bit of trouble with the idea of her only child spending the night with a Lemurian warrior.

One who'd just looked her in the eye and as much as admitted he wanted her.

Which wouldn't be so dangerous if Mari didn't want him every bit as much.

Chapter 6

"Everything's fine. I'll open at ten as usual, but don't expect me for breakfast. I've got some errands to run first. Give Dad my love, and I'll try and get over to see you tomorrow after I close. I love you, too."

"That was your mother?" Darius leaned back on the couch and watched as Mari turned off her communication device.

She nodded. "Yeah. Mom always calls at night to check on me. She used to call every night after I moved to San Francisco, at least until she got comfortable with me living so far away."

"You didn't tell her about me . . . or the demons."

Mari slowly shook her head, and her silky blond hair whispered across her shoulders. "No. I don't want to worry her. She's got enough on her plate with Dad's recovery going so slowly. He had surgery on his back and he's . . ." Her voice trailed off when Darius stood up and walked across the room to stand in front of her.

"You don't need to be afraid of me, Mari. I will not deny the very powerful attraction I feel for you, but I don't intend to act on it." He lifted her chin with his finger. Her smile was uncertain, confused. "At least, not tonight. You are safe with me. I mean it when I tell you I am here to protect you. I don't want you to fear me."

Her eyes were wide, shimmering pools of blue sky and dark onyx. Her lips trembled and he sensed her desire like a living, breathing entity between them.

It was almost as powerful as his need for her.

Mari shook her head. "I don't fear you, Darius. I've never felt as safe with any man in my life as I do with you."

She laughed, a short, sharp bark that echoed the frustration he was feeling. "Maybe you should fear me," she said, and he knew she meant to tease, to make a joke of what they both understood but couldn't pursue. There was an edge to her voice that skittered along his nerves. A sultry, sensual edge that purred through his groin and wound its way across the base of his spine.

She turned her head and rested her cheek against his palm. "I know you're a big boy, Darius, but I've already proved I can bring you to your knees. How do you know your virtue is safe with me?" Then she grinned, a wide, heartfelt gamine's smile.

The tension flowed out of him like water from a jug. He met her grin with one of his own. "Because I am a mighty warrior and I will be strong enough for both of us." Then he chuckled and shook his head. It hurt to admit the truth. "Besides, it's not my virtue I'm worried about. My balls still ache as if the gods used them for bowling. I think you've ruined me."

"Oh, God." Her smile disappeared and she hung her head. "I am so sorry. I really, really am sorry. I forgot about that."

He rolled his eyes. "I haven't. Believe me."

"Will you ever forgive me?" She wasn't teasing at all. In fact, she looked horribly upset.

"Ah, Mari. Of course you're forgiven. Truth? You were

magnificent. Your attack was perfectly executed. A little too perfectly from my point of view, but you're definitely forgiven. Besides, you've taught me an important lesson. Never again will I underestimate a woman warrior."

"I promise never to do it again."

"I should hope not." He glowered at her.

She covered her lips to stifle a giggle and he grabbed her hand. "Come," he said. She wrapped her fingers in his and it felt right. Natural. "Let's look again at your book of spells. I may be a mighty warrior, but even I might need help fighting the demons should they come during the night."

"Do you expect them tonight?" Still clutching his hand, she stopped and her eyes went wide once again.

He nodded. "Demons are stronger at night. They are nocturnal and thrive on fear and in darkness. I want to sleep for a while, and then I intend to stand guard. You will be safe from me, Mari. And I promise, on my honor as a Lemurian soldier, to keep you safe from demonkind."

There was no way in hell she could just curl up and sleep as if she didn't have a care in the world. Besides, sitting here in the darkness, watching Darius as he slept on her makeshift bed that was nothing more than a mattress on the floor put together with her own bedding from home, was more satisfying than she could have imagined.

He'd only argued a little when she suggested he take her bed. Once she'd convinced him she was staying up to read for a while, he finally admitted he'd been awake for more than twenty-four hours.

Then Mari did more than suggest. She insisted.

He'd fallen asleep within minutes.

Now she sat on the couch with the rest of the room in shadow. She'd twisted the pole lamp so that it focused on the pages of her mother's book of spells.

Mari's attention, however, was focused on the man in her bed.

Darius slept silently, as graceful in sleep as he was when wielding his crystal sword. Where Brad had snored and mumbled and twitched at night, Darius slept on his back with his arms folded over his chest and his long black hair fanned out across the pillow.

The mattress was queen-size, but he slept diagonally across it in order to fit. Even so, his feet almost hung off the end. Mari tried to imagine how she'd fit if she chose to join him. She'd need to curl up close beside him.

Really close.

For now, she merely watched and wondered at all that had happened over the past few hours. Wondered what would happen tomorrow. Besides, it was more pleasant watching Darius sleep than trying to figure out her mother's spells.

But pleasant wasn't going to fight demons. She ran her fingers over the pages of Spirit's book and tried to ignore the frustration she felt. The spells her mother had written down were for specific types of demons, yet nothing seemed appropriate for the actual threat Mari and Darius faced.

"How the hell do I know what kind of demons we're dealing with?" Mumbling softly so she wouldn't disturb Darius, Mari pulled her attention away from his sleeping form and read through one spell after another.

This one claimed to banish succubae, that one dealt with incubi. One exorcised demons of anger and greed with sea salt and thyme, but she'd need holy water for demons of fate.

Sheesh. She was just getting used to the whole idea of demons in general, and now they wanted specifics? Mari read page after page, but nothing felt right. Her eyes grew heavy and the hour late. Darius slept quietly, but the room was getting colder. The big mattress and the down comforter and the big man beneath it looked too inviting to ignore.

Finally Mari put the book aside and turned out the light.

Then she carefully, quietly crawled into bed beside Darius, slipped beneath the comforter, and curled up close enough to absorb the warmth from his body.

He was so close. He smelled wonderful. He was warm and so damned sexy, she thought she'd have trouble falling asleep.

She didn't.

Some soldier you are. Darius propped himself up on his elbow beside Mari and stared at her as she slept. He couldn't believe she'd crawled into bed without waking him, couldn't believe he'd not gotten up and stood guard as he'd planned, that he'd slept beside her throughout the entire night without even knowing she was curled up so close beside him.

In all his long years of life, he'd never spent a night beside a woman. Not once. He'd taken lovers on occasion, but they'd been brief, purely physical affairs. Not one single woman had actually slept the night beside him.

He lay back down beside Mari. Drew her into his arms so that she sprawled across his chest like a warm, sweet-smelling blanket. She mumbled something, nuzzled the hair covering his pectoral muscles, and relaxed back into sleep.

Relaxed was not how he'd describe himself. No. More like aroused, amazed, and content. He'd never felt such contentment, merely from lying close to another soul.

As he lay there with Mari covering his body, Darius stared into the darkness. Before long, shadows would flee beneath the rising sun. He'd never seen a sunrise, yet holding Mari was more important than getting out of bed and looking out the window. He'd watch it tomorrow. He'd still be here. He realized he wasn't going anywhere soon.

Demons should not be about in daylight, but Darius had every intention of remaining by Mari's side.

She moved her leg across his thighs. He hoped his erection wouldn't frighten her, but there was no controlling his reaction to the warmth of her body, the sweet scent of her hair, the beat of her heart thudding against his abdomen.

She moved again and her lips parted. Her breath lifted the hairs around his nipple and his arousal spiked to another level. Gods, she was killing him here. Innocent in sleep, her every move seemed designed to incite him further.

She stretched and yawned, and suddenly jerked into awareness. Her head popped up.

"Good morning." He raised his head and smiled at her.

Her face was mere inches from his, her eyes wide, her lips parted in a perfect *O* of surprise. Mari blinked.

Darius did the only thing possible.

He kissed her. Her body went stiff against his. Then she melted against him and her lips softened against his mouth. Softened and parted as she kissed him back.

She was warm and sleepy-sweet and he wrapped his arms around her slim back and held her close as they explored each other with lips and tongues. She wriggled and turned, aligning their bodies until she lay full upon him, trapping his erection between the firm muscles of her thighs, teasing him with the slide of her full breasts over his chest, the sweep of her lips across his.

This was heaven. Heaven and hell, all at the same time.

Many minutes later, as much as he hated doing it, Darius was the one to break the kiss. He nuzzled her chin and her throat, letting her know with his continued touch, the soft strokes over her hips and the rounded curve of her buttocks, that he would have preferred more kissing.

What he wanted and what was right, however, were two very different things.

Then, with a soft, almost apologetic laugh, Mari raised her head and stared directly into his eyes. Still sleepy and warm, she radiated a needy tension that he felt wherever their bodies connected. There was a definite glitter of arousal in her beautiful blue eyes, and when she lowered her mouth to his, when her lips parted and her tongue tentatively tested the seam of his, Darius knew he was lost.

This was right—this simple joining of two souls who needed, who wanted the connection, the beautiful sense of two bodies perfectly aligned, two souls in sync. Darius bent his knees and planted his feet firmly against the mattress, trapping Mari between his thighs. He cupped her face in his palms and gently held her, kissing her thoroughly, tasting her. She moaned against his mouth, kissing him deeper. Her fingers threaded through his tangled hair and she held him even as he held her.

The thick length of his cock rode between her thighs as she rubbed herself against him. Her nipples were hard points against his chest, her heart thundering so frantically he felt its staccato beat. Arousal exploded between them, desire so powerful, so immediate, there was no denying what each of them wanted . . . needed.

Suddenly Mari scrambled lower, hooked her fingers in the cotton sweatpants and tugged them over his thighs, past his knees, off his feet. He slipped his hands beneath her camisole top and drew it up. She raised her arms as he slipped it over her head. She shoved her own pants down her long legs, off over her feet.

Darius wished for the sun. Wished the dawn would come faster, the shadows not linger so long. He wanted to see her, to worship the long, lean, lines he felt so clearly beneath his hands, but she didn't give him a chance. Already she was sliding over him, kneeling, raising up and grasping his painfully erect length in her long fingers, holding him still as she slowly, so slowly lowered herself over his erection.

He wrapped his hands around her slim hips and held

her—gritted his teeth and prayed for control. Her eyes went wide as she slowly, carefully, took him inside. He was an unusually big man by human standards, a well-endowed man among Lemurians, and he fought the raging desire to thrust, to force himself deeper inside her honeyed warmth.

Mari's head was thrown back, her eyes closed, lips parted, but it wasn't pain he read in her expression. No. It was pleasure verging on rapture. She wriggled her hips and seated him fully. Then she sighed and began to move.

He felt as if she grasped his member in a tight, hot fist. Her inner muscles rippled along his full length, her fingers curled into the hair on his chest and she rode him with a smile on her face, an expression of conquest as much as pleasure.

As well she should. He'd not intended this intimacy so soon, though he'd wanted it. Dear gods, how he'd wanted it. Her lips parted, her smile stretched into a grimace as orgasm claimed her. She rose up and came down on him harder, faster. He heard her cry, felt it as the sound blossomed into a scream of passion and release that set him free.

Darius arched his hips, driving deeper, grasping her hips, lifting her and then pulling her close again and then again. A shock of pure fire raced from his spine to his balls to his cock—fire and a feeling so amazing, so unbelievably sweet he was afraid to question what it could possibly mean.

But he knew, as she whimpered his name and collapsed forward against his chest, that something special had just happened. Something he'd never experienced before.

Something he had to believe was part of Mari's magic.

Long moments later, Mari kissed his chin and lowered her forehead to his chest once again. Her body shuddered as her vaginal muscles continued to pulse and ripple around him.

"Oh. My." She raised her head and grinned at him. "I do like your method of waking me up."

He chuckled. His laughter bounced Mari up and down. "My method? Oh, Mari. That was all yours. All you."

She bit her lip. Then she took a deep breath, kissed his nose and rolled off of him. Distancing herself from such an intimate connection, though her smile was firmly in place. "It appears you're miraculously healed. This is good to know, right?"

He growled and reached for her. "It appears you've healed me, witch."

Laughing, she rolled out of his reach, stood up and headed toward the bathroom. "Give me a minute and I'll be ready to go. Later we can get breakfast at the café down the street. I have to open the shop at ten, but we have a lot to do before then."

Darius watched as Mari disappeared behind the closed door. For some reason, she didn't want to discuss what they'd just done, what they'd shared. So be it. Maybe things were different for women of Earth. There was no one he could ask.

No one but Mari. Hopefully he'd figure her out before too long. Smiling as he considered all the things he wanted to learn about her, he cast his thoughts wide, searching for Roland, but there was no sense of his cousin. Lazily he scratched his chest and studied the way the sunlight moved across the ceiling. He felt replete . . . whole.

What a beautiful world Earth was. How could his people have given up their place in it so easily?

How could they have chosen a life that was nothing more than prison? He thought of all the years he'd lived within his world, within the confines of a dimension without a real sun, without stars. He'd read about them, watched film of them, experienced the artificial days and nights designed to copy what existed right here on Earth.

It was too depressing to dwell upon. He glanced toward the closed bathroom door. Toward Mari. The thought of returning to Lemuria after his brief visit to this world made him want to weep. Somehow he had to find a way to remain here, in Earth's dimension. Here. With Mari. He lay there on the comfortable mattress, thinking about the morning so far, about the day ahead, thinking of walking in sunlight for the first time in his life, wondering if there would be more demons again tonight.

If demons won this fight, all this could be lost. *And what of Mari?* He almost understood the Council of Nine's lack of interest in fighting demonkind. What did they have to lose? They merely existed in the shadows of what they'd already given up.

Darius had never had so much to lose. Never before. And with that thought, he wondered again about Roland, if his cousin was looking for him. Had an alarm gone out? He'd been missing now for almost twelve hours and he hated to think he might be worrying his fellow soldiers.

Even so, lying here listening to the sound of running water in the small bathroom as Mari made ready to meet the day, hearing birdsong outside the window, and thinking of sunshine and blue sky overhead, he hoped it took his cousin a long time to find him. A long, long time.

When Evergreen Feed and Tack opened at eight, Mari was waiting at the door with Darius's measurements in hand, and very low expectations of actually finding clothes that would fit him.

She'd been absolutely shocked to find everything she needed, right down to the pair of hiking boots, size sixteen. It had taken her less than half an hour. The moment she returned to the apartment, she'd turned her packages over to Darius and he'd disappeared into the bathroom to change.

He'd looked like a little kid at Christmas, and she couldn't wait to see him. It was easier to shop for him, to give him things, than to think of what they'd done this morning.

What she wanted to do again.

He stepped out of the bathroom, fully dressed.

And took her breath, along with her ability to form cohesive words. After a moment of staring she softly said, "Wow. You look amazing."

He filled out the faded, prewashed jeans perfectly, and the green and blue plaid flannel shirt turned his eyes the color of a dark forest. The thick soles of his boots added a good inch or more to his already impressive height. He'd pulled his long hair back into a single thick braid that hung past his waist, and positioned his Evergreen Feed and Tack ballcap low on his brow.

"Do I look okay? Really?"

The hesitancy in his voice surprised her. He actually seemed to need her approval, but after a lifetime wearing nothing but robes and sandals, she figured this must feel really strange.

"Oh. Yeah. Turn around. I want to see everything." Mari parked her hands on her hips and waited while he did a slow spin. "Perfect. I think you're ready to go out in public. You're still going to draw attention, but at least it won't be from people who think you're a bit weird."

"What will they think?" He'd already reached for the door, but now he turned and frowned.

Mari grabbed her purse and stepped through the open door ahead of him. She glanced over her shoulder and grinned. "They'll think you're gorgeous, and that I'm too damned lucky for my own good."

Darius looked as if he didn't know quite how to answer her, which was probably just as well.

She couldn't believe she'd had the nerve to say what she'd

said. Of course, she still couldn't believe she'd taken on such a sexually aggressive role this morning. She bit back a grin. She was so not like this!

He followed close behind as they went down the stairs and out through the back door. Everything in the shop looked just fine. They still had an hour before she needed to open—time to grab breakfast at the café just down the street. Hopefully, they'd hear if there was any gossip of unusual activities.

Darius reached out and took her hand. Mari wrapped her fingers around his and shot him a quick glance. He smiled at her, and the image of how they'd awakened this morning flashed into her mind.

She couldn't have hidden her blush if she'd tried. Luckily, they'd almost reached their destination. "I'll feel a lot better if I hear other people are seeing strange things," she said.

Darius paused outside the door. "Why?"

She shook her head. "I don't want to think I'm a target. I'd rather think what happened last night was random. It's too scary, otherwise."

He took a deep breath, gazed at the snow-covered volcano looming over the small town, and shook his head. "I don't think it's random," he said. "What happened should frighten you." He tugged her hand and drew her through the door. "Come. We'll have breakfast and forget about demonkind for now."

Mari snorted. Darius turned and stared at her. "What?"

"You make a statement like that and expect me to forget? Darius, my friend, you really need to work on your people skills."

"I imagine you're right."

At least he was grinning.

They took seats at the counter. Mari figured they were more apt to hear what was going on if they sat up front.

When the waitress poured coffee for Darius, he looked at the cup and then at Mari and raised an eyebrow.

"Try it and see what you think," she said, taking a sip of hers. "It's a mild stimulant. Helps wake you up in the morning."

He raised an eyebrow. "I prefer your method of waking me up in the morning."

Then he tasted it and made a face.

Blushing, Mari laughed. "Here. Try this." She opened four packets of sugar and a little container of cream, dumped them in his cup, and stirred.

Darius tried it again and sighed. "Much better. Thank you."

The waitress took their order. Mari noticed that, while she was the one speaking, the waitress only had eyes for Darius.

She couldn't blame her. As soon as the woman left, Mari gazed around the restaurant, curious to see whom she recognized. An older couple walked through the door. The man smiled at Mari and led his wife over to her.

"Good morning, Dr. Franklin." Mari grabbed Darius's hand. "Darius, I want you to meet Dr. and Mrs. Franklin. Dr. Franklin was my mom's obstetrician when I was born."

Darius nodded and smiled at the couple, though Mari figured he probably didn't have a clue what an obstetrician was. The doctor stared at him and frowned. "Darius? I thought your mother said your young man's name was Bradley."

Oh, crap. "Wrong young man, Doctor. Bradley and I broke it off awhile back."

"You did?" Mrs. Franklin stared at Darius. "Weren't you planning to marry him? What happened? Your mother hasn't said a word about you breaking up with him."

"I, uh . . ."

Darius's arm slipped around her waist. "Mari changed her

mind," he said. "That's all that matters." His look didn't in-
vite further comment.

"Oh. I see." Mrs. Franklin's nose went higher in the air.
She stepped back, obviously offended.

Mari groaned. She figured her mother would know all
about Darius before lunch. She wouldn't be surprised to see
Spirit at the shop before the day ended. Mrs. Franklin was a
horrible snoop, though as usual the conversation appeared to
have flown right over her husband's head. He leaned close
and patted Mari's knee.

"Well, don't take too much longer to find the right man,
Mari. Not if you intend to give Spirit and Freedom those
grandbabies they're so anxious for. You're not getting any
younger." With that, he turned and guided his wife to a booth
toward the back.

Mari turned around, planted her elbows on the counter
and leaned her head in her hands. Groaning, she shook her
head. "I so did not need to hear that this morning."

Darius laughed. "So. You're not getting any younger?
How old are you, Marigold Moonbeam Schwartz?"

Her head popped up. "How did you know my name?"

He leaned close and planted a kiss on the end of her nose.
"I saw it written on a piece of paper in the kitchen and figured it must be you. I like it. Being named after moonbeams
and flowers is wonderful. Are you going to tell me your
age?"

"I'm thirty-three. That makes me an old maid in Dr.
Franklin's estimation. I think he's delivered every baby in
town for the past fifty years and he wants to deliver mine. So
how old are you?" She poked him in the ribs.

He sighed and looked away. "It doesn't matter," he said.

"Hey! Fair's fair. I told."

Darius glanced around, as if checking to make sure no
one heard. Mari felt like giggling. He really seemed bothered.

When he finally answered, he spoke softly. "We judge time differently in Lemuria. By your calendar, I was born a little over ten thousand years ago, but I'm considered a very young man in my world."

She shook her head. Obviously something got lost in translation. "You wanna run that by me one more time?"

He smiled and shrugged. "Lemurians are immortal. Sort of. We can be killed, and no one really lives forever. Our older members eventually grow tired of life and choose the spirit world, but I won't reach middle age until I'm at least fifteen thousand of your years old."

The waitress set their plates down in front of them. Scrambled eggs, hash-brown potatoes, thick strips of bacon. She refilled their coffee cups. When neither Darius nor Mari acknowledged her, she turned away to the next customer.

Mari felt as if her brains were as scrambled as the eggs, but so far, she'd seen no proof that Darius had ever lied to her. What he said was outrageous, but . . . She shook her head. "I had no idea. So when I'm old and wrinkled and gray, you'll still look like you do now?"

He nodded, but he didn't look very happy. "I will."

"Eat your breakfast," she said, chagrined at how sharp she sounded. More softly, she added, "We need to get going so I can open up the shop by ten."

Darius stared at her a moment. Obviously, he was surprised by her non sequitur. He'd probably expected her to comment on the immortality thing, to say something besides ordering him to eat his breakfast.

There was nothing she could say. Nothing at all, especially after what they'd shared this morning.

He nodded, an almost imperceptible gesture. Then he dug into his breakfast. Mari spun around on her stool and stared at her plate. She didn't want to think of what she'd just learned. The idea of growing old and ugly while Darius remained as young and perfect as he was now left a foul taste in her mouth. She felt like throwing up.

Instead, she methodically ate her breakfast and wondered at the stupid dreams she'd had all morning. Dreams of keeping Darius here with her. Dreams of finally finding the perfect man to tie her star to, to spend her life with.

She'd actually thought seriously of Dr. Franklin's comment about babies. Experienced a short, sweet dream of holding Darius's son in her arms. Of raising his daughter.

So much for dreams.

Chapter 7

Darius spent the day exploring Evergreen. Occasionally he checked in to see how things were going at the shop and he kept his senses open for any hint of demon activity. He listened for messages from Roland, but so far he'd heard nothing from his cousin. Still, he felt no need to worry. He was enjoying himself more than he'd imagined possible.

He liked Evergreen. The town was small, the people friendly, and the sunshine a blessing. For a man raised beneath an artificial sky, the limitless blue canopy and the brilliant sun, the occasional white, puffy cloud overhead, and the sounds of birds singing in trees of all shapes and sizes was close to overwhelming.

He was filled with questions, filled with joy, and depressed. More depressed than he'd imagined possible.

What to do about Mari? He found himself returning time and again to the little shop, merely to reassure himself she was okay, to see her, hear her speak, watch her move.

Since learning of his immortality, she'd thrown up a wall between them, one he had no right to break through, to tear down, or to climb over.

So why did he hope to do exactly that?

The sun was sinking behind the horizon when he realized his new boots were giving him blisters and his legs were somewhat raw from the unfamiliar chafing of fabric against tender skin. He ended his exploration and walked slowly back to the shop. The sound of angry voices brought him to a halt outside the door. When he glanced through the window, he saw Mari speaking with a small, round woman with long gray hair.

Mari had her arms wrapped tightly around her chest in the defensive posture he'd already learned to recognize. The older woman leaned forward, shaking her finger in Mari's face, berating her about something.

Darius stepped into the shop. Mari raised her head and her eyes went wide. The older woman spun around.

"You!" she said, shaking her finger at him now, instead of at Mari. "Just who do you think you are, moving in on my daughter and filling her head with foolish stories? You're no more a Lemurian than I am. Everyone knows Lemurians are at least twelve feet tall with a horn in the middle of their foreheads. You are nothing more than an oversized interloper."

Darius glanced at Mari. He wasn't sure if she was going to laugh or cry, but something was ready to give. He swept his hand in front of the woman who claimed to be Mari's mother.

Her mouth snapped shut. Her eyes glazed over and she stared blankly into space.

"Mari, what—"

"What did you do to my mother?" Horrified, Mari raced around the counter and reached for her mother.

"No! Don't touch her." He shook his head. "She's fine. I merely used a compulsion on her to give me a minute alone with you. I wanted to find out what's going on."

"A compulsion? Like you do with your sword?" Mari leaned down to look directly into her mother's glazed eyes.

Darius shrugged. "Well, what I do to my sword is actually a glamour, which is a bit different, but yes, sort of the same. It's a mild form of hypnotism, but this won't last long. What's going on?"

Mari sighed. "Mrs. Franklin called Mom and told her I'd broken up with Brad, something I hadn't mentioned yet because I didn't want to worry her while Dad's recovering. She also told her about the man I was having breakfast with, which obviously meant we'd spent the night together."

Darius frowned. "We did spend the night together."

"Well, it's none of her business! Anyway, Mom came charging into the shop yelling at me like I'd lost my mind, I tried to explain the demons and you, and she went nuts." She huffed out a big breath and added, "Which isn't all that unusual for my mother."

"I can help her accept what you've told her, or I can remove her memories. It might be easier if she doesn't know my origins or anything about the demons, at least not yet."

"Anything. Please?"

He laughed, altered the compulsion to remove the memories of Lemurians and demons, and slowly released Mari's mother.

Spirit blinked, turned to Darius, and smiled. "So you're Darius," she said, holding out her hand. "It's a pleasure to meet you." She glanced at Mari and then up at Darius. "Where did you say you met him, Mari?"

"In San Francisco, Mom. Through friends. I'm sorry I didn't tell you about Brad, but it all happened around the time Dad fell and you were so busy at the hospital, I didn't want to worry you."

Spirit nodded. "I understand, sweetie. I never liked Brad anyway. Will you and Darius be joining us for dinner?"

Darius interrupted. "Not tonight, thank you. I was planning to take Mari out this evening."

Spirit beamed. "Wonderful. Please, though, before you leave Evergreen, you must stop by and meet Marigold's father. He'll be so glad for company. He's not used to all this inactivity."

When Spirit finally left, Darius closed the door firmly behind her and turned toward Mari. He wasn't sure what to expect.

She burst out laughing. "Damn. I wish I'd had that compulsion thing of yours while I was growing up! It would have really come in handy. My mother can be like a dog with a bone."

"How is a dog with a bone? We have no dogs in Lemuria."

"No dogs? How sad." Mari shook her head. "It means she can be very, very persistent. As in, unwilling to give up, ever. I hadn't intended to tell her anything about you or demonkind, but she managed to get it out of me. She could always do that. She just sort of wears a person down until you spill everything."

"I hope you don't mind that I lied to her." He stepped close and took Mari by both hands. "I'm not planning to take you out tonight." He looked into her unbelievable blue eyes and softly added, "I thought we'd stay in."

She looked at their clasped hands and then raised her head and stared so directly at him, he felt as if she read his very thoughts. "What are we going to do about . . . ?"

Mari didn't need to say the words. He knew exactly what she meant. Her mortality and his immortality would be an issue for as long as she lived. "Do we have to do anything? Can't we just wait and see what happens?"

She smiled. "I think we both know what will happen, but it's tough." She shrugged and pulled her hands free of his grasp. "There can't be any future for us. I'm not the kind of person to get involved with a man, knowing it won't go anywhere."

"Who's to say it won't? I hope to be around for a while. I will have to return to Lemuria at some point, if only to check in, but I don't know that I can ever live there again. Not knowing what I know now of Earth. Of you."

"Darius, even if you're around forever, I won't be. I'll grow old and ugly and you'll still be the gorgeous young man you are today. I'd hate that. You'd hate it. It won't work."

He shook his head. "It's a long way off. Your body might age, but the woman you are will remain the same. That woman is the one who's caught my heart. Don't write us off as impossible. Not yet."

Darius! Where are you?

Roland? Darius glanced at Mari. "Hold that thought. My sergeant is finally contacting me."

Mari nodded and looked away.

Darius concentrated on his cousin's voice. Then he answered. *I'm in Evergreen, a small town at the base of the volcano. I fought demons last night. They appear to have targeted a young woman who lives here.*

Darius smiled at Roland's audible yet cerebral sigh of relief. *Thank the gods I found you! Protect the woman from demonkind. Unexpected events will keep me in Lemuria. Leland and Matthias are coming to you as soon as they can. I closed the portal yesterday, but demons reopened it this evening. It's sealed once again, but I don't know for how long. Many demons have passed through. We're fighting them now, on the upper flank of the mountain. Once everything is under control and the portal secured, Leland and Matthias will join you. It may not be until much later tonight.*

Darius gave Roland the coordinates for the shop and wished him well. Then he turned his attention to Mari. "It's almost time to close, isn't it?" He glanced out the window, at the shadows deepening along the street outside.

Mari nodded. She flipped the sign on the door to show they were closed and then counted out the cash drawer, collected the register receipts, and stuck everything in a zippered pouch as she'd done the night before. "Are you ready?"

Darius nodded. He checked the area around the front of the store for signs of demonkind, but all was quiet. Together they made the short walk to the bank, but tonight he held Mari's hand as they walked down the dark and quiet street.

"I hardly saw you today. I mean, I saw you checking in through the window, but you hardly ever stopped in." She glanced at him and her fingers tightened around his.

"I did not want to bother you while you worked. I walked around town, went into many of the shops, talked to some of the people." He ran his thumb over her hand. "You have a wonderful town. Was it hard to choose to live elsewhere?"

Mari shook her head. "No. Not so hard. I wanted to experience life in a city and I do love San Francisco. Plus, the kind of work I do, I really can't do here in Evergreen. There aren't any big banks or investment houses."

They reached the bank. The sun was gone now and street lamps cast a glow over the parking lot. Mari slipped the deposit bag through the slot and stood there a moment with her hand against the metal. Then she turned to Darius. He was surprised to see tears in her eyes.

"Who am I kidding?" She shook her head. "I couldn't wait to get away from my parents and the town. All I saw were the bad things. My mother and father seemed like such flakes to me. They were so caught up in their drugs and their off-center thinking that I often felt as if I was just an obstacle in their path to further enlightenment."

She laughed and shook her head. "I had to live away to

realize how much good was here, too, but growing up with parents like mine . . ." She shook her head and her shoulders slumped. "It's hard to explain."

Darius tilted her chin up with his fingertip. "I could feel your mother's love for you. She worries."

"I know. I couldn't see that for a long time. I saw it as interference, saw their flamboyance as something embarrassing. I was always expecting them to get arrested, and it was an honest worry. I was terrified child protective services would come and take me away, at the same time hoping it would happen. Somehow they managed to skirt the rules without ever getting caught."

She looked so sad, like a lost child staring across the empty parking lot. Darius cupped her face in his hands and turned her toward him. "And yet they managed to raise a beautiful daughter like you. One who knows the rules, yet who thinks for herself, who is brave and beautiful and very, very exceptional."

She gazed at him with such longing it broke his heart.

"How can you say that? You hardly know me."

"Ah, Mari. I know you better than you think." And standing there beside the bank, beneath the bright overhead lights, he leaned close and kissed her.

He'd wanted to taste her lips all day long. Wanted to hold her close and feel her heart beat against his chest, the way he'd felt her this morning, but he'd stayed away. He'd honored her unspoken request for space—had given her time to think.

And yet he'd been the one thinking all day. Thinking of holding Mari in his arms. Of kissing her, the way he was kissing her now. He'd dreamed of how it would feel if she kissed him back.

Just as she was doing now. Kissing him. Holding him close, opening her heart even as she parted her lips. Letting him know she was willing, if only for a little bit, to put aside her fears for the future. She was willing to experience the moment, to experience Darius, if only for now.

Darius might have been the one to kiss her, but Mari was really proud of herself for finding the strength, finally, to pull away and put a bit of space between them.

A very tiny bit. It took her a moment to bring the world back into focus, to remember that they were standing in the parking lot of Evergreen Community Bank, that it was dark outside, and that there were demons about.

Probably not a very good idea to be so caught up in kissing the man that she'd not noticed there were people coming and going, cars pulling in and out of the nearby grocery store, a world passing by outside their embrace.

Damn. She'd never been kissed by anyone the way she'd been kissed by Darius. She licked her lips and raised her head. He stared at her with a bemused expression on his face, as if she'd maybe rocked his world a little bit, too.

"Let's go." He reached for her hand. When she placed her fingers within his grasp, Mari felt as if she'd somehow made a huge concession, as if she'd agreed to much more than merely holding his hand for the walk back to Crystal Dreams.

And oddly, she didn't mind at all. The misgivings she'd had earlier today, when she'd learned of his immortality, somehow seemed unimportant now. Not that there was a practical way to actually work through them, but maybe she could just sort of shove all those issues aside for now.

When they got back to the shop, it was quiet. There was no stench of demon, and the stray cats that showed up when she filled the bowl with kibble were the usual strays she always saw—even the big tom that had cornered her last night.

Was it only a day ago? Mari flashed a grin at Darius as

they locked the front door. "I just realized that you showed up about this time last night. It's been a busy twenty-four hours."

He nodded, but he hardly took his gaze off her. Then he shook his head and shot a quick glance around the store. "I expected the demons by now. Maybe Leland and Matthias have stopped all of them at the portal." He gazed longingly toward the door leading upstairs.

Mari laughed. "I need a shower and something to eat. We can come back down here later and make sure everything is okay."

"That works." Darius grabbed the book of spells off the counter where Mari had left it. "Have you learned anything today?"

She laughed as she led him up to her apartment. "Only that all of my mother's spells rhyme, not to mention she's a lousy poet. Rhyme seems to be the only common denominator. There's one she wrote for calling forth rain that I remember." Mari lowered her voice and ponderously recited, "Clouds roil and water rise, let rain fall down from heaven's skies. Water flowers, water trees . . . this I ask, so mote it be."

" 'So mote it be'? What's that for?"

"I read that it's a sorcerer's phrase for 'because I said so.'" She laughed. "I think it's to add validity to the spell. Who knows? Most of the spells are my mom's, and Lord only knows what was going on in her mind."

She thought about all the spells she'd read, the thoughts she'd had as she'd slowly worked her way through the book. She'd ignored the published spells and concentrated on the ones her mother had written. They filled the margins and every other blank space on the pages. "Ya know, at first I thought they were just silly poems. Then today I asked Mom if she'd ever cast a spell that worked."

"What did she say?"

A shiver passed along Mari's spine. She turned and stared at Darius. He'd stopped a few steps beneath her, which put him at eye level. "Mom said that's how she caught my father and why Crystal Dreams has always been a success. Because of her spells. She also said she cast a spell that would bring me home when Dad was hurt. And another to show me Brad's true colors. She never did like him."

"What did you say?"

"What could I say? I thanked her for taking care of Brad. At the time I was joking, but the more I think about it, the more I wonder if it's true." She opened the door and stepped into the apartment. "Maybe those stupid rhyming words do have power of some sort."

Darius glanced out the window. "It's raining," he said. He pulled the curtains aside so Mari could see the rain falling gently from what had, only moments ago, been a perfectly clear sky. Then he turned the curtains loose and carefully set the book down on the kitchen table. "Maybe we need to read those demon spells a little closer."

"Maybe we do." She glanced at him and the first thought that flitted through her mind had nothing to do with rain or demons. No, it was exactly what she'd been thinking this morning—how glad she was that she hadn't quit taking her birth control pills when she and Brad split up. Need rose in her like a bloom opening its petals.

Then she smiled at Darius and very softly added, "Later."

Chapter 8

That one word skittered across his nerve endings like a physical caress. *Later?* If Mari wanted to discuss the spells later, he hoped she wanted to do the same thing he did, now.

She stepped up close, and he sighed. It appeared she did. Mari ran her fingers down the buttons at the front of his shirt. Lemurian robes had no buttons, but as he watched, almost mesmerized while she slowly unbuttoned the top one that rested against the base of his throat, he realized how sorely lacking were the buttonless robes his people wore.

"I'm going to take a shower." She raised her head and looked him straight in the eye. "Would you like to join me?"

He tried to answer, but nothing came out of his mouth.

Mari chuckled. "I'll take that for a yes." She finished unbuttoning his shirt, flipping open one button after the next, exposing his bare chest to her fingertips, the sharp edges of her nails.

He drew in a shuddering breath, and then another. She slipped her hands beneath his shirt. Her palms were hot as she slid the shirt back over his shoulders and tugged it down his arms. Then she ran her fingers through the dark hair covering his chest.

"I've wanted to do this since I first saw you after your shower last night." She nuzzled his chest and then glanced at him with a huge grin on her face. "We were in too big a rush this morning. It's so soft. Like silk. I thought it would feel coarse."

She ran her fingers over his chest again and he tilted his head back and groaned. "You're trying to kill me, right?"

"Not at all. Just helping you get out of all these clothes."

"If that's what you're after . . ." He ripped the shirt off and tossed it over the kitchen chair. Unbuttoned his jeans and slid them down his legs. As soon as they stuck at the tops of his boots he realized his mistake.

Mari's giggles didn't help any. "Oh, Darius. There's a system to undressing when you're wearing jeans. Boots first. Then pants."

"I can see that. Now." He sat on the floor in his boxer shorts with his pants around his ankles and untied the laces on his boots. Slipped them off and tugged off the socks, tugged the jeans off, and left everything in a heap on the cracked linoleum. When he looked up, Mari was already out of her shirt and shoes and had her hands at the waistband of her jeans.

The tiny little bra she wore barely covered her breasts, and when she peeled her jeans down over her underpants, Darius sucked in a breath. There was hardly enough fabric to cover her feminine mound. Her long legs were sleek and smooth. She stepped close to him, close enough for him to reach out and run his fingers across the soft curve of her belly, just above the elastic band of her panties.

Her skin rippled beneath his touch and a soft little gasp hissed between her lips. She swallowed, took a deep breath, and grabbed his hand. "C'mon. The shower's big enough if we get real close."

He stood up and followed her into the little bathroom, watching while she leaned over and turned on the water. She waited for the hot water, adjusted the temperature, and then grabbed a towel and looped it over the curtain rod.

Steam billowed up and out of the shower stall. Mari stepped away, but she didn't even look at Darius when she unhooked her bra's front closure and slipped the thing over her shoulders. Nor did she look when she peeled her tiny pink panties over her hips and down her legs. She stepped out of them and left them lying on the floor, a tiny wisp of pink silk.

He couldn't have not looked if his life depended on it. It took an act of will to keep his hands to himself as she stood there, so close and so perfectly naked. Darius shoved his boxer shorts down over his legs without another thought, though he appreciated the way her eyes flashed the moment his pants were down and his erection finally freed. It had been much too dark this morning to appreciate each other's bodies. Now he reveled in the light.

Mari quickly pulled the shower curtain back and stepped beneath the spray. Darius followed her, standing to one side so he didn't block the water. It was a tight fit, thank goodness. Tight enough that when Mari grabbed a cloth and covered it with soap, it was easier for her to wash him than to bathe herself.

Following her lead, Darius grabbed a second washcloth and ran it over her shoulders and breasts. She washed his back and then his waist, down his arms, over and under, scrubbing so gently the friction made him shiver with all the sensations she was raising on his overly sensitized skin.

She washed her own hair, he washed his, they both rinsed. He soaped the cloth again and washed her buttocks and her legs, kneeling in the small shower to run the soapy cloth over her feet as she lifted first one and then the other.

He wondered if her skin tingled as much as his did. If her heart was pounding as hard, her need growing as desperate. Darius raised his eyes and gazed at Mari. Neither of them had said a word and yet Darius felt as if every question he'd ever asked was being answered in this moment.

As if every need he'd ever felt, every desire he'd wanted fulfilled were suddenly encapsulated here, in this time, in this tiny shower, with this one perfect woman.

The water continued to beat against his back and buttocks. His long hair, loosened from its braid, covered his arms and tangled in the swirling water. He grasped Mari's flanks in his big hands and drew her close, nuzzled the soft, wet tuft of blond curls at the apex of her thighs, and used the tip of his tongue to separate the sweet folds between her legs.

She cried out and clutched his shoulders. He felt the bite of her nails scraping his skin. The sharp pain sparked a bolt of energy that shot straight to his groin.

He licked deeper, harder, using teeth and tongue now to claim her, using his big hands and his long, strong fingers to mold the firm muscles of her buttocks, to hold her even as her legs trembled and her body arched against his mouth.

He concentrated on the tiny nub at the top of her cleft, suckling and licking, stabbing deep with his tongue and then sucking her gently between his lips.

Mari's breath escaped in harsh pants, her grip on his shoulders tightened, and she screamed. He tasted the warm rush of her fluids, felt the convulsive shudders of her climax, but he kept his mouth against her, licking gently, nuzzling softly, slowly bringing her down.

When he stood up, finished rinsing, and turned off the tap, Mari leaned against him as if she'd lost the ability to stand. He dried her off, supporting her with one arm, drying her from head to foot with the towel she'd hung over the shower curtain rod.

Then he dried himself as best he could with one hand and a damp towel, lifted Mari easily in his arms, and carried her to the bed where they'd awakened together this morning—where they'd made love this morning. He laid her gently on the mattress. Then he knelt beside her, hard and ready and utterly confused.

He had to know—did she really want him, want this? This morning they'd made love without really thinking of where it might lead. Tonight was different. Tonight had meaning.

Was she ready to take a leap of faith with a man who was already falling more than a little in love with her? Nine hells, he hoped so, because it was killing him to be so close, and yet not at all close enough.

Her ears were actually buzzing. They hadn't even made love yet, and her body felt replete and yet so needy she wanted to grab him and tell him to quit staring already and get busy! Then she remembered how he'd waited at meal-time—waited again this morning, and then followed her lead.

She reached for him. Held out her hand and almost giggled at the relieved look on his face when he took her hand in both of his, kissed her fingers, and then turned his attention to her breasts, her belly, her legs, her shoulders, and even her toes.

There wasn't a part of Mari's body that hadn't been touched or kissed or rubbed or loved by the time he settled himself between her thighs. He sat back on his heels and just smiled at her, running his hands over her arms, linking their fingers together.

His body glimmered with a fine sheen of sweat as he leaned close and kissed her gently, but even though his lips barely touched hers, she felt the tension in the soft pressure, knew Darius was strung tight enough to explode. She planted her feet and lifted her hips, offering herself.

He closed his eyes for a moment, almost as if he whispered a brief prayer. Then he leaned forward and pressed the broad crown of his erection between her swollen labia. She was so wet, so ready, that when he pushed inside her tight channel, there was no pain. He was bigger than any man she'd ever been with, longer and thicker than any lover ever, and yet once again, her body adjusted, took him deep, welcomed him with a rippling embrace.

Slowly, in and out and back in again, deeper with each roll of his hips, he worked his way inside her passage until he'd seated himself fully, until his patience and her need won out.

After a moment, he began to thrust. Faster, deeper—harder than she'd expected after his gentle entry. It was as if, once he'd gained her full compliance, he set himself free, taking her as a conquest, as the prize he'd fought for and won. This was no civilized lover—he was a primal force, his lips drawn back, eyes narrowed, nostrils flaring. His breath was harsh upon her breasts, his hands hot where he held her.

She lifted to him, begged for more, and rolled her hips to meet his on each downward thrust. Her nails raked his back and buttocks. Her lungs burned with the effort to draw enough air, and she felt each powerful thrust like a brand, a mark of ownership, a claiming. This was so primitive, such a visceral mating, she wanted to cry out with the power of it.

Her body was pliant, receptive to his every move. A frown marred his forehead and from the tight clench of his jaw she knew he fought for control, fought the spiraling desire that pulled him closer to completion with each slap of thighs and bellies and breasts.

His long black hair draped all around them, a midnight curtain of silk trailing over Mari's breasts and shoulders, tickling her thighs. Then he reared back on his heels, easily lifting her in his arms. She locked her heels behind his back, tightened her arms around his neck, and reveled in the powerful rhythm, the lovemaking that was so much more than mere sex, so far beyond anything she'd ever experienced in her life.

She wasn't a woman who found completion in the sex act alone. It always took more—lips or hands or even toys to take her over the edge. Not this morning and not now. All it took was Darius—filling her, loving her, taking her to the edge and over in a screaming free fall awash in sensation, a clenching, throbbing, burning blast of pleasure shared.

Her climax slammed into her and took her breath. Mari's scream and Darius's growling release echoed in the small room, shook the mattress against the wall, left them both sated and laughing with the shocking power of two bodies joined, of hearts thundering and lungs laboring.

Long moments later he lowered Mari to the mattress and followed her down. Their bodies were still connected—all sweat-slick and trembling with the aftereffects of their powerful shared orgasm. Darius held his weight off of her, resting on his elbows and nuzzling her breasts, kissing her chin, her shoulder.

It hit Mari like a body blow. Pure, straightforward, powerful—a knowledge so true, so deeply planted within her heart, there was no doubt at all. She loved him. No matter the problems they faced, she would never give him up. Somehow they'd make it work. As impossible as it might be, as impossible as *they* might be, she finally understood what love really was.

And it wasn't anything at all like she'd imagined.

Darius dried the last dish and set it in the cupboard while Mari wiped down the counter. He knew that if she were to ask him what he'd eaten for dinner, he probably wouldn't be able to answer, though whatever it was had filled him. He certainly wasn't hungry—for food.

How could he possibly want her again? But he did. She'd said her mother was a witch. Maybe that was true, but he knew for certain Mari was. How else could she have bewitched him so?

It was almost midnight. They'd made love for hours—the most glorious hours he'd ever spent in his life. They'd showered once more and eaten and all he wanted to do was bury himself in her perfect body once again. Mari glanced his way, and from the sparkle in her eyes he knew she was thinking the same thing.

Suddenly her eyes went wide as she stared past him, toward the couch. "Darius? Your sword is glowing. Look!"

He spun around and was almost blinded by the brilliant flash of blue light. "It's warning of demons nearby. I wonder if they're getting into the shop?"

All he wore were the cut-off sweats. He slipped on his sandals and tightened the straps as Mari grabbed her book of spells and opened the door.

"I'll go first," he said. "Stay close." He drew his sword and raced down the stairs, paused at the door into the shop, and flung it open.

Black demon mist boiled and swirled within the small shop. Broken glass lay on the floor in front of the door, and more demons spilled in through the missing window. They seemed drawn to something on the counter. Mari dodged under Darius's arm and reached straight into the swirling mass. She pulled her hand out, firmly clutching the ruby geode.

Darius sent out a mental call for help. Where the hell were Matthias and Leland?

Leland's voice popped into Darius's head as he swung his crystal blade through the seething mist.

We've almost reached the coordinates you sent us. We've battled demonkind all the way down the mountain. For some reason Roland can't keep the portal closed, but you were right. Something here is drawing them. They're all headed your direction. Hang on.

Sharp talons slashed Darius's arm, drawing blood. He swung his sword and the demon died in a shower of sparks, but for a moment he was certain he saw an image within the mist—wicked fangs, multiple arms, scales, and wings.

Something else bumped into him and he felt the slice of teeth biting into his calf. He swung again and yet another demon died, but blood poured from Darius's wounds. "Mari! Stay back. They're gaining corporeal form without avatars. Somehow they had the strength to break the window. Something's happening. I can't explain it."

Mari cursed and he glanced her way. She held the geode out in front of her face. Demonkind, still in mist form, swirled and dove, but they went for the geode, not Mari. She flipped through the pages of the spell book, unharmed.

Sharp teeth latched onto Darius's thigh. He cursed and swung his sword again.

Something kept drawing her to pick up the ruby geode, but the geode appeared to attract the demons. What was it about the damned thing? Mari was almost certain it was linked to the demon attacks, but she couldn't explain how. There had to be something in this blasted book!

Darius was hopelessly outnumbered. More of the dark wraiths streamed through the broken window. The brief rain had ended and the roiling black cloud outside the shop had nothing to do with the weather she might have called with her mother's stupid spell. It was demonkind, massing in front of Crystal Dreams.

Frantically searching for answers, Mari swung the geode at the demons and skimmed from one page to the next.

She heard a shout and spun around just as two large men

burst through the back door. Darius yelled out a greeting to Leland and Matthias, his fellow guards. Mari's breath caught in her throat as the two new Lemurian guardsmen filled her mother's small shop. Swords flashed and sparks flew. Dressed in dark blue robes as Darius had been—was it only yesterday?—they moved with the same powerful grace as only highly trained warriors could.

More demons swirled through the broken glass. The air reeked, thick with their sulfuric stench. The walls echoed with banshee cries and Lemurian oaths and the battle went on for what felt like forever.

Darius's bare chest and back were streaked with blood. All three men were bleeding now. Still fighting bravely, still killing demonkind, yet their strikes were coming slower, their strength beginning to fade.

Mari held the geode out from her body, hoping to call the demons to her and give the men a break, but after the demon mist flowed over and through the ruby crystals, they sped back into battle against the three Lemurian warriors.

No wonder. She skimmed page after page in her mother's book until it all made sense. The ruby geode! It wasn't merely drawing the demons, pulling them all the way from the mountain portal to her mother's shop. It was energizing them. Giving them the strength to exist in this dimension without an avatar.

Damn! She wasn't helping. She was making things worse! But how to destroy it? According to the text, breaking the geode would merely free the evil power held within. It could only be stopped by magic—magic powered by blood and sacrifice.

She read the lines again, unwilling to believe the answer printed so plainly in the published text in front of her.

When Evil inhabits the ruby's red heart, true love's blood and sacrifice take it apart.

The spell, written beneath the lines, was in her mother's

neat hand. Mari glanced up as Darius cursed and ducked away from a demon's slashing claw. There was no denying that the demon mist was changing—demons were beginning to show their true form.

All three men bled from numerous wounds, yet they fought on without pause. Even so, as they grew weaker, the demons seemed to gain strength. Mari glanced at the geode she still clasped tightly in her hand. The rubies inside glowed and pulsed, beating like a living heart.

"Leland!" Darius shouted as Leland went down beneath a writhing cloud of demons. Part mist, part demon, they covered the young guard in a seething mass of teeth and claws and black, oily smoke. Leland cried out in pain and frustration. Darius's sword slashed back and forth through the demons, leaving flashes of light, sparking flames, and the stench of sulfur.

Dozens died, but there were more to take their place.

A shouted curse was all the warning given before Matthias disappeared beneath even more of the demons. Darius fought with frantic thrusts and slashes of his crystal blade, but there were too many, and they were too strong.

No matter the sacrifice, Mari knew she was the only one who could make it. Tears streaked her cheeks as Mari held the geode in front of her, grasping it with both hands. She'd read the spell only once, but the words seemed imprinted on her brain. She closed her eyes and chanted, "Heart's desire and heart's blood true, power of crystal for payment due."

She raised the ruby geode high over her head. "This sacrifice I freely give, that these brave men I love will live."

Clasping the geode against her heart, oblivious to the hundreds of demons screaming and shrieking as they suddenly swarmed over and around her, she shouted, "Evil burn and demons die. These ruby crystals cannot lie."

The screeching reached a crescendo. Mari held the geode out and pointed it toward the demons. They massed now, as if to attack her. Energy flowed through and over her body and her long hair stood on end as she screamed the final verse. "My heart, my soul, take all of me. Let Evil die. So mote it be."

Everything stopped. The strands of her hair floated slowly to her shoulders. Mari had time to wonder if the spell had failed, if they were all lost. Then the geode exploded. The loud concussion deafened her. Brilliant crimson light flashed, demons shrieked and, as if it happened in slow motion, thousands of red crystal shards spun and twisted and flew through the air, targeting each of the demons.

She heard Darius shout as if from far, far away.

"Mari! No! Gods, no!"

Pain sliced into Mari—unimaginable pain that went straight through her heart. Darkness overwhelmed her. Darkness and a sense of peace, that she had not given her life in vain.

As she fell, she knew the demons were gone.

Chapter 9

The flash blinded him for a moment. The concussion made his ears ring, but the silence that followed was deafening. Darius raced to Mari as she crumpled slowly to the ground.

"Mari! Gods, Mari. No!" There was blood. So much blood spilling from a wound in her chest, a deep puncture directly over her heart. He grabbed a white silk scarf off a sales rack beside her, wadded it up, and put pressure on the gaping hole, but blood pulsed out around his fingers and pooled on the floor.

Bright red heart's blood. There was nothing he could do for her. No way to save her. Her eyes were closed, her lips already growing pale as her life's blood spilled out of the wound, pumping slower now as she bled out and her heart failed.

Lifting her in his arms, he held Mari against his chest. Willing her to live, silently begging her not to die. Leland dragged himself close, and Matthias stumbled to his feet and joined them.

"What happened? The demons had me down. I was a dead man." Leland rested his hand on Darius's shoulder. "Who is she, Darius? How did she stop them?"

"She is the woman I love. She stopped them with magic. With love." His voice broke. He couldn't imagine losing her. Not when he'd just found her. Tears blinded him and his heart felt as if it were being ripped asunder.

"Darius. Pay heed."

He raised his head. A woman's voice? "Who speaks?"

"Nine hells, man." Matthias gaped at him. "It's your sword."

"Hold me against your true love's heart. Now, quickly, before it is too late."

He moved like a man in a dream, grasped his sword, and pressed the crystal blade against Mari's bloodied chest, over her heart.

A black mist seeped out of the open wound, hissing as it blossomed above her body. Working purely on instinct, Darius twisted the blade through the oily mist and it burst into flame with an eerie shriek and the stink of sulfur. The moment it disappeared, he pressed the shimmering blade against Mari once again, praying to his gods for all he was worth.

Long moments later, Mari's eyelids fluttered and slowly opened. "Darius?"

"Dear Gods. Thank you." His voice cracked and failed him as he gathered her close, weeping without shame, holding her in his arms as he felt her chilled body slowly grow warm once again.

"What happened?"

Darius couldn't answer her at first. His throat was too tight, his chest burning. Finally he whispered, "You cast a spell. A powerful spell. Whatever it was, it worked."

She licked her lips. Leland grabbed a metal bottle from his pouch and handed it to Darius. He opened the top and tipped it so that Mari could drink. After a few swallows, she struggled to sit up. Darius pulled her into his lap and supported her against his chest.

"Thank you." She reached over her shoulder and touched his cheek, as if to reassure herself he was still there. He kissed her fingers.

"It was the geode," she said. "I don't know how I missed the information, as much as I've read through that spell book, but the geode was drawing the demons. Empowering them. Giving them corporeal bodies without the need for avatars."

Darius ran his fingers over the healed wound above her left breast. "When the spell exploded the geode, a sliver of crystal must have gone into your heart."

He still couldn't believe she lived.

"Evil hitched a ride on the crystal. She would have lost her soul and become his avatar."

Mari blinked. "Who was that?"

Darius grasped his sword. "I'm not entirely certain. She hasn't properly introduced herself."

The blade pulsed in shades of blue and silver. "I am EarthFire, Darius of Kronus. The spirit within your blade. You have fought well, as have your comrades. I suspect their swords will speak to them soon."

"I did not expect a woman warrior." Darius glanced at Mari, and then at his sword once again. "You honor me, EarthFire."

"I do more than honor you, Darius of Kronus. I give you the gift of love everlasting. A spelled crystal remains buried deep within your true love's heart. A heart she was willing to sacrifice to save you and your comrades. Bravery is honorable, whether human or Lemurian. I have used my power to bond the ruby crystal within the fabric of Mari's soul, where it will give her eternal life—and the chance of love everlasting."

The blade lost its glow. Mari didn't lose hers. She stared at Darius, eyes wide, lips parted. "Does that mean what I think it means?"

Darius rested his forehead on hers. "It does. You and me, together. Always. Are you okay with that?"

Slowly she nodded her head. "I am. More than okay."

Darius and Mari took the mattress. Leland took the couch after a flip of a coin, while Matthias threw his bedroll on the floor. Exhausted from battling demons and blood loss, the two guardsmen were asleep within minutes.

Darius held Mari close against his chest. Occasionally his body trembled when he thought of how close he'd come to losing her today. How much he would have lost.

How much both of them had gained. The battle was far from over. Demonkind appeared to be increasing in strength, but the small army of demon slayers was growing. His sword had gained her sentience today, and they had added a new warrior, a powerful woman warrior able to fight demonkind with magic.

Mari wielded stronger magic than either of them had suspected. She'd called the rain with a simple spell. She'd shattered the geode and turned it against the very demons it empowered. They'd discovered a simple truth: It wasn't just the words in the spell—it was the innate power of the one speaking those words. It was Mari and the magic she'd been born with.

She'd never realized her abilities before tonight. Darius should have known. She'd bewitched him from the very beginning.

She was the key to a future he'd never truly considered. He would gladly bind himself to her for all time. She ruled his heart. Owned his very soul.

"Go to sleep, my love. We'll find answers for all our questions later. Tomorrow will arrive exactly as it should, even if we sleep." Mari planted a kiss on his chin.

With his lips buried against her tousled hair and her slim form tucked close beside him, Darius closed his eyes and did exactly as she said.

SPARK OF TEMPTATION

By Jess Haines

Chapter 1

I couldn't stop fidgeting. Mostly I was bored, but I was also a bit nervous about the vampire and mage sitting on the uncomfortable plastic chairs across from me. It was getting hard to stay nonchalant about not staring at them.

Like me, they were in the intensive care waiting area of a hospital in Queens, twiddling their thumbs while the nurses finished unhooking our friend (and my business partner), Shiarra Waynest, from all the gadgets monitoring her vitals. She was being shifted to a different ward today as her doctor thought she was out of the life-threatening stage and into the world-of-hurt-to-get-over-somewhere-else stage.

Shiarra's parents, brothers, and boyfriend, Chaz, were all in the room with her. Since Arnold (the aforementioned mage) Royce (the aforementioned vampire), and I weren't family, we were banished to wait outside. The place reeked of astringent and was empty save for the nurse tapping furiously at a keyboard across the room.

"Ms. Halloway," Royce purred, drawing my attention. He'd been so quiet and still, it caught me unawares. I only remembered at the last second not to meet his gaze and open myself up to being bespelled. "I wonder if I might enlist your services."

I was tempted to laugh in his face at the request. He didn't *look* dangerous in those Italian loafers and that dreadfully out of place Armani suit, but it was all part of the camouflage he used to hide his true nature. It was partly his fault that Shiarra was here in intensive care. Instead of insulting the ancient, influential vampire, I cleared my throat and mustered a more cordial refusal.

"No offense, Mr. Royce, but I don't think Shiarra would take it too well if I accepted a job working for you."

"None taken. I understand your concern but I can promise that you wouldn't be in any danger."

Arnold glanced at us over the top of a paperback he'd brought with him, shifting a little in his seat. The mage was cute in a geeky, bookish sort of way, but he was also an Other—and therefore dangerous. A magic user like the guy who'd put Shiarra in the hospital and who'd come very close to sacrificing me to whatever nether creatures he worshipped. Even though I knew Arnold wasn't anything like that monster, being in his proximity made me nervous. Almost more so than the vampire.

Yet, Arnold had been one of the few at Shiarra's back, helping to save us from the crazy guy out to take control of all the supernatural critters that call New York home. It was hard to stay afraid of him after all that, but the aura of magic that surrounded him never failed to give me the shivers.

"That's a crock of shit. Haven't you caused enough damage? Leave the girls alone."

Royce shot the mage an affronted look, which Arnold ignored by the simple expedient of going back to reading his book. Irritated, the vampire returned his attention to me and paid no mind to Arnold's snort of amusement.

"I need someone of your talents to assist me. A gentleman has been most persistent in his efforts to sneak into employee-only areas and interview the staff at some of my clubs. He flees whenever one of my security team attempts to question him or throw him out, so somehow he knows who they are. I don't want you to address the matter with him directly, just find out who he is and what he's after."

Working around Royce had proven extremely hazardous to Shiarra's health. Most times I wasn't deterred by danger, but humans rarely came out in one piece when Others were involved.

"No, thank you. There are a couple hundred private investigators in Manhattan alone. I'm sure you can find one who's willing to help you."

"True, but I have no guarantee of their competence or willingness to interact with my staff in a tactful or respectful manner. Make no mistake, your capture only proved your courage. You remained levelheaded and acted appropriately in the heat of a battle that would have sent most of your compatriots fleeing for their lives." One coal-black brow arched sardonically, and I shifted to look away. "You sit here holding conversation with me rather than retreating to Shiarra's bedside or avoiding me entirely. It only proves that you perfectly suit my needs for this task."

"Oh, please. You can't honestly believe that load of bull," Arnold interjected. "I wouldn't do it, Sara."

Royce determinedly ignored him. "I can provide you with adequate compensation for your services."

"I'm sure," I said, doing my best to keep my expression from betraying that I was with Arnold on this.

Royce frowned, studying me with an intensity that made me thankful he was one of those "good," law-abiding vampires who believed in following the rules. Those rules clearly stated that no vampire or werewolf could touch me without a signed and notarized contract lodged with the courts beforehand—and there was no way I'd ever sign a *Notice of Mutual Consent to Human/Other Citizen Relation-*

ship and Contractual Binding Agreement. Not after what I'd been through.

"What can I offer that would interest you?" he asked. Persistent bastard. "Anything within my means—within reason, of course. Protection for your sister, perhaps?"

"What?" More of a squeak than I intended was startled out of me. How did he know about my sister? "What's Janine got to do with this?"

"She has been garnering some attention from one of my following. I'll ensure she never finds out and that she's left alone in the future if you will work for me."

"You keep your hands off her!"

"It's not me you need worry about. I simply cannot promise that the several hundred vampires who answer to me will *all* know to stay away from her. Not without proper incentive. Without your assistance, what reason do I have to go to the effort of guaranteeing her safety?"

It was cold but I could see his point. I shot a look at Arnold, hoping he might have something helpful to add. He shook his head, frowning but not saying anything. No assistance from that end. Damn it.

I raggedly ran a hand through my hair, keeping my eyes off the leech as much as I could. His hypnotic gaze might tempt me into doing something I'd regret. Not that I wasn't already considering the possibilities.

Was taking the risk of leaving my weak, neurotic sister to fend for herself worth it? She'd be easy prey to a sweet-talking leech. When not on stage, she was reclusive and stayed at home or at the studio rehearsing. However, she also had a tendency to latch onto whomever she befriended, and vampires were nothing if not masters at making you trust them. How else would they get a human to open a vein for them?

No, I was only fooling myself to think, even for a moment, that Janine could handle herself. Not against a determined vampire. Until now, I hadn't understood how Shiarra

had gotten herself tangled up so thoroughly with these creatures. I hadn't thought Royce had anything on me, and yet
here he was, neatly manipulating me into doing what he
wanted. This job would undoubtedly be dangerous, no matter his assurances—but I couldn't bring myself to risk Janine's life.

"If I agree to work for you, will you make sure Janine is
safe—starting now? Tell whoever is sniffing after her to back
off? Even if they talk her into a contract, nobody will touch
her?"

"If you agree and see this job through, I will make sure of
it," Royce answered, his frown once again shifting to a sly
smile. "My people will protect you—and your sister. I realize that may be of little comfort. Might I offer additional
compensation to dispel any hard feelings?"

I reluctantly conceded. Blackmailing bastard. I'd make
him pay through the nose for this. "As long as you keep your
people off her back, I'll do it. I know the Moonwalker Tribe
is helping pay for Shia's medical bills, but will you pay the
remainder? In a way she can't trace? If I did it, she'd pick up
on it in no time. You owe her anyway."

"Yes, I do. I already planned to assist Ms. Waynest. Is
there anything else you need?"

It would be no small chunk of change for him to pay those
medical bills. That he was offering additional exchange for
my services was worrisome, but I didn't know what else to
ask for. I was by no means destitute and couldn't imagine
what a vampire—even one as well-to-do as Royce—could
give me. Aside from ensuring Janine's safety, that is. Maybe
having the vampire owe me a favor wasn't such a bad idea.

"I'll have to get back to you on that."

"All right. Come by The Underground tomorrow night
around ten and I'll give you the details."

I nodded, though I was uncomfortable about the idea of
skipping my scheduled date with my boyfriend, Mark, to go

to the vampire's nightclub. Not to mention how off balance I was from Royce's mixture of solicitousness and extortion. Arnold's pitying looks weren't helping. Mark wouldn't be happy, though as a cop he'd understand better than most when I told him I'd have to reschedule due to work. Though I was still left wondering what on earth the vampire had to gain by hiring me.

"Hey, Sara, good to see you."

Shiarra's weak voice penetrated the dull haze of worry. I rushed over to Shiarra's wheelchair being nudged along by a nurse; Arnold and Royce followed at a more sedate pace. I reached out to take the hand not wrapped in bandages as Chaz and Carol, Shiarra's mom, shifted aside and made room for me. Arnold's grip was warm and comforting on my shoulder as he leaned over me to ruffle Shiarra's fire engine-red curls.

"Good to see you up and about, Speed Racer. I take it you're feeling better?"

"Not well enough to kick your ass yet, but give me a few days." Weak as her voice was, I was glad to see she hadn't lost her sense of humor or boisterous attitude. She and Arnold shared grins while her mom tsked at their banter.

Royce followed at a respectful distance, unnoticed by Shiarra and unperturbed by the vicious glare Robert Waynest gave him for daring to approach his daughter. Carol made the sign of the cross and kept her eyes carefully averted from the vampire. Shiarra's brothers, Mikey and Damien, and Chaz, her boyfriend, barely paid him a glance.

"Easy now, guys, give her some breathing room," the nurse scolded. "That's it, just back up a bit."

"What's he doing here?" Shiarra asked, her voice a dry whisper after her bloodshot amber eyes spotted Royce.

"Don't you mind him, honey," Carol said, her mouth thinning to a hard white line.

Shiarra didn't say anything else, though her fingers tightened in mine when Royce afforded her a nod. He stayed behind when everyone else piled into the elevator, shaking his head when the nurse paused in the door to see if he was coming.

I couldn't suppress a shiver when the doors closed, cutting off the sight of those knowing black eyes staring past everyone else—straight at me.

Chapter 2

The next night, I was staring unhappily at the black-painted ceiling of one of the quieter lounges in The Underground, cradling a drink I hadn't touched to avoid letting anyone see how badly my hands were trembling. I was doing my best to keep my eyes off the show on the stage across the room. The S&M theme gave me the willies.

It wasn't crowded and I wasn't dressed for the club, and yet, even in my relatively conservative blue jeans and black long-sleeved top, I'd racked up three propositions and five free drinks while waiting. I hadn't accepted any, because God only knew what kind of offers were attached to drinks in a place like this. Royce was ten minutes late. I was strongly considering leaving.

"What's a pretty thing like you doing all alone?" trilled a smooth voice. I shifted on the barstool to examine the latest freak to accost me.

He was thin and wiry, with sandy brown hair that he'd slicked back in an attempt to reduce the boyishness of his features. It didn't work very well. His brown eyes were too sharp and probing to match the carefully casual stance or easy smile he affected, showing a glint of tiny, sharp canines.

He looked more overdone than menacing in his black leather pants and billowy white shirt, which created the illusion of broader arms and shoulders. The shirt combined with the bluish tint of the bar lights washed out his already pallid features. He was like a guy from one of those boy bands; he had the potential to be cute if he didn't try so hard to be cool and suave.

Judging by the look he was going for, I was willing to bet he was some teenager posing as a vampire for the night to pick up girls. Shaking my head in disgust, I pushed back from the bar and picked up my purse. This was the last straw. It was time to leave.

"Ah, I didn't send the little bird into flight, did I? At least give me a chance. Let me get you a drink," he offered, rising to follow. Exasperated by his persistence and off balance by the creep-tacular number of passes that had already been made at me tonight, I turned on my heel, folded my arms, and did my level best not to glare at him.

"Look, I'm not here to get picked up. Back off, okay?"

"Ah, is this place making you nervous? I could take you somewhere else. Perhaps you'd prefer the atmosphere at *La Petite Boisson?*"

If I had been, well, pretty much anyone else, I might have been flattered—okay, floored—by the offer. *La Petite Boisson* was another of Royce's properties; a ridiculously pricey, upper-crusty restaurant. I'd heard somewhere the waiting list to get a table was up to four months—for A-list celebrities. Not my kind of place. As Shiarra could attest, I may have come from old money but I was doing my best to stay out of that world. Who the hell was this guy that he could get a table there so quickly?

Well, whoever he was, it didn't matter. If he was hanging around a place like The Underground, he was bad news. Plus, I'd had my fill of rich, good-looking, snobbish assholes before I graduated college. It put me in mind of a T-shirt Shiarra once bought me as a gag gift, which perfectly described my tempestuous and occasionally disastrous love life: "Princess, having had sufficient experience with princes, seeks frog."

"I'm sorry, no. I'm not interested."

He opened his mouth to reply—man, this guy didn't know the meaning of "no"—but before he could get any more cheesy pickup lines out, his eyes widened and he ducked his head deferentially. Wow, did he finally get the message?

"Not leaving, are you?" Royce asked from behind me, touching my shoulder.

I jumped and gasped in shock. I whirled to face him, withdrawing until my lower back dug into the bar.

Like the guy who couldn't take no for an answer, Royce was wearing leather pants, though there was nothing ridiculous about his getup. His toned upper body was on display in a matching vest, leaving his corded arms bare. His dark hair was left loose to brush his shoulders and occasionally mask his eyes. It was a shocking contrast to the business suits and conservative attire I'd always seen him wearing in the magazines and on the news. Bloodsuckers aren't my type but my, was he easy on the eyes.

It only made me more determined to hold my ground. If Janine laid eyes on a vampire like this, she'd never find the willpower to resist him.

"I do hope my associate didn't scare you off."

The smile on the other guy's features rapidly fell into a scowl, interest sliding into disappointment. I didn't know whether to be relieved or horrified.

"She was here to meet you? Sorry, sir."

"Not to worry. I wasn't going to bother you with the details of my calendar on your night off. John, this is Sara Halloway, Ms. Waynest's business partner. She's the PI I hired to find out about that person who's been nosing around the clubs. Sara, meet John Torrance. He's my second-in-command. He may end up working with you some nights if I am not available."

That seemed to perk John right up. I did my best to suppress a grimace, schooling my features into a carefully blank expression before extending my hand. John took it in both his own, bowing theatrically to place a kiss on my knuckles. His fingers were cold, his grip carrying an unpleasant undertone of possessiveness.

"A pleasure, Ms. Halloway. I look forward to working with you."

"Likewise," I gritted through my teeth.

"If you'll follow me," Royce interjected, saving me from further come-ons, "I'll introduce you to my head of security and give you the file on what we've compiled so far. John, you can come along, too."

I did as Royce asked, shaking my head when his assistant gallantly offered his arm. I'd felt how chill the guy's touch was, cold enough to make my skin crawl, and I was sure Royce wouldn't employ a human as his second. Ridiculous as he looked and acted, John was clearly a vampire. He radiated teenage awkwardness instead of the mystique I associated with his kind, but that could be his hunting method, designed to make him appear charming and harmless. Whatever it was, I wasn't interested.

A few minutes later, we arrived at a tiny office tucked away in the back of the first floor. It was filled with papers, security monitors, and a very large, very hairy man sitting behind, and dwarfing, a cluttered desk. The redheaded giant rose to greet us, a few stray strands and unruly curls sticking up from his ponytail. He looked like he should've been wearing a kilt and swinging around a claymore, not wearing a navy business suit and shuffling papers.

"Angus," Royce said, ushering me to stand beside him. My hand was completely engulfed by the big man's own as he reached across the desk. "This is Sara from H&W Investigations, the firm I told you about. She'll need the file."

"A pleasure, lass." The thick Scottish accent was distract-

ing. More so was the chill to his grip; another vampire. His
bushy beard bristled when he smiled at me, revealing frighteningly long fangs. Hard to believe he was a vamp and not a
Were, what with the thick, coppery tufts sticking out of his
shirt collar and on the backs of his hands.

It took every ounce of willpower I could muster not to
flinch away upon realizing what he was. He might be
friendly, but being the lone human in a tiny room with three
leeches wasn't a situation I was comfortable with. As long as
I didn't take any chances and kept my eyes off their own, I
should be okay. Even though Royce and his people followed
the rules, my experiences with them had me wary of any further blackmail or traps. Royce's promise they'd keep me and
my sister safe was about as good as a pack of wolves promising to guard spring lambs.

Not trusting my voice, all I did was nod in response, praying they hadn't taken note of my sudden surge of fear and
accelerated heartbeat.

The security chief and his boss shared a bemused look.
Once Angus released my hand, he picked up a manila folder
from his desk and passed it to me. Glad to have an excuse
not to meet anyone's eyes, I flipped it open and skimmed
through the papers inside.

At first, I had a hard time concentrating enough to focus on
the photographs. Once the initial burst of fear from being in a
room full of predators faded, I frowned and pulled the file closer
to squint at some of the grainy pictures. They were all printouts
from security monitors. It was a trifle difficult to make out the
man's face until I flipped to one where the cameras had caught
him at an angle, looking up. That startled some shaky laughter
out of me, as much relieved by figuring out who the shady man
was as to have an excuse not to stick around much longer. I
snapped the folder shut and tossed it back down on the desk.

"You're not in any danger. That's Joe Finnegan from Pro-
Detection in Levittown. He's H&W's competition."

Nonplussed, John picked up the folder, flipping it back open. "Your competition?"

"Yeah. Finnegan's a braggart, slick as a used car salesman, but he does what we do at H&W—skip tracing, surveillance, that sort of thing. He was probably hired to watch somebody or look for something. He's as skeezy as they come, but he's not dangerous. Most likely one of your people is late paying a bill and he's tracking them down for a collection agency."

"Well then, half your job is done." Royce smiled winningly, and my good spirits faded. I'd hoped Royce would take care of the rest of his problems himself once I identified the creep. The idea of talking to Joe was about as enticing as working for the vampire. "If you can find out exactly what it is he's looking for—better yet, who he's working for—I'll see that it's made very much worth your time."

"We've run across each other a couple of times at business functions. He might remember me. I'll give him a call and see if I can get him to tell me what's up."

Though it wasn't a call I was looking forward to making, I was fairly confident I could get Joe to tell me what he was after. He wouldn't divulge who his client was, but he might be willing to tell me what he was looking for. If I was lucky and this really was nothing more than a simple skip tracing assignment, H&W might even get a cut of the profits for finding the wayward debtor.

"If ye find out what he wants or run into any trouble, tell me at once," Angus said in a deep rumble, thrusting a business card at me. "That's my business line and my cell number. If anything goes wrong, don't wait. Just call."

I took the card, eyeing it dubiously. "What if something comes up during the day?"

"Call the business line," Angus advised, unperturbed. "We have agents we can send to assist you no matter the hour."

Okay, *that* was creepy. Suppressing a shiver, I stuffed the card in the pocket of my jeans.

"I'll show you out," John said.

Royce frowned at his second but didn't say anything more. Rather than come off as bitchy, I decided it wouldn't hurt to take John's arm when he offered this time, doing my best to hide my misgivings. The youthful vampire smiled at me in what I imagine was supposed to be a reassuring manner, placing his other hand lightly over mine once I settled it on his arm.

"I'll be in touch," Royce called after us, staying behind to speak to Angus.

John didn't ply me with questions or come-ons this time, leading me to the dance floor we'd have to cross to reach the exit. Aside from the somewhat possessive way he took my hand, he was polite and cordial. However, once we reached the edge of the dance floor he did ask rather hopefully if I'd be staying a little longer.

"Sorry. I'm going to go home and get some sleep."

He nodded, clearly disappointed but not pushing the issue. I was grateful for that. His attention, while flattering, was also giving me a good case of the heebie-jeebies.

I knew he couldn't bespell me unless I signed papers giving up my legal rights to recourse against any form of physical, mental, or spiritual damage he might cause. But that didn't allay my misgivings about dealing with him, or Others in general.

After the fall of the Twin Towers, werewolves and vampires and other such dangerous creatures had revealed their existence to the world at large. These creatures of fairy tales were citizens now, with all the rights and privileges that entailed, save that their feeding habits were carefully regulated. The new laws were our way of thanking the Others for all they'd done: the werewolves' searches for survivors in the rubble of Ground Zero; the impressive spellwork done by magi to improve our defenses around major cities and airports; and the vampires' much-needed economic boosts in the days following the terrorist attacks.

Congress hadn't quite finished tweaking all the laws involving our new, daylight-impaired, citizens, but the contracts had been hurriedly made into a requirement by federal law within a couple of months of the Others' appearance. The contracts meant Others had to go the more traditional route of courtship and seduction instead of simply taking what they wanted. If one didn't go the legal route and the victim filed a complaint, after a short, low-hassle trial the offender would be hunted down and killed.

There were enough people out there desperately hoping to be some vamp's Renfield that finding fresh blood and willing victims wasn't a problem—for most. Though I am certainly not as phobic as Shiarra, I had zero interest in being some vamp's plaything. I presumed John's attention was because he'd recently lost a donor or something; nothing I was going to concern myself with.

When we reached the exit, he insisted on waiting with me, intent on seeing me to my car. It was charming, if pushy. Once the valet brought my car around, he released my arm, but not before bowing low over my hand to brush his lips over the backs of my knuckles.

" 'Til we meet again, my little bird."

"Yeah. 'Til then," I said, vowing to wash my hands ten times with antibacterial soap as soon as I got home. Dead man's lips on my skin? Ugh!

As I pulled away from the curb, I glanced in the side mirror. John still stood under the flickering red sign for The Underground, watching me go. His eyes glittered strangely and his face held an emotion I could not place. I quickly looked away, driving off as rapidly as I dared.

Chapter 3

On the way to the office the next morning, I put in a call to my boyfriend. Mark picked up after a couple of rings.

"What's up, sweetie? How come you couldn't make it last night? You didn't say much in your message."

"Sorry," I replied, tapping my nails on the steering wheel while I waited for the light to shift. "Business kept me later than I expected. Are you at work?"

"No. I've got a couple of hours before the next shift. I'm off at eight, though. What about you? Want to catch a movie?"

"I can't. Duty calls," I said, trying to think of a kosher way to ask him if he'd heard any rumors about someone gunning for Royce. The incessant worrying about Royce, that creep John, and Janine's dubious safety were making it hard to concentrate.

"Again? What is it this time?"

"You know I can't talk about that."

"Yeah, yeah. So when can I see you?"

"Not sure. Tomorrow afternoon, maybe? By the way, do you know Joe Finnegan, that guy who runs Pro-Detection?"

"Heard of him. Not in my precinct, though." Mark paused, suspicious. "Why? This have something to do with last night?"

Much as I didn't want to start up an old argument, I couldn't skirt around it. Mark would get even angrier at me for avoiding the subject. His cop instincts flared up at the strangest things. Bracing myself for the inevitable, I resignedly told him as much as I safely could.

"Alec Royce hired me to find out why Finnegan is digging into his affairs."

"What?!"

"Yeah. It's not a big deal. Finnegan is small fry. I doubt it's anything dangerous. Like I told Royce last night, he's probably just hunting down someone who skipped out paying a bill. No big deal."

"Sara," Mark started, his voice gone dangerously low, "we've discussed this before. I don't want you hanging around those things. You could get hurt."

"The 'thing' you're referring to is a person. Who is paying me good money to find out what Joe is after. Will you relax and let me do my job?"

"Dealing with the Others isn't your job, Sara, it's mine. Look what happened to Shiarra."

"Damn it, Mark, don't start that again! It's my job. My choice."

"You stay away from those things, you hear me? I absolutely forbid—"

"Oh, grow up!" Angry and upset, I hung up on him—just in time to swerve out of the way of an oncoming truck. The sting of something in my eyes must have made me lose track of the road.

Yeah, that was it.

My eyes were dry by the time I got to the office. A familiar face greeted me in our tiny reception area.

"Arnold!" I exclaimed. Considering my mood, I found it

surprisingly easy to return his smile, though I took a quick step back when he rose and reached out to me. At his puzzled look, I shook my head and inwardly berated myself for the lapse in manners, belatedly taking his hand and tensing against the tingling, electric jolt I felt at his touch. "What are you doing here?"

The mage didn't come around to visit very often these days. He hadn't been hurt in the battle, but he'd taken a lot of time off from work to try to help speed up Shiarra's healing process. His magical capabilities leaned more toward defensive shielding and wards, but he'd done everything he could to help her recover. After he saved my life, and seeing him at Shiarra's bedside in the hospital every day for two weeks, my nervousness around him had lessened quite a bit. He was also the only Other I'd ever considered a friend—though, most of the time, being near him still gave me the jitters.

His smile turned sheepish, releasing my hand to rub the back of his neck and glance at H&W's receptionist. Jenny was watching us over the rims of her glasses with interest, her hands stilled over her computer keyboard.

"I wanted to stop by and see how you're doing, and drop something off. Can we go in your office?"

"Of course."

Once the door shut behind us, the tension in Arnold's skinny shoulders relaxed and his green eyes lit up with excitement. He dug through the pockets of his jacket, producing a rumpled envelope and passing it over as I took a seat on the edge of my desk. He paced back and forth in the small office, watching my brows shoot up as I withdrew a check made out to H&W Investigations for just shy of a hundred grand. It was more money than Shiarra and I usually made in six months.

Arnold was smug when he answered my questioning look. "Payment for services rendered. Since Veronica is dead and the *Dominari* Focus was destroyed, the Financial

Planning Committee tried to table it. I had to fight tooth and nail to get the purchase order pushed through."

"Lord. I didn't think we'd ever have anything to show for it," I said, shaking my head incredulously. "When I called a few weeks ago, the receptionist passed me around a bit, but nobody ever answered my questions or got back to me."

"Yeah. I figured something like that was happening when I overheard the new VP of acquisitions laughing about it. You two went through a lot of trouble for The Circle. It's only fair since it was our fault Shiarra got mixed up with Royce to begin with. She did her job. She deserves to get paid for it."

I grinned, putting the check down and hopping off the desk to wrap my arms around Arnold in a hug, appreciating the firm play of muscles in his shoulders, hardly noticing the ever-present tingling I felt whenever I touched him. He was lean but strong. At first he stiffened at the touch, but as soon as he got over the shock he returned the gesture, sliding his arms around me. He radiated warmth and the scent of ash, though it wasn't unpleasant. In fact, after being around the vampires last night, it was positively refreshing.

When I abruptly recalled the ink-stained hands on me belonged to a mage, I pulled away, fighting a shudder.

"Sorry," he said, though he appeared more puzzled than apologetic.

Ducking my head to hide the blush to my cheeks, I shrugged and took as brisk and nonchalant a tone as I could. "No, I should be the one apologizing. That was a bit forward of me."

"Don't mention it."

"Well. Thank you for everything."

"Sure," he replied, brows furrowing. "Wow, that really got weird, didn't it?"

I smiled ruefully, regretting my impulsiveness. It was completely unlike me and very unprofessional. Even if he'd helped save my life, I didn't know him well enough to be fa-

miliarizing myself with the firmness of his muscles or contours of his body.

"I'm sorry," I stammered. "I don't know what came over
me."

That wasn't true. John's heavy advances and the worry
about being surrounded by undead things made me appreciate Arnold's presence more than usual. He was a mage, but
he was also more human than monster.

Also, geeky as he was, right now I found him easier to get
along with than my boyfriend. That last conversation with
Mark had left me stinging. We'd had arguments plenty of
times before, often along the lines of him demanding I stop
risking my life with "that silly PI business" and me telling
him what an uptight, sexist prig he was being. It never failed
to make me cry. He used the same points my parents had
when we argued over my going into business with Shiarra.

Arnold's supportive actions put him in a different light.
We hadn't had much time to get to know each other while
we'd been fighting for our lives a couple of months earlier,
and though we'd chatted now and again at the hospital, neither one of us had made any special effort to see each other.
Yet he obviously cared about me. Even now, he was being
apologetic when I was the one who'd acted like an ass.

Maybe I needed more friends like him around. Why
couldn't Mark see what Shiarra and I did was important, like
Arnold did?

"Look," I said, rubbing at my temples, "I'm not handling
this very well. My boyfriend and I had a little spat while I
was on my way over, so I know I'm acting a bit weird. But
I'd like to do something to thank you for what you've done
for Shia. And for me. I just can't think of something that
doesn't come off like I'm asking you on a date—so bear
with me here."

He blinked rather owlishly at me from behind the thick
lenses of his glasses before cracking a smile. "Don't sweat

it. We can go for the platonic approach. Why don't you come out with me and a few of my buddies tonight? We'll go see a movie or something. Should be a nice change without vampires and werewolves coming along to stir things up."

"Er, about that. I'm still doing that job for Royce. I might have to work tonight."

He hesitated, and I got the feeling he was gathering his thoughts to start spouting the same hyperbole Mark always threw at me when I accepted a dangerous job.

Rather than give him the opportunity to chastise me, I was quick to reassure him. "Don't worry, I know what it's about now and it's nothing serious. Some other PI has been nosing around in his business. I just have to find out what he's after and report back. As soon as I find out, my job is done."

"Any idea how you're going to do that?"

"Sort of. It shouldn't be too hard. Just don't tell Shia about this, please?"

"I won't. Look, it's not like you don't already know vamps are dangerous, but I don't want anything bad to happen to you. Do you mind if I work with you on this one? I can make sure they don't try any funny stuff."

I bit my lower lip to keep from saying something that would win me an award for best foot-in-mouth performance, opting for a nod in reply. He grinned at my reaction.

"Good," he said. "I'll be in touch."

Chapter 4

Arnold had to go back to work for a while, but he promised to meet me afterward. As he left, Jen watched us with the kind of interest and attention to detail I wished she'd apply to those ledgers she was supposed to be working on. When Arnold noticed her avid curiosity, he affected a comically exaggerated male swagger. Both of us watched him go with wide eyes. Though Arnold and I hadn't been doing anything to merit it, I blushed at Jen's raucous wolf whistle after the mage was gone.

"What a butt on that one. Yowzah! Hey, what happened to Officer What's-his-name?"

"Officer What's-his-name is still my boyfriend. Arnold's just a friend." I frowned at her knowing look. "Go on, get back to work. You can daydream about somebody else's butt while you get those spreadsheets done."

She sighed theatrically and made a big production about getting back to balancing the accounts.

Grinning, I returned to my office. With Arnold to back me up, this crappy job for Royce should be done before the end of the night. Even knowing the next item on my to-do list was to call Joe Finnegan couldn't drag me down.

A quick search through my Rolodex brought up Pro-Detection, and I tapped my nails lightly on the desk as I waited for someone to pick up. I was starting to think Joe must have changed his number when a gruff voice came on the other end of the line.

"Pro-Detection. This is Finnegan."

"Joe," I said, doing my best to sound friendly and cordial, "this is Sara Halloway from H&W. You remember me?"

"Yeah. You and Sheena or Sheila or whatever her name is were on the news every night for a month. How could I forget?"

I ignored his sour tone as best I could.

"It's Shiarra. Hey, listen, I know it's not really any of my business, but I want to ask a favor, one professional to another." I grimaced at the bitter harrumph on the other end of the line. There was no love lost between H&W and Pro-Detection, but I pressed on anyway, hoping for the best. "We might be able to exchange some info and both get paid."

"You gonna pay my bills, sweet cheeks?"

I had to stop and take a breath, silently counting to ten before continuing. If I didn't, I might say something I'd regret. Joe was just trying to rile me, that was all. If I kept my head, I'd be okay. I might even get everything I needed in this phone call. My false cheeriness was replaced by cool, professional dislike. There wasn't any point in sugarcoating my words anymore. It wasn't like he didn't already know I detested him.

"Alec Royce hired me to find out what you're after. Up for a trade?"

Joe laughed derisively. I held the phone away from my ear until his hoarse guffaws settled down.

"Man, you aren't shy about asking for what you want. I doubt you could get me what I need, girlie."

I loosened my grip on the phone when the plastic squeaked in protest. "I'll give it my best. What do you need?" *Aside from a boot up the ass,* I carefully didn't add.

"I need info from the inside, not a hired hand."

"Try me."

"That an offer, doll-face?" He laughed at my stony silence. "Tell me something first. You contracted to that leech?"

I started, leaning forward in the squeaky office chair. The guy was despicable, but even with the snide remarks and undisguised innuendos, he was getting to the point. Despite the disgustingly personal nature of the question, it must be important.

"Of course not. What does that have to do with anything?"

"Everything and nothing. Here's your professional favor. Take my advice and stay as far from Alec Royce as you can get. Don't be seen anywhere near him or his people. And, before you go, you can tell him the Anti-Others are coming."

"What?" I asked the question to a dead line. Joe had hung up on me.

"Bastard," I muttered, putting the phone back on the cradle and leaning back in the chair to consider his words.

If Joe's employer was the Anti-Other Alliance, Royce was in some serious peril. Members of the AOA were considerably more dangerous than the White Hats.

The White Hats were a bunch of vigilante Other hunters. Shiarra had gotten a few of her vampire-hunting weapons from them a while back. The leader of the local chapter, Jack, had attempted to recruit her to their cause at knifepoint. It didn't matter to the White Hats that any supernatural creatures who valued their (un)lives legally contracted the humans they took to be their honey, their lunch, or made into another Other. It also didn't deter some of the more extremist White Hats that in forty or so states it was illegal to kill Others without a signed warrant. The hunters hated anything humanoid with fur, fangs, or claws, and would gladly use every dirty trick they could to hunt one down. News reports where the White Hats proudly claimed responsibility for burning down buildings, defacing Other-owned properties or Other-sympathizers' homes, and staging violent protests outside Other-run establishments were not uncommon.

The White Hats considered members of the AOA too extreme to be part of their organization.

Oh well. The AOA didn't have problems with full-blood humans unless we showed very publicly that we were sympathetic to Others. Unless they showed up on my doorstep, the hunters weren't my problem. Knowing they were Joe's employers should be enough information to turn over to Angus and call this job quits. Joe must have been searching for information on which of Royce's employees were vampires, their schedules, that sort of thing, to pass on to the Anti-Other Alliance. It was unlikely the hunters were interested in anything else.

The lecherous prick was right about one thing—I needed to stay away from the vamps. That thought in mind, I dug Angus's business card out of my purse and called the daytime number, intending to leave a message and be done with it. Hopefully Royce would consider the information enough not to need me for anything else.

"Hello?" The voice on the other end wasn't deep or accented enough to be Angus's.

I frowned down at the card, noting the name and title above the phone number. "Hi, this is Sara Halloway from H&W Investigations. Is Mr. MacLeod in?"

"Sorry, no, he's resting at the moment. He told me you might call. Did you get any word about that guy? I can pass it on to Mr. Royce."

"Yes, I did. Joe Finnegan was hired by the Anti-Other Alliance to investigate the clubs. He didn't say specifically what he's after but I imagine he's trying to find out which employees are Others and what their work habits are."

"Gotcha. I'll let him know," the man said. "He'll be at The Underground at nine tonight; meet him there. Thanks for calling."

Before I could ask the guy's name, protest about having to meet Royce again, or anything else, he'd hung up. Miffed at the treatment, I dropped the phone and glared at it.

"Fucking fantastic," I growled. Maybe Arnold would come with me when I went to meet with the vampires tonight. Hopefully the AOA wouldn't notice me, John would get the hint, and Arnold would keep me safe.

Maybe I should ask Shiarra if I could borrow her guns and vampire-slaying belt. Ugh.

Chapter 5

Jen left early for a dentist appointment. I didn't mind holding the fort by myself. Shiarra, when she wasn't in the hospital, took the bulk of the surveillance and undercover jobs. My specialty—locating missing people, referred to as skip tracing in the industry—usually kept me in the office. With the advent of the Internet, my job had become much easier.

Of course, there were times when I had to get off my butt to verify leads and I did take on the occasional surveillance gig myself. With Shiarra out of commission, Jen got a lot of overtime, which H&W couldn't really support, to handle the research I normally did, and I ended up doing all the foot-work. While I'd always appreciated her hard work, I hadn't realized how much I depended on Shiarra to handle the more confrontational end of the business until her unexpected "vacation" in the hospital.

Without Jen on the phones, I couldn't leave the office today until close of business. I used the time to catch up on outstanding status reports to clients, checking and returning a handful of voice mails, wrapping up the only skip tracing job Jen wasn't able to do, and fitting in a few rousing games of solitaire.

Right as I was considering calling it a day and locking up early, three men walked in, peering around the tiny lobby. I've usually got a good memory for faces; the short reddish hair and sharp facial planes of the guy in the lead triggered something, but I wasn't sure where I'd seen him before. They were all dressed casually: jeans, T-shirts, light jackets. Clean-cut, nothing alarming about them at first glance, save for the unmistakable lumps of concealed firearms on the two flanking the one I'd recognized and a barely visible boot knife on the leader. Rising, I called out a hasty greeting.

"Good afternoon. Can I help you gentlemen?"

The two bigger guys settled into a classic bodyguard stance on either side of the front door, arms folded across their chests. The leader approached my office, gesturing for me to sit back down. There was a strange scar on his palm, like he'd been branded, but I didn't get a close enough look to see what it was before he lowered his hand. His smile was friendly, cordial; the predatory glitter to his eyes was anything but.

"Ms. Halloway? Ms. Sara Jane Halloway?"

"Yes," I said, frowning and remaining on my feet. He settled easily into the chair in front of my desk, unperturbed by my wary reaction. "Who are you? What can I do for you?"

"That's not important. I'm just here to deliver a message." His eyes reminded me of a snake; he never blinked, just stared. "A friend of yours asked us to leave you alone, as a professional favor. We won't be able to keep our promise if you keep meddling in our business."

"What's your business, then?" His threat wasn't terribly well veiled, but if he meant to hurt me, he would've done it already. I settled down in my seat, folding my hands together as I leaned forward against the desk. "And who's the friend you're talking about?"

Instead of answering, he pulled a pack of cigarettes and a lighter out of his breast pocket, ignoring my look of distaste as he lit up. Only after the pack was tucked away and a ring of foul-smelling smoke wafted toward me did he answer. My eyes watered, but I didn't give him the satisfaction of drawing away.

"You've attracted the attention of the Anti-Other Alliance, little lady."

My heart skipped a beat at his answer. It took all I had not to jerk away from him. The AOA—live and in person at my office. Just how I wanted to end my day.

"You're running with a dangerous crowd. Your buddy Jack asked Mr. Morgan to have us give you and your redheaded friend a wide berth. This is just a friendly reminder to stay the fuck away from the leeches so we don't have to mow you down on our way to them. Understand?"

My mouth was so dry, my voice rasped when I answered. "I understand."

His pleasant smile widened. I gasped and pulled back when he reached for me, but his fingers tangled in my shirt before I could get very far. His guards did nothing, watching with identical bored expressions as he yanked me sprawling on top of my desk, pinning me there. He plucked the cigarette from his lips and held the glowing tip less than an inch from my left eye as he continued, the heat and smoke making it sting.

"You're a pretty thing. I should do you a favor—make you less pretty, so the leeches don't take you, too. Jack would agree."

"Please don't," I whispered, too afraid to struggle. What if he jabbed me with that thing? The heat, I could feel the heat pulsing right by my eye. A few stray strands of hair against my cheek were curling and blackening from the proximity of that cherry glow. Oh, God, if I moved—

"No," he said, more an afterthought than anything. "No, I think you get the point. Don't you?"

"I get it! Let go!"

He did. As soon as his fingers loosened, I thrust myself back until I was tripping over my own chair, pressed against the far wall. His expression never changed.

"Remember, stay away from the vampires. If you don't . . ."

I cringed as he put out the cigarette on my desk, leaving an ashy smear on the polished surface.

Without a backward glance, he left, his two goons following in his wake. One of them had the gall to wink and leer at me before closing the door behind him, the hunters' shadows against the beveled glass quickly fading out of view.

Shaking, I pulled my chair over and slowly lowered myself into it, my gaze sliding to the burn mark on the faded oak. That could have been my face. My eye. Shuddering, I plucked the butt off the desk and put it in the trash to get it out of my sight, then picked up the phone and dialed Mark. Maybe he'd know what to do. The phone rang nine times before he picked up.

". . . and go get that Eleven Ninety-Two Jeff called in, will you? Sorry, Sara, hold on a sec. *Kevin!* The Eleven Ninety-Two!"

Dimly, I heard another voice in the background—his partner, Harry. "Who're you trying to impress? We don't use the numbers anymore, remember?"

"Fine, whatever."

"Just call it a goddamn DUI. The rookie doesn't know an Eleven Ninety-Two from a Ten-Two."

Mark swore. If I hadn't been frightened out of my wits, I might have found their banter funny. "The new kid is driving me nuts. What is it, Sara?"

I was starting to feel a bit stupid for calling. The guy from the AOA had threatened me, but hadn't actually hurt me. He was gone now. What could Mark do about it anyway? I couldn't tell him everything; it would mean revealing Royce was blackmailing me. I weighed my words carefully, hating that I couldn't let Mark know what was going on, why the AOA was showing up at my office. My desire to close the growing rift between us wasn't as strong as my desire to keep Janine safe.

"Um, I'm sorry for bothering you. I just—this guy just came into the office. He threatened me."

"What?!" I cringed at the panic in Mark's voice. "Who? Is he still there?"

"I don't know his name. He's gone."

"What did he want? Do you know?"

"I'm not totally sure," I lied. "He said he's from the Anti-Other Alliance."

"Sara!"

"What?" I asked, going on the defensive. "He was a nut-job! He walked into my office with two goons backing him up, and threatened me to stay away from the Others. Okay? I don't know why he needed to pay me a personal visit for that, but he's gone now. I just thought you should know."

Mark went quiet for a minute. I could hear shuffling sounds through the phone, the sound of a door shutting. He must have been going somewhere for privacy. The hum of background noise faded and his voice dropped to a harsh whisper, cutting even through the distortion of the cell phone line.

"Sara, I never thought I'd say this, but I agree with that terrorist. Stay the hell away from the Others. How many times do we have to go over this? You're just inviting trouble!"

"God, stop it already! I called you for help, not another lecture."

"This is connected to that vampire. You know it is. Drop the case. Let someone else take it."

Mark's insistence was grating away the few nerves I had

left. It didn't help that I knew I wasn't being totally honest with him. There wasn't any way for me to tell him everything that was going on. Royce would let his leeches loose on Janine if I brought the police into his affairs. Much as I loved her, my sister was not smart or crafty enough to outwit a vampire. I had no doubt she'd be used and discarded if one of Royce's people took an interest in her.

No matter what Mark said, I had to finish this job for the vampire while somehow staying out of the way of the Anti-Other Alliance. There didn't seem to be any way out of this without losing Janine or endangering myself. The whole situation was sheer lunacy. Whatever way this turned out, either my sister or I would suffer for it in the end. If it came down to it, I'd take the fall before letting Janine get hurt.

Even if it meant trading my life for hers.

"Look, Mark, I know this may not make a lot of sense right now, but I can't drop it. It's my job. I have to see this through."

His frustrated sigh crackled over the phone. The fierce protectiveness he'd been radiating faded into an easy lilt. It was the same kind of tone he'd taken when I first fell for him.

"Don't think anyone can get you to do something you don't want to. I sure can't."

The admiration behind the statement was the only thing that saved me from wanting to hit him the next time I saw him.

"Listen, love," he said, sliding into a more persuasive pitch. Though I didn't really mean to, I felt my scowl crumble into a smile at that sweet, husky inflection, teasing me with his voice. It brought to mind better times, times when we didn't have so many secrets and disagreements tearing us apart. "What do you say we hit the road tonight? Just for a few days, you and me. I'll call in sick, you tell Jen to hold your calls, and we'll leave all this messy business behind us for a while. We can go out to Montauk. Maybe take the ferry out to Block Island again, stick around for a day or two."

Under any other circumstances, it would have been tempting. When it was just the two of us, no worries about work or friends or other commitments, things were great between us. The last time we'd gone out to Block Island, we ended up staying for a week longer than expected. We did everything the island had to offer—from bird-watching to night fishing on the beach to some drunken karaoke with the locals. The candlelit meal we had on our last night was followed by one of the most intense, passionate nights we'd ever spent together.

But giving in to him now would be as good as signing Janine's death warrant.

"I can't, Mark. Not yet. Please just see if you can have a black-and-white pass by the office a few times to make sure those guys stay away?"

"All right. We need to talk, though." Uh-oh. That sounded ominous. "Head home. I'll meet you there later."

Rather than wait for my response, he hung up. I stared at the phone before setting it down, closing my eyes and taking a deep, steadying breath. Those last words meant more trouble would be waiting for me once I saw him again. The real fight would start as soon as he showed up at my house.

I picked up my purse, intending to go home and wait behind locked doors for Mark to get off work, but I paused before setting the strap on my shoulder. There was one other thing I needed to do.

I reached for my phone again.

"Sara? What's up?"

Arnold sounded surprised at my call. I shifted to hold the phone between my ear and shoulder, digging through my purse for some aspirin. Hopefully I'd be able to swallow it around the lump in my throat.

"Hi, Arnold. I've got a problem. The Anti-Other Alliance paid me a visit."

"Oh, great. I hate those guys."

A laugh that sounded suspiciously like a sob was startled out of me. I cut it off as quickly as I could, speaking fast to keep from betraying how upset I was. I'm not sure it worked.

"Yeah, me too. I just wanted to let you know I don't think it'd be a good idea for us to meet up tonight, especially since I have to go see Royce again. Don't want to drag you into this mess too."

"Too late. I already promised to help, remember?"

"Yeah, but—"

"No 'buts' about it. Let me guess—you're headed home?"

"Yeah, in just a minute."

"Okay. I remember where your house is. I'll meet you there in an hour and take you to meet with Royce. Maybe see if there's anything I can do to help you figure out what the AOA is up to."

"Thanks, Arnold," I said, fighting back the lump in my throat.

"Don't sweat it. Stay inside, lock your doors, and try not to worry. I'll see you soon."

As I ended the call, I bit my lower lip, closing my eyes against the sting of tears.

Why couldn't Mark be more like that?

Chapter 6

Despite my bankroll, I don't care for flashy cars or big, sprawling properties to show off my wealth. My indulgences run more toward the latest imported Swiss chocolates than the newest Bugatti model or this season's line of Manolo Blahnik strappy heels. Most of the time, I spent my tax write-offs on charity functions or new equipment for the office. Which is not to say I never indulged myself. My latest big purchase was spy sunglasses that held a video recorder and doubled as an MP3 player. Why not listen to some tunes while gathering evidence on cheating spouses or deadbeat business partners?

Another example of the disparity in how I could be living versus how I did get by was the two-story house in Manhasset Hills I'd moved into shortly before my parents died. My surviving family hates it, thank God. It's in a typical middle-class suburban neighborhood. Lots of families, kids, and friendly neighbors. The brick front and white shutters hide a cozy, intriguingly built interior. It's a far cry from the extensive, but rarely visited, beachfront property left to me in the will. My Aunt Beth and her husband, Richard, up in Boston no longer expect to see me except at Christmas and Thanks-giving, which means her tirade against my refusal to carry on the family business comes only twice a year.

To further discourage prying relatives from dropping by, I have a pair of American pit bulls to keep me company and guard the house when I'm out during the day. They wouldn't attack a soul, but their intimidating size and proclivity to bark at anything that moves make Buster and Roxie great guard dogs.

When I parked under the sugar maple in front of my house, the dogs had their paws up between the slats on the picket fence. They were both showing their teeth at a guy in a trench coat pacing in front of the gate. Strange. The dogs usually bark rather than bite or snarl at strangers. I warily sized him up, reaching for the pepper spray in my purse.

"Can I help you?"

The man whirled at my question, flinching when my car door slammed shut. His drawn, unshaven face was twisted in alarm, but his expression eased at the sight of me. It took a moment to recognize him, though the gruff voice and blatant once-over confirmed my suspicions and had me easing up my grip on the spray.

"Jesus, girl, don't sneak up on me like that. Could give a guy a heart attack."

"Hi, Joe," I said, hefting my purse on my shoulder and scooting around him to reach the gate. "What are you doing here? Thought you never left Levittown unless there was money in it for you."

"I don't usually," he admitted, then shifted into a serious tone I wasn't used to hearing from the lecher. The thunder-ing approach of a motorcycle was drowning out his words. "I don't want blood on my hands. You're too close to this one. Stay away from the vampire. Please, for your own safety."

Before I could respond, he grabbed my shoulders. The dogs started barking and snapping again, but they couldn't reach us. His fingers dug in hard enough to hurt. As he opened his mouth, red and blue flashes illuminated the scene and the wail of a siren drowned out whatever he was trying to tell me.

As Mark pulled up before the gate at my driveway and leapt off his patrol cycle, Joe shoved me away from him and ran off down the street. I stumbled against the fence, clinging to it, ignoring the worried whines of the dogs as they jumped up to put their paws on me and lick my face. Torn, Mark paused, looking back and forth between me and Joe's fleeing form.

"Forget about him, he's not trouble," I panted, rubbing at my shoulder. Damn, the guy had a good grip. "That was Finnegan."

"Goddamn it, Sara!" Mark hauled me up against his chest. His fingers were shaking as he ran them through my hair, tangling in the pale gold strands. "When are you going to let this job go? How much more is it going to take for you to see that it's dangerous?"

At first, I yielded to the protection of his arms. By the time the last word left his mouth, I was pushing him away. My resentment from earlier settled back into place as if it had never left.

Hefting up my purse, I whirled away from him and slammed the gate open, storming up to my door. He followed close at my heels, sputtering. The dogs whined and backed out of our way.

"Mark, we've had this discussion. Multiple times. It. Is. My. Job. Your job is dangerous but you don't see me giving you grief for it. Leave it alone."

He caught the edge of the door before I could slam that, too, and followed me inside. His swarthy skin was darker than usual, flushed with anger.

"Your job isn't worth your life. You don't take my advice. You don't talk to me about what you're doing—"

"Has it occurred to you that I may not *need* advice? When I asked for your help, I thought you were going to be there for me and give me your support. You know I have confidentiality clauses I can't ignore. I can't talk about everything I do!"

"That's not the point! You've never *listened* to me, Sara. Never. How many times have I told you to leave the business to Shiarra? I've told you—"

"See, that's the problem. You *told* me. You never *asked* me. Why can't we just discuss this like civilized people?"

"I *am* discussing this with you!" he shouted. Buster and Roxie howled outside, a mournful baying. "I am telling you that it's not a choice! If you want to stay with me, you need to leave H&W. Why the hell are you hanging on to this so hard? It's not like it's brought you anything but grief! You really think what you're doing is going to make a difference?"

"You ass! Of course it makes a difference!" I cried, seething. "Let me live my own life, for God's sake! I can make my own decisions!"

"No, you can't. Are you blind? What do you think that guy Joe was doing? What do you think those dirtbags were doing at your office, huh? You've made it obvious you can't keep out of trouble. This childish shit has to stop."

"Are you done yet?" I snarled at him. It stung when I realized that if Janine's safety wasn't on the line, I might have agreed with him—about the job for Royce, anyway.

His eyes narrowed to thin slivers, mouth set in a hard line. "Look, when you're through being a pretend cop, you can call me."

"You—you self-important, unmitigated asshole! This job is my *life!* Can't you see it's important to me?" I didn't mean to cry. I didn't mean to let the tears fall. They spilled anyway, blinding me. "Why can't you understand that this job means everything to me?"

"Oh, I see it," he said, his voice suddenly turning low, even, and controlled. "Yes, I see it does. Goodbye, Sara."

"You're leaving me?" I grabbed his arm as he turned for the door. He looked at me over his shoulder, dark eyes narrowed before he shrugged my hand off. I didn't think anything could have hurt more than that cold gesture until he opened up his mouth again.

"We're done, Sara. I've had enough of this shit. You don't have any idea how dangerous the world you're playing in can be. I work in it *every day*. You aren't tough enough to take it. No one is. And I won't sit by and wait to see the girl I love get hurt because she won't wake up and stop messing with things that can kill her."

Anger, hot and intense, burned in me. Words spilled out of my mouth before I could stop myself.

"At least I'm solving cases, you asshole!"

He stopped. Turned around. "What did you just say?"

My brain-to-mouth function seemed to have shorted. "You heard me."

His jaw tightened, hands curling into fists at his sides as he glared at me. When he stalked forward, at first I thought he was going to hit me. Instead, all he did was bump me, hard, on his way past, storming upstairs to the bedroom. Once I caught my balance, I followed in his wake, my temper flaring anew. "What do you think you're doing? Get the hell out of my house!"

"Oh, I will," he promised, slamming my bedroom door open so hard, it left a dent in the wall.

I stood speechless in the doorway, watching as he yanked open my dresser and pulled out his clothes. He ducked into the bathroom next, not saying a word as he collected his razor and toothbrush. He breezed past with the armful of personal items, the few things he left here for those occasional nights he didn't go home.

I didn't follow him as he stomped down the stairs. When the door banged shut below, I sank to my knees. As his motorcycle roared to life, the dogs yelping after the thick rumble that chugged off into the distance, I lowered my head into my hands and wept.

Chapter 7

My back against the bed and a pillow in my arms, I'd settled into hiccups punctuated by the occasional wracking cry when a hand settled on my shoulder. Startled, I flailed, sending Arnold sprawling in surprise.

"What are you doing here?" I squeaked, wiping furiously at my eyes. God, the pillow was soaked. "How did you get in?"

"The front door was open. I saw your car—never mind that. What happened? Are you okay?"

My laugh came out more like a sob than I intended. "No, I'm not okay. My boyfriend just left me because he can't stand to see me do my job."

Arnold scooted over until his back rested against the bed next to me, enfolding me in the scent of incense and peppermint. I flinched when he put an arm around my shoulder to hug me, a shiver running down my spine. His frown of concern deepened, his other hand gently tilting my head back to meet his gaze when I looked away.

"Did he hit you?"

I flushed at that, pushing his hand back. "No. Mark would never do that."

"Then why are you so afraid every time I try to touch you?"

His question took me so off balance I didn't know how to answer him right away. He waited patiently, watching as I struggled to come up with a response.

"Arnold—I—look, I'm sorry. It's not you. Well, it is, sort of. It's just—"

When his fingers dropped from my cheek to my hand, cradling my shaking fingers in his, I paused. His clear concern made it harder to explain what was wrong. It took some courage to work my way up to coming clean, particularly considering this was coming on the heels of one of the worst breakup fights I'd ever had. My eyes still stung, and I was too exhausted to think of any tactful way to explain to Arnold that it wasn't abuse from Mark, but another source, that made it so hard for me to accept his touch.

Arnold had always been honest with me. He deserved better than social lies, or some other form of deceit.

"Please don't take this the wrong way, but you're a mage."

Understanding dawned. He started to speak, but I held up a hand for him to quiet and let me speak. "Sara, I—"

"I know you're not David, but when he used me to get to Shia he did things I'll never be able to forget. Even if the scars fade, every time you touch me I can't help but wonder if you'll do the same."

Not to mention that weird pins-and-needles sensation against my skin every time he touched me.

Arnold didn't respond right away, his thumb lightly rubbing against my knuckles. He carefully turned our hands over and pushed up the cuff of my sleeve to see the web-work tracery of scars on my left arm. Runes carved into my skin, trailing from wrist to elbow. Fae runes that no one but Mark and my doctor had seen since that psychotic sorcerer,

David Borowsky, had carved them into me. Even Shiarra hadn't seen them.

When I drew my arm away, he took hold of my hand again. Keeping our fingers twined, Arnold nudged my chin so I'd look at him. His expression betrayed a touch of anger, though his eyes radiated concern. The ember of crackling energy glimmering in their depths was more menacing than reassuring.

"Sara, I can't undo the bad things that happened to you— but I can promise I won't ever let them happen again."

"How can you know?" I asked, tugging my sleeve back down. "I don't know what they are, or what they mean. How can you expect me to believe that, Arnold?"

"Those rune scars—that's nothing like what I do. I don't even know what they are for sure. Whatever David did to you goes against everything I was ever taught. Magi don't use that kind of blood magic—only sorcerers do that." He took a steadying breath, and some of the fae light died out of his eyes. "You and Shia are my friends. Maybe more than anyone at The Circle. I value that friendship, and I'd never do anything to compromise it. I promise."

"I'm sorry," I whispered, leaning into his embrace and relaxing just a trifle. Now that I'd spent some time close to him, that freaky tingling seemed to lessen. His arm around my shoulder tightened a little, a reassuring squeeze. "I know you're not him. I just can't not think about it, you know? Knowing what you are."

He chuckled, a soft, pained sound. It was entirely unlike him.

"Sara, let me tell you a little story."

I closed my eyes and rested my cheek against his chest, listening to his heartbeat as his voice rose and fell with the cadence of a lullaby.

"Once there was a kid who got beat up a lot in school. He was short, skinny, with big glasses and good grades. His family wanted him to have the best education possible so he'd be able to get by in the real world. They thought he needed it since he didn't have the spark—the inherited trait of a magic user."

"Did he also have reddish-brown hair and green eyes?" I asked, smiling at the thought of Arnold in school, wearing a pocket protector and carrying a heap of books.

"Shh. Who's telling the story here?"

"Sorry."

"One day his older brother decided to show off the latest spell he'd learned from his mentor by testing it out on the kid. A simple conjuration of wind, barely a beginner's cantrip. The showing off was nothing new; neither was tormenting his little brother. He used his power to scatter the kid's final report for his history class all over the street right after the first bell, when they were all supposed to get to class. The report that the kid had spent half the semester scraping up the information on and putting together until it was a perfect masterpiece, which accounted for a third of his grade and guaranteed he'd ace the class.

"It had rained the night before, and most of the pages landed in puddles or on wet grass, so the ink started to bleed. The kid's brother and his friends laughed and laughed at him as he ran all over the front of the school, collecting up his ruined report. That's when the kid got mad."

Arnold quieted, tilting his head back against the bed. I opened my eyes and glanced up at his face, relieved to see he was smiling rather than getting angry at retelling the tale.

"What happened next?" I asked, lightly poking his ribs. He laughed and rubbed my shoulder, then resumed his story.

"The kid got pissed off and used the same cantrip to shove his big brother into a locker. When his brother got out, he beat the snot out of him. Both of them got two weeks' detention. His mangled report got tossed, but the teacher gave him four extra days to put it back together. Their parents grounded them both and enrolled the kid in the same evening magic classes as his brother."

"So the moral of the story is, when you get beat up in school, use magic to get back at the bullies? And then irony wins the day?"

"No." He laughed again, giving a playful tug on my hair. "Actually, I don't know if there is a moral. I continued to study under the wizard through high school and college and even for a couple of years after I graduated. He taught me the same lesson Ben Parker taught Peter—'with great power, there must also come great responsibility'—so, among other things, I stopped shoving my brother into lockers. Got my degrees in mathematics and engineering and still hold the rank as my old mentor's number-one student. I outclassed my big bro in the supernatural a long time ago. Doug went on to be a cardiologist. He didn't pursue the art the way I did, with the intention of being a full-time mage. My parents are proud of us both, though I think for a while they were worried I was going to pull a Lone Ranger and run my own wizarding business instead of using what I learned to get ahead in corporate life."

"I know that feeling," I said, Arnold arching a brow in question at my dry tone. I wasn't interested in explaining how my parents felt about me going into business with Shiarra. That argument had gone on right up until the day they died. "How did your brother get away with using magic out in the open like that, anyway?"

"He didn't. Though I don't regret what I did for an instant, my parents grounded us both for a year, almost ended up pulling us out of school. Especially after the principal called to find out what was going on. See, my parents are the types who think showing the mundanes you know a little witchcraft means you've opened yourself up to public ridicule, angry mobs, and a possible lynching. This was before September 11, so they still had good reason to be wary.

People weren't supposed to know we existed. Hell, to this day, their neighbors still don't know what we are. If I had set out a shingle in Seattle for Potions, Spells & Other Hocus-pocus, they would've disowned me."

"Yet they're okay with you working for The Circle?"

"Sure. Greater numbers equals greater protection. It's a bit different from going solo."

"Weird," I muttered.

"Yeah. So, feel better? I've learned to control my temper since high school."

"As long as you don't shove me into any lockers."

"You got it." He grinned, then stretched and clambered to his feet. "Hey, it's past nightfall. We should get going. Traffic to The Underground is going to be abysmal."

"Ugh, yeah." I scrubbed at my eyes with the heels of my hands before getting to my feet and tossing the damp pillow on the bed. Arnold sat on the edge while I went into the bathroom, calling out over the running water of the sink as I washed my face to remove any lingering signs of my tears. "Thank you, Arnold. I'm sorry I was being a bitch."

"Don't sweat it. Like I said—you're my friend. I don't want to see you hurt."

I thought about what to say to that as I toweled off my face, frowning into the soft cotton. Arnold had done more for me in the past few days than Mark had done in the past year and a half of our tempestuous on-again, off-again relationship. The mage was supportive of my friends and my work. He'd also saved my life—something Mark had never done.

"Arnold?"

"Yeah?"

"How do you feel about playing the rebound guy?"

He didn't answer right away, and I had to stop myself from taking a step back when he appeared in the door. Instead, I leaned my hip against the edge of the sink, meeting his thoughtful gaze with difficulty.

"Well," he said, tones slow and measured, "I'm not sure. I've never been the rebound guy before."

"If it's too awkward . . ."

"No, it's fine." He cut me off, taking my hand in his and placing a feather-light kiss on my fingertips, sending a little electric jolt of pleasure through me—an entirely different sensation than what usually prickled over my skin when I touched him. It sent a thrill of nervous fear down my spine. This impulsiveness was unlike me, and putting so much trust in the mage was approaching a line I had never intended to cross.

"Tell you what," he continued. "Let's handle this mess with Royce first. Then we'll plan something. Just you and me. Okay? We'll take it slow and see how it goes."

"Okay," I agreed, inordinately pleased. Arnold had never done anything to hurt me, only to support me and my friends. There was a world of difference between him and Mark, a gap I was glad to cross. Another surge of emotion—joyful this time, rather than pained or angry—brought the tingle of tears back to my eyes. "Just you and me."

Chapter 8

"The little bird's come back, I see," John observed as Arnold and I entered the same lounge I'd met Royce in the night before. The vampire's eyes narrowed as the mage following in my wake halted beside me. "I don't recall Mr. Royce retaining the services of The Circle."

"He didn't," Arnold replied, smiling down at the much shorter vampire. "H&W occasionally needs a little extra muscle. So here I am."

I had to restrain laughter. Arnold, while tall, was hardly Mr. Universe. Then again, he was a mage. He could probably flatten John with a snap of his fingers.

John set aside his displeasure long enough to bow theatrically before me, keeping his gaze steady on mine. "Regardless, it is wonderful to see you again, my dear. I don't suppose you'll—what are you doing?"

Arnold had put his hand over my eyes. After the initial surprise, I started plucking at his fingers. "Uh, Arnold? Creepy much?"

"Don't meet his eyes. This is *exactly* why you need me along."

John was clearly offended, straightening and folding his arms. "I'm not so ill-mannered that I'd entice the lady against her will, spark."

A few people at the bar and lazing on the couches scattered through the room turned to stare, wondering at the epithet. I yanked Arnold's hand off my face by the wrist and turned a glare on John—soon shifting the look of mixed surprise and distaste to Arnold as he responded to the vampire in kind.

"That's nice, leech. Why don't you go slither off to your master and let him know we're here?"

While Others traditionally don't get along well with those outside their own species, it was rare for them to resort to such outright hostility in front of witnesses. Neither one seemed to care. John lifted his lip, showing his fangs in warning. Arnold tensed, the whispered words behind whatever spell he was casting lost in the throbbing bass of the music coming from the dance floor next door.

Before things could get any worse, I stepped between them, placing a hand against each man's chest.

"That is *it!* Knock it off, you two!"

The men glared at each other until I laid into Arnold, to John's intense satisfaction.

"You're here to help me, not embarrass me in front of a client! Stop it!"

The smirk on John's face quickly shifted to alarm as I turned on him, putting his palms up to ward me off.

"And *you!* For the love of God, can you please keep your nasty little remarks to yourself? I'm here to help your boss, in case you've forgotten. Arnold is on our side, so can it!"

Every eye in the room was on us. I'd backed John all the way up to the bar. He was extremely careful not to touch me. So careful, in fact, that he was practically bent over backward on the bar, his fingers tightly wrapped around the edge so he wouldn't risk laying a hand on me.

His panic was understandable. Without a signed contract, if he did anything to me that could be construed as assault—particularly before so many witnesses in a crowded bar—his butt was toast. Despite that, I had no sympathy for the slime-ball. He was putting moves on me to either get me in the sack or drink my blood. Maybe both. That didn't inspire warm and fuzzy feelings on my part. Not at all.

"'Ere, now," rumbled a deep voice as a hand settled on my shoulder. "We'll have none of that."

Angus's grip was uncomfortably strong, and I didn't resist his urging to back off.

As I pulled away, John hissed a few hateful words. "Pity you're not as amenable as your sister."

Ice-cold shock froze me in place. This disgusting twit was the vampire Royce would have to keep away from Janine? Though I saw through his unthreatening demeanor and over-the-top charm, Janine was too naive to realize someone like him could be a danger to her. Not until it was too late. From his words, he was already familiar with her.

Damn him. If not for Angus's grip tightening in warning, I might very well have attacked John myself. Instead, I had to make do with baring my teeth in a silent, frustrated snarl, and content myself with the foolish hope that Royce would keep to his promise. This blackmail was detestable, but the idea of leaving Janine to fend for herself against John was terrifying.

After I backed up, John moved from arched against the bar to halfway across the dance floor in a flash, his eyes gleaming crimson as he watched us. I ignored him as best I could. Angus drew away and gestured for John and me to follow him. Looking sheepish, though still bristling with hostility, Arnold stayed quietly by my side the entire way to the security office in the back.

The cramped office positively crackled with unseen energy as John and Arnold were forced into close proximity.

Something about the power they were radiating made the runes on my arm itch like mad. I clenched my hands into fists at my sides to keep from scratching, and pressed close to Arnold.

Angus paid them no mind, so I did my best to do the same, leaning over to see what he was pointing at in the thick manila folder he had spread open on his desk.

"Was this what you wanted me to come here for?"

John answered me instead of the Scot, his voice once again smooth and charming. "We have a few things to give you. Since the AOA is involved, we thought we might assign a bodyguard. Show you the location of a couple of safe houses if needed."

I was going to respond but Arnold cut me off. He was all confidence, his green eyes glinting with fae light as he folded his arms across his chest. The tingle on my arm got worse. "That's not necessary. I'm on the job."

John glowered at him but didn't reply.

"Now then," Angus said, bringing my attention to a few highlighted points on the papers, "your information was very helpful. We've put together a report on the Anti-Other Alliance for you. Most of this is from the Internet, but one of Mr. Royce's contacts in the NYPD and a few of his colleagues from the South gave us some additional information. The founder and many of the key members of the AOA used to be White Hats. I've heard your mage friend"— Arnold stopped glaring at John long enough to pay some mind to what Angus was saying—"has some contacts with them, so maybe he can find out more about what they want."

"Isn't it obvious?" I asked, surreptitiously rubbing my wrist to ease the prickling. "You guys *are* vampires. . . ."

Angus's tone was patient as he collected the papers up and handed me the manila folder. "Aye, but what is their plan, lass? Are they looking to attack Alec—or someone else? Blow up some property? Disrupt our business? We need more data to counter whatever they're planning. That's what you were hired for."

I managed a sheepish "Oh!" as he handed me the folder.

"They're a violent lot. We don't expect ye to get yourself killed, so see if ye can get that PI they're using, Finnegan, to contact me. Mayhap we can negotiate something." He turned to Arnold, one bushy brow arching. "Or would ye be willing to check with your White Hat friends if they know anything?"

"Sure. I'll call them later tonight."

"Be careful. White Hats are bad, but the AOA is worse," John warned.

"I know," I said, suppressing a shudder at the memory of the cigarette being held so close to my eye.

"Are you sure you don't want me to show you to one of our safe locations?"

The solicitous tone didn't do a thing to conceal John's eagerness for my response. How he thought I might be interested after his barbed comments about Janine was beyond me. Perhaps he was only eager to get his hands on me because Royce had put Janine off limits. Clearing my throat, I held up the file and gestured at Arnold with it. "Thanks, but we should get going. Start studying this thing. I'll be okay."

Arnold seemed just as relieved as the vampire was disappointed.

"Let me see you out."

I accepted John's offer with a nod. Before I could leave, Angus pressed a bit more into my hands—a list of phone numbers and an address, and a key.

"Take this with ye. If ye run into trouble, the numbers are sorted under the times we're available. Any of these people can help. Ye can also hide out at the address written there if ye need to—no need to call ahead. Security's been alerted that ye may drop by. Don't make any copies of the key; return it to me after we get this mess under control."

"Thanks," I said, and surprised myself by meaning it. "I appreciate it. Really."

He smiled at me, fangs peeking out behind the coppery tangles of his beard and blue eyes twinkling with something very much like mirth. "Anytime, lass. Stay out of trouble, now, and do call if ye need us."

"I will."

John gave the Highlander a disapproving look, tapping his foot in the doorway until I tucked everything under my arm and made to follow him. Arnold took his place by my side one more time.

We had a lot of work ahead of us.

Chapter 9

John escorted us to the parking lot but didn't wait to see me to the car this time. I leaned against a street lamp on the sidewalk and thumbed through the pages of the file while we waited for one of the attendants to bring the car around. It was early for people to be leaving, so a couple of valets were chatting amiably nearby instead of paying much mind to the lot. Arnold had his hands in his pockets, watching the passersby on their way in and out of the club.

"That guy has a problem," Arnold commented. The anger in his voice drew my attention off the papers in my hands. "The vampire, I mean."

"John?"

"Yeah. I met him once, when I did a consultation for Royce on additional security measures for his art collection. John's a cheapskate and a sleaze. Cost me a good commission. Hurt a girl who used to work with us at The Circle. Be careful around him, okay?"

"Sure," I replied absently, frowning as I flipped to a photograph. It was the man with the strange eyes and scarred palm who'd visited me in my office, but the photo wasn't attached to any of the reports and didn't have a name on it. Who *was* that guy?

Just as I closed the file and tucked it under my arm, someone pushed me from behind. I stumbled against the valet's podium and set the keys on their hooks to jingling like dozens of tiny bells. A small cluster of men in ski masks herded Arnold, the attendants, and the few other startled pedestrians away, cutting me off from the others. A sharp pain at my neck made me lash out, braining the guy behind me on the temple. He cursed and made a grab for the file, but I pulled it up against my chest, refusing to let go.

"Sara, don't move!" Arnold shouted, his hand flinging out as strange words slipped over his tongue. The runes on my arm *burned* as a flash of bright bluish-white light raced from his fingertips. I stood stock still, more out of shock than because of Arnold's order, as the guy grabbing me staggered back and screamed.

The people around us also screamed cries of "Magic!" "Look out!" and "Don't let it touch you!" as they scattered and fled.

Shock waves of force pressed against my skin, pushing me up against the podium a second time. The runes tingled so painfully I couldn't move or feel my fingers. A rush of air blew my hair into my face, obscuring my vision. Once I collected my balance, I brushed the strands out of my eyes and stared.

Several of our assailants were sprawled on the ground, groaning or clutching at their ribs. The fading sparkle of magic clung to their limbs, tracing their extremities in glittering arcs. The rest of them were running away, pushing people aside as they booked it down the street. Two of the attendants were on the ground, one not moving, the other on his butt and staring wide-eyed at Arnold.

"Holy *shit*," the young guy in a rumpled uniform managed. "What the fuck was *that?*"

"Sara!" Ignoring the kid, Arnold rushed to my side and reached for me. "Are you okay? Does it hurt?"

At first, I shrank back. His expression wavered, sorrow and anger coloring the concern. He waited, one hand outstretched, but not touching me.

Ashamed for hesitating, I reached for him, pulled him close. "I'm sorry. Yes, I'm okay."

His other hand came up, fingers brushing against my neck. Though I hadn't felt the injury at first, once he touched it, it hurt. The itch up and down my arm grew painful again, then faded. His fingertips came away red.

"That should do for now. Doesn't look like it needs stitches."

I settled into the comfort of his arms, though I stiffened when I turned my attention to where the muggers had fallen. They were gone—disappeared while Arnold inspected the cut on my throat.

The valet who'd been so afraid of Arnold was on his knees, gently shaking the shoulder of the guy facedown on the pavement, hesitating to turn him over. I hadn't seen it at first, but there was a spreading pool of blood soaking into the knees of the other attendant's slacks.

Angus was by our side moments later, barking orders, instructing the flock of men in security T-shirts to fan out and make sure no one else was attacked. He checked that we were okay before rushing away to question some of the other witnesses, herding us together so we could all give our reports when the cops arrived.

The guy who'd spoken to us earlier was growing frantic; one of the vampires urged him away from his friend while another knelt down to examine the body. I hid my face between Arnold's neck and shoulder, but not before catching a glimpse of the poor kid's slit throat as the vamp turned him onto his back.

When I got around to peeking out, the vampires didn't

seem fazed by the sight or smell of the blood. They were industriously directing people around the scene and keeping an eye on anyone who had witnessed the debacle. Angus was still giving orders, listening to various reports, and cursing a blue streak as he took stock. The sound of sirens growing in the distance brought with it a sense of dread; I sorely hoped neither Mark nor any of his friends would be among the cops to investigate the scene.

"Bold as brass, they are," Angus muttered as he came to a stop beside us. His gaze was suddenly sharp upon me, thick caterpillar brows lowering in a scowl. "Is Sara bleeding?"

Arnold held me close while Angus eyed my neck, though I wasn't as afraid of him as I should have been. Too busy having the shivers as I stared at the body on the ground. Someone had put a coat over the dead boy, but it didn't stop me from envisioning what could've happened if I had been just a little slower ducking away from the man who attacked me. I'd be on the ground in a pool of my own blood, just like that kid.

"I'm okay. It's just a little scratch."

"Make sure the paramedics see ye before they leave. Get it looked at." Angus switched his attention from me to Arnold once I nodded agreement. "That light show shorted out our security cameras during the fight. Did ye catch any of their faces? I didn't have time to check before I came out here."

"No. They were wearing masks," Arnold said.

"They tried to take the folder. Probably AOA members," I said, glancing down at the papers in my hand. What was in them that was worth murdering an innocent kid? Almost killing me?

Angus swore. "Just our luck, then. Give the folder to the police if they ask for it, but not the list with the address or the key. I'll provide you with a new copy when they're gone."

It didn't take very long for the first round of police to arrive. Though I'd dreaded the possibility of seeing Mark or one of his friends, we were outside his precinct. Officers I didn't know taped off the section of the lot and sidewalk where we'd fought, and took the statements of all witnesses.

No one recognized me, though I got a few disapproving looks when they heard I was a PI. The questions turned brief and perfunctory after that. Nothing new there. I was grateful that H&W Investigations didn't ring anyone's bells. Surprising, considering how much media time Shiarra had bought with her stunt at the Embassy followed by the Borowsky incident. They might pull something up when they got back to the station, but none of the cops connected my name with the Other-waged battle from just a few months ago that had involved a number of innocent—human—bystanders. Myself included.

As expected, the officers wanted to take the file. I didn't argue, gave them everything they asked for. I dumped all of the papers—save for the one with the address and phone numbers tucked in my pocket—into the evidence bag one of them held open for me. Another took my business card and advised me to expect to be called in as a witness to the homicide at a later date. It was "too early in the investigation" to have any idea who the AOA members were or why they had attacked us in such an open, public location.

Some reporters had set up camp at the fringes of the police-made barricaded area but Arnold and I managed to get by without attracting their attention once the police were done taking our statements. Arnold's statement took a bit longer as they had more questions for him when they found out he was a mage, but they didn't have enough to go on to request his presence at the station.

I was too shaky to drive, so Arnold took the wheel. We didn't speak much on the way back to my house. He glanced at me in concern now and again but mostly concentrated on the road.

I spent most of the ride thinking about the heavy file on my lap Angus had slipped me before we left. A duplicate of the one the AOA had just committed murder for.

I hoped it held some answers.

Chapter 10

Oddly enough, the dogs didn't bark at Arnold when we arrived, instead sniffing him and wagging their tails. They accepted his patting, licking his hands and following docilely at his heels. Feeling ashamed for neglecting them earlier, I let them inside to lie at our feet while we perused the file's contents over mugs of coffee and hastily made sandwiches.

There was a pitifully short list of names of known Anti-Other Alliance members. A couple came from Web articles and police reports, but others were on photocopies of handwritten notes. Two were written on the backs of photographs. Other pictures didn't have any names at all, only dates and locations matched to newspaper articles to show their connection.

One of the photos with a name on the back was the guy who'd held the cigarette to my eye. All it said was "Ace." Not a name I would've given to the creepy weirdo, but I suppose there's no accounting for taste.

Aside from a few tidbits about the backgrounds of the known members, there wasn't much useful information. Some guy named Russell Morgan ran the show. The same "Mr. Morgan" that Ace had mentioned in my office, perhaps? He was an ex–White Hat, and he'd broken off from the New York chapter after a falling-out a couple years ago. Since then, he'd formed an elite corps of the most murderous and psychotic former White Hats he could find. They renamed themselves the Anti-Other Alliance and opened up a base of operations a few states away, staying away from White Hat territories like New York and Miami. Though their ultimate goals were unknown, the AOA didn't flinch at mowing down a few innocent bystanders on their way to the monsters they targeted.

The AOA had stuck to individual vampire nests and werewolf packs to begin with, but lately had been selecting businesses and higher profile victims to destroy. There were a few maps in the file that showed they were working their way from Atlanta back up the East Coast, toward New York.

The pattern shown by the comparison of the maps against the news clippings was disturbing. They seemed to fan out once they reached a large city; only small instances of individual assaults would occur on the fringes of city limits. Then, seemingly unrelated events spiraled deeper into the city, leading up to one or two bigger attacks, gradually growing in scope until the target was eliminated by whatever means necessary. They'd already taken down two werewolf pack leaders and a good chunk of the D.C. vampire coven, leaving a swath of destruction in their wake.

Judging by the information in the file, they were breaking some sort of unspoken rule to stay away from White Hat territory. Something was drawing them back to Morgan's hometown. Their interest in Royce's businesses wasn't singular; they'd also been spotted at some werewolf-run dive in Brooklyn, and evidence pointed to an AOA member defacing the office of a privately practicing mage in Jersey City.

What the hell were they after?

"This is getting us nowhere. I'm going to call Jack," Arnold announced, setting down his coffee. Roxie stuck her head in his lap to be scratched when he sat down and he absently obliged her.

I regarded him dubiously, wondering what the leader of the White Hats might have to say about Russell Morgan. White Hats and AOA members didn't mix, from what I understood. Plus, Jack was clearly unstable. Shiarra had told me about his efforts to make her more amenable to helping them hunting down vampires by threatening to kill her if she didn't join their cause.

"Are you sure that's a good idea?"

"I already told Angus I would. Besides, that Morgan guy is an ex–White Hat. Jack's bound to know him."

Arnold dialed Jack with his cell phone. Once the White Hat answered, Arnold put it on speakerphone so I could join the conversation.

"Ms. Halloway," Jack acknowledged once Arnold introduced us, "I've heard your name mentioned but I don't think we've had the pleasure of meeting. How can I assist you?"

Arnold spoke up and I sat back to let him ask the questions. "We need to know about Russell Morgan and the AOA. What can you tell us?"

Jack was silent for so long, Arnold checked to make sure the line hadn't disconnected.

"Russell Morgan is . . . an unpleasant character. I'm not sure this is something I can discuss with you, Arnold."

"Have I ever betrayed your confidence? Come on, help me out here."

Jack growled something distorted over the cell phone line. Arnold leaned forward on the couch, furrows appearing between his brows.

"Your secret's safe," Arnold said, giving me a warning look when I opened my mouth. I quieted, rolling my eyes, though I was terribly curious how Arnold knew so much about Jack and how they had met. What was the hunter's secret? "This is trouble. You know I wouldn't ask if I didn't need to know."

Jack growled something again, this time resigned instead of angry. "You're going to get me killed if he ever finds out I talked to you."

"He won't."

"Look, Russ is bad news. He used to be part of our team out here, but he got violent. Unnecessarily so. He managed to cover it up from the cops, but he and another guy killed some furball's wife and kids in the process of hunting the Other down. Sure, they were sympathizers, but the girl was human and we don't know for sure if the kids carried the virus. They didn't deserve to die for that. The guy who was with him that night told me what happened.

"Russ admitted to it when I confronted him but disagreed that he'd done anything wrong. He wasn't caught by the police, so it was okay."

I was gaping by this time but Arnold wasn't fazed. He pulled out one of the papers spread out on the table and studied it, nodding along as Jack talked. "Go on."

"He knows too much about us to turn him over for his crimes, but we wouldn't have anything more to do with him. Having him stay or ratting him out was too dangerous, either way. When he left, he took a few of our less inhibited members with him and formed the Anti-Other Alliance. Some real gems in that outfit. Can't say as I was sorry to see most of them go. He still calls up here now and then looking for new members. Last I heard, the AOA was concentrating on ousting that one leech from D.C. They wanted to relocate there after they ran into so much trouble getting rid of the one in Atlanta. I hear it took Van Alstyne halving their numbers before they gave up and started looking for a new city to work out of."

"Van Alstyne?" I whispered.

"The vamp in charge of Atlanta," Arnold answered, his

attention still centered on the paper in his hands. "Jack, did you know the AOA is in New York?"

"What?!" the White Hat exclaimed, his shock turning to anger and demand in an instant. "Where? How do you know it was them?"

Judging by Jack's reaction, either Ace had lied to me in my office, or Russell Morgan had lied to his henchman. Interesting and potentially useful information, though it was nothing that would yield any clues as to what they were after.

"They attacked Sara and me outside of The Underground tonight. Check the news. I'll text you some names, dates, and locations after we hang up."

"Damn it!" It sounded like Jack hit something. The distortion of the cell phone made it hard to tell. "Shit, Arnold, why didn't you say so in the first place? Morgan isn't supposed to cross the state line. We had an agreement. I'll see if I can reach him. I need to find him before he does something drastic."

"Too late," I muttered.

"What?" Jack must have overheard me.

"I said, 'too late.' They killed a bystander outside the club."

Another thump, this time more like a head hitting a desk. "Please tell me it wasn't a human."

"Sorry," I said, clearing my throat as I rubbed at the scab that had formed on my neck. It was too shallow to require stitches, and after cleaning away the crusted blood the paramedics hadn't even bothered to put a bandage on it. Too neat a cut to need it, they said. "It was one of the attendants outside the club."

"Probably a donor. Salvageable, if you can get to them before they get addicted or bound to a vamp." After a brief lull, I jumped at Jack's venomous snarl. "We're not supposed to kill *them,* just their masters! God*damn,* Russ never learned the difference."

"Jack," Arnold cut in, "can you help us out? We need to find this guy before he hurts somebody else."

The hunter went quiet briefly, probably considering his words before responding. "I'll help you. You can't connect the White Hats to this, understand? If I find out where he is, you can't tell the police you found out from me. Tell them you used a spell or something."

"I will. Thanks, Jack."

"Don't thank me yet. I'll call when I've got something."

He hung up without saying goodbye. Arnold put the phone back in his pocket and started shuffling the papers back into a neat pile.

"That went well," I said, collecting the plates. Buster perked up at that, getting up to follow me hopefully to the kitchen. Roxie stayed where she was, happily curled at Arnold's feet. "What's the big secret, anyway?"

"Not mine to tell." Arnold smiled to soften the blunt words. "Don't worry. Jack's got some skewed priorities but he's not a bad guy. He's good at what he does, too. He'll track Morgan down."

I nodded and walked out of the room, Buster bouncing like an overgrown puppy at my heels, begging for scraps. I tossed the remains of our sandwiches into his bowl before putting the dishes in the sink and pausing to stare out the window into the shadowed yard.

Some of the White Hat's comments were bugging me, sticking with me despite the fact that there wasn't anything I could do about them. The casual admission of covered-up murder wasn't sitting easy. No matter how the hunters may have justified it, there was a Were-something out there whose wife and kids were taken away from him because he wasn't human. He'd never know why or how, because Jack couldn't bring himself to go to the cops and turn in their killer. There had to be a pretty damned convincing reason for the hunter to keep his silence.

I really hoped Jack was as good a guy as Arnold thought he was.

Chapter 11

Another hour spent studying the contents of the file didn't yield anything else of use. Arnold didn't object when I got up to check my messages. The dogs stayed at his feet. Odd, they usually followed me everywhere when I let them in the house.

My desk upstairs felt strangely empty after I tilted the framed picture of Mark down on its face. Doing my best to resist the urge to smash the frame and tear up the photo, I tapped the play button on the answering machine. I didn't pay close attention to the messages at first, more interested in my e-mails than listening to Janine take five minutes to get around to asking me to come over for dinner next week.

Soon my attention was dragged off my computer monitor by a familiar and entirely unwelcome voice.

"Sara, listen"—Finnegan's rough Brooklynese was unmistakable. How he got my unlisted number was questionable, but his obvious panic was enough for me to put aside my bristling at his lack of professional ethics—for now—"you've got to come down to my office. Something's gone wrong. Please, I need—shit! They're coming!"

A few seconds of recorded scuffling and a series of heavy thumps were followed by the sound of someone picking up the receiver. They didn't say anything, just breathed into the phone. A click, then nothing. The message ended; it had been left a couple of hours ago.

I sat in silence, chilled to the bone. I had the sinking feeling the AOA was behind this. Joe could be hurt. Maybe dead. As much as I disliked the guy, I couldn't ignore the fact that he'd called me for help.

Enough time had passed that the assailants were likely long gone. Chances were good there was something at Pro-Detection documenting what the AOA was after, too. I knew Arnold and I should check it out. If nothing else, maybe we would find some clues that would lead us to where Russell Morgan was hiding.

We couldn't report it—calling authorities over the break-in might mean losing our only shot at finding out where the AOAs were and what they really wanted. The red tape tying up the investigation would take too long and the police would be looking at break-and-enter charges, not a murder rap. Whatever else happened, I needed to track down enough information to tie Russell Morgan to the dead kid outside of The Underground. The cops could be called in—*after* I got the evidence I needed to solve the case.

That in mind, I rushed down the stairs. The dogs jumped up, barking excitedly and following me around the living room as I collected my purse and keys. "Finnegan's in trouble. Let's go."

"Wait, hold on a sec!" Arnold exclaimed, pulling back as I grabbed his arm. "Who is he? What do you mean, he's in trouble? Where are we going?"

"I just got a message from him that he left a couple hours ago. He's the PI the AOA hired to look into Royce's business. Sounded like someone broke into his office. Come on, we have to get down there and see if he's okay."

Arnold shook his head, frowning. "That's not a good idea. What if it's a trap? We should call the police."

"I'd rather not. This might be our one chance to find out exactly where the AOA are hiding." I gestured at all the papers spread out on the table, not bothering to hide my frustration. "We've been at this for hours. There's nothing here that will help us—but Joe would've had Morgan or whoever from the AOA fill out paperwork to do the job. He'll have something that says how they can be reached, maybe even what they've been looking for all this time. I want to get to it before the police do."

Arnold eyed the paperwork. Rather than argue, he shrugged and came around the coffee table to join me. "Okay."

I blinked, surprised. "Okay?"

"Yeah. Let's go." He put his arm around my waist, smiling at my flustered expression. "What, you expected me to argue?"

"Well, yes," I stammered. "Mark would've."

He leaned in to press a kiss to my temple. "I'm not Mark. Don't worry, I've got your back."

His words sent a little thrill through me. No, he wasn't Mark. Nothing like him.

Things didn't seem quite so dire on the trip to Finnegan's. While I was concerned, I wasn't so afraid or feeling a constant pressuring need to justify my actions.

It was a short trip to Levittown. Pro-Detection was located in a squat, boxy building with a tiny parking lot, sandwiched between a liquor store and an optometrist's office. There was a beat-up sedan parked in front with tinted windows and a faded bumper sticker reading: IF WE ARE WHAT WE EAT, I COULD BE YOU BY MORNING! Clue enough the car was Joe's, but Pro-Detection's windows were shuttered and dark.

"Wait," Arnold called out when I reached for the front door, giving me pause. "Let me go first. I'll see if there's anyone inside."

When I stepped aside, Arnold didn't do as I expected. Instead of trying the door, he knelt down in front of it, cupping his hands and whispering something under his breath. A few seconds later, a tiny black mouse peeked from between his fingers.

"Go check it out. See if anybody's inside."

The mouse squeaked and hopped to the ground, scampering over to the door and squeezing between the cracks.

"Forgot you had Bob," I said, chuckling. I'd only seen the familiar a handful of times, and hadn't realized he could do reconnaissance.

Arnold winked and stepped back to wait. "Of course. He'll let me know in a sec if anyone's in there."

It didn't take long. The mouse crept out from under the door, shaking his tiny head. He made a few squeaks and clicks, whiskers twitching, before rushing out and climbing up Arnold's outstretched arm to perch on his shoulder.

"He says there's the smell of a cat and rat poison inside, so he didn't go very far. It looks like the front is clear of people."

"Okay. Let's check it out."

Arnold shrugged and tried the door. It was unlocked, swinging open on creaky hinges. Papers rustled on the floor and the streetlight outside didn't offer much illumination in the dark room. Arnold fumbled for a switch but no lights came on when he flipped it.

He lifted his hand, saying something that sounded like a weird mix of Latin and Greek. *"Smæl leukós handus."*

A ball of blue-white light formed in his palm, illuminating the office. A large gray tomcat hissed at us. It was in the corner, back arched and fur fluffed out.

Baleful yellow eyes glared at us as we looked over the

papers and Rolodex cards on the floor and scattered on the desk. The line to the phone was cut, the computer monitor smashed on the floor. A large reddish-brown smear on the papers and desk was worrisome, but there was no sign of Joe.

Another door leading to the back offices was closed. I dropped the file I was looking at when a muted thump came from behind it. Arnold and I looked at each other before he extinguished the light, closing his fist around it. We waited, but aside from the cat hissing at us and Bob's disapproving chitters, there was no other sound.

Arnold moved first; I could hear his footsteps shuffling through the papers, even if I was still too light-blinded to see him do it. I held my breath, listening and straining to see. The door he opened clicked but the hinges didn't squeal like the front door's. It was dim in the hallway but a light from an open door at the end of the hall illuminated a figure gagged and bound, slumped in a chair.

Despite the five o'clock shadow and blood that had trickled from a wound at his scalp, drying to a tacky coat on half his face, I recognized the craggy features under the mess.

Joe.

Arnold passed through the door, reaching for something in a pocket. I didn't have enough time to call out a warning when a slender shadow whipped out from between the wall and door, cracking him on the back of the skull.

As Arnold collapsed, I backpedaled and fumbled for my cell phone. The dark shape broke away from the door and came at me too fast. Before I could reach the phone to call for help, the guy had my wrists in a bruisingly tight grip.

My knee connected to his groin and he gasped a curse, one hand losing its hold on me as he grabbed at his family jewels. I shoved at him but he refused to let go, pulling me off balance as he simultaneously cradled himself and tightened his grip on my wrist. He didn't let go until I kicked him in the stomach.

He wasn't alone. In the time it took for me to break away, half a dozen more burly men dressed in dark colors and ski masks had surrounded us. They swarmed out of one of the offices to drag Arnold deeper into the trap, taking me with him.

Chapter 12

While Arnold was unconscious, two of the men took their time binding his legs, tying his hands at the small of his back, and gagging him as they had Joe. They emptied his pockets, dumping his keys, wallet, cell phone, and a small bag onto a rickety break-room table. The bag contained a few colored dice, nothing more. One of the guys snickered at the sight.

I was given the same treatment, save for the gag. I kept my mouth shut as they shoved me into a chair, watching as they poked through our IDs and credit cards and examined our cell phones. A gasp escaped me when one of the men tugged his ski mask off, smiling genially. That warmth never reached his eyes.

"Ms. Halloway. I thought I made myself clear back in your office. What are you doing here?"

My voice stuck in my throat. No plausible lies came to mind. The man with the scarred palm reached for me and, though I shrank back, there was nowhere for me to go. His fingers curled in my shirt, jerking me forward and bringing to mind visions of the bright glow of a cigarette held up to my eye.

"Are you the one Joe called? Is that it?"

At my mute nod, he laughed and shoved me back. My chair tipped precariously before righting itself. Ace gave the other PI a look of bemused tolerance; Joe was semiconscious. His glazed eyes watched us from the hallway, bound fists clenching in his lap. One of the other hunters stepped out of the room to give him a smack on the head, making me wince in sympathy.

Ace reached for my cell. He tapped some buttons on it while he talked, looking at the screen instead of watching us.

"Why would he call you? You're the competition. Trying to stop him, I'll bet. That's what you were doing with that file outside The Underground, wasn't it?"

"Yes," I said, my voice coming out as a harsh whisper. Him. He was the one who'd tried to slit my throat. "He knew I was looking for you."

The hunter's gaze was suddenly sharp upon me. "Were you, now?"

"Yes," I said again, stronger this time. "Royce wanted to know what you were after. He hired me to do it. I'm doing my job."

"That's truly a pity. I was hoping he'd called those monsters to tell them what we were doing. Well, plans change. I suppose you'll do just as well."

"What do you want me for?"

"Bait, Ms. Halloway. You're not a donor but I assume you're invested enough in the leech's mess to warrant him sending a few people to look for you, given reason."

"Hey, should you be telling her that shit?" one of the other hunters queried. Ace didn't look pleased at the interruption.

"She needs to know enough to pass on to the leech before we get rid of her."

The other guy shrugged, adjusting his shoulder holster before leaning back against the door frame. "Just doesn't seem like a good idea, man. What if she gets away? She knows what you look like. We haven't found the stuff yet. She could get the cops before we finish the cleanup job."

"How about you just shut the fuck up and let me work?"

The guy lifted his hands in surrender, looking away. "Sure, whatever."

"Now," the man with the scarred palm said, pinning me in place with the intensity of his gaze, "you don't have to die tonight, Ms. Halloway. Play your part in our little game, and you can walk away from this."

"Is that your choice to make, Ace?" a new voice drawled. A large man stood in the doorway, radiating the kind of presence I was more accustomed to feeling around Others. His chiseled features were too roughly hewn and muscular, the tangled mane of dirty brown strands too unkempt, to be considered handsome. As he swaggered into the room, the space seemed to get smaller, retracting around his strangely graceful bulk. "You should've told me you caught a donor. And a spark to boot!"

"I'm not a donor," I muttered, though at this point I wasn't sure I wanted to call attention to myself.

Ace backhanded me and blood gushed into my mouth as pain exploded across my jaw. I shut my eyes against the tears of pain, refusing to cry out. His tone was as casual as the way he wiped my blood off his knuckles and onto my shirt. "Russ, this is Sara Halloway. That investigator the master leech hired."

Ace edged out of his way as the big man moved closer to kneel in front of me. One calloused thumb wiped at the blood trickling at the corner of my mouth. I jerked back from the touch, but he kept his hand at my cheek.

"You're not a donor, you said? Not contracted?"

I didn't answer, just glared. His fingers dug into the bruise forming on my jaw, making my eyes water.

"If you want to live to see morning, sweetheart, answer me."

I spat blood in his face, but he didn't flinch. "I'm not a fucking donor, asshole! What the hell does that have to do with anything?"

He wiped his face with one ham-fisted hand, examining the red streaks. He touched his tongue to it, tasting my blood. Ugh, gross.

"Not contracted, and no taste of fae or sucker high in your blood. Lucky girl. That means we don't have to kill you. The leeches run out of willing food, they'll have to start hunting people who aren't contracted. They do that, and the rest of this doped-up nation will wake up to the fact that they've been holding hands with monsters. Maybe this time it'll be enough to spur the government to do the job of getting rid of them for us." He grinned at my startled look, thick fingers brushing the hair out of my face, meeting my gaze. The intelligence I saw there clearly wasn't enough to counter the insanity of his plan. "Looks like you get to see sunrise, pretty lady."

He rose to his feet, towering over me as he took the rag Ace offered him and rubbed his face clean. Morgan toed Arnold's prone form, not getting so much as a groan out of him. He was still out like a light.

"This must be the spark. You feel that crackle in the air? He cast something recently."

"He won't be casting anything else," Ace assured him. "We might need him, though. He's been working with the girl."

Morgan nodded. He gestured to the other men in the room. They all snapped to attention. "Let's head up and move out. We've got a lot of work to do tonight if we're going to hit the next batch of donors before the leeches catch on. Bring the girl and the spark; we'll see if that's enough to keep security at the club distracted."

With my wrists and ankles bound, there wasn't much I could do to brace myself when one of the goons pulled me out of the chair. He hefted me over his shoulder and filed out behind a few of the others. I could only watch, cursing quietly to myself, as Ace collected our stuff from the table, putting them in his pockets. Others picked up Joe and Arnold, carrying their limp forms in a fireman's carry.

These guys were certifiable—but also wickedly clever. Their trap had worked for us, and the next one might work just as well on the vampires. Angus, John, and Royce had all shown some concern for my well-being, which meant they might actually fall for the plan the AOA had to use me as bait.

If they succeeded in keeping the vampires distracted, they would target the unprotected donors. The hunters would kill the donors just as surely as they had murdered that poor kid whose only crime had been working as a valet for a vampire-run club. If they killed enough donors—and, judging by Morgan's comment and John's very overt advances toward me, they must have already succeeded in getting to a few— the vampires would have no choice but to break the law in order to feed and survive.

The Other-Citizen Amendment to the Constitution, Article XIV-1(B), said that any Other born or turned in the United States or living within the United States since September 11, 2001, was awarded citizenship under the amended terms of naturalization. It also provided strict regulations on their feeding habits, hunting methods, and turning humans into one of their own.

It also meant Morgan was right. The only thing that gave vampires the same rights as people was that strict set of laws requiring them to keep their fangs very much to themselves— unless the victim was contracted. If a bunch of them started feeding on people who weren't . . . well, it might be enough to spur another amendment, changing vampires from private citizens to an exception to Article XIV-1(B). "Varmint" laws allowed for killing Others who went rogue and broke the rules—and Others who broke the rules tended to take their hunters down with them. Mark had spoken about it occasionally, when liquored up enough, after some of his buddies on the force were injured or killed while bringing in a werewolf who had savaged someone outside of a contract. Though he'd never stated it outright, I was sure that was why Mark had always pushed me so hard to stay away from Others.

If Royce and the few hundred vampires who answered to him were labeled rogue, it would be a bloodbath.

Chapter 13

The AOAs took us out through a back door and into a dark alley, dumping Arnold, Joe, and me through the double doors of a van. Ace and a couple of other hunters got in the back with us. Morgan and the rest took separate cars.

Nobody said much, except when Ace gave the driver directions now and again. My fear didn't lessen when I recognized the route he was taking. We'd end up somewhere near The Underground. New York City was big, but I knew my stomping grounds well; we'd be within blocks of the vampires' club.

Judging by the tightness of his expression, Arnold must have been coming around. I scooted as close to him as I could get. It didn't accomplish much other than to get a vicious kick from a hunter who growled a command to stop moving.

Though he was grimacing and gasping for air, I managed to note that Arnold opened his eyes to thin slits. Fae light glimmered in their depths, but there wasn't much he could do with his hands bound and his mouth stuffed with cloth.

Bob was peering out from under the collar of Arnold's

light jacket, the mouse's beady eyes glinting in the dark. He crept down Arnold's shirt and scuttled up by my head. If the guards noticed him, they didn't do anything about it.

I flinched when I felt the little furball moving around in my hair, though, stifling the urge to jerk away. Before long, he was inching down my arm instead, the barely there pressure turning into a tiny, warm body creeping between my fingers. I cupped my hands around him when I felt a minute tugging on the ropes. He was chewing his way through.

After what felt like an interminable ride, the van ground to a halt. Bob stopped his efforts, worming his way up one of my sleeves while the hunters got to their feet and filed out.

A cold wash of air and the brackish scent of the river entered the van when they opened the back doors. We were somewhere out in the warehouse district, in the rapidly shrinking section that hadn't yet been overrun by overpriced boutiques, restaurants, and nightclubs, but not so far off that I couldn't detect the sound of heavy bass coming from somewhere down the street.

When I was dragged out of the back and hefted up on someone's shoulder—now becoming an uncomfortably familiar position—I spotted the Statue of Liberty far off across the water. We were close to some docks, too. At a rough guess, we were maybe a mile away from The Underground. The time it would take for Angus and the others to get here would be more than enough for Morgan and the other AOAs with him to sneak into the club and carry out their plan.

We were carried inside the warehouse. Someone had brought lanterns, their electric glow only making the deeper pools of shadow around us emphasize how large and empty the place was. The copper scent of old blood lingered, even though this place couldn't have seen any meat to pack in a decade or more. Enough dust puffed up to make me sneeze. Joe, Arnold, and I were dumped unceremoniously on the floor, the cold cement giving me the shivers. It was all I could do not to drop Bob, who fell into my hands after the jarring landing.

Joe made an inarticulate sound behind his gag and was cuffed for it. Once again, I huddled against Arnold, who rested his brow against mine before closing his eyes. The marks on my arm started tingling again, but I was more concerned about Bob. He'd stopped moving, though I could feel his whiskers tickling my palms.

Bob and I both squeaked when someone grabbed my hair and yanked me upright. Ace held me in place, holding up my cell phone as he took a conversational pitch.

"Which number will get me through to one of the leeches you've been working with?"

I glared, not answering until he started twisting his wrist, pulling some of my hair out by the roots. Wincing, I spat out an answer. "Angus! His name is Angus."

"Good. When I hold out the phone, you'll beg Angus to come save you." He pulled away, leaving me to fall heavily back to the floor.

I was afraid I'd crushed Bob until I felt him wriggle frantically in my hands. He went back to work at the ropes around my wrists while Ace pulled Angus up on my phone.

The hunter paced slowly nearby, glancing down at us every now and then. A slight smile widened to a predatory grin as someone picked up on the other end.

"No, this isn't Sara. She's here, though."

Ace crouched down and held the phone by my face. I screamed out as quickly as I could, "Don't listen to him, it's a trap!"

The hunter backhanded me. I vaguely heard him continue speaking through the starbursts of pain flashing in my skull.

"Listen, leech, and listen close. If you want her to live, and you don't want a media frenzy on your hands, you'll come to the old Bessie's Best Meats Building by the waterfront in the next hour. Bring five hundred grand, cash, and leave the cops out of it, or this old packing plant is going to see some fresh blood tonight. Get it?"

Without waiting for an answer, he hung up and grinned down at me. "Well, that should do for starters. Do what I say next time. Less pain in it for you."

A strange clicking sound echoed in the darkness. Ace's attention jerked around as he and his three henchmen spread around us in a semicircle, lifting their weapons. A voice floated out of the shadows, echoing in the empty space.

"Next time you want to spill innocent blood, do it on someone else's turf."

"Jack," Ace said, the tension running out of his shoulders. He sounded genuinely glad to see the White Hat, he and his men lowering their weapons. "What are you doing out here? Didn't Morgan tell you we were going to be using the place tonight?"

Jack stepped into the light, holding what I was fairly certain was an illegal assault rifle on Ace. He was followed by a number of other White Hats; far more men than Ace had at his back. None of them looked happy to see the AOAs, and all of them were brandishing weapons.

Ace frowned. "What's going on here, Jack?"

"Morgan didn't get my permission. He was never supposed to come back here." Jack's eyes narrowed to thin slivers, icy blue orbs glinting dangerously. "Neither were you."

The other hunter took a step back, raising his hands. "Hey, hey, let's talk this over. We're right in the middle of—"

Jack cut him off. "I know what you're in the middle of. I won't have you or Morgan killing more innocent people. That's not what we stand for. You knew that when we kicked you out of New York, just like Morgan did. You've just violated the terms of your amnesty."

With a curse, Ace dove to the side, tossing my phone away as he went for a weapon. I grimaced as the cell shattered into pieces, skittering out of sight into the dark. Before

I had time to mourn the loss of my phone, the place was suddenly ringing out with gunshots. I squeezed my eyes shut and huddled against Arnold, praying it would be over soon.

One of the AOAs tripped and fell over me. Bullets pinged off the cement, the weapons' firing punctuated by screams and curses.

In a moment it was over, though it was hard to tell through the ringing in my ears. I opened my eyes at a renewed tugging on my wrist. Just before Jack knelt down to cut the bonds off my ankles, the ones at my wrists snapped free, and Bob rushed back to huddle by Arnold's cheek.

The White Hat didn't say anything, though he arched a brow at the sight of the mouse. While he went to work on Arnold, one of his buddies freed Joe. I rubbed my wrists and looked around.

Through the lingering haze of gun smoke, I could see one of the AOAs had fallen to the ground behind us. A spreading pool of blood and his stillness told me he was dead. Two others were on their knees with their hands up, a number of White Hats holding weapons on them.

Ace was also under heavy guard, lying on the ground a few yards away and clutching at his shoulder. He was snarling and spitting curses, but not moving from where he'd fallen. Another White Hat was frisking him, tossing an extraordinary number of weapons into a growing pile out of his reach.

I jerked around at a touch to my shoulder. "Are you okay?"

Arnold's worried gaze turned to surprise as I threw my arms around him, pulling him into a ragged kiss. It hurt, but the pain was soon forgotten when he started kissing me back, lips tasting of peppermint moving hungrily over mine as his hands tangled in my hair. His touch felt like fire against my skin, a different kind of warmth and electric buzz that quickly built between us, making all the pain and fear fade away into an afterthought. I breathed in his scent, the pleasant tickle of ash now mixed with the ozone of unspent magic and tang of sweat.

In that moment, I knew that Arnold was right—he was nothing like the sorcerer, David, and nothing at all like Mark. Pressed so close, feeling the minute tremble of his limbs and the desperation in his touch matching mine, we were as much acknowledging our survival as our need for each other. That uncomfortable sensation when we touched was suddenly something deliciously pleasant, tracing strange patterns over my skin. Intimacy with a mage was a totally new experience for me, one I was suddenly eager to investigate. His urgency was mine, sparking a keen sense of desire to know every line and curve and contour of his body.

A loud "ahem!" interrupted us, and we reluctantly parted, turning matching sheepish looks to Jack.

"Well. I'm glad to see you two are all right," Jack said. He seemed to be trying to hide a smile, though he wasn't doing a terribly good job of it.

"How the hell did you find us?" Arnold asked.

"One of my sources got the information on Morgan's plan. I know he's headed to The Underground, but when I heard he was sending someone here, I knew he was planning to repeat history. I didn't know you were the ones involved, but I didn't want any more dead people on my turf." Jack held out a hand to each of us, helping Arnold and me to our feet. Joe was already standing shakily to one side, another White Hat holding his arm to steady him. "We had this warehouse long before Morgan joined the White Hats. I knew he'd come back here because it's one of the few places he could use for a setup like this."

"It's not over," I said, sliding an arm around Arnold's waist. "He's planning on killing a bunch of people at The Underground. We've got to stop him."

"Not our problem," Jack said, heading over to where Ace

was struggling and busying himself with helping another White Hat tie up and gag the AOA.

I gaped at him. "What do you mean, 'not our problem'? Why are you even here, then?"

"I meant to save the innocents and I did," Jack replied, not bothering to look at me as he tightened the knots around Ace's wrists. "Anyone at that club knew they were walking into the lion's den."

Stumbling, I pulled away from Arnold and grabbed Jack by the back of his shirt. His men started muttering, hands going to their weapons, but he waved them off and looked up at me.

"You self-righteous son of a bitch. You think saving us exempts you from what happened with Morgan before? Not just one or two, but *dozens* of people could die tonight. Just because they're hanging out at a vamp-run bar doesn't mean they don't deserve to be saved. What kind of excuse do you need to help them, huh?"

He looked up at me, the twinkle in his eye completely at odds with the fierce grin twisting his lips. "Thought you'd never ask. Owe us—the White Hats—a favor. One to be called in at a later time."

That gave me pause. Owing a favor to these crazy hunters could be detrimental to my health. Maybe more so than it had been when Shiarra worked for The Circle. Still—if owing them a debt meant saving lives, it was a burden I was willing to endure.

Scowling, I nodded.

Jack stood up and thrust some things at me—the personal items Ace had taken from us back at Joe's office. "Good. Devon, call the cops." A guy in a deep-red bomber jacket nodded, pulling out a cell phone. "Tell them there's a package here waiting for pickup."

While Devon made the call, Jack dragged Ace by the collar over to the other trussed-up AOAs. Once he'd dropped his burden, Jack brushed off his jeans and hefted his rifle up on his shoulder. "Let's go."

"Wait."

The command was soft, gravelly, but we all paused in our tracks as Joe shuffled forward. One of his eyes was swollen shut, his grimace more pitiful than frightening under the mask of dried blood. He limped over to where Ace was twisting halfheartedly in his bonds and glaring at us.

The PI kicked Ace in the face, blood spraying from the hunter's nose as he fell to the side.

Joe smiled, rolling his shoulders and standing up straight. Dried chips of blood flaked off as he rubbed a hand over his stubble.

"Man, that felt good. Okay, *now* we can go."

Chapter 14

We hurried into the White Hats' waiting cars. A couple of the hunters loaned Joe and me weapons: a hefty-looking Desert Eagle and a machete for Joe, and a couple of daggers and a Smith & Wesson 500 for me. Arnold declined when they offered him a gun, sharing an inscrutable look with Jack.

Traffic made it take forever to crawl the measly distance between the old warehouse and The Underground. Weekend revelers were out for a night on the town, leaving the streets of the meatpacking district jammed. When we were within a couple blocks of the club, idling at a light, Jack told the driver to find parking and gestured for us to follow as he jumped out of the car.

I was vaguely aware of other White Hats around us, following in our wake. When I noticed they held their jackets and flannel shirts closed, hiding their weapons, I did the same. We ran the rest of the way to the club, though there was no sign anything untoward had happened—yet. People were lined up out front, waiting to get in, and men whose security shirts strained across massive chests guarded the door and directed people around the yellow caution tape from the earlier crime scene. Valets scurried this way and that as they tended to visitors' cars.

Clearly the murder hadn't done much to hurt business.

People in the line shifted and muttered, quieting once we halted in front of the guards. One of them frowned down at me, his eyes widening in recognition. "Aren't you—"

"Yes, I am." I frantically gestured at the door. "We've got to get inside! The Anti-Other Alliance is here, they were just waiting for Angus to leave. Is he still here?"

He shook his head, patting down his pockets and pulling out a cell phone. "Miss, those are White Hats behind you. We've got standing orders not to allow them on the premises. Jack Thornton, you're violating the terms of the restraining order Mr. Royce filed against you. I'm going to have to ask you all to leave."

Jack smiled, the expression more a vicious baring of teeth than a friendly overture. "We're here to help Sara. Just for tonight, we're on your side. The AOA should have infiltrated this club and started killing people already. Are you sure you don't want us here?"

The guard didn't answer right away, fingering his phone before stepping aside to call someone. Jack didn't wait; he ducked past and inside, the rest of us following despite the protests and shouts behind us. Some of the other White Hats kept security busy while the rest of us rushed down the hall that led into the club proper and toward the first bar.

Inside, there was no sign of panic. A few patrons were mingling near the entrance, watching us over their drinks. A multitude of brows, many encrusted with metal and jewels that winked and shone in the muted lighting, rose upon our entrance, making it clear our presence was hardly welcome. Our jeans, pressed slacks, T-shirts, and button-downs looked entirely out of place in this crowd. The murmur of voices was drowned out against a heavy techno beat, though a few exclamations could be heard when some of the White Hats drew their weapons.

One of the bartenders brushed Day-Glo green tendrils out of his eyes, glaring at us as he shouted over the pulse of music. "You people don't belong in here! Head out before I call the cops."

Jack ignored him, scanning faces at and around the bar. Not satisfied, he dashed off, the rest of us following. The bartender picked up a phone before we were out of the room, watching us go with a mixture of fright and defiance.

For some reason, the White Hat knew the layout of the club very well. After shoving his way through a crowd of startled, angry dancers, he led us straight to a "Staff Only" door beside a stage. Without pause, he kicked it in, splintering the cheap wood around the lock and rushing inside. The hall was lined with doors, and as we passed, I noted many of them were labeled as dressing rooms. Protesting shouts and pounding feet sounded behind us, but when I looked back, all I saw were a few shocked, half-dressed people peering into the passage.

There was a sound of scuffling and a few shouts before Arnold and I reached the end of the hall. There were two doors—one for storage, and one for a staff break room. A couple of White Hats checked the storage room while Jack went into the break room. Arnold and I had barely cleared the door before several White Hats pinned a couple of guys whom I assumed were AOA members on the floor. When I glanced in the other direction, I had to cover my mouth not to be sick at the sight.

We were too late; they'd gotten to some of the donors already, shoving them like an afterthought into the back of the storage closet. I recognized one of the attendants from the parking lot earlier in the evening, his features distorted with panic behind the clear plastic bag over his head. Suffocated so no scent of spilled blood would draw the attention of vampires. It was the same kid who had freaked out when he saw his dead friend on the ground.

Someone who wouldn't have been missed.

I closed my eyes and turned away. It took a few deep breaths taken slow and easy to keep from hyperventilating. Arnold's arms sliding around my waist was a comfort, but a small one. We were too late.

"Cold bastards," Joe remarked, wheezing. He was holding his gun with both hands, but it still trembled. "Damn it, I never should've given them floor plans. This is my fault."

"No, it isn't. They would've done this with or without your help," Jack said, clapping the PI lightly on the shoulder. He urged Joe into a chair, and the man sat down without protest. From his gray-faced pallor, shock was catching up with him.

Some new security guards caught up with us, weapons held at the ready as they shouted commands from the end of the hall.

Jack waved everyone else aside and stepped out of the break room, holding his hands up. He called out, calm and reasonable, nothing like I would've expected after what Shiarra and Arnold had told me about him. Those on the security team who weren't busy clearing some space on the dance floor seemed surprised, stopping their shouting long enough to listen to what Jack had to say.

"Hey, we're here to help. Look in the closet—we caught a couple of the guys responsible."

After a brief debate with each other, one of the guards edged his way down, keeping his gun on us. We backed out of the way, giving him room to see. At the sight of the bodies in the closet, he stumbled back, putting up his weapon.

"Holy shit! You know who did this?"

"The Anti-Other Alliance," Jack said, slowly lowering his hands.

The other guards cautiously made their way down the

hall. Some of the people in the changing rooms were peering
out at us again, curiosity written all over their features.

"Russell Morgan is here somewhere. He's the one behind
this."

"The cops will be here soon," the first guard said, his features gone pasty white. He couldn't drag his gaze off the
floor of the storage closet. "Somebody else call Angus, tell
him to get back here, *now*."

"We need to keep looking. Morgan and the others are
probably still here."

"No need," someone growled from one of the changing
rooms. Morgan stepped into view, a gun held to the temple
of a slender, immaculately dressed vampire whose eyes were
shot through with red. The vampire looked thin and frail
next to the hunter's bulk, trembling as he stumbled forward.
"Keep these people out of my way, and no one else will get
hurt."

"Ken!" someone squealed.

The vampire flinched when the gun pressed harder
against his temple. The burly hunter held him by the back of
his collar, dragging him along as he edged toward the doorway leading onto the dance floor. Morgan's dark eyes flashed
with anger from behind stray strands of unkempt hair, his
rough features twisted in a snarl. The worried security
guards lowered their weapons and backed up out of the way,
giving Morgan room.

"You shouldn't have come here, Jack," Morgan said,
scowling at the White Hat. Jack didn't reply, except for the
slight twitch of his hand over the handle of a hunting knife
on his belt. "After tonight, walk away. Don't involve yourself
in this any more than you have."

"It's too late for that," Jack replied, darting forward.
Arnold and I stumbled out of his way as he pushed us aside.
Bob dropped off Arnold's shoulder, but I didn't see where he

disappeared to in the scuffle. My attention was focused on Morgan and his hostage.

Morgan whipped the gun off the vampire's temple, but his first shot went wide as Jack plowed into him. Instead of catching him in the chest, the bullet nicked the White Hat's arm. The blond vampire skittered back into his dressing room and screams sounded from the dance floor, lingering revelers rushing away as the two hunters grappled. The pounding music was replaced with shouted orders to be calm and head to the nearest exit, overlaid by the cries of panicked patrons.

The security guards had their weapons out but couldn't shoot for risk of hitting Jack or one of their own people farther down the hall. Jack was fast and strong, but Morgan was bigger and tougher, and had no qualms about fighting dirty. Morgan got Jack's feet out from under him and followed him to the floor, though they were still too busy fighting over the gun to go for other weapons. Jack's arms were shaking, the gun slowly working its way to his face; Morgan's superior strength, coupled with the wound and blood loss, were overpowering him.

There were too many people in the hallway behind us for me or Arnold to escape. I would've gone for my own gun, but Arnold pulled me up tight against him, one arm around my waist, the other held out in front of us as he chanted something under his breath. A wall of energy lifted between us and the hunters just before Morgan's pistol went off a second time, the bullet whining in ricochet as it bounced off the shield.

It proved to be enough of a distraction for Angus to dash forward, bodily yanking Morgan off of Jack and pinning him up against the wall. The vampire moved so fast, he was nothing more than a blur until he came to a stop with the human held so high the top of his head brushed the ceiling. Eyes that matched the bright red of his beard and wild locks glared into the vainly struggling AOA's own.

"That's enough o' yer shenanigans, bucko," he snarled, ignoring the faint choking sounds Morgan was making. "Ye'll be goin' away for a long time, I wager."

Arnold let the shield drop, and I sagged in relief before pulling away to see to Jack, who was sitting up and clutching his injured arm. He didn't take his eyes off of Angus, who was barking out orders at the guards clustering around us.

"You okay, Jack?"

He finally looked at me, a mix of hatred and terror settling into an expression of pain and sheepishness instead. "I'll be fine. 'Tis but a scratch; I've had worse."

Nonplussed at his *Holy Grail* reference, I shook my head and helped him up to his feet, Arnold coming up on the other side of him to help support his weight. As we headed back to the break room to get some chairs and wait for the police, some of the bystanders who'd been watching from the changing rooms came out to follow us. Words of thanks and admiration for our help made me smile, and I detected the rosy hue of a blush high on Jack's otherwise pale cheeks.

He didn't say anything the entire time, keeping his eyes averted even after we found a chair next to Joe for him to settle in. His blush deepened when Ken, the vampire he'd saved from Morgan, enthusiastically pumped his good hand and sang his praises, particularly at the part about how brave he was for facing off against "that awful brute." Most of the other White Hats in the room were having difficulty keeping a straight face as Ken clucked over his wound, fussing at Jack's reticence to let him see to it. A few of the hunters didn't bother to mask their snickers.

Jack looked to Arnold in horror when the vampire offered to take him to dinner and introduce him to his better half, a gentleman by the name of Reece Castle.

Chuckling, Arnold pressed a kiss to my cheek and pulled away. "I'll be back in a moment."

With all the people crowding into the room, I hadn't noticed John right away. He'd waited until Arnold busied himself elsewhere to sidle over, the vampire's cold fingers closing around my hand, startling me.

"Forgive me, I didn't mean to frighten you," he said, radiating false warmth and sincerity. I barely resisted the urge to curl my lip in distaste. "I was worried something happened to you after Angus got that call. Are you all right? You weren't hurt, were you?"

I pulled out of his grip, shoving my hands in my pockets and focusing intently on Arnold's wry conversation with Ken. Though I was surprised to see that in the short time I'd looked away, Jack and the other White Hats had left the room. The only people still in the crowded kitchen were Joe, some of the people from the dressing rooms, the security guards, and the trussed-up AOA members. The tingle of ozone in the air made me wonder if Arnold had something to do with their little disappearing act.

"I'm fine. Thank you for asking."

John leaned in close, keeping his voice low. "I'm sure this must have been upsetting for you. Can I get you a drink to settle your nerves? Maybe take you someplace a little quieter?"

I couldn't help it. I laughed.

"How's this for an answer?"

Pushing off the counter, I walked over to Arnold, cutting him off midsentence as I yanked him down to press my lips to his. He was startled at first but soon reciprocated in kind. I poured every ounce of relief and passion into the gesture that was left to me after the crazy night we'd had. He cradled me against him, the hard lines of his muscles arching and sliding under my fingertips, and I sensed a matching desperation and relief in his touch. The electric tingle on my arm matched the sensation of our lips crushed together, thrills of pleasure tracing wicked fingers along my spine.

It took awhile for us to finish, and this time it was to the sounds of catcalls and a few cheers. Joe was laughing, a rough guffaw that no longer grated on my nerves. When I looked up, John's envious expression was soon replaced by resignation.

I barely noticed. For that moment, with Arnold holding me so tight, nothing else mattered. Not the dead people left behind by the AOAs. Not the people in the room with us. Not even the prospect of dealing with the police in the near future or having to explain what happened tonight could bring me down.

The worry and fear of getting hurt, of dying, of losing him—all of it was washed away in that simple, ardent kiss.

Chapter 15

We waited about a week to visit Shiarra in the hospital again, giving excuses about work and "an unexpected emergency we didn't want her to worry herself over."

Arnold was skilled at defensive magic, but he claimed not to have his brother's gift at healing. Unskilled or not, thanks to his help, the swelling and bruises on my face faded remarkably fast. It took longer for the worst of the aches and pains to die away.

By the time we saw Shiarra, every outward sign of the fight was gone. She was suspicious—no PI worth her salt wouldn't be at our lame excuses—but since we were being cagey about what had happened and she was still abed, there wasn't much she could do to investigate. Thank God.

"So, when did that start?" Shiarra asked, gesturing at our entwined fingers with the hand that wasn't wrapped in bandages.

Arnold smiled and lifted our hands to brush his lips over the backs of my knuckles. "A few days ago. It just sort of happened."

"Right," she said, rolling her eyes before giving me a

pointed look. "Does this mean Officer Shithead is out of the picture for good?"

I answered without the slightest hesitation. "You bet."

A knock drew our attention to the door where a nurse held a large bouquet of white roses. Judging by the twinkle in her eyes and her cherubic grin, she'd been star struck by whoever talked her into delivering them. "A gentleman just dropped this off for you. Mr. Royce sends his regards. Make sure you read that card. It's very sweet."

Expression darkening, Shiarra gestured vaguely at the mountain of flowers overflowing from the furniture to the floor. Most had been dropped off by the myriad well-wishers she'd saved, directly or indirectly, from the crazy sorcerer. "Thanks."

The nurse placed the roses prominently before the other flowers, briefly fussing with the arrangement before leaving us alone. Shiarra cursed once she was gone.

"Will you please take that with you when you leave?"

"Nope," I said, grinning at her. "They're all yours. Anyway, we should get going. I'll come back tomorrow."

"Bring me some chocolate next time! This hospital food is killing me."

Laughing, I agreed, and Arnold and I got up to go. Shiarra called out one more time before we made it out the door. "Arnold?"

"Yeah?"

"If you make her cry, I am so kicking your ass."

He placed his free hand over his heart, an unusually solemn expression crossing his features. "Shia, believe me, that's the last thing I want to make her do. Don't worry, I'll take good care of her."

Shiarra gave him the stink eye. When he didn't break under her distrustful look, keeping the serious mien, she eventually broke into a grin that brought new life to her pallid features.

"Good. I think I owe you too much to beat you up anyway."

We all smiled at that, and Arnold and I walked out into the hall with a lighter step, though our good cheer faltered at the sight of Alec Royce at the end of the hall, waiting patiently by the elevators.

With a last look over my shoulder at Shiarra's room, I led the way to where the vampire stood with his head bowed and hands clasped together at the small of his back. His black eyes gleamed with some strange emotion when he lifted his head to regard us, staring at me. It took me a moment to remember to avert my gaze.

"Ms. Halloway. You're looking well."

I inclined my head, leaning into Arnold's warmth. "Yes, I'm doing better. The club reopen yet?"

"No. The police need a little more time before I can send in a cleaning crew." He straightened, glancing in the direction of Shiarra's room down the hall. "Did she accept the flowers?"

"Sort of."

"Hmm. Well, I do hope she'll be back on her feet soon. We have some matters to discuss."

Both brows shot up toward my hairline. That didn't sound good. Arnold's grip around my waist tightened, his muscles stiffening. Royce smiled at our reactions, some tension in his frame easing away.

"Don't worry, Ms. Halloway. I don't intend to draw her into my affairs the way I did with you. We simply have some unfinished business," he said, his mild tone at odds with the wicked gleam in his eye. "Speaking of which, I've made the arrangements for the hospital bills, and to ensure all of my people know that your sister is off limits to them. I do hope that is satisfactory."

Relief surged through me, and I might very well have sunk to my knees if Arnold hadn't had his arm around my waist. Janine would be okay. John would stay away from her. It made the whole crazy business worthwhile.

"You have my gratitude, Ms. Halloway, and that of my people. You did a far better job than expected, and I feel I owe you a debt for going above and beyond what was asked of you. Call Angus if you need his services or my connections."

Still weak with relief, being handed that bit of news was too much for me to roll with. I simply nodded and did my best not to gape or stare. Royce turned to Arnold, laughter edging his words.

"If you see him, be sure to tell Jack that Ken was disappointed at his rapid exit. The invitation still stands."

Amusement colored Arnold's response. "I'll do that."

Royce nodded and turned his attention back down the hall to Shiarra's room, clearly dismissing us as he resumed his earlier stance. Though it was unnerving how intently focused he was, I had the feeling he was here out of a sense of obligation. I'd seen him hovering around the halls and waiting rooms in the hospital several times before, but he never actually approached my partner. Whether he was worried about what Shiarra's reaction to his presence might be, or simply felt it best to give her time and distance before seeing her about that "unfinished business," there was an undeniable protective air about his demeanor. No crazed sorcerers, angry werewolves, or rogue vampires would be bothering her with him hanging around, I was sure.

Arnold and I continued past him to the elevators. Once inside and alone, he rubbed my shoulder, bringing my attention off my thoughts about what Royce had said and up to green eyes glinting with mischief.

"Hey, the night is still young. How about that date we were supposed to go on? Just you and me, remember?"

I replied by yanking him into a kiss, stealing his breath as

I pulled him down to meet my lips. A hot, electric tingle raced over the places our skin met, matching the somehow pleasant fire quivering along the runes etched into my arm. When we finally broke apart, I waggled my brows, the two of us grinning foolishly at each other. "Answer enough?"

"Oh, yeah."

MY SOUL TO TAKE

By Clare Willis

Chapter 1

"Oh yeah, and the guy in 148 is possessed." Rashad Simpkins yawned so wide I could count the silver fillings in his molars. His eyes squeezed shut and his forehead wrinkled halfway up his shaved pate. Stubble peppered his almond-hued skin.

"Possessed by what?" I took a sip of my venti mocha as I flipped open the medical chart. It was seven a.m., the start of my shift at the inpatient psychiatric unit at Pacific University Hospital, and the end of Rashad's. He was giving me the overnight report, filling me in on the new admits.

"I don't know, Johnny Depp in *Pirates of the Caribbean?*" He gulped from his aluminum go-cup.

"You mean he sounds like Keith Richards talking through a mouthful of marbles?"

He shook his head. "Not the accent. The look."

Rashad smelled of disinfectant and coffee, but all in all he'd had a good night, judging from the sparse stack of charts in front of me. He might even have gotten a couple of hours of shut-eye.

The nursing station was a beehive of activity, bleary-eyed

nurses and techs on their way out exchanging small talk and official business with their neatly coiffed and fresh-faced replacements. Ambulatory patients in regulation hospital gowns wandered past, some talking to nurses or family members, others conversing with invisible companions. Phones rang, fax machines buzzed. My heart rate ratcheted up as I prepared to leap into the whirl of activity. If this day was going to be like all the others, I would barely have time to pee before the night shift came on again.

I scanned Rashad's notes on the possessed man. It had taken three years of shared residency for me to decipher the chicken scratch he called writing. "He's a suicide attempt? 5150?"

"Yup. Mr. Fielding will be our guest for seventy-two hours of spa treatments and organic gourmet meals. His parents are around here somewhere, by the way."

Between yawns and sips of coffee, Rashad filled me in on the rest of our guests as I flipped through their charts. There was a forty-five-year-old female manic-depressive who'd gone off her meds, and a teenager whose parents had caught her cutting herself when they went into her room to tuck her in. We had a frequent flyer, a homeless man by the name of Slice who wound up either here or in city lockup a couple of times a month. The *Chronicle* had recently reported that Mr. Slice had personally cost the city of San Francisco $150,000 in the past year in hospitalization and ambulance costs. This news had caused a spirited discussion in the break room about the obligations of government to its citizens, which I steadfastly refused to join. Decisions about the rationing of health care were way above my pay grade.

"A good night's work, Rashad," I said. "Now get some rest."

"I will," he replied, popping his pen into the breast pocket of his wrinkled white coat. He smoothed his hands over his shiny head. "I have a date tonight, gotta be fresh."

"Who would date *you?*" I was joking. Rashad was young, handsome, buff, and gay, and this was San Francisco.

"Oh, there's plenty of fish in the sea." Rashad elbowed me in the side. "Even for a shark like you, Maggie. When was the last time you went on a date, by the way?"

Rashad's cool, clinical gaze forced me to assess myself as an impartial observer might. My long brown hair was clean, but it was pulled back into a utilitarian ponytail that emphasized the sharpness of my chin rather than my large hazel eyes and shapely dark eyebrows. Speaking of eyebrows, how long had it been since I'd had them waxed? I rubbed my dry lips together. The only makeup I was wearing was SPF 15 moisturizer. When had I dropped my customary lipstick and mascara? Probably somewhere around the second year of a grueling work schedule that left me so tired I was constantly rubbing my eyes, leaving racoon rings. Makeup was another thing I had decided to put off until I graduated, along with sleeping, buying clothes, and having a decent sex life.

I squared my shoulders and returned Rashad's stare, eye to eye, as we were almost the same height. "I'm busy." I hoisted the charts to emphasize my point. "I'm chief resident, in case you hadn't noticed."

Rashad smiled. "Seriously, Maggie, you need to get laid."

"Amen," said a voice from the nurses' station. I recognized its alto pitch as belonging to Wanda, one of the longest-serving nurses on staff, but she never looked up from her desk or slowed the tapping of her fingers on the keyboard.

"What's that supposed to mean?" I snapped.

Wanda's shoulders lifted in a slight shrug.

"All work and no play makes Jack a dull boy," Rashad said. "Haven't you seen *The Shining?*"

"You bring that up when I'm about to go see a patient who says he's possessed?"

* * *

I read the rest of Mr. Fielding's chart on the way to his room. Rashad had made an initial diagnosis and ordered meds. Derek Fielding was the right age and gender for the onset of schizophrenia, and his clinical presentation was indicative of that diagnosis. The parents, who lived in Oakland, had come to the hospital last night, and Rashad had written up his interview with them. According to the parents, Derek Fielding had no previous psychiatric history. He had the foresight to buy medical insurance. He was a successful folk musician about to go out on tour to support a new album. This suicide attempt was a complete and shocking surprise to them.

I felt a wave of sympathy at the thought of another life lost to the all-consuming wildfire of mental illness, but I pushed the feeling away. After seven years in the medical profession I was getting better at putting my emotions in a box. I always intended to take the box out later, because I knew from clinical experience that pent-up emotions were harmful, but the right time never seemed to come. I had seen so many patients crash and burn that if I paused to mourn them all I would never get anything done. Mr. Fielding didn't need my sympathy; he needed my expertise. I tucked the chart under my arm, spilling coffee on my white coat in the process, and opened the door.

I heard him before I saw him. A tenor voice of unearthly beauty was singing a lullaby, one I knew intimately but hadn't heard in years. In an instant the pale yellow hospital walls fell away, replaced by fading wallpaper adorned with roses and creeping vines. I was in my childhood bedroom, on the second floor of a shotgun house in the Garden District of New Orleans. The window was open to catch any breeze that might blow in to relieve the stultifying August heat. The setting sun tinted the room rose gold, a color I could see even through my closed eyelids.

Lying on my narrow iron bed, with Aloysius the teddy

bear under my chin, I tucked my light cotton nightgown between my sweaty legs to keep them from sticking together.
My sister Eva tossed and turned in her matching bed, trying
to find a cool spot on the sheets. Between us was a rocking
chair, creaking as it moved in time to the lullaby. Mama was
on the last verse, one I rarely heard because I was usually
asleep. But that night it was too hot to sleep, so I listened to
the words, which were beautiful but frightening.

> Hark, a solemn bell is ringing
> Clear through the night
> Thou, my love, art heavenward winging
> Home through the night.

> Earthly dust from off thee shaken
> Soul immortal shalt thou awaken
> With thy last dim journey taken
> Home through the night.

Just as Mama reached the last, trilling note, a bird flew in
the window. It fluttered, confused, near the steeple ceiling of
our attic bedroom. Mama launched into another tune, this
one about *birdeens* singing a fluting song. My sister and I
jumped out of bed. Laughing and tumbling over each other,
the three of us managed to shoo the bird out the window.

The hospital room went silent. Like a pebble dropped in a
pond, I tumbled through my insubstantial memories, back to
the hard ground of reality. I turned eight that summer, and
that night was one of the last times I heard Mama singing.
She died the same year, two days before Christmas.

I pulled the door shut and surveyed the room. The bed
was empty. The heavy old visitor's chair was turned to face
the back wall. Nothing to look at, but that was where he was.

His head drooped onto his chest as if he was asleep. I walked around the chair to face him and felt a tiny shock at seeing his eyes open and staring.

A pale blue hospital gown stretched over his spread knees. The hair that hid his face was beautiful—wavy, shoulder-length locks of light-brown shot through with gold, so shiny you wanted to touch it to see if it was real. Well, someone might want to touch it. Not me, I was a professional. He balanced his arms on his thighs with the palms facing up, protecting the wounds on his wrists. Stark white cotton bandages contrasted with his tanned skin. A tattooed green snake seemed to be escaping out of the left-hand bandage.

He smelled of cigarettes overlaid with an acrid stench. In the acting profession they called it "flop sweat": the cold, drenching perspiration that came on when you went blank on stage or knew your performance was bad. Fielding's odor, which I'd smelled many times in patients having a psychotic break, was also produced by fear, but the patients weren't scared of forgetting lines. Their fear went much deeper than that.

"Mr. Fielding?" I said quietly.

He slowly lifted his head. He had Bambi eyes: chocolate brown, ringed with lashes so thick they looked like eyeliner. His features were delicate: dark, defined eyebrows; narrow, straight nose; a sharp jaw adorned with three days of dark stubble. Rashad was right on the money with the Johnny Depp comparison. On stage, in a bar or an intimate music hall, with a guitar on his lap, Derek Fielding would be irresistible. This of course was simply a clinical observation.

He stared at me for a minute as if he was deciding whether I was worth the effort of speech. Apparently I wasn't, because he stood up and walked away. Mostly to keep my gaze from drifting down to where his hospital gown gaped open at his hips, I focused on a Celtic cross tattoo on his bicep. Which made me wonder what other body parts were tattooed, which didn't help my focus at all.

He sat on the bed and propped up his pillow, wincing as his bandaged wrists brushed the stiff fabric. When he was situated he looked at me again. His expression was calm, but his eyes glinted with unshed tears. A muscle twitched in his jaw.

"Do you have a cigarette?" he asked.

"You can't smoke in here, I'm afraid."

"I don't smoke."

"Okay, then. I'm Dr. Dillon, the chief resident here." I didn't offer my hand, knowing that even light pressure might cause pain to his wounds. I imagined his wrists under the bandages—the guy had more stitches than a patchwork quilt. He had lost two liters of blood, according to his chart. This was no "cry for help." Derek Fielding had meant business.

"You have a beautiful voice," I said.

He looked away.

"Can you tell me what happened last night?"

Fielding began singing again, this time very quietly. I looked at his hands, which were tapping the sheet in intricate rhythms. His fingers were slender and delicately tapered. The nails on his right hand were long, filed into neat ovals, while those on his left were short and square. Guitar-playing hands.

Some people say music transports them, but the only time it had happened to me was when my mother sang. I could feel it happening again as I listened to Derek Fielding. It was like an angel was singing just for me. The song contained everything I'd ever known and done, and all I could and would be in the future.

Even though one part of my mind screamed that it was completely against protocol, I sat down on the bed. I needed to be close to his mouth so that I could hear the words. Now I noticed his eyes had a golden ring around the pupil that glowed like fire.

Derek lifted a bandaged hand and stroked my cheek, still singing that siren song. When his lips were an inch from mine he stopped, but I didn't. In a moment we were kissing. It was the most passionate kiss I'd ever had. I lost myself in the sensation of soft and hard—the firm, insistent pressure of his lips opening mine, the velvet texture of his tongue, the grassy odor of his breath . . .

When I opened my eyes I was still standing against the wall. Derek was three feet away from me in the bed. I heaved a deep sigh of relief. My job was still intact.

I often told my patients in therapy that any fantasy was fine, the only thing they needed to control were their actions in the real world. I told myself that now, but somehow it didn't help. My fantasy had been so vivid that it left me damp and trembling. My legs were shaking so hard I had to press my hands against the wall to keep from slipping to the floor.

This is not helping your patient.

I sat down and opened the chart, clicking my pen several times to remind myself what I was doing there.

"Mr. Fielding, do you know where you are right now?"

"Hell."

Hmm, not the answer I was looking for.

"Can you tell me what day it is?"

"I think it's Friday, but it doesn't matter." He turned to me, his eyes wide and glassy. "Who did you say you are?"

"I'm Dr. Dillon. I'm going to help you."

He smiled, but in an off-kilter way that set my nerves jangling. "You can't help me. He's trying to take over my body."

"Who's trying to take over your body?" I imagined the answer would be the devil, given that Fielding seemed to be having religious delusions.

"Edgar." The muscle in his jaw twitched faster as his fingers danced over the sheet. "When he does it, I'm still there, but I can't control my body. He wants to kill people; wants *me* to kill people. But I won't do it." His head pulled away as if someone had grabbed his chin.

"I'll kill myself first," he muttered. His head jerked back toward me.

"Was it, um, *Edgar,* who tried to kill himself?"

He shook his head impatiently. "No, I was trying to kill Edgar."

"But Edgar was in your body?"

"Yes." The smell of sweat filled my nostrils. Moisture stippled his forehead. This conversation was making Derek Fielding very nervous.

"You've got to help me, Doctor. You're an expert in these things, right? You can make him go away."

"Well, first let's focus on making you comfortable and more secure. Then we'll see what we can do about making Edgar go away."

I looked at the file to check what medications Rashad had prescribed.

"Tell him the truth, Maggie. You can't make me go away."

There was a sudden chill in the air, as if someone had just opened a refrigerator door, but nothing had changed in the room, so the chill had to be coming from inside me. I kept my head down while I processed what was happening. Derek's voice had changed radically. Instead of his normal soft tenor voice, this new voice was low and raspy, originating deep inside his chest. But there was something else that was turning my skin clammy. He had called me Maggie, when he had no way of knowing my first name. My nametag had only my surname on it, not even a first initial.

Well, surely there was a reasonable explanation. He had overheard one of the other doctors or nurses talking about me. I arranged my face into a mask of calm and looked up.

"So they're letting broads be doctors now, are they?"

The new voice even had an accent that wasn't Derek's. It was nasal, with hard consonants, maybe from the East Coast. This wasn't an average case of schizophrenia, not if Derek was sharing his body with other personalities. This was looking more like dissociative identity disorder. It was a rare and controversial diagnosis, even after the name was changed from multiple personality disorder to the more conciliatory DID, and I was going to catch flak from some of the more conservative doctors on staff for even suggesting it. But in the face of this kind of transformation, it seemed self-evident.

"Is that you, Derek?" I asked.

The smile he gave me made my stomach lurch. It was patently false, a twisted, angry leer.

"What do *you* think, Maggie?"

"Okay, are you Edgar?"

The smile widened. "At your service."

Derek was doing a remarkable job of looking and moving like someone else, and I was both fascinated and repulsed. I'd never seen a real case of DID, and I was impressed by how thorough the transformation was. His fingers had stopped tapping. Instead they lay curled into loose fists in his lap. When he saw me looking at them he cracked a knuckle so loudly I winced.

"Are there others that you know of, Edgar, besides you and Derek?"

He made a noise I could only describe as a cackle. "You're on the wrong track, girly."

"Why don't you put me on the right track?" I smiled, although I knew my own attempt was as false as Edgar's.

The eyes grew even narrower, until they were barely slits. "I think you can figure it out, Maggie. You're a smart cookie, you understand these things. Even though you've tried to block it out with all this"—he waved a hand to take in the hospital room—"you know what's really going on here, don't you?"

He swung his legs over the side of the bed, lurched forward, and grabbed my hand. His fingers were freezing. Our eyes locked. I felt something so horrible that it froze every muscle in my body. I was deeply, truly frightened of this person, whoever he was.

Derek suddenly closed his eyes. His face twisted, contorted, and then relaxed. When he opened his eyes he was Derek again. He released my hand. The fear rushed out of me like air from a popped balloon, leaving my body prickling with adrenaline.

"I'm sorry, Doctor, that you had to see that. I hope he didn't frighten you too much."

I blinked hard a couple of times. "No, it's fine. You don't have to apologize. And you, I mean he, didn't frighten me."

I shifted uncomfortably in my chair, the lie sitting between us like a big pink elephant.

"He knows everything. He can see into your soul."

Out of my peripheral vision I saw Derek's fingers begin anew their intricate dance across the sheets, and I felt immense relief.

I stood up, trying to control my shaky legs. "Well, I've got to go now, Mr. Fielding. I'll check in on you later."

Chapter 2

The consultation room had a lovely view of the Golden Gate Bridge, but Derek's parents weren't seeing it, nor were they looking at me. Neil stared at the floor with a glazed expression on his narrow, sharp-featured face. Drina focused on the iPhone in her lap. She was close enough to me that I could see the screen. It held a photo of Derek in better days, standing with a guitar against a backdrop of trees and blue sky.

"He could have been rich by now," Drina was saying, "if he'd taken that recording contract with Atlantic."

Of the two of them, Drina looked the most like Derek. She had the same slender, feline grace, the golden undertone in her skin, and the doe eyes. He got his height from his father, however. Drina's head barely reached my shoulder.

"He wanted to stay independent. You know he's always been that way, Drina." Neil looked at me, seeking approval. "He refused to be a sellout, as he called it. He was going to do it his own way. And he did. He's got his own label, does his own distribution. He has his own recording studio, which he rents out to other musicians." He chewed his lip. "Or he did, until it burned down."

"That's when the symptoms started, when his studio burned down?" I asked, folding my empty hands. I never took notes during a therapy session, since I had an excellent memory.

"He barely got out alive. It was an old building and it went up like a box of matches," Neil said.

"Was he injured?"

"Smoke inhalation. He couldn't sing for three months." He winced at the memory. "He lived with us for a couple of months. He seemed okay. He was busy with the insurance, trying to replace everything, and finding a new place to live."

"Yes, it wasn't until he moved to that place, *il castello*." When Drina switched to Italian, her hands gestured expressively.

Neil sighed impatiently. "Let's not get melodramatic, Drina."

She snorted. "Always the scientist."

Time to redirect. "But you agree, Neil, his symptoms began when he moved to this new house?"

He nodded. "He found it on Craig's List; they were advertising for a caretaker. The place is a real castle, made of huge stones, with two towers, crenellations, the whole nine yards. It has a throne in the living room, I kid you not." He shook his head, causing his wispy, white-blond hair to flap like wings.

Drina twisted her engagement and wedding rings around her slender finger. "There's a *malumore* there." She shivered.

Neil clenched his jaw.

"What does *malumore* mean, Drina?" I asked, mangling the pronunciation.

Her eyebrows knit. "It means a bad feeling. A bad spirit. You understand?"

As I looked into Drina's brown eyes, so similar to Derek's, I shivered, just as she was doing. I hadn't been able to get warm ever since I left Derek's room, even though I'd gone to the staff room and put on an extra sweater under my white coat. Much as I hated to admit it, I knew exactly what Drina was talking about.

After they left I placed a call to Dr. Frederick Kay, the chief of psychiatry. He didn't answer his phone, so I left a message. I was back in the nurses' station talking to a social worker about Mr. Slice, the homeless man, when he called me back. The social worker was used to these interruptions. She turned to her paperwork while I took the call.

"What's up, Mags?" He was driving his BMW convertible with the top down, judging from the sounds of wind and engine. I pictured him on the Golden Gate Bridge with his second wife, Trisha, her blond hair whipping around her face, as they headed to their waterfront estate on Belvedere Island. It was an enviable life, but not one I was destined for, although we shared the same profession. Dr. Kay had been on the cutting edge of research on serotonin uptake inhibitors, and when Prozac was approved by the FDA in 1987, Kay cashed in on a heavy investment in Eli Lilly stock.

"It's about a patient, Derek Fielding. Thirty-two-year-old white male, admitted last night after a suicide attempt."

"What's the differential diagnosis?"

"Rashad admitted him, diagnosed him as schizophrenic, but I think it's DID."

"Are you sure you want to go there?" Dr. Kay asked. "DID is quite a can of worms, diagnostically speaking. Did the patient display other personalities?"

"Yes, one other."

"That's very interesting. So, what are you recommending for treatment, Mags?"

I pulled my long brown hair out of its coated rubber band and twisted a lock around my finger. It was an old habit I indulged only when I was really stressed. "Actually, I'd like you to take his case, Dr. Kay. If you're not too busy."

Dr. Kay saw very few patients at this point in his career, and only those who presented with unusual symptoms or who might be good candidates for drug trials or studies that he was running. Derek Fielding was none of those things, so I needed a damn good reason to turf him. The truth, that Derek Fielding had unsettled me, both as a woman and as a doctor, was not only a bad reason, it was a dangerous one.

"Why do I need to take this case? And talk fast, I'm heading into a tunnel."

Playing to a superior's vanity was a gambit that often met with success in the medical field. It probably worked in the rest of the world, as well.

"I have a feeling that his case is going to be particularly complex and delicate. I think the patient requires a doctor with your level of expertise."

His phone crackled.

"What did you say?" I asked. There was more crackling. I waited, tapping my foot and signing a couple of discharge reports the social worker slid under my pen.

Kay came back on the line. ". . . need to interview, but don't worry. I'm going to put in a good word for you with Edelstein."

I pressed the phone harder against my ear. "Hold on, we got cut off. What were you talking about?"

"The staff position."

"What staff position?"

"You didn't hear me? I said that Dr. Carlyle is retiring next year and there's going to be an opening in the department. I'm going to recommend you as his replacement."

I knew Kay favored me, it was why I was chief resident, but I had never imagined staying at Pacific University Hospital for my whole career. Positions came up so infrequently that almost no one who graduated from the program continued on. Most had to leave San Francisco to find work. I was immensely flattered, so I tamped down the secondary feeling of anxiety that fluttered up from my stomach into my throat.

"I don't know what to say. I'm honored."

"Say thank you, and make an appointment with my secretary for an interview with the committee."

"Thank you, I'll do that. And did you say you would take Derek Fielding's case?"

"Yes, I'll take him, but no more favors, Mags. You may be my heir apparent, but I'm not the fucking Genie of the Lamp."

I couldn't think of anything I'd ever asked him for before, but I certainly wasn't going to contradict him. Doctors like Kay—in practice for years, at the top of their profession—weren't average human beings anymore. They were icons, high priests whose every pronouncement was accepted as gospel. Some of them handled this responsibility with humility and intelligence. Some of them believed the hype.

"Thanks, Dr. Kay."

The line crackled again and went dead.

"What do you mean he didn't show up?" I crossed the nursing station to peer into Derek's chart.

Wanda gazed at me over her shoulder, her plump, wrinkled face managing to be impassive and scornful at the same time. "I mean he didn't show up for his appointment with Dr. Kay. It happens, Dr. Dillon."

For the rest of Derek's seventy-two-hour hold I'd kept my distance, allowing only the occasional glance through the window of his hospital room to assure myself that he was all right. And every time I looked at him the same things happened: My heart lurched in my chest, my palms got sweaty, and I felt like a seventh grader suffering through her first crush. I also felt frightened. All reasons to keep away from him, but still my hand reached out for Derek's chart. Wanda happily handed it over.

I scanned the notes, written in several different hands. "Did a social worker visit him?"

"He's on the schedule, but you know how overbooked they are. But this guy's got parents, a support system. He'll be all right." Wanda snapped open another folder and turned away, clearly finished with our discussion.

I committed Neil Fielding's cell number to my short-term memory and found an empty consultation room where I could make a private phone call. He answered after the second ring.

"Hi, this is Dr. Dillon, from Pacific University Hospital. I'm calling to follow up on Derek."

"Oh, thank goodness you called. I was worried no one was going to call me back."

My stomach seized up at the anxiety in his voice. "What happened?"

"Derek insisted that we take him back to the castle when he was released. He opened the door, turned around, and told us to go home. He said he'd be in touch when he was done."

"Done with what?"

"I have no idea. But he won't answer the phone now. We drove over there and he didn't answer the door either. I'm worried about him, Dr. Dillon."

"Did you call the police? He was on suicide watch; they should be notified."

"I did. They sent a patrol car out. He talked to them. They told me he seemed stable and that was all they could do."

"Did you talk to Dr. Kay?"

Neil sighed. "He said to call the police."

"Okay, I'll see what I can do."

After I hung up the phone I sat for a few minutes, twisting my hair. When my mother "took sick," as the family called her depression, at first we had either ignored it or made crass attempts to cheer her up. She had always been prone to moodiness, and this just seemed a particularly bad patch. But when she stopped eating and then stopped getting out of bed, our father and assorted relatives all began to try to help. Mama was in and out of the hospital for months. Then came the terrible day I arrived home from school and found Eva on the front steps, crying like her world had broken in half, which of course it had.

I think my sister Eva and I both went into our chosen professions because of Mama. We were too late to help her, but we thought maybe we could help others so that their families wouldn't have to suffer like ours. Although we approached it from entirely different angles, we shared the same purpose, to ease the mental suffering of our fellow human beings.

That was all I was doing, I told myself. Just helping a fellow human being who was suffering. The fact that this particular human had a voice so beautiful it seemed capable of shifting time and space, and that he was so attractive he was causing fantasies that felt as real as anything in my current life, well, these were just feelings, easily managed with a strong dose of reason. And I was only being reasonable when my shift ended and I took a minute to apply mascara and lipstick and brush out my hair before I pointed my Honda Civic toward the address in Pacifica that had been noted in Derek's chart.

Chapter 3

The massive wooden door was covered with iron buckles and buttons, but none of them appeared to be a knocker or a doorbell. Finally I found a button, not on the door itself, but tucked into the mortar between two stones. After pushing it I stepped back and took in a full view of the castle. It was one of the most forbidding places I'd ever seen. Three stories of rough stones set in mortar, topped by towers and crenellations that wouldn't have looked out of place on top of a German or Irish mountain. There were no windows, except for the narrow arrow slits in the towers. There was no moat, but a high stone wall surrounded a yard filled with dead trees and shrubbery. Set in the center of a neighborhood of 1950s ranch-style houses, the place couldn't have been more incongruous.

The door opened with a long, resistant creak. My heart pounded at the sight of Derek Fielding. He was still as attractive as before, but he looked exhausted to the point of dropping. I wondered how long it had been since he'd had a decent night's sleep. He held the door open, but looked past me down the path, as if checking to make sure I'd come alone.

"Dr. Dillon," he said. "This is a surprise." He met my eyes and gave me a tentative smile. "To what do I owe the pleasure?"

"You never followed up with Dr. Kay."

He raised his eyebrows. "Do you make house calls for all your patients?"

I smiled through my nervousness. "Only the ones who can sing."

He stood still, staring at me with a strange look on his face.

"Can I come in?"

"Well, I . . . ," He looked back into the house.

"Oh, do you have company?" I'd never thought about whether he had a girlfriend, but surely someone as handsome as him would have one. I stepped back from the doorstep.

He laughed, just a tiny bit. "You might say that. But not the kind you're thinking of." He opened the door wider. "Please come in."

I stepped inside and touched his arm, trying to ignore the tingle I felt when my hand contacted his silken skin. "Your parents are worried about you."

Before I could move my hand he laid his own on top of it. "And you? Are you worried, Dr. Dillon?"

"I'm not your doctor anymore, so please call me Maggie. And yes, I was worried. That's why I'm here."

I followed him through the dim, oak-paneled foyer to a cavernous rectangular room, mostly empty. It bore a striking resemblance to the Hall of Mirrors at Versailles. Arched windows on the ocean side were reflected in arched mirrors on the opposite wall. The coved ceiling was adorned with paintings, crisscrossed with gold molding, culminating in busts of maidens at the corners. Crystal chandeliers hung at three-foot intervals. It was a rococo monstrosity, built by a person with more money than taste.

An oil painting hung over the gilt and marble fireplace. Although it was in a seventeenth-century style gilt frame, the subject was a man from the early twentieth century. He wore a suit and a thin red tie, and had slicked-back dark hair, heavy brows, and a broad, bulbous nose. But he was handsome, and the smile on his face was wide and jovial. The painting had a generic quality, like the photos that are already in a frame when you buy it: a happy couple, a kid with a dog.

"Is that the guy who built the house?" I asked.

"Yeah, but he doesn't really look like that."

I thought of asking how Derek knew that, but then decided to let it go for now.

The only things that obviously belonged to Derek were three guitars, hanging in racks next to a dais. On the dais was an oversized gilt and velvet chair. From its height the sitter could view the city of Pacifica and the ocean that gave it its name, both on the ocean side and multiplied hundreds of times in the mirrors.

I walked over to the guitars. "Which one is your favorite?" I asked.

His eyes lit up. "That one in the middle. It's a 1954 Gibson Les Paul." He pointed to an electric guitar with a fin on the side and four gold buttons. The varnish on it was metallic gold, but darkened and burnished with age to a deep honey color.

"Will you play something for me?" I asked.

When he put the strap over his shoulder I noticed his guitar was singed under the strings and gave off a faint smell of melted glue. I remembered the fire in Derek's studio and wondered what else had been damaged or destroyed.

Derek perched on the edge of the dais and plugged the guitar into an amp. He stretched his fingers across the strings, wincing as the tendons in his wrists put tension on his stitches. I started to tell him that he didn't need to play, but then he began and I forgot everything but the music.

He played a blues tune, something so heartfelt and resonant that it brought tears to my eyes. His face was even more beautiful when he played. I sat down on the floor near him, closed my eyes, and let the music wash over me. He finished one song and moved seamlessly into another.

But then something started to go wrong. He played a sour note, recovered, and then faltered again. More wrong notes dropped in, discordant and painful to the ear. His expression turned from joy to confusion to dismay. Finally he stopped. His head dropped until his forehead touched the guitar.

"What happened?" I asked.

Derek lifted his head. Fear seized my body, turning my guts to liquid. He began to change before my eyes, all the features slowly sifting, as if his face was made of sand instead of flesh. His eyebrows drifted low onto a ridged Neanderthal forehead. His eyes darkened by several shades. He smiled, but the expression was sardonic and malevolent. I squeezed my eyes shut, but when I opened them again, the changes were still happening.

"I don't know how to play the guitar." Derek's breath was fogging up, as if he'd walked outside into a cold day. The puff of vaporized breath continued to grow, turning into a white mist that wreathed his head. I shivered from the sudden chill in the air.

It was almost unbearable to look at him, but I forced myself to keep my eyes steady, my face calm. "What's your name?" I asked.

He threw his head back and laughed. His movements were jerky and stiff, while Derek's were smooth and graceful.

"I'm a figment of his imagination, is that what you believe? Hah! I'm as real as you are, girly. You think the drugs you gave him will drive me away? Derek could be as doped up as a shanghaied sailor and I'd still be here. It's only a matter of time. Every time I take him over it's harder for him to come back. Eventually he just won't." He looked down at the guitar in his lap.

"I think while I'm here . . ." He stood up, grabbed the guitar by the neck and swung it over his shoulder like a giant hammer.

"No!" I ran over and grabbed the guitar, just as it began its downward arc.

We struggled. The guitar was pulled out of my hands. Again, he lifted it high and swung it toward the floor. I closed my eyes and held out my arms, bracing for the pain that was coming.

Nothing happened. I looked up to see Derek cradling the Gibson like a baby. Tears ran down his face as he placed it gently in the stand. As quickly as it had come on, the episode that Derek had just experienced was over.

"Derek?" I reached for him, but grabbed air instead.

"No! I'll kill you first. I'll kill both of us if I have to!" Derek was running for the fireplace. He leaped and grabbed the painting off the wall.

A hoarse, wordless cry came from deep inside his body as he smashed his heavy boot into Edgar's face. Over and over he pounded the painting. When the ornate gilt frame split into pieces he picked one up and used it to tear the canvas and break up the stretchers and remaining pieces of frame. I stood nearby, helpless in the face of his hysteria.

All at once Derek stopped kicking the painting. "Do you hear that?" he cried out. "He's laughing at me."

He pressed his palms against his ears. "Stop it!" he screamed.

I gasped as bright red blood seeped through the bandages

on his wrists. "Derek, you've got to stop." I grabbed his hands and pressed them down gently but firmly. He finally looked at me, his eyes wild and desperate.

"Maggie, help me. Oh, God, help me." He collapsed onto my shoulder. I held him tightly while his body shuddered helplessly.

"Derek," I spoke quietly into his ear, "you've got to go see Dr. Kay."

He moved his head back so he could look at me. His expression was bitter and sad. "You don't believe me. You don't believe this is real."

I stroked his arm. "Of course it's real."

He moved quickly out of my reach, his arms crossed protectively over his chest. "Don't twist my words. You know what I mean."

I looked away so I didn't have to meet his piercing gaze. "I know what you mean."

He grabbed my chin and forced me to look at him. His breath smelled of cigarettes, which was odd, since I hadn't seen him smoke. "So, is it real or isn't it? Because if you just think I'm crazy then we have nothing more to say to each other."

He held my chin, lightly but firmly. I would have given anything at that moment not to have to answer him.

"It's real, Derek, it's as real as anything I've seen. If you want to get into some existential philosophy about what reality is, that's up to you. What's important is that I believe, just like you do, that this thing will kill you."

He let go of my chin and dropped his forehead to my shoulder.

"I'll go see Dr. Kay," he said.

I stroked his hair and then cupped the back of his head in my hand. His breath smelled of cigarettes, but his hair smelled like a hippie commune—sandalwood and warm

spices, like cloves and cinnamon. I took a long whiff and let
my lips rest against his smooth neck, just for a moment.

I lay sprawled on the couch in the tidy, some might say
sparse, living room of my flat above a veterinary hospital on
Seventh Avenue. I'd come home at eight p.m. after a nonstop
shift where everything was moving so fast it started to seem
slow. It was almost to the full moon, and although none of us
would admit it to anyone outside of the profession, that's
when the crazies came out. I'd taken a shower and put on my
favorite pajamas, made of T-shirt material with cats on
them. I climbed into bed but sleep wouldn't come, so now I
was staring at the TV.

My mind kept drifting back to Derek Fielding, as it had
more or less every twenty minutes since I'd left him the day
before. Even the half-naked man who came in screaming that
aliens had stolen his invention (an artificial bladder) out of
his backpack couldn't keep my thoughts from eventually cir-
cling back to Derek. I'd told him to call me if it was an emergency, but otherwise to make an appointment with Dr. Kay
for today and I'd see him tomorrow, which was my day off.

My favorite hospital drama was on TiVo, but I'd had to re-
play the same scene three times. It was a scene where my favorite dreamy doctor was making love to his current intern
during an earthquake. If I couldn't concentrate on that, I
couldn't concentrate on anything. I clicked the TV off and
went to the kitchen for a snack. My refrigerator contained
only beer, mustard, pickles, and a half-full container of cake
frosting, which I ate with a spoon after particularly difficult
shifts at the hospital. I chose alcohol instead of sugar and
popped the cap off a beer as I walked to my bedroom. My
dirty clothes lay in piles as high as a Maine snowdrift. If I
couldn't sleep or watch TV I could at least get a load of laundry started.

With my arms full of clothes, I stopped in front of the long staircase down to my front door. Someone was tapping insistently on the glass. I went downstairs and pulled the curtain, only to meet the wide, dark eyes of Derek Fielding. I opened the door a crack.

"How did you find me?" I asked. Vestigial self-protectiveness born of years of psychiatric training had kept me from giving him my address, and I was more than unlisted. All the doctors at Pacific University kept their home addresses and phone numbers locked up like Fort Knox.

He shrugged. "I just got in the car, and I knew your address."

"You just *knew* it?"

Derek grabbed the door frame. "He knows things about people, and when he's inside me I know them too. Like he knew your name."

I was speechless.

"Can I come in?" His wavy hair standing up in wild tufts, as if he'd been pulling on it. Tricholtillomania, my clinical mind said, before I told it to shut up.

"Well," I said hesitantly. Conflicting emotions staged a full-scale war in my body, concentrating in my stomach and chest.

Derek's long eyelashes fluttered as he slowly blinked. "Don't worry," he said quietly, "he won't hurt you. He likes you. It's me he wants to get rid of."

I opened the door. Derek had a guitar in a bag strapped to his back. His eyes were wet and bloodshot, as if he'd been crying. I resisted the urge to pull him into my arms and comfort him, instead ushering him ahead of me up the stairs.

Derek ignored my offer to sit. He leaned his guitar against the wall and hugged the window overlooking Seventh Avenue, staring down as if he'd never seen sushi restaurants and liquor stores before. I deliberately chose the couch instead of the armchair, sitting cross-legged so I wouldn't look like a shrink.

After a minute or two Derek turned to me. He gave me a small, pained smile. "You look terrible," he said. "Are you all right?"

Well, I guess I could give him points for honesty. "I had a rough day at the hospital, that's all."

"Hmm. I bet you have a lot of those. Have you eaten?"

I shook my head.

"Want to go out?" He glanced at my pajamas. "Why don't I cook us something?"

"You cook?"

"Pretty well, in fact. My mom made sure of that. Where's your kitchen?"

I pointed. "It's back there, but there isn't much to work with."

"Oh, I can work miracles." I followed him down the hall, trying not to stare, but his well-worn T-shirt did nothing to hide the way his sinewy back muscles flexed as he walked. The snake tattoo undulated across his gleaming skin before diving under the bandage on his wrist.

He opened my refrigerator, glanced at the contents, and closed it again. He turned to me and raised his eyebrows. "How do you survive?"

"Coffee and Clif bars."

He pushed his gold-flecked hair behind his ears. "Where's the closest grocery store?"

Twenty minutes later I was sitting at the tiny table in my kitchen watching a culinary miracle. From one pot and a dented frying pan, Derek had conjured fresh fettuccini and a sauce called *sugo alla puttanesca,* an Italian name he refused to translate. Steam rose from the stove along with a heavenly spicy tomato aroma. I sipped a fruity Zinfandel

while he sprinkled chopped basil over slices of fresh moz-
zarella and tomatoes on top of grilled ciabatta bread.

"Do you have any plates?" he asked.

"Of course!" I glanced sheepishly into the sink. "I'll need
to wash them, though."

When the plates were clean, Derek ladled out saucy ribbons of pasta for both of us, topped with a light grating of
fresh Parmesan cheese. For a few minutes silence reigned as
we shoveled food into our mouths.

"This is really delicious," I said.

He winked at me. "You sound surprised."

"I haven't met too many men who can cook."

"Do you have a boyfriend, Maggie?" he asked.

I shook my head, looking down at my plate. "No."

"Why is a beautiful, accomplished woman like you not
taken?"

A warm flush overpowered my normally pale cheeks. "I
could say I'm too busy, but that doesn't begin to cover it. The
job I do, it taps you out: mentally, physically, and emotionally. I just don't have the energy for a commitment."

The intensity of his gaze did nothing to ease my embar-
rassment. "Maggie, a job should fuel you, not tap you out."

A jolt of righteous anger shot through me. "That's easy
for you to say."

"What do you mean?"

"You're a singer. What you do is not exactly life and
death."

Now it was his turn to blush. Chagrined, I encircled his
wrist just above the bandage. "I'm sorry. I didn't mean it like
that."

He shrugged and placed his hand on top of mine. "You're
right. What's going on now is the first life-and-death thing
I've ever dealt with."

I pushed my plate away. "Why don't we go into the living
room?"

* * *

"Remember that song you were singing at the hospital, Derek? It's an Irish lullaby, right?" I'd never learned the name, I realized, even though my mother had sung it dozens of times. I hummed a few bars.

He nodded. He was perched on the edge of the armchair while I was back on the couch. He looked as anxious as he had when he arrived at the door, but he smiled through it. "Yes, I love that song. It's from an album of Irish lullabies I did a few years ago. It sold about six copies."

I perked up. "I bought an album of Irish lullabies about three years ago. It was called *Home through the Night.*"

"That's it. Only five more copies to account for," he said drily, but I saw a tiny hint of a smile.

"But I don't remember your name being on it." I thought for a moment. "It was by the Fieldstone Brothers."

"It was a combination of our names—Derek Fielding and Eric Stone, a friend of mine. We just did the one project together."

"That was a great album. I wished I could have given it to my mother."

"Why didn't you?"

My eyelids were suddenly heavy with the weight of tears. "She died when I was eight. Killed herself."

"Oh. I'm sorry." Derek folded his arms as if he was trying to hide his bandages from me.

"My mother used to sing that song to me when I was a little girl."

He smiled ruefully. "Not mine, I'm afraid. Drina's not much of a singer."

"Have you been playing much music yourself?" I asked, pointing to the guitar.

All pleasure washed out of his face, leaving the same blank misery I'd seen in the hospital. "I still can't play anything. Not since you were at my house."

"Have you been taking your medication?"

"Yes, Maggie. I'm taking the pills."

"Have you had any more, um, visits from Edgar?"

He shook his head.

"Well, that's good. Now, this thing with the music, it must be some kind of temporary aphasia brought on by stress. I'm sure if you give it time it will fix itself."

He looked at that moment as if he pitied my sad, closed mind. "No, Maggie, Edgar did something to me. It's like he wiped that part of my brain clean."

"So why did you bring your guitar with you tonight?"

"I thought maybe here, with you, something might come back to me. I loved the way your face looked when I was playing."

"Well, give it a try," I said, patting the sofa cushion next to me.

He sat next to me with the acoustic guitar on his lap, nervously chewing his lower lip and running his fingers across the strings. A couple of times he looked up at me, and I smiled, projecting encouragement. He strummed the guitar. A few discordant notes echoed through the room, sounding like a cat had run over the strings.

"It's okay," I said. "Maybe you should stop for now. . . ."

The guitar skittered across the hardwood floor until it stopped at the opposite wall.

"I can't do it! The most important thing in the world to me, and the bastard took it." He dropped his head into his hands, his shoulders convulsing with silent sobs.

Normally I considered the consequences before I took any action, however small. It often took me five minutes to decide between nonfat and 1 percent milk. But I didn't think at all before putting my arms around Derek. He returned my embrace, pulling me so tight my breasts were squeezed against his slender, muscular frame. His long, curly hair, smelling of cloves and sandalwood, tickled my cheek. He pressed his lips against my neck. His breath was warm and damp. My heart was so loud it echoed in my head, and I could feel Derek's heartbeat pounding equally wildly against my chest.

Then we were kissing, and it was just like my fantasy at the hospital. He kissed me like it was the last kiss he'd ever have. His tongue probed deeply as my own glided over the slick polish of his teeth, then they entwined, first softly, then with eager pressure. He encircled my neck and pulled my hair free from its band while the other hand lit fires over every inch of my skin.

I pulled back, suddenly frightened of what we were doing, of how important it felt. When he sensed my hesitation he kissed me harder. With one hand lost in my hair and the other under my pajama top, he deftly flipped me onto my back and pressed me into the couch. He positioned himself so that our bodies met at every point that ignited heat, and he savaged my neck and chest with licks, kisses, and nips.

The hard length of him, studded by the buttons of his jeans, ground against me through the thin cotton of my pajamas. The intense pleasure was tinged with pain, but when he lifted himself off me I was desperate to make him keep going. I grabbed his hips to try to move him back. Instead he slid his cool hand into the waistband of my pajamas, stroking tiny circles on my abdomen before continuing downward. My thighs tightened in anticipation as his hand slipped under my panties and between my legs.

Nothing else existed but his fingers as they glided over my damp and yearning flesh. My breath caught raggedly in my throat as he tortured me with hovering, feather-light touches. When my hips jerked upward, slamming against him, he groaned again, and then dived deeply into me. His talented fingers played me with strength and dexterity. Gasping with pleasure, on the edge of release, I opened my eyes. I wanted to see his face, to reassure myself that he was enjoying himself as much as I was. But when I looked up everything that was moving in me slammed to a halt. My blood stopped flowing, my heart ceased beating, the joy I was about to express died in my throat.

The face I was looking at wasn't Derek's.

Chapter 4

As adrenaline flooded my body, all I could think of was how to escape. I tried to slide out from under him but the weight of his body, seconds earlier a pleasure, was now a trap. I pushed at his shoulders but his body felt like it was made of iron. Desperate, I freed one leg and kneed him in the groin. He curled into a ball, grunting softly. I scrabbled with my socked feet, flailing for purchase against the slick leather sofa. Finally I was able to push him enough that I could roll onto the floor. I crawled across the room and huddled against the wall, clutching my knees, panting raggedly.

In a minute or two the person who was no longer Derek recovered from his injury and sat up. With jerky movements that were the opposite of Derek's feline grace, he adjusted a nonexistent collar on the neck band of his T-shirt. He balanced his right ankle on his left knee and stroked his chin while he observed my shivering, clenched-up body. A thin white mist surrounded his head and shoulders, and more vapor emerged from his mouth each time the creature breathed.

The face I'd seen at the castle was strange and different, but I could see some of Derek in it. Now he was completely transformed. The lips were thicker, while the chin was more pointed. Derek's delicate straight nose had become broad and cauliflower-shaped, like a career boxer's. His chocolate-brown eyes were now shiny and black, with the iridescent glimmer of an oil slick. And the expression on this unfamiliar face! The evil, malicious countenance made a mockery of the human smile. It was as if someone had cut a U-shaped gash in Derek's face and pulled the sides of his mouth up with hooks.

I blinked several times, trying to clear my vision. My mind was playing tricks on me. Guilt over kissing a patient, even a former patient, was taking the handsome features of Derek Fielding and distorting them into something repugnant. But once I acknowledged this and understood it my sight should have returned to normal. Well, then, why wasn't that happening?

"What's wrong, Maggie? I thought you were enjoying yourself. It felt like you were enjoying yourself." The person I couldn't call Derek wagged his heavy eyebrows lasciviously.

"Do you have a last name?" My voice came out as a mousy squeak. Dissociative identity disorder, my clinical mind said, but the primitive, animal part of my brain recoiled in horror, trusting only the evidence of my eyes.

"Edgar Templeton, at your service." Speaking in the same raspy, cigarette-scorched voice I'd heard in the hospital, he touched his hand to his waist and bowed slightly. It was an incongruous, courtly gesture, completely at odds with the scornful smile on his face.

I scanned the room for anything that could be used as a weapon. Unfortunately my spare, bachelorette pad apartment was severely lacking in brass candlesticks and loose hammers. I eyed a heavy biology textbook that had been gathering dust on the floor.

"Do you know Derek Fielding, Mr. Templeton?" I asked,

as my fingers clamped onto the book and slowly pulled it close.

The iridescent sheen on his black eyes shifted as he followed my movements. At first he had appeared to have no pupils, but now I could discern an area of darker black in the center, shaped like a long, pointed oval. He had the eyes of a lizard.

"You find him handsome, don't you, Maggie?"

I struggled to keep my face neutral. Inside I was longing to scream and babble like a two-year-old, but only my rational mind could help Derek and me now. Growing up in New Orleans, I'd been fed the typical diet of ghost stories. Calamitous events always followed ghost sightings. A man cut off his feet to escape a ghost who had dropped a coffin on them, a woman jumped off a bridge because a ghost in a car was driving toward her. It wasn't the ghosts that killed them; it was their own stupidity. I told myself all through my childhood that if I ever saw a ghost I'd stay calm and ask them the location of Mama's lost wedding ring.

"I'll ask the questions, and call me Dr. Dillon."

He inclined his head in acquiescence. "As you wish. But I would appreciate it if you would call me Edgar. After all, we should be on a first-name basis, don't you think, after what we've shared?"

"When were you born, Mr. Templeton?"

He patted the left side of his T-shirt, as if searching a coat pocket. "Do you have a cigar?"

I shook my head.

"Cigarette?"

"No."

"Too bad. That stupid bastard doesn't smoke either. I buy them, he throws them out." He sighed. "Where were we? I was born in 1895, right here in San Francisco. Barbary Coast, you know it? I built the castle in 1925. I made a lot of money in those years."

"And now?"

"Now?" His obsidian eyes glinted as he leaned toward me. "Dr. Dillon, I'm dead. There is no now."

I couldn't suppress a sudden shudder. Patients with DID usually didn't present dead people as alters.

"When did you, um, pass away?"

"New Year's Day, 1932."

"Where have you been since then?"

He patted his chest again, and when he found nothing, chewed on a thumbnail with the relish of someone who hadn't had these small comforts in a long time. "Here and there."

"What do you want now?" This was not a question a psychiatrist would ask a patient. It was a question my sister asked when she was ridding a house of a pesky poltergeist. But Edgar Templeton seemed to appreciate it. The arrogant grin he gave me looked nothing like Derek's warm, humble smile.

"I'm rich, Dr. Dillon. I have a beautiful home and many interests to occupy my time. But I am, alas, missing one thing."

"What's that?" I cringed, thinking of the way he'd leered at me.

"A body, of course," he hissed. "I am incorporeal, in case you failed to notice. Although I am not without resources."

The heavy book slid out from under my hand, flew through the air, and smashed against the opposite wall. I gasped, clutching at the floor.

"I intend to have Derek's fine young body as my own, so I can live again, and enjoy the pleasures of the flesh." His lizard eyes dragged insinuatingly down the length of my body. Gooseflesh erupted all over my freezing skin.

"What will happen to Derek?" My normal calm, authoritative tone had disappeared, replaced by a plaintive little girl voice that I hated but couldn't control.

"His soul will wander, rootless and destitute, for all eternity. Perhaps it will haunt you for the rest of your life. Have you ever wanted your own personal ghost?" His cackle made my flesh crawl.

Edgar stood up. His movements were disjointed and awkward, like a marionette being directed by several different hands. "I'm going home," he said.

"You're what?"

His lower lip turned down in mock pity. "You keep hoping I'll give up, don't you? But I'm stronger than he is, Maggie. He can't win."

"With my help he can."

When he laughed this time he sounded genuinely amused. "Oh, dear me, you have great confidence in yourself, little lady. Why would that be?"

He moved closer, lurching as if his knees didn't work. One of his shoulders was pulled up around his ear. I backed up until I hit the TV.

He stopped a foot away from me. The white mist floated in tendrils around his head, swayed by an invisible breeze. There was an unearthly power coming from this entity, so strong it was visible in the room. It radiated out of him in waves, like looking at a tarmac road on a hot summer day.

"You couldn't save your mother, could you?"

His words hit me like a punch in the solar plexus. "I was only eight," I whispered. "I couldn't have done anything."

When he touched me it felt as if he'd pressed a Popsicle against my cheek. "Yes, that's what you tell yourself. But you don't really believe it, do you?"

My head moved side to side without any help from my conscious mind.

"And you can't help Derek. But stay out of my way, girly, and you might just survive this."

He tapped his forehead as if he was tipping an invisible hat, and then he left. Closing my eyes, I listened to him careen down the hall like a drunk, his body bouncing off the walls as he stumbled down the staircase. Only when the door was closed and everything was silent did I allow myself to cry.

Dr. Kay steepled his fingers and stared at me impassively. From my position on the leather couch in his handsomely appointed office I could read all of his diplomas. They'd been carefully positioned behind his head for optimum visibility.

"You saw a mist coming out of his mouth, you say?"

I nodded, resisting the urge to break our shared gaze. His steel-blue eyes were hard to look at, even though his demeanor was resolutely professional.

"How much sleep are you getting, Maggie?"

"I'm a resident, Dr. Kay. Which is to say, not enough. But sleep deprivation is not a new thing for me. This is."

"Are you religious?" He tapped his Waterford pen on the legal pad in his lap.

"What does that have to do with anything?"

"Do you believe in the immortal soul?"

I shrugged. This was a conversation I would have enjoyed having with my Catholic mother, if she hadn't died before we got the chance. "I'm not sure. Do you?"

He gave me a tight smile. "We're talking about you right now."

"Yes, I know."

Dr. Kay glanced to my right, where I knew there was a clock on the side table. My time was running out.

"It's countertransference, Mags."

Was this what he'd been thinking all along, slapping me with that Freudian label while pretending to listen to my talk of morphing faces and unexplained cold spots?

"But I—"

"You have feelings for the man, don't you?"

I pressed my lips together tightly while my mind floundered for the right answer, if not the true one.

Dr. Kay waved a dismissive hand. "Don't worry, you're not going to get in trouble. You did the right thing, sending him to me when you knew that your feelings were making you less than impartial. He's a nice-looking fellow, I'll give you that."

My cheeks grew hot. This conversation was getting more and more uncomfortable. "But if he's not my patient anymore, how could it be countertransference? Isn't that only for therapists who fall for their patients?"

"Countertransference can refer to a therapist developing erotic feelings for a patient, but also when a therapist takes on the psychosis of a patient. In your case, both of these."

I grabbed a tissue. Under the cover of wiping my nose I cleared away a few tears. "So what do I do about it?"

"You need to stay away from Mr. Fielding. I'll take good care of him, I promise you. Concentrate on your work. Can you do that?"

I blinked hard. "Yes, I can do that."

Dr. Kay put his pad down on the side table and leaned forward. The calm, neutral expression was gone, replaced by steely determination. "Good. Because if you don't, I might have reason to question your professional judgment. Then I might have to think twice about recommending you to the selection committee, and that could affect your career in a very negative way. We don't want that to happen, do we?" His sharp blue eyes pinned me down like a dead insect on a specimen board.

I swallowed hard and shook my head.

He patted his knees and glanced at the clock again. "Good, I'm glad we understand each other. And I'm afraid our time is up."

* * *

I sat at the table, staring at a framed photograph on my kitchen wall. The Cliff House was a historic hotel and restaurant on Ocean Beach that had burned down twice. My photo was of the second Cliff House, taken on the day of the fire, in 1907. In my left hand was a glass of the Zinfandel that Derek had left behind. If I breathed deeply I could still smell his spicy tomato sauce. Its aura was buried somewhere in the walls, and I certainly hadn't cooked anything else since then to bury it. I spun my BlackBerry like a dreidel. In the twenty-four hours since my appointment with Dr. Kay, Derek had called twice and texted twice.

I'd been sitting at the table, looking from the phone to the photograph, for over an hour, paralyzed with indecision. I wanted to call Derek so badly I felt it through my whole body, like the flu. To defy Dr. Kay would be to kiss my career goodbye, but the only thing I was really worried about now was Derek. He had gone back to see Dr. Kay, so I couldn't claim any therapeutic benefits for my presence in his life. Perhaps dealing with me would only distract him, interfere with his healing process, as Dr. Kay believed.

Or perhaps I was the only one who could really help Derek.

I hadn't been able to get Edgar Templeton out of my mind. The image of his face was so clear, I could have picked him out of a police line-up. If this had been New Orleans rather than San Francisco I could have easily found people, including my sister, who would have believed Derek's story of ghostly possession without question. But here in San Francisco, among my colleagues at Pacific University Hospital, I would risk being labeled mentally ill myself if I so much as mentioned the possibility that Derek's perceptions might be real.

I'd been poised on the edge of this particular knife since I was a child, precariously balanced between the worlds of fact and faith. The former was the realm of science, where I lived now, and the latter was the province of my mother and sister. The world of my childhood was a dark place full of misty intangibles, where death was a transfer station on the journey to another plane, and souls who got lost on the way could be found in every old house, chapel, or barn. They might even be driving ghost cars on a bridge.

I was a product of both of these worlds, but I had found them irreconcilable. So I had packed the world of my childhood away, like my emotions, in a box that I always intended to open but never did. Until now. Ever since not-Derek lurched out of my house like a zombie from a George Romero film, I had been thinking of the two men as separate entities. Countertransference or not, some part of me already believed Edgar and Derek's story.

I swirled the wine until it coated the inside of the glass and then I took a deep inhalation, as Derek had taught me. If only there was a way to prove that Edgar Templeton was real, to use the methods of science to bolster my case, rather than refute it. My eyes drifted back to the phone, then to the photograph of the Cliff House. Smoke and flames were coming out of the roof, encircling the belvedere and winging into the sky. A Victorian era family, in suits and long dresses, posed on the beach in the foreground. They smiled for the camera, commemorating the historic day. As I looked at their long-dead faces an idea occurred to me. I grabbed my phone and my purse and ran out of the house.

I walked right past the San Francisco Historical Society on my first pass down the block. The squat, two-story redbrick building, tucked between two skyscrapers, was the architectural equivalent of a pair of old shoes in the back of your closet being slowly buried by subsequent purchases of more expensive and higher-heeled versions. The lobby was showing an exhibit about camping in the nineteenth century. I passed it with barely a glance, looking only for the signs that directed me to the photography archives.

A middle-age woman, with wispy blond hair and a blanket-sized red scarf coiled around her neck, was clicking away on a computer behind the archives counter. She smiled cheerily when I reached her, as if this were a regular day and I was a regular customer looking for some relic of history that existed now only in her dusty archives. How could she imagine that what I was looking for was as alive as either of us, maybe more so?

"I'm looking for a photograph," I said.

The woman nodded. "Any particular subject?"

"A man named Edgar Templeton. He built a house in Pacifica that looks like a castle."

"Eddie's Folly," she said, reaching for a set of shelves on her right.

"You've heard of it?" I didn't know whether to be glad or horrified.

The librarian handed me a printed form and a pen. "Yes, I've got some pictures. If you could just fill this out and show me some ID, I'll pull them for you."

While I was waiting I wandered the room, checking out the framed photos on the walls. In a single circumlocution I discovered that Haight Street had once had an amusement park with a rickety waterslide called The Chutes that occasionally ejected people onto the sidewalk at high speed, and that a bar called Abe Warner's Cobweb Palace once housed monkeys, parrots, and bears. And people thought San Francisco was weird now.

The librarian brought out a cloth-covered accordion folder, placed it on one of the tables and handed me a pair of white cotton gloves. My legs suddenly felt weak, so I sat down and took a few deep breaths as I donned the gloves. The faded folder bore a typewritten sticker: TEMPLETON, EDGAR, 1895–1932. My hand trembled as I reached for the clasp.

The first file held a scratched black-and-white photo of Templeton's house when it was new. A crowd of men in broad-shouldered, pin-striped suits and women in flapper dresses milled around the courtyard, which at that point in time was beautifully landscaped and dotted with iron tables and chairs. Some people were standing on the roof, hanging over the parapets, smoking and drinking.

The next file slot yielded a yellowed article clipped from the *San Francisco Chronicle*, dated January 2, 1932.

Notorious Bootlegger Edgar Templeton Murdered in Little Italy

Suspected bootlegger and gang leader Edgar Templeton was shot and killed while dining at Vesuvio restaurant on Columbus Avenue last night. Also killed were his wife, Claudia, two associates, Melvin Purvis and Angelo Ciccone, and a bystander, Juanita James. Three other people were wounded.

The cold-blooded killings have stunned the populace of San Francisco. Witnesses stated that as Templeton and his party were dining at the front of the restaurant, a black Ford without license plates pulled up on Columbus Avenue. Several gunmen opened fire through the plate glass windows, sending patrons scurrying for cover amid a hail of bullets and shattered glass. At least three gunmen were involved, according to eyewitnesses. Police have recovered at least 160 shell casings inside the restaurant.

Police chief Francis Gibb speculated that the killings may have been in retaliation for another spectacular shooting that occurred in Half Moon Bay, at a

*beachside location known as a rendezvous point for
liquor smugglers from Canada. Two weeks ago, on De-
cember 15, two unidentified Canadian men and an
American, Joseph Margolis, were shot and killed
while unloading a shipment of whisky that subse-
quently went missing. There are no suspects in this
murder, but rumors have flown that it was perpetrated
by Edgar Templeton, whose reputation as a bloodthirsty gangster includes at least three murders al-
legedly perpetrated by his own hand.*

*The establishment in Half Moon Bay, reputedly a
speakeasy, was said to be in competition with one in
Pacifica owned by Mr. Templeton. Templeton maintained that the large and impressive building, modeled
after a European castle, was solely his private residence.*

The article was accompanied by two gruesome photographs that would never have run in a twenty-first-century
newspaper. One was a shot of Templeton and the other dead
people lying on the floor of the restaurant amid shattered
plates and overturned furniture. The men had on suits and
ties, while the woman, who was petite and dark-haired, wore
a floral print dress that was bunched up around her shapely
thighs, revealing the garters that held up her stockings. The
other photo was of Edgar Templeton, lying on the floor with
an overturned chair next to him. He held a fork in his right
hand. His wide-open eyes stared upward and his mouth
seemed to be smiling. There was a neat hole the size of a
quarter in his forehead and a pool of sticky-looking black
blood under his head.

The file also held an eight-by-ten print of Templeton's
mug shot: side-by-side front and side views, with a five-digit
prison number in the lower left corner. He was again wearing a suit and tie, the white shirt dark with grime around the

collar. It was an excellent likeness of him, so clear that I could distinguish individual smallpox scars on his cheeks and chin. The living Edgar Templeton was handsome, in an Al Capone sort of way. His expression—even in a mug shot— was insolent and vaguely amused, as if his incarceration were a practical joke he was playing on the prison guards. His eyes were dark, but not the depthless black I remembered. In the photo they had some translucence that indicated they might have been brown or hazel. But the splayed-out nose, sharp cheekbones, and heavy eyebrows low on the ridged forehead—they all belonged to the man I had seen in my apartment, the man who had turned an expression of love into a repellant sexual violation.

I put out one gloved finger and touched the face, but I didn't need tactile evidence to know it was real. The blood drained out of my head, leaving me dizzy and nauseated, gripping the table to stay upright. The evidence was here, as plain as the nose on Edgar's face, that we were dealing with a ghost. But what to do now? No drugs, no shock treatments, no amount of talk therapy or hypnosis or biofeedback was going to make Edgar go away. I knew what I needed, and it wasn't going to be found in the *Diagnostic and Statistical Manual of Mental Disorders*.

Chapter 5

"Lady Eva's House of Gris Gris. New Orleans Cemetery Tours every Tuesday night." The girl's tone was bored and perfunctory. She ended the recitation with a sharp snap of her chewing gum.

"May I speak to Lady Eva?" I asked. Even after ten years I still choked on my sister's "professional" name.

"Who's callin'?" the girl asked.

Her New Orleans drawl was as familiar to me as my own name. I had talked the same way when I came to California, but after the twentieth person described my accent as "cute," I decided I had to get rid of it. I traded my car for lessons from a graduate student in speech therapy. I had been relatively successful, but the accent slipped back whenever I was exhausted or drunk or overwhelmed.

"This is Eva's sister, Maggie."

"I didn't know Eva had a sister."

"I'm not surprised."

While the girl went to look for her boss I was treated to the rolling piano notes of "Basin Street Blues," played by Dr. John. The bearded pianist was part of the New Orleans musical canon, heard in every establishment in the French Quarter, including Eva's store on Rue St. Anne. After a pause long enough to finish Dr. John and move on to the Neville Brothers, the receiver rattled.

"Maggie Dillon, as I live and breathe!" Eva said cheerily.

I winced at her choice of words. Our mother had used that phrase whenever she ran into an acquaintance. It was usually accompanied by a hug and an invitation to tea. Eva sounded so much like Mama that it twisted my heart like a wet dishrag.

"Hi, Eva, how are you?"

"Fine as a fiddle. It's been awhile, Sissy, so I have to figure that you're not calling to pass the idle minutes. Did someone die?"

"Who would die that I would know about first? You're the one living within six blocks of our every known relative."

Eva's laugh was still husky. Boys had been loving that laugh since Eva turned fourteen. "The president, maybe? I don't follow the news much." There was a jingling sound, followed by a click, then an exhalation. I pictured my sister, lifting an armful of gold bangles to light a cigarette.

"Actually, I'm calling for professional reasons."

"Your profession or mine?"

"Both, I suppose. I have a patient . . . I *had* a patient, past tense."

"He's passed over to the other side?"

"No, he's not dead, he's just not a patient anymore. Now he's a friend. He thinks he's possessed by a ghost."

Eva's exhalation made a hissing noise. "So give him his meds and send him on his way. Isn't that what y'all do up there every day?"

I chewed my lip. "Eva, this one is different."

"Love potions are on the bottom shelf, in the red glass bottles." Eva was yelling at someone in the store. "Sorry, Maggie. You were saying?"

"This one is really possessed." I had never said those words out loud. I could hardly believe I was saying them now.

Eva whistled. "Well, hellfire and tarnation. That must be a kick in the britches for you."

"You could say that."

"Listen, Maggie, if this guy is really possessed you should run the other way as fast as your little legs will carry you. I'm serious." Eva's voice echoed in my ear. She was holding the receiver very close to her mouth, as if to keep anyone from overhearing. "In all my years in this business I've only seen a few real cases, I have to tell you. And they scared the shit out of me."

"I really care about this guy." I pressed my arm against my stomach, which was full of butterflies with knife-edged wings.

There was a long pause on Eva's end. The silence was filled with the Preservation Hall Jazz Band's version of "When the Saints Go Marching In." I listened to the melancholy undertone below the rollicking notes and remembered that these bands played at funerals in New Orleans, another reminder that the dividing line between life and death was a lot more amorphous down there.

"I want you to come out here, Eva. I need your help." The words stuck in my throat, but for Derek's sake I spat them out. "Blood is thicker than water," our mother always said, and although I never knew what it meant when I was a child, I understood it now.

"I'll be there by tomorrow," my sister said. "In the meantime, don't be alone with him."

The weather was frigid and overcast, typical for February in Pacifica. Fog from the ocean filled the air with drifting specters, and the wind-beaten trees leaned precariously to the east, waving skeletal black arms. On a day like this Eddie's Folly looked even more sinister. I pressed the doorbell, and when that produced no response I pounded on the door. I didn't know what I would do if he didn't answer. If it had been an ordinary house I would have broken a window to get in, I was that desperate to see Derek, but this house was as impenetrable as the fortresses on which it was modeled. Luckily I didn't have to figure out how to storm the castle, because the door opened with a familiar creak.

I barely recognized Derek, and it wasn't because he was wearing Edward's face. He had a black eye, bruised and bloody cheeks, and an upper lip that was so swollen it looked like it might burst.

"What the hell happened?" My fingers fluttered over his black eye and scabby cheek, lingering near his lip without quite touching it.

"I'm all right," he said, but he didn't sound convinced.

I grabbed his arm and pulled him into the foyer. "We need to get some ice on that lip."

The kitchen was small for such a grand residence, appointed with avocado-colored 1970s-era appliances and a breakfast nook with a table covered in checkered oilcloth. Derek leaned against the white tiled counter, cradling his injured face while he watched me rummage through the drawers for a plastic bag. I filled it with ice cubes from the old-fashioned trays in the freezer. We sat next to each other in the nook, our thighs pressed together, while Derek put the ice on his lip.

I held back tears as I examined the blue and purple flesh around Derek's gentle brown eyes. I picked up his hand and examined his raw and scraped knuckles. Had he actually punched himself in the face? Who had he been when he did it—Derek or Edgar?

"What happened?" I whispered.

"He's an evil man, Maggie," Derek said, closing his hand around mine.

"I know that. What he's doing to you is unconscionable."

He shook his head. "He didn't do this to me. I did it to him."

"Why?"

"Because I can't let him get control of my body." He winced as he moved the bag of ice to another tender spot. "He wants to kill people."

"You better read this." I pulled the photocopy of the *Chronicle* article from my purse and let go of his hand so he could read it.

"So there it is," Derek said when he was finished. "He wants the gang that killed him and his wife."

I knitted my eyebrows. "But Templeton was killed in the 1930s. Nobody involved could still be alive."

An internal struggle was going on inside Derek, I'd seen the look countless times on the faces of my patients. He was trying to decide whether to tell me something terrible.

"They're not," he finally said. "He's going to kill their children."

I jumped like I'd been given an electric shock. Even after what I'd already learned about Templeton, this seemed outrageous. "He can't do that. They're innocent people."

He shrugged. "So was I."

Picking up a dish towel I'd found in one of the drawers, I dabbed at a cut on Derek's lip that had started bleeding again.

"How did this happen?" I asked gently.

He stared at a spot just beyond me, as if he couldn't bear to meet my eyes. "When he's in me, Maggie, it's like I'm trapped in a cage. I can see what he's doing and I can tell what he's thinking, but I can't stop him. Except sometimes, when I get angry enough, I can take back control."

Hot anger rose up in me as I gazed at his battered face, a face that was growing increasingly precious to me. "But you know it's your body. What the hell were you doing, punching your own face?"

"I was trying to kill him."

I clutched Derek's hands, squeezing hard in spite of his injuries. "Please, Derek, promise me you won't try to harm yourself again."

Derek eyed me suspiciously. "Is this coming from Dr. Dillon?" he asked. "You don't want to lose a patient?"

I shook my head vehemently. "No, it's coming from my heart. I care about you, Derek. There's a connection between us, and I know you feel it too. I just want time to get to know you better."

His face softened. "I want that too."

"I want to kiss you," I said, "but your lips look like they're going to pop."

He laughed. "I don't give a damn about my lips."

Even so, I kissed him as gently as possible. Our tongues met, still with only the lightest of pressure, and then we hugged. My head fit perfectly in the curve of Derek's neck. He stroked my hair gently, causing tears to spring to my eyes. There was some part of myself that I'd been hiding away from people for years, maybe ever since I lost my mother. But with Derek the barrier was falling down, as easily and naturally as a wave pulls sand from the beach. With him I wanted to share every part of myself.

"I'm thirty-two years old," he whispered, his lips pressing against my temple. "I've been writing love songs for twenty years and I've never been in love—can you believe that? I didn't really know what I was talking about." He hesitated, and I felt his chest fill with a deep sigh. "Until now."

Suddenly he pulled away. I looked up to see his expression change from passion to bitterness. He stabbed a finger into the bag of ice on the table. "I've finally found someone

I think I could love, and I'm not going to live long enough to enjoy it." He looked up and gave me a strange, unhappy smile. "That would make a nice ballad, wouldn't it?"

I put my arms around his neck, sliding my fingers into his thick hair, trying to bring him back to me. "You're alive now," I said. I kissed him gently but insistently, stroking his lips with mine.

He grabbed me, pressing me hard into his body. The breath whooshed out of my lungs, and I couldn't get it back. He returned my kiss so passionately that the blood from his cut dripped into my mouth, tasting salty and metallic. I pulled away, staunching his bloody lip with my fingers.

"I'm sorry, I didn't mean to hurt you," I blurted out.

He made a noise that startled me. Halfway between a groan and a growl, it came from low in his chest. Suddenly afraid, I searched his face for indications that Edgar might be taking over. But all I saw was Derek, gazing at me with what I could only call naked lust. Without another word he scooped me up and nestled me against his chest, all the way through the foyer, the living room, and up two flights of stairs.

The bedroom Derek took me to must have originally been a maid's room. It was small and simple, containing little but a double bed, a stool, a rustic desk, and two more guitars on stands. The desk was scattered with papers filled with hand-written musical notes, but I didn't have a chance to look more closely because Derek took me straight to the bed.

Lying side by side with his leg over mine, he kissed me with slow delicacy, starting at my collarbone. He opened my shirt one button at a time, caressing each inch of skin with his mouth before undoing the next button. Then he unsnapped my bra and applied his diligent attention to my breasts, building the pleasure bit by bit until I was sure I couldn't stand it anymore. If I sighed with delight at something he was doing, he increased it. If I inclined even slightly away, he moved to a different spot. He was learning me, as if I was a new instrument he had never touched before, and he was going to take all the time in the world to play me perfectly.

When it was over we lay entwined in each other's arms. I pressed my cheek against Derek's heart, which was beating calmly now, his breathing slow and steady. I hoped he would let himself sleep a little while. My gaze wandered around the room. Our clothes had been tossed wildly: My shirt was hanging from the neck of a guitar, and Derek's pants were on the other side of the room, sprawled like an ash corpse at Vesuvius. I was glad that I couldn't see Derek's face right now, handsome as it was.

When we were making love, he'd maneuvered me so that I was on top, riding him with my hips. While I moved faster and faster, increasing his pleasure and mine, I couldn't stop examining his face. Even when the lovemaking reached its height and he clutched me in his final release, I *still* couldn't close my eyes, for fear that if I did, I'd open them to see another man inhabiting my lover's body. Edgar couldn't prevent me from making love with Derek, but he had stopped me from truly being present. If I didn't hate him before, I certainly did now.

"Maggie?" Derek whispered. "Are you awake?"

"Yup."

"I hope you don't mind my asking, but you didn't have an orgasm, did you?"

I shook my head slightly. "It doesn't matter, though."

He deftly slid out from under me, putting his palm under my head and maneuvering so that we were eye to eye. "It matters to me. Tell me what I need to do better."

I laughed, gazing into his warm brown eyes with their fiery golden ring. The man was a god. How could he think he'd done anything wrong?

"You did everything just right, Derek. It was me."

"I've heard that women say that when they don't want to hurt your feelings."

I sat up, pulling the sheet with me. "No! That's not it."

He smiled. "So you *do* want to hurt my feelings."

"Okay, here's the truth." I grabbed his cheeks in exasperation. "I couldn't concentrate because I kept looking for *him*."

He rolled away, giving me a view of the Celtic cross tattoo on his bicep. "Oh, fuck me. He really has ruined everything, hasn't he?"

"But listen. I'm going to help you."

"I'm not taking any more drugs, Maggie. I told Dr. Kay that already. You're a doctor, you think you can fix me, but I'm not crazy."

I pulled his shoulders, turning him to face me. "I'm way past all that. I thought you'd realized that when I gave you the *Chronicle* article. I believe you, Derek. God help me, I believe everything you've told me. I've seen it with my own eyes."

He ran a hand through his long, messy hair, a gesture that never failed to touch my heart. "So how can you help?"

"My sister's coming today, and she's going to help us."

He looked skeptical. "What is she? How can she help me?"

I stroked his cheek, avoiding the scabs and bruises as best I could. "She's a, um, well, how can I put this so it won't sound crazy?" I paused and then threw my hands in the air. "I can't. She's a voodoo priestess in New Orleans."

His eyes widened and his eyebrows shot into the stratosphere. "*Your* sister is a voodoo priestess?"

"She's done exorcisms before."

He sat up in one fluid movement, swinging his feet to the floor. "Some two-bit huckster from the French Quarter is going to come and light sage over me—that's your solution?"

"Derek! That's a little harsh, don't you think?"

He narrowed his eyes. "You're a scientist. Do *you* believe in her?"

Eva had been dabbling in the supernatural since we were teenagers. After school, instead of hanging out with other girls, painting her nails and phoning boys, she holed up with our housekeeper, Nelida, and learned to cast spells. My father and I were constantly finding little cloth bundles—hidden behind books on shelves, tucked under pillows, or dug up from the backyard by the family dog. Every one was a unique combination of herbs, crystals, feathers, hair, twigs, and sometimes malodorous, unsavory-looking substances. My father always shook the contents into the toilet and flushed them away.

The year I was fourteen, Eva announced that she was going to contact our mother. She asked me if I wanted to participate. How could I say no? The longing to see Mama one more time, to feel her arms around me and tell her that I loved her, was so strong it overpowered every other thought in my head.

At midnight during a full moon, we went to the graveyard where our mother was buried. Eva created an altar on her gravestone and lit some candles. She began chanting, all the while shaking a bundle of dried herbs tied with a piece of red thread that Eva had unraveled from one of our mother's nightgowns. I stared at my mother's name in the gravestone until my eyes burned.

Eva spread her arms wide. "Spirits of the nether world, we are seeking the one who was known in life as Elizabeth Dillon. If she is out there please send her to us now."

The very air around us seemed to fill with shimmering, pulsating energy. I caught sight of something in my peripheral vision, something whitish, with blurred edges, but when I turned it faded away behind a neighboring gravestone.

"She's here," Eva said. "I can feel her."

"I can feel her, too," I said, as my skin prickled with excitement.

Eva called out in a clear, bell-like voice, "Mama, if you can hear us, give us a sign."

Although the sultry New Orleans air was completely still, all the candles wavered. Two of them went out. Eva increased her effort, dropping to her knees, chanting louder and louder, shaking the herb bundle until its leaves fell into the neatly trimmed grass. Hope leaped in my chest, and I leaned forward with such joy and anticipation that I could scarcely contain myself.

And that was when I noticed Eva snuffing out one of the flames with her fingers while surreptitiously fanning the flames with her skirt so that they appeared to be wavering. I stood up, knocked over the remaining candles, and ran out of the graveyard.

The following fall, when high school started, I took every science class that St. Mary's offered, surprising the nuns and offending the boys by getting the highest score on every exam. Four years later I left for Stanford. The incident in the graveyard was never mentioned again.

I turned to Derek and answered him as honestly as I could. "I think she's our only chance."

Derek crossed the room and grabbed his jeans, pulling them on impatiently. "Why are you doing this, Maggie?"

"Why? Because I want to help you."

He plucked my shirt off the guitar and sat back down on

the bed. "I'm not sure there is a me anymore. Think of what I've become, Maggie. Doesn't it make you want to run the other way?"

"No! Don't say that."

"He could hurt you, you know." He spread his long fingers and held his hands in front of my face. The bandages on his wrists were dirty and starting to unravel. "He could use these to hurt you and I wouldn't be able to stop him."

I grabbed his hands and pressed them down. "Don't say that. That's not going to happen."

I leaned in and kissed him, long and hard, holding his hands tightly in mine. He kissed me back, but when it was over he wouldn't meet my eyes. Instead he looked at the floor, his expression distant and sad, as if he was looking into the future and not liking what he saw.

Chapter 6

My sister had always entered a room like a . . .

Well, no one from New Orleans would ever use the word "hurricane" lightly. Let's say she came in like a force of nature. The years had done nothing to diminish her impact. If anything she was more impressive now, sweeping through the airport hallway, than she'd been at age twenty when I saw her last, waving goodbye as I boarded a bus for California.

A flowered scarf trapped the hair around her face, but irrepressible masses of red curls flowed down her back. Abundant cleavage peeked out of a form-fitting purple silk blouse, but her lower half was disguised with several layers of lacy skirts, from which black lace-up boots peeked as she walked, pulling two wheelie suitcases. Almost everyone gave her a longer than usual glance as they passed. The men's expressions were admiring, the women's were inquisitive, sometimes critical.

I waved and jumped, trying to clear the shoulders of a tall man in front of me. The crowd parted as if a truck had been driven into their midst, and Eva arrived, trailing clouds of perfume and jingling from head to toe with jewelry.

"Hey, y'all, I made it!" Eva grabbed me around the waist and twirled me in a circle, simultaneously charming and infantilizing me.

"Where's your man?" she asked, checking behind me as if I'd hidden him somewhere.

"He said he had a few things to do and he'd meet us at my place later."

I had tried to get Derek to come with me to the airport but he refused. His face had looked strange when he said goodbye, set and emotionless. I was trying not to let it worry me, but of course it was all I could think about.

Eva raised a shapely eyebrow. "Did you follow my advice about not being alone with him?"

"Of course not."

She snorted. "Well, you're still alive. That's a good sign."

"He doesn't seem to be interested in hurting me."

"*Yet*. We'll see when he feels threatened." Eva handed me the handle of one of her suitcases. "Pull that for me, would you, sweetheart?"

I eyed her bulging bags. "How long are you staying?"

"One's got my equipment in it."

Eva and I sat on the couch drinking wine and eating Chinese from my favorite take-out place out of the cardboard boxes. Every few minutes I checked my cell phone. I'd already left three messages for Derek. I folded a pancake filled with mu shu pork and plum sauce into a burrito shape, while suspiciously eyeing the contents of Eva's suitcase, which was spread over my floor.

"Can I look at that stuff?" I asked.

Eva nodded as she spooned hoisin string beans into her mouth. "This food is really good," she said.

I shoved the last bite of mu shu pork into my mouth and slid onto the floor. There was an abundance of odors coming

from the suitcase, everything in the spectrum from sweet floral to rotting carcass. I must have been very hungry to be
able to eat with this in the room with me. I examined the
items one by one, sniffing and then sorting them into piles.
There were pillar candles of all different colors, beaded neck-
laces, silk drawstring bags holding substances that ranged
from powder to plant leaves, and glass tubes filled with oil.
The most disturbing items were several mud-encrusted roots
that resembled mummified fetuses. Perhaps they really were
mummified fetuses; it wouldn't have surprised me.

"When Derek gets here we have to put all this stuff away.
He shouldn't see it or touch it," Eva said.

"Why are you letting me touch it, then?" I picked up a
handful of peacock feathers and tickled Eva's bare leg.

Eva didn't smile. "You're the sister of a voodoo priestess," she answered. "It's in your blood. Derek, well, I don't
know what would happen if he got his hands on objects of
power in his current state. Could be the ghost might take the
power from them."

Eva had brought several small knives in leather sheaths. I
removed one and tested it on my finger. A big mistake, it
turned out, because I gave myself a nasty little cut.

"Ouch!" I shrieked.

Eva laughed.

I stood up to go into the bathroom and get a bandage.
That's when I noticed them. At the bottom of the suitcase,
under the stuff I'd dislodged, was a canvas bag that looked
like it was filled with coils of rope. But the bag was trembling.

"Eva, what's in there?" I whispered, taking a cautionary
step backward.

My sister sipped her wine as she peeked over the table
into the suitcase. "Oh, my babies are waking up," she said.
Her smile did look like that of a proud mother.

"Your babies?"

Eva opened her mouth to answer, but I held up my bleeding hand. "Never mind, don't tell me. Don't tell me how you managed to get this shit through airport security. Don't tell me what you plan to do with it. Don't tell me anything. Just please, have this case closed up by the time I get back from the bathroom."

I turned to go.

"Sissy, look at me."

I turned around, holding the wound on my finger. "What?"

"Do you trust me?"

I looked at the floor. "Does that really matter?"

She set her glass down and walked over, and then she put her hands on my shoulders, forcing me to meet her gaze. My eyes were hazel: pretty, but nothing to write home about. Eva's eyes, on the other hand, were a light green that shone so brightly in her pale face they seemed otherworldly. When she fixed you with that stare it was impossible to look away, and ten years of being a voodoo priestess had only intensified the effect. I felt like she was burning twin holes into my face.

"I know you're thinking about what happened with Mama."

I shuffled my feet but returned her gaze. "Nothing happened with Mama."

"I was a child then, Maggie, I didn't know what I was doing. I didn't know my power, just like you don't know yours."

"I know my power," I grumbled.

She raised her eyebrows, and then she gave my shoulders a little shake. "It is essential that you believe in what we're doing. Derek is in grave danger from this spirit. Spirits like this have an 'if I can't have him, no one will' attitude. If, during the procedure, he perceives that we are winning, he will most likely kill Derek. It will take all of our strength to keep him from doing this."

I stepped away from her hands. "You're just trying to scare me," I said uncertainly.

Eva flicked back her long red hair, making her earrings jingle. "Do I give a shit whether you're scared or not? This isn't play-acting for the tourists on Bourbon Street. This is serious, Sissy. Serious as a heart attack."

My phone buzzed. I scrambled back to the table to grab it. "Here's a text from Derek now," I said. "Probably telling me when he's going to meet us . . . Oh, shit." My voice trailed off. Eva pushed her head close to mine so she could read along.

I don't want you in danger. Don't try to look for me. If I can get rid of him, I'll come back for you. If I can't, have a good life.

Chapter 7

After a half dozen phone calls, starting with Derek and ending with Dr. Kay, I put down the phone and turned to Eva. "Dr. Kay hasn't heard from him," I said, "and neither have his parents. I don't know who else to call."

"Let's go to the castle," Eva said. "Maybe he's holed up there."

I couldn't imagine Derek staying there, given that the castle was the site of his most destructive encounters with the ghost, but then again, maybe he was there for that very reason.

"Okay, let's go."

I drove way too fast down Highway One, but Eva still had time to enjoy the view of silvery moonlight reflected in the Pacific Ocean.

"You sure live in a beautiful place," she commented.

"I can't make small talk right now," I said.

"Of course you can. Bet you do it all the time at your work. Comes with the territory."

"I guess you're right," I sighed. "Well, New Orleans is beautiful too."

I'd always thought so, although it was a different kind of beauty than California. New Orleans had an intimate kind of beauty, like peeking into the artfully decorated parlor of an eccentric doyenne, while California sported grand vistas and natural splendor. I slowed down a bit and took a quick glance at the ocean. "I don't get to see much of California besides the inside of Pacific University Hospital."

"You're working too hard. But do you like it?"

I hadn't stopped to ask myself that question since I'd started residency. No one asked themselves if they liked residency. That was like asking if you liked getting vaccinations. They were painful but necessary. But did I like psychiatry? That was a question that had been nibbling at the inside of my mind, trying to get my attention, while I avoided it with the business, and busyness, of the work itself.

"You haven't answered me," Eva prodded.

"I know. What about you, do you like your work?"

Even in the dim light I could see the glint in her emerald-green eyes. "My work is me, Maggie."

"So do you like yourself?"

Eva tossed her abundant red hair over her shoulder, setting her bracelets jingling. "I love myself, of course."

"Okay, now that we've dispensed with the small talk, I have a question."

I knew the tone of my voice had changed, and from my peripheral vision I could see Eva's shoulders tighten.

"Go ahead," she said.

"If ghosts are real, why have I never seen Mama?"

"I told you, Sissy, I couldn't call her that night because I lacked the knowledge—"

I held up a hand. "I'm not talking about that night. I mean in general, why hasn't she appeared to me?"

Eva was silent.

"How could she just leave us like that?" My voice was thick with tears.

Eva put her warm hand on my thigh. "I have no doubt that she watches over us, Maggie."

"Oh, that's religious bullshit." I scrubbed a tear off my cheek.

"Not to me." Eva heaved a deep sigh. "I've seen her."

I wasn't sure how to respond to that, but I didn't have to, because at that moment the hulking form of the castle appeared, backlit by the full moon so it looked like a spotlight was pointing it out. I parked in the courtyard and we walked through the garden of dead trees and bushes. Eva moved more and more slowly the closer we got to the door. She put one hand up to her chest.

"Bad mojo," she said.

I snapped my fingers. "That's what Derek's mother said, but she used an Italian word. I assume it means the same thing, though." I tilted my head up and pretended to read a sign above the door. "Abandon hope, all ye who enter here."

Eva linked arms with me as I pushed the doorbell.

"He's not going to answer," I said. "He knew we were coming."

"Let me." Eva put her hand on the iron latch. She closed her eyes and said a few words under her breath.

"Oh, come on," I protested.

The door opened with its trademark creak. Eva looked at me triumphantly.

"It was already unlocked, wasn't it?"

She didn't answer.

We made our way into the living room, calling out for Derek. Everything was just as it had been before, from the three guitars on their stands to the crushed painting of the idealized Edgar Templeton. Derek was sitting on the throne, staring out the window at the ocean. He didn't turn around as we approached, which reminded me of the day I met him in the hospital.

A cluster of emotions hit me: relief at seeing him safe and not Edgar, mixed with anger and hurt that he could have left me so cavalierly. Half of me wanted to hug him, and the other half wanted to smack him silly.

"You shouldn't have come," Derek said.

"Nice to meet you too," Eva said. She climbed onto the dais and bent over Derek, examining him like he was a used car she was thinking about buying. "Tall drink of water, this one." She turned and winked at me.

"Come on, Derek," Eva said. "We need to do this tonight, while there's a full moon."

He looked up, his expression resolute. "I'm not going. I can't be sure Edgar won't hurt Maggie, so I have to stay away from her until I'm sure it's safe."

"Oh, you don't have to worry about that. I won't let you hurt her."

Derek smiled ruefully. "You haven't seen me when he takes over."

Eva took something out of her skirt pocket. When she turned toward the mirrors I saw her reflected into infinity, pointing a shiny silver gun. Even in the first reflection it was so small it looked like a toy or a souvenir from a Wild West show.

"I'm not going to let anybody hurt my sister, Derek. Or me, for that matter. Much as I know about the other side, I'm still pretty attached to the here and now."

"So you'll kill me if it looks like Maggie is in danger? You promise?"

"What the hell?" I took an awkward step forward, but with that gun pointed at Derek's head I didn't want to make any sudden moves. I was fairly sure it wasn't loaded, but I knew not to underestimate Eva.

"I promise," Eva said, ignoring me.

"How do I know you're not just putting on a show?"
Derek asked. "After all, isn't that what you do for a living?"

There was a loud click as Eva cocked the pistol.

"I guess we're just gonna have to trust each other, aren't
we?"

Normally I would have used my high beams on the winding road to Muir Woods, but the fog created a wall that reflected the light back into my eyes. Derek sat silently in the
passenger seat with his eyes closed, but I knew he wasn't
asleep because his fingers were tapping. In the backseat Eva
used a tiny flashlight to dig around in her suitcase, doing
things I couldn't see but that were emitting a miasma of
strange odors into the car.

After an hour my neck was cramped from the strain of
peering into the dark road to follow the centerline, so I was
relieved when we reached the entrance to the state park. The
large parking lot was empty. Giant redwoods rose up on all
sides of us, so tall it was impossible to see their tops from inside the car. The fog was so thick it vaporized into fat water
drops that plunked onto the windshield. Instinctively I
turned the car toward the visitor center and gift shop.

"What are you doing?" Eva snapped.

"I don't know. What do you want me to do?"

"Go that way." She pointed toward a road at the other end
of the parking lot, with a chain across the entrance and a
sign that read NO ADMITTANCE.

Derek stirred and stretched. "Are we there yet?"

"Apparently not," I said, driving to the blocked-off road.

The chain wasn't locked. Derek replaced it after I drove
through and then jumped back into the front seat. The road
inclined through the forest, passing trees on both sides that
were wider than the length of my Honda Civic. Some of
these giants had burn holes straight through them; some

were cut down, leaving only a broad, flat base that looked like a stage for late-night fairy shows. Many were surrounded by children, a protective circle of smaller trees. These whippersnappers were probably only a few hundred years old, compared to their millennial mothers.

The family trees made me think about children, and the fact that Eva and I didn't have any. If our mother had been alive to see us at ages twenty-eight and thirty, with no children and no prospects for any, she would have tortured us about it every day. She always said that people who don't have children or animals are missing out on the "zest of life." After growing up in a small shotgun house with one sibling, two dogs, a three-legged cat, and a turtle that lived in the bathtub, I decided I'd had enough zest to last me the rest of my comfortable, solitary life.

But now, sneaking a peek at Derek, who was securing his hair with one of my rubber bands in anticipation of whatever was coming next, I realized that the life I'd thought of as merely solitary was now starting to seem lonely. Having Eva around contributed to that feeling. She had an infectious liveliness that reminded me of the way I'd been once, before seventy-hour workweeks and a seemingly endless supply of human misery had worn me down. Sometimes I felt I was nothing more than a human calculator, tallying up the costs of mental illness—insurance reimbursements, medicine dosages, number of inpatient days required.

"Turn off here," Eva yelled.

"Where?" I couldn't see anything except trees in the direction she was pointing.

"Right between those two big trees. There's an energetic point somewhere in there, I can feel it."

My Honda bumped and shuddered as I negotiated a path between the redwoods. The turns were so tight I had to haul the steering wheel right and left with my whole body. Branches and other detritus caught in the undercarriage, making tearing noises. I wasn't sure we'd have a car to return in if we had to go much farther in this direction.

"Maybe I should drive," Derek said helpfully.

I rolled my eyes, which of course he couldn't see, as the only light was coming from the headlights. "*Now* you turn into Mr. Macho?"

"Just a suggestion," he replied.

"There," Eva said, thumping me on the shoulder. Her hand appeared in my peripheral vision, pointing to the right. A hundred yards ahead I could detect a very particular kind of emptiness. The headlights, rather than reflecting back at us off the trees, petered out when confronted with that darkness. I drove to where the trees stopped and parked the car. My heart was pounding like a piston, and I wasn't sure whether it had just started or had been caused by the adrenaline of the drive. Either way, I didn't like the look of this glade.

"Turn off the headlights," Eva commanded.

"Don't you think I should leave them on until we've—"

"Off!" Eva was using a voice I hadn't heard before, commanding and imperious.

I thought that we would be plunged into darkness when I turned off the headlights, but we weren't. The glade was bathed in a silvery glow that resembled moonlight, but dark clouds obscured any celestial illumination. The light was coming from the glade itself, from everywhere and nowhere at once.

After my eyes began to adjust I saw the contours of the land: soft, undulating grassy hillocks, with a small stream running down the center. I thought I could even detect wildflowers, stripped of their colors, gleaming white in the strange light.

Eva pushed a canvas bag into my hands. "Let's go," she said.

"I can carry something," Derek suggested.

"No, you can't. Don't touch anything unless I tell you to. In your condition it could backfire and be dangerous to all of us."

"Okay, then." Derek climbed out of the car, zipping up his down jacket against the fierce chill.

Eva led us near the center of the glade, to a flat rock that resembled a table. She handed me an armful of candles and a lighter, then directed me to create a circle around the stone, placing the lit votives an equal distance apart. Out of her own bag she pulled two vaguely oval-shaped black objects and placed them at opposite ends of the rock. I took a lit candle and moved closer to examine one. When I realized what it was I shrieked, dropping my candle into the grass.

Derek jumped forward, scooping up the candle before it had a chance to light the grass on fire. He stood next to me while we both contemplated the black objects in horror.

"Is that real?" Derek asked.

Eva, still busy with her preparations, didn't answer.

I touched the thing with one finger. The fur was silky. The cat appeared to have a slight smile on its face, because its fangs were showing.

"Yeah, they're real," I whispered.

"Don't touch my mediums," Eva said. "They don't like to come in contact with misbelievers."

I turned around to see Eva laying out several baskets and bowls made of gourds, and a large bunch of dried twigs.

Derek slid his hand into mine.

"What are we doing here?" he asked quietly.

"What other option do we have?" I asked, but then I looked at his bandaged wrists. "Don't answer that."

Eva came over and handed Derek a vial. "Drink this."

He held it up to a candle, swirling the brown and viscous substance. "What is it?"

"Truth serum." Eva didn't smile when she said this.

Derek looked at me questioningly. I gave a small nod. He

lifted the vial and tossed the stuff down. His eyes bulged and he clutched at his throat.

"Oaky, with a hint of sulfur," he said, and shuddered violently.

"Lie down and close your eyes," Eva said, pointing to the rock.

Derek cupped my face in his hands and kissed me hard without opening his mouth.

"See you on the other side," he said.

Chapter 8

Holding one of the gourd bowls and the bundle of twigs, Eva circled the rock several times, chanting in a language I didn't recognize. Every few steps she dipped the twigs into the bowl and sprinkled Derek with liquid. When she did this she stopped chanting and muttered quietly, as if she didn't want me to hear what she was saying.

Derek was absolutely still. I couldn't even tell if he was breathing.

"Play the drum, Maggie." Eva pointed into the darkness.

I turned around. There was a large drum sitting on the grass that I hadn't seen Eva put there.

"I don't know how," I said.

"Just play in rhythm to my incantation."

I sat on the drum and banged it with the flats of my hands, keeping time with the increasingly fast pace of Eva's chanting. She whirled around the rock, jumping on it and over it, splashing Derek with the liquid until rivulets ran down his face. Still he didn't move. She crouched at his head, opened his mouth, and placed something in it that looked like a large lozenge, a small pebble, or maybe a shiny black bug. Then she opened a bag at her waist and began winding a yellow and black checkered rope around her upper arm.

My hands froze in mid-air. Something about that pattern had awakened a deep and hidden fear, presumably some childhood lesson about poisonous snakes that had been lying dormant in my hippocampus.

"Play!" Eva's voice brooked no argument.

I hit the drum heedlessly while the snake slithered around Eva's arms. She lowered her hands, letting it slide onto Derek's neck. I gasped as it slipped under his shirt and disappeared. Her chanting was so fast now it didn't sound human. I couldn't keep up with it on the drum and I didn't try.

Eva pulled Derek's mouth open, removed the pebble and tossed it away. Derek's chest heaved. Spasms wracked his body, lifting him up and then banging him down onto the rock over and over. If Eva hadn't been holding his head he might have knocked himself unconscious.

Derek choked, gasping and clutching at his chest as if he couldn't breathe. I started forward. Eva held up one hand.

"Don't."

The coughing and choking got worse, as specks of white foam spewed from his open mouth. His arms and legs were stiff as boards, but the rest of his body jerked spasmodically. I ignored Eva and rushed over, grabbing Derek's wrist to check his pulse.

"I told you to sit down." Eva's voice was low, but her tone was biting.

"Eva, his pulse is dropping. What the hell was in that liquid you gave him?"

"Mandrake root."

I stared at her in disbelief, remembering the fetus-shaped roots from her suitcase. "But that's poison."

"We must drive the malevolent spirit from his body."

Derek's pulse was getting slower and more arrhythmic by the second. I grabbed my sister by the arm. "You poisoned him!"

"Maggie, step back." Eva stared in my direction, causing my heart to lurch and my stomach to roil. Her normally emerald-green eyes were obscured by a bluish-white membrane. That or I was hallucinating.

The grip she applied in return caused me to yelp with pain. She spoke slowly and calmly, squeezing my arm so hard that my hand went numb and then lost all feeling.

"If you do not believe, then Derek will die."

I sobbed with pain and fear, staring into Derek's lifeless face. "How can I, Eva?"

"Let go of Derek. Open your mind to Edgar Templeton. Let him come to you as he comes out of Derek. Whatever happens, don't touch either of us until it's over."

With a choking sob I released Derek's wrist and backed away. I had no idea whether I believed, or whether my belief was strong enough to save Derek. I was full of doubts, and terrified of what was going to happen next. Was I killing the only man I'd ever loved, or saving him?

As soon as I let go of Derek Eva's body stiffened. Her mouth flew open in a silent scream. She fell backward as heavily as a statue and lay sprawled and unconscious, but with her milky eyes open, staring up at the sky.

In the middle of a spasm Derek's chest was pulled toward the sky as if by an invisible hand. His body continued to rise until he hung, suspended, with just his hands and feet touching the ground. There was a strange whimpering sound, which I eventually realized was coming from me. Derek's mouth opened wider than seemed anatomically possible. A white cloud gushed out. It gathered above his head and then condensed, becoming more opaque as the stream emerging from Derek's mouth grew thinner and paler. When the last of its molecules were gone, Derek flopped back onto the rock like an empty sack. The urge to run to him was almost overwhelming, but I held back, thinking of Eva's warning.

The miasma stretched into a long rope and whipped through the sky. Its movement reminded me of those acrobats who perform with ribbons on sticks. The whitish cloud circled wildly, darting through the air in a dance that was both beautiful and horrifying. I was having so much trouble breathing through my fear that I was close to joining Eva and Derek in oblivion. The cloud shot into the sky like a firecracker, burst apart, and then drew back together, only to dive back down and chase its own tail through the trees on the edge of the glade. Whatever the misty substance was, it had consciousness, and it was enjoying itself.

For a moment I lost sight of it. A second later it reappeared directly in front of my face. As I screamed and jumped backward I heard a familiar maniacal cackle. The cloud divided into thousands of dots, and then the dots transformed. Some lightened, others darkened, some grew while others shrank. They became like pixels in a graphic, and the image that appeared was Edgar Templeton's face, adorned with his trademark smirk. But I could see the trees through it, and it wavered as if he was having trouble holding the image together.

"Fancy meeting you here," the ghost said.

"Get out of here. Disappear. My sister is far more powerful than you," I replied with much more bravado than I felt. It was getting colder by the second. I started to shiver uncontrollably.

The ghost turned its transparent face toward my sister's prostrate body. "It doesn't look that way to me."

I took a step backward, feeling more frightened and vulnerable by the second. And Edgar could feel my fear, because the more scared I got, the more solid he became.

"I have to have a body, Maggie, that's all there is to it. Any young, healthy one will do. It doesn't have to be Derek's. In fact, yours is preferable, in a way." The cloud drew closer. "I've never been a woman before. I hear you can have several orgasms in a row, is that true?"

I gulped thickly.

He chuckled. "But it would have to be with someone besides Derek, because he doesn't do that for you, does he?"

"Oh, good God." I pressed my hands over my eyes. My body shivered until my teeth clattered. Every part of me was being assaulted: my mind, my body, and my emotions. Only my desire to rid Derek of this demon held me in place.

"Let's horse trade, Maggie. You love Derek, don't you?"

I nodded without moving my hands from my face.

"Enough to die for him?"

I nodded again. Yes, I was willing to die for Derek, but I didn't intend to go gently into that good night. I was going to fight Edgar with all my strength. If that wasn't good enough, at least I'd tried. I put my hands down and stared at the ghost.

"Open your mouth." Even in his transparent state he managed to make the simple command sound smutty.

I obeyed. The ghostly apparition thinned and lengthened into the shape of a knife. It stabbed its way down my throat and into my chest. His essence burned through my body with every beat of my heart. My blood felt like it was made of battery acid. My knees crumbled and I sank to the ground, landing on my side halfway up the rock where Derek and Eva lay.

At that point my death began in earnest.

Chapter 9

I couldn't move any part of my body, but I was aware of being cold, of pain in my flank and my cheek, of the uneven surface of the rock pressing into my hip and rib and thigh. I could hear the rustle of wind high in the trees. I could smell the mineral tang of the rock, the damp grass, and the burning candle wax. I could taste blood in my mouth from when I fell.

But slowly, like sand out of an hourglass, my ability to experience physical sensation faded, until I was left with only the memory of being cold, of lying on a rock, of smelling grass and candles. I had become a miasma like Edgar, floating somewhere inside the universe of my own body.

Once he had stolen my five senses, he began to work on my memories. He flipped through my mind like the archivist at the Historical Society, setting up a slide show of scenes from my life. Then he showed me the images, one by one. I saw them, although I couldn't say what I was seeing them *with,* since I had no control over my eyes, or even my brain, as far as I could tell.

My father holding me up to see the lions at the Audubon Zoo.

My mother helping me to light a candle in church.

My sister and I walking to school on a fresh spring morning, and seeing a tiny green frog on the sidewalk.

Kissing my father goodbye as I boarded a bus to leave New Orleans.

Putting the name tag on my white coat that finally said Doctor *Dillon.*

Edgar had presented the moments that I would have chosen myself if I had only a minute left to relive my life, but probably he already knew that. Each of the images hovered for a moment and then dropped away, like candles being snuffed, and when they were gone I couldn't remember them. Piece by piece, everything that I was and ever would be was being siphoned out and destroyed. I still wanted to fight, but there was nothing left to fight with. I had no body, no soul, no humanity. Soon there would be no reason to fight. I would be an empty vessel, ready for Edgar Templeton to move in and take possession.

Then Edgar made a mistake. He showed me an image of Derek.

He was in the psychiatric hospital, his wrists wrapped in bandages, singing the song I'd heard when I first walked in. As I listened to Derek sing that beautiful song which held so much meaning for me, I begin to reincorporate. Awareness and physical sensation crept back in, and soon I had enough control over my body to realize that the song was not a memory, plucked out of my mind by Edgar like a photo that he was about to toss in the trash.

Derek was singing to me, here and now.

I struggled to open my eyes but they felt like they were melted shut. So I concentrated on listening.

"No, no, no!" Edgar screeched.

A crushing weight ground me into the unyielding rock, squeezing the breath out of my lungs. Red sparks exploded behind my eyelids. As sensation flooded back in, so did pain. It was worse than anything I'd ever imagined, much less experienced. I felt as if my limbs were being severed from the inside out, every joint and ligament disconnected and pulverized like I was in a giant mortar and pestle.

"If I can't have you nobody will."

Edgar Templeton's voice was inside my head. It echoed and multiplied, driving out the sweet sound of Derek's voice. The experience of Edgar Templeton taking my body was like being filled with hot molten lava. I felt my heart begin to slow down. My life was fading out.

But then I heard the singing again, and this time another voice had joined in. It was my sister's sweet soprano, singing harmony with Derek's tenor. The sound was so lovely it almost broke my heart, and that was when I realized that my heart was my own to break. My eyes began to open, and Edgar Templeton flowed out of me as easily as water down a cliff.

The first thing I saw when my vision returned was Derek, sitting on the edge of the rock, clutching his knees.

"Maggie?"

I nodded. "Yes, it's really me."

I tried to stand up and go to him, but all my body parts were not yet under my control. From the way Derek was struggling I could tell that the same thing was happening to him. We moved toward each other like a couple of lurching zombies, but when we met our lips functioned just fine.

"Thank God you're okay. I wasn't sure we'd be able to . . . ," I blurted.

Derek squeezed my arm. "It's not over yet."

He pointed into the sky. The ghostly cloud was above our heads, glowing and pulsating with malevolent light. My heart sank down to my heels. I didn't have the strength to fight Edgar again and I was sure Derek didn't, either.

But then I heard Eva. Turning toward the sound, I saw her standing in the center of the rock. Her arms were outstretched and her head tipped toward the sky. She was chanting in that unintelligible tongue. A white cloud surrounded her. As I watched, she seemed to spread out and become insubstantial, as if her body was vaporizing. The chant continued, but it grew quieter, as if Eva was on the back of a truck driving away. There was a battle going on between Edgar and Eva, a molecular tug of war, as each of them tried to drive the other out of existence.

All the candles in the circle went out at the same moment, although I hadn't felt a breeze. The ghostly mist concentrated above Eva's head, darkening and lengthening into the knife shape it had used to enter my body. Eva's head began to tilt upward, toward the ghost.

"Let's sing the lullaby," I said quickly, clutching Derek's arm.

We joined hands and approached Eva, getting as close as we could without entering Edgar's miasma. Derek sang in his beautiful tenor, and I harmonized as best I could. My voice was nothing like Eva's, but I didn't think it mattered whether I was on pitch or not. It was the emotion that counted.

> Hark, a solemn bell is ringing
> Clear through the night
> Thou, my love, art heavenward winging
> Home through the night.

Eva stopped chanting and joined in our song, although her voice seemed to be coming from somewhere deep un-

derground. The white cloud pulsated angrily and then pixi-
lated, breaking into millions of tiny dots. Edgar was trying to
incorporate again.

At that moment my eye was drawn to the edge of the
woods, where a light had appeared. As it drew closer I saw
that it was another miasma, similar in substance to Edgar
and yet entirely different. While Edgar whipped through the
air like an angry hornet, this cloud bobbed gently, like a but-
terfly. Instead of being white, it had a rosy-pink hue, the
color of a sunset. And this entity filled me with joy and comfort. It didn't have to take on human form for me to know
who it was.

Mama surrounded us, breathing warmth into my frozen
body. Derek and I joined hands with Eva and we quietly repeated the song. The rosy cloud pulsated rhythmically, like a
giant transparent heart. I felt strength flow back into my
body, and I could see that Eva looked rejuvenated as well.

As we sang, the dots that made up Edgar separated and
pulled farther and farther apart. Millions of white specks
flew high into the air and hung there for a few moments,
looking like a sky full of stars, and then one by one they
winked out, until there was nothing left.

Eva slumped and started to fall, but Derek caught her and
held her under the arms. I checked her pulse and found it
strong and steady.

"She'll be all right," I said.

I turned around, looking for the rosy cloud, hoping that it
had incorporated into something I could hold in my arms,
but she was gone. The sky and the air were empty and quiet.

"Mama!" I ran to the edge of the glade, peering into the
opaque darkness for some tiny sign, a winking firefly light
that said she was still there, but I already knew she wasn't.

Derek slid his strong arm around my waist. "Are you all
right, Maggie?"

I leaned back against his chest, letting his strength support me. "Yeah, I'm okay."

When we got back to the rock, Eva was waiting. We each kissed her on the cheek, and then, laughing like children, we joined hands and skipped in a circle on the rock until we all collapsed, exhausted, in a heap.

Chapter 10

As soon as the door closed behind us I ran. When I reached the bed I collapsed onto my stomach and closed my burning eyes. A moment later Derek dropped down beside me. His hand felt around until it found mine.

"This is a really nice duvet," Derek said.

I stroked the silky surface. "It should be, at that price."

The manager of the Inverness Inn had stared at us in disbelief when we banged on the door of his upscale establishment at two a.m., covered with dirt and bloody scratches, but he had enough discretion not to ask any questions, especially after Derek produced a platinum AmEx card to cover two rooms at five hundred dollars each.

"I don't think I've ever been so tired," I said.

"For you, that's saying something." Derek stroked my hand. I turned my head and met his smiling brown eyes.

"Thank you, Maggie," he said.

"You don't have to thank me."

"Why not? You risked your life for me."

"I did it for myself as much as for you."

"How's that?"

I couldn't look at him when I said this, for fear of what I might see, so I turned my face toward the window. The fog had cleared, and the moon smiled in on us from a purple sky. "I couldn't bear to lose you. I need you, Derek."

He touched my cheek and turned me to face him. Tears glimmered in his eyes. "I love you."

Now it was my turn to cry. So much had happened in such a short time that my head was still reeling from it all. I felt like I'd been living inside an egg, self-contained and protected, with no idea how tiny my circumscribed world was compared to what was outside it. And then the egg cracked and I emerged into a world that contained other people, and wide horizons, and love.

"I love you too."

Derek enfolded me in his arms and kissed me gently. He molded my hips to his, and I could feel that he was hard and ready.

"I want to make love to you again," he whispered into my ear before he licked the tender skin behind it.

"And I would too," I replied.

"But I'm too tired," we both said simultaneously.

We barely managed to crawl under the covers before we both fell asleep.

The next morning we were awakened by an insistent tap on the door.

"Did you order anything?" I grumbled.

"How could I?" he answered. "I was asleep."

He stumbled to the door, still in the dirty jeans and T-shirt he'd worn the night before. A hotel employee was waiting with a plate under a silver dome and a pot of delicious-smelling coffee.

"That smells awfully good," Derek said, "but I didn't order it. Besides, there's two of us here."

"Oh!" The young man looked chagrined as he checked the ticket. "This is for the room next door. Please accept my apologies, and if you would like breakfast today, of course it will be on the house."

Derek shut the door on his retreating back and turned to me. "Do you want breakfast?"

I lifted a corner of the duvet. "Maybe later."

Derek didn't immediately climb into bed. Instead he treated me to a slow striptease as he removed the clothes he'd been too tired to take off the night before. We had forgotten to close the curtains, and the sun gleamed through puffy cumulus clouds, surrounding Derek with a honey-colored halo. When the T-shirt came off my gaze lingered on his taut chest muscles and chiseled abdomen. He turned slightly, revealing the tattoo of the Celtic cross on his bicep that I'd first seen at the hospital. Then I'd tried to avoid looking at his sinewy back and high, round buttocks, but now I was free to feast my eyes. My mouth went dry as he unbuttoned his jeans, tantalizing me with their slow progress down his jutting hipbones. Finally he revealed his manhood in all its glory.

"That is a beautiful picture," I said.

"Do you want me to stay like this?" He flexed a bicep and struck a pose, turning his head so that the sun burnished the long waves of his hair.

"Hell, no, I want you to come here."

He slid between the sheets. After a bit of scrambling I was divested of my own clothes, down to my bra and panties. Derek kissed me so deeply I felt it all the way down to my curling toes, which he trapped between his own feet as he flipped me onto my back. He held my hands down, rendering me immobile. I could do nothing but gasp as he slid up and down, pressing himself into the cleft between my legs, the silk of my panties generating a delicious friction between us.

"Oh, yes," I moaned, as he stripped the panties off my legs. "Come inside."

"No, not yet." He freed my hands so that he could slide down the length of my body, kissing and licking all the way. "I'm going to make sure this gets done right."

I tossed the duvet aside so that I could look at him. His hair fell in a curtain around his face, and the ends swept my skin, causing a tickling pleasure that was so exquisite it made me laugh out loud. Digging my fingers deep into his curly hair as he dove between my legs, I started to guide him with my hands, but quickly realized he needed no assistance. He found the spot where I wanted him to go and worked it expertly with tongue and teeth until shooting stars appeared behind my eyelids. My world contracted until nothing was left but that tiny knob of flesh and the sensation pulsing through it. Then everything exploded. The world expanded again, and I felt it all, in every part of me. I sobbed with the pure joy of it, of being alive and having Derek with me, wholly and entirely himself.

"Are you okay?" he asked, lifting his head. "You're crying."

"No, I'm not," I said. I hauled him up, locking my ankles around his thighs and pulling him in hard, so that he had no choice but to slip inside me.

He gasped as he went in. "Are you sure?"

"Yes. Move with me, Derek."

He did. We rocked together in flawless rhythm and perfect harmony, performing a duet that was timeless, ageless, shared by all humans and yet entirely unique to us. It was our song of love.

Epilogue

Six months later

The music seemed to be coming from inside my head.

For a moment this sensation frightened me, until I realized I'd fallen asleep with the iPod headphones on, listening to the latest track of Derek's new album. It seemed I was falling asleep all the time now, but that was understandable, since I was six months pregnant. I stood up slowly, to avoid the dizziness that hit me every time I moved from horizontal to vertical. Being pregnant had slowed me down considerably. Or maybe it was being back in New Orleans. Something about the thick, magnolia-scented air seemed to cause everything and everybody to move at a more leisurely pace.

I checked the clock and was startled to realize I'd been asleep for an hour. I was seeing a client at two o'clock, a half hour from now, but since my commute was only about sixty steps I had plenty of time. I went to the bathroom, combed my hair, and touched up my lipstick. Standing sideways, I checked out my belly in the full-length mirror. As always, I was awestruck at the miracle that was occurring inside me. The baby had started kicking a month ago, and since then he or she had kept up an almost constant marathon of calisthenics that made my belly ripple and pucker like Eva's bag of snakes.

When I first found out I was pregnant, three weeks after the exorcism in the forest, I was worried that I would conflate the experience of being pregnant with being occupied by Edgar's ghost. After all, the only experience I'd ever had of having another soul inside my body was a profoundly distressing one. But after the first sonogram, when the tiny, ghostly white apparition of our baby appeared on the screen and its rapid heartbeat echoed out of the sonogram machine, and Derek and I cried together, I knew that I would welcome this soul, and nurture it happily inside my body until it was ready to make its own way in the world. This baby, and Derek, had given me my life back and allowed me to shape it into just the right life for me.

After locking the apartment I crossed the balcony, running my fingers along the ornate eighteenth-century ironwork, and waddled downstairs. Derek's music studio was on the first floor of our carriage house, which was behind a brick-lined courtyard containing a burbling fountain and several overarching oak trees. I didn't bother to knock, since I knew he'd have headphones on, and I was able to watch him undetected as he sat at the recording console, adjusting dials and sliders while his head bobbed in time to the music.

I snuck up behind him and put one hand on his chest. He startled, and then relaxed, leaning back into his chair. I slid my fingers under his T-shirt, cupping his hard pectoral muscle. Even six months after Edgar had left Derek's body, it was still reassuring to feel his steady heartbeat under my hand. I pinched his nipple lightly and it tightened at my touch.

"Can't you see I'm working?" he groaned. "You pregnant women are insatiable."

"Don't flatter yourself," I said. "I have a client in twenty minutes."

He pulled my hand until I bent over him, and then he grabbed the back of my head. He kissed me, long and deep, until the fluttering in my belly made me wonder if he was right—if I was, in fact, insatiable.

He stood up so abruptly the headphones pulled off his ears and fell onto the console. He put both arms around me and grabbed my behind, pulling me tightly against him, fitting himself expertly around the swell in my belly. All the while he kept kissing me, his tongue alternately swirling and probing, first soft, then hard and insistent. I stumbled backward until I hit the wall, and still he was grinding against me, massaging my flesh, pulling my skirt up my legs . . .

"Derek, Eva's waiting for me in the store. Maybe if I hadn't fallen asleep, or if you'd woken me up, but I don't have time to go back home."

"Who said anything about going back?" His hand slipped insistently down my abdomen. He lifted the upper edge of my panties and then paused, his lips on my neck, hot breath blowing down my collar.

"What are you waiting for?" I moaned.

"For you to say yes." His fingertips tickled my hair, skimmed my outer lips.

I waited, torturing myself with the pleasure of anticipation. He bit my neck, just fiercely enough for me to cry out. There was a yes in the cry, and his fingers plunged downward. I came instantly, and he supported my weight with his other arm as my legs gave way underneath me. He held me tenderly, whispering how much he loved me into the cup of my ear, until I stopped shuddering. Then he straightened up and adjusted his jeans to accommodate the extra bulk at the front. There was a wicked smile on his face.

"What about you?" I said, reaching for his belt buckle.

"Oh no." He spun toward the console and picked up his headphones. "Let it be known that I did not make Dr. Maggie Fielding late for her appointment." He turned back and kissed me once, lightly. "I'll see you tonight."

I eyed him like he was a plate of the French Market beignets I'd recently rediscovered.

"You're evil, Derek Fielding. But in a good way."

The water in the fountain sparkled in the shafts of bright summer sunlight that found their way through the shelter of the oak trees. I dipped my hand in the water and splashed it onto my hot face, drying it with the sleeve of my shirt. We allowed customers to sit in the courtyard, so there was a sign on both the front and back doors.

Two Sisters House of Spiritual Counseling

I had voted against the drippy gothic lettering, but both Derek and Eva liked it, so I'd been outvoted. And now that I'd lived with it for a few months, I realized that it did fit the French Quarter milieu better than the sterile sans serif font I had wanted to use. I was still getting used to my new identity as the ghost-whispering psychiatrist, whose arsenal included everything from Prozac to pentacles, but as each day passed I became more comfortable and more accepting that this was my true calling.

Even though it was shaded, the courtyard was blisteringly hot, so I was happy for the cool blast of air conditioning as I entered the store. I breathed in the heady aroma of incense, herbs, and candles. Carmel, the clerk I'd spoken to from California, was at the counter unpacking a box of jewelry. I picked up a necklace of assorted semiprecious stones and worked it through my fingers like a rosary, happy to find I could recount the healing and spiritual properties of each of the stones. I was wearing a necklace of carnelian and citrine. Carnelian was associated with reproduction, rebirth, and reincarnation, and citrine was useful in helping people find their way along the path of life. Eva favored malachite because it was a money attractor, and Carmel was into moss agate because she was on the hunt for a decent boyfriend.

"Rashad Simpkins called," Carmel said, as she draped a necklace over a riser in the black velvet display case.

"Oh, really?" Rashad had been given the staff position at the hospital after I made it clear to Dr. Kay that after graduation I was taking my career in a different direction. "What did he want?"

"He wants to consult with you about a patient."

I couldn't help but smile. Only three months out and I was already getting consultations from mainstream practitioners? Maybe this new gig was going to work out even better than I had hoped.

The bell over the front door jingled, and a woman stepped inside. She looked to be in her sixties. Her long, thick hair, secured at the back of her head in a messy bun, was mostly gray, but had probably been red or auburn. She had sparkly green eyes and beautiful ivory skin with hardly any wrinkles. She was what I imagined Mama might have looked like as an older lady.

She wasn't the first woman who'd given me that impression. Derek and I occasionally went to Mass on Sundays, and there was always at least one lady there who made my heart lurch with yearning because something about her—the tilt of her head, the way she held her hymn book, a throaty laugh— reminded me of Mama. I didn't shy away from these feelings; in fact I welcomed them. For too long I had packed my emotions away while I tried to solve everyone else's problems, wrongly assuming that by chasing other people's demons

I could keep my own at bay. No, the only way a demon would be vanquished was by facing him head-on. I'd learned that from Edgar Templeton, and for that I was thankful to him.

"I have an appointment with Dr. Fielding," the woman said.

"That's me," I said, shaking the woman's hand. "But you can call me Maggie."

Please turn the page for an exciting sneak peek of
Jacquelyn Frank's
DRINK OF ME,
coming in November 2010!

Sorrow.

It beat at him like a relentless drum, throbbing through his mind and vibrating into his soul until he felt it burning in his body as though it were his own. Stunned by the intensity of the intrusion, Reule actually hesitated several moments, distracting himself at the worst possible time. He felt the purity of the devastating emotion shuddering through him. Too pure, and too disturbing, Reule realized very quickly as he flung up well-practiced and powerful mental barricades, the imposing walls blotting out most of the wild despair that had stained his concentration.

Careless of him to let something like that intrude on such a crucial moment. Lines of disconcertion etched themselves into his forehead and around his mouth. The source of that unsettling intrusion was a mystery. It tempted him. But that, he realized, might very well be the point. It could be intentional bait.

Reule dismissed the idea straightaway, confident he could tell the difference between deception and honesty. Though he'd never felt such overwhelming sadness before in his life, it had been brutally honest. Pushing it all away to focus back on his goal of the moment, he lifted his head and sought the scents of the others, marking their positions in silence as they kept their mental communication minimalized. Their prey would sense their approach if they picked up on the power of their pursuers' thoughts flying back and forth along the telepathic channels between them.

Reule marked the identifications and locations of the other males of the Pack. Rye, to the north along the stone wall in the underbrush. Darcio, to his rear by several yards, low against the trunk of a thick and ancient oak. Delano, of course, on point ahead of them and moving slowly along the perimeter of the hostile territory they sought to enter. Reule focused next on the house hidden deep in the darkness, concentrating until his vision altered to pierce the veil of the brick walls, picking up the greenish-white blobs of movement that indicated life in one form or another. It was easy to differentiate their target, seated centrally and surrounded by others like bees buzzing over their precious queen. All of this activity took place on the second floor.

Reule turned his attention to Delano, watching the sleek speed the male used to breech the property line. In concert, the rest of the pack moved forward, their senses sharply attuned to the rhythm it would take to succeed at their task. He could have closed his eyes and still known that Rye leapt the stone wall with ease, and that Darcio kept every step timed to match perfectly with his own as Reule advanced.

Each member of the pack neared the structure with caution. Reule crouched low on the balls of his feet, sharply alert, and he became as still and invisible as a shadow. His stillness was timed perfectly. His target came through the near door, so close he nearly tripped over Reule. When the unfortunate crossed in front of him, Reule struck with the speed of a cobra. His fangs exploded into full, glorious length as he attacked, but they wouldn't taste of this repugnant creature. He could control the impulse, sparing himself the disgust of such an experience.

Instead, it was his extending claws that struck, and even that attack was conservative. Reule grabbed his victim over his mouth, jerking his head back and puncturing his shoulder with needle-sharp nails right through his shirt, the cotton fabric no protection from the invasion. Reule's muscles flexed as his prey struggled and fought, but they both knew it was a futile effort. Once the paralytic tipping his nails broke beyond the skin, it was only a matter of time. Still, Reule held him to keep him quiet until the drug took effect, using his mental power to stifle his victim so he could raise no alarms. When the male finally became deadweight in his hold, he released him. The body of his enemy dropped to the ground like a sack of rocks, thudding sickly as bone impacted earth. Reule kicked him away in contempt. The toxin wouldn't kill him, but if Reule didn't like what he found when he entered the house, he'd be back to finish the job.

Reule straightened and eased toward the door. He was vigilant for other stragglers as he sought the heat and motion of others. They were all upstairs in that central room, and now Reule understood why. He heard shouts of laughter and cajoling, cheering and jeering, and he suddenly realized why there were insufficient guards staged to protect the place. He snarled low in loathing and the sound was echoed by his Shadow, Darcio. The others didn't respond, but they felt Reule's rage and he felt their agreeing emotion.

And that opened him up to the sorrow once more.

It slammed into him, stronger than before—a devastating sadness that stole his breath away and nearly stopped his heart. Chills rushed up under his flesh until it crawled with agonizing emotional response. Never, in all his many years, had he felt anything like it. He'd shared thoughts and emotions with his Pack for all of his existence, and never had they, *his family,* been able to project such powerful emotion into him. If he couldn't feel such things from his family, who could force it upon him? More, what caused such agony? He was the most powerful, the most sensitive when it came to sensing these things, but surely one of his caste had felt deep, abiding pain before! What made this so incredibly intense to him? How did it invade him so easily in spite of his skill and power to resist such things?

Reule tried to shake off the sensations even as he fell back unsteadily against a near wall. Darcio leapt forward, instantly at his side when he sensed his distress. Reule quickly fended off his friend's concern, recovering and pushing the alien anguish hard away from himself so he could project confidence and strength to the Pack. They were being distracted in dangerous territory and he'd be responsible if any of them was injured because of it. Reule silently realigned their attention with a powerful emanation and he felt them draw back into formation swiftly. Only Darcio, who had seen him falter physically, hesitated. Reule ignored his concern and reached for the door.

Entering from three different portals, Reule felt Rye and Delano both engage hostiles, swiftly taking them out and discarding them so they could move rapidly to the stairs leading to the next floor. Reule scanned the first floor to be sure they wouldn't leave anyone at their backs and sent Darcio after a stray with silent command. Then he and the rest of the Pack moved upward.

As soon as they reached the second floor, Reule felt a ripple of awareness go through half of the crowd in the central room. Now they were close enough that emotions, projected or not, gave their presence away. Reule moved like lightning, as did the others, knowing that surprise, such as it was, was key.

Before the Jakals became fully aware of the danger approaching, half of them staggered back from paralyzing puncture wounds and debilitating hand-to-hand combat.

Reule moved so fast that he went through three victims before he met with his first resistance. With about a half dozen Jakals on the floor, or slipping numbly toward it, the Pack faced the remaining enemy, which was now fully on guard. It wouldn't be so easy to incapacitate them. Six Jakals were standing alert and in perfect fighting form. Reule took only a moment to survey the room with quick, accurate eyes, and what he saw seared his brain with wrath.

Besides the Jakals, in the center of the room was a metal chair, bolted to the floor and made of gleaming steel that had to feel as cold as it looked. The sight of it alone chilled Reule's spine. However, it was nothing compared to what he felt when he saw the figure slumped forward in it as far as his bound wrists and feet would allow; the former manacled to the flat metal arms and the latter to the legs. Blood drained in a steady stream from his mouth and nose, both of which had been battered to a pulpy mess. Steel spikes had been driven through his forearms and calves, as if the manacles wouldn't be enough to hold him. The Jakals were right. Manacles alone would never have held their prisoner. Although now, with the pool of blood growing in an ever-widening circle beneath that sterile chair of metal, the prisoner within was not even strong enough to lift his head, never mind escape. The Jakals had been taking their pleasure torturing him, and they'd made a spectator sport of it.

This time the snarl that vibrated out of Reule was violent enough to reverberate against the four walls of the room. His eyes turned from their normal hazel to a reflective green as he lowered into a crouch and bared his fangs. His Pack, including Darcio, who had caught up to them, imitated both the sound and the predatory motion in perfect synchronicity. Reule almost smiled when he heard a fifth growl join weakly with them from the chair in the center of the room.

Jakals on the defensive, however, were no easy targets. The Jakals' slender forms were made for speed, their skin smooth to the point of slickness. They were impossible to grapple with. The wily creatures could twist and strike before you even saw them. Discordant hisses and taunting laughter radiated from their midst as venom dripped from fangs. They were prepared to strike or spit the acidic compound at their attackers, and unlike Reule's people's paralytic, Jakal poison was mortal if the skin was punctured; and a more brutal death to suffer had yet to be invented.

Reule wasn't overly concerned about that. What concerned him was that they were between his Packmates and the prisoner in the chair. If he hadn't already been envenomated, the enemy might take the opportunity to do so before they could be stopped. Since there was no known cure for envenomation, this was Reule's primary worry. He could tell by the look in the eyes of the Jakal facing him that his enemy was well aware of it.

As a rule, Jakals were the more powerful empaths of all the known species of the wilderness, only Reule's breed strong enough to block them. However, as a man of significant ability, he had learned that with strong powers of the mind came strong sensitivities. That had been proven just this evening as he himself had been bombarded by a stranger's overwhelming grief and been caught unaware by it. Surely these empaths before him had heard those cries of anguish from whoever it was projected them? He knew it was no Jakal feeling those emotions, for though they could sense every feeling any creature was capable of, they didn't have the ability to generate such deep feeling themselves. They certainly didn't understand its true value. It was a terrible irony, and it was what made them such vicious little monsters; monsters who found glee in glutting themselves on the intense emotions of others. Like the emotions generated by torture, rape, or any number of things Reule refused to imagine lest he give way to a rage that would blot his focus and potentially feed his avaricious enemies.

This information did allow Reule an advantage. He was the most powerful sensor of his kind, one without measure in the history of his people. He was willing to bet these lowly gypsy Jakals had never seen his type before and would never be expecting him. That would be his advantage, and that would save the Packmate who had fallen prey to these depraved beasts.

And to think, others considered *his* people were the lowest of breeds, Reule thought with disgust.

Reule sent an emanation to his Packmates, steadying them and preparing them silently, including a reassurance to the barely conscious one in the center of the room. Then he slowly unfolded the layers of protection over his mind so he could release his concealed power.

This time he was better prepared for the anguish that struck him, but still it was bordering on all-consuming. It was just the kind of emotional inundation that a Jakal would take gluttonous pleasure in. He could easily amplify the already overwhelming feeling and overload his enemies with the rawness of it, but Reule dismissed the idea instantly. There was something far too personal and *innocent* about the stark grief. To feed it to the Jakals somehow felt as though it would be a betrayal. Reule didn't understand his reluctance, but he didn't have time to do any soul-searching.

With a mere glance he commanded Rye, who nodded his head and slid closer to one of the paralyzed Jakals. The enemy lay helpless but conscious, staring up as the hunter contemplated him with a wicked little smile that bared a fine set of fangs. Loosing an intimidating vocalization, Rye reached over to the sheath attached to his bicep on the right and withdrew the blade slowly. The blue metal gleam of the *rubkar*'s blade caught the overhead lighting and made it look even more menacing as Rye lowered himself into a crouch next to the helpless male.

There. That moment. That fear and terror in one of their

own, *that* was what Reule caught hold of, magnified, and used to net the sensitive enemy before him. His fingers curled into fists, his chin dipping down as he focused ferociously on manipulating all of them at once. He couldn't allow a single one to escape the bombardment, giving them a chance to further harm his kinsman.

The effect was more than he would have expected or even hoped for. The Jakals standing in the center of the room suddenly recoiled in horror and began to scream. They clapped bony fingers over their skulls as males and females alike wailed to a pitch high enough to shatter glass. Reule ignored it, pushing and pushing, refusing to let go lest they try to push back and incapacitate him, which they could do just by virtue of his being fiercely outnumbered.

As he drilled into them their compatriot's horror of impending death, and his helplessness to do anything about it, he felt as though he were stronger than he ever had been before. He was an awesome force to contend with under any circumstances, but there was no mistaking the surge of vitalizing strength sliding into the well within him that he drew his ability out of.

Reule kept the conduit open; from victim Jakal, to amplification within himself, and back to the small crowd of compatriot Jakals in the center of the room, pouring it out as Rye's knife lowered to a mark. His Packmate closed both his hands around the haft of the blade in a ritualistic manner. Reule prepared for the death strike, knowing that he could put these bastards in a comatose state for the rest of their lives, even though there was a good deal of jeopardy to himself as well if he channeled the imminent death throes. But he felt supremely confident that he would remain only the messenger, untouched by what was about to happen.

Rye looked straight into the eyes of the Jakal whose throat lay under the tip of his razor-sharp, dual-edged blade. With the scent of battle and impending bloodletting on him,

Rye's eyes were nearly glowing with green-yellow anticipation and his fangs pushed out both his upper and lower lips so they could be seen even without his purposeful sneer.

"Abak tu mefritt," he hissed.

Death to my enemy. Rye spat the battle cry just before plunging deep and with so much rage-filled power that the blade went clean through and was imbedded in the wood of the floor. He left it like that and leapt to his feet before the Jakal's blood could touch him. He spat on his victim in obvious contempt.

Reule felt every moment of both the death and the victory, but it was the last minutes of suffering that he passed on. He broke out in a drenching sweat, every last muscle in his taut, powerful body shuddering as he closed himself off from being dragged into the dark of oblivion along with the dying Jakal. Instead he forced himself to magnify the last pulses, the last breaths, and the last horrified thoughts of the Jakals' kin as he drilled it all into the entire group of them. The effect was so potent that Reule was aware of even his mentally guarded Packmates staggering back from his onslaught. But he couldn't gear back the intensity of it. They would be all right, he reassured himself, so long as they weren't his direct targets.

His direct targets, however, were not so fortunate. Reule strove for total incapacitation, but he got much more. All six Jakals tumbled to the floor, some landing on their knees, others flat on their backs or faces. They all began to seize violently, clawing at their throats as though a wicked blue blade had pinned them to the floor. Some coughed up blood; others gasped out strangled breaths.

Then, with a communal, convulsive sigh, each exhaled one last breath.

Reule felt the group of target minds shut down all at once and there was an instant whiplash effect, impacting him physically so that he fell back as if he'd been playing tug-of-war and the other team had suddenly let go. Darcio caught him, but Reule was no light weight, his build thick with a warrior's muscle and his height stretching to over six feet. Darcio was determined, however, to at least keep his Pack leader from landing in an undignified heap, easing him to the floor.

The death was gone, purged from Reule's mind with the break in his concentration, although the metallic ghost of it would cling to him for a long time to come. Darcio knelt on a single knee beside him, steadying him even though he sat, a disturbed furrow creasing his brow.

Darcio had every right to be concerned. The Packmates had seen Reule do some pretty amazing things over time, had even come to expect to be amazed regularly by the sheer potency of their leader's unique power, but never had Darcio seen any one man strike such a devastating blow to an enemy at six-to-one odds. The Jakals weren't just comatose, they were *dead*. Dead by the power of Reule's thoughts. Darcio felt the heavy silence of the Pack, only the captive Chayne making noise as he rasped for breath. Otherwise, the Pack guarded their thoughts from Reule. However, because they were a Pack, Reule would be aware of their collective discomfort.

It wasn't his Pack's disturbance that struck Reule's weakened mental defenses, though. His mind was now stripped of the strength to defend itself, and that allowed the desperate sorrow to bombard him again. Reule had also carefully blocked out Chayne's agony and humiliation so it wouldn't interfere with his concentration. Now it washed over him in burning waves, clearly differentiating itself from the sadness that swirled around him. No, it wasn't his suffering Packmate that Reule felt in deep, assailing eddies. There was another, and whomever it was had to be close.

"Reule, don't do it," Darcio warned him, his kin now free to exchange thoughts with him as his mental walls lay crumbled. "It could be a trap. You will end up like them." Darcio flicked a hand at the pile of dead Jakals.

"No," Reule rasped as he struggled to regain his balance and physical coordination. "This is something else. Someone is in pain."

"It's no concern of ours," Darcio hissed softly, his worry coming through despite his attempts to be coldhearted. Reule knew Darcio well. His Packmate had one concern in all the world, and that was Reule's safety and well-being.

"Darcio, if it were you, would you appreciate others turning their backs on you and abandoning you to your fate? She is close. In this house, I believe." Reule stopped suddenly, realizing that he was right. What he felt originated from a female. Strange he should know that. Stranger still that he could sense only this tide of one particular feeling, but no others. No thoughts, nothing to identify her, just . . . sadness.

"You see?" his companion persisted. "Even your own mind tells you that something is wrong about this."

Reule frowned irritably, disliking the defenselessness of his mind, which allowed Darcio to read his every thought. He struggled to erect even the slightest of barriers against the intrusion, a filter at the very least. To his surprise he got a monumental wall of protection. It was so strong and abrupt that he felt Darcio stiffen with shock as he was booted out of Reule's mind with perfunctory force. Reule quickly reached up to grasp his friend's shoulder, giving it an apologetic squeeze.

"Your advice is always valued, Darcio. Remember that. But I will act in accord with my instincts on this." The gesture of camaraderie seemed to ease the other male's bruised feelings, and Darcio reached to help haul Reule to his feet. No easy task that, Reule weighing several stones more than the leaner man. He felt Rye under his other arm helping to steady him within moments, though.

"Chayne?" he asked.

"We won't know until we get him back home. The apothecary will tell us the whole of it," Rye said softly.

"Go, help Delano with Chayne. I'm well enough," he instructed Rye. To prove the point, he took his weight onto his own two feet and pushed Rye away with a guiding hand. Rye hesitated only a moment before nodding and moving away to do as his Pack leader commanded.

Feeling increasingly steady, Reule directed his focus away from the fearful, paralyzed Jakals that yet remained alive, and the noisy thoughts of his Packmates. It wasn't hard to hone in on the sorrow. Adjusting his vision once more to detect heated shapes, he began to scan the house more slowly. He was in the central-most point of the structure, one floor above him and one below. Wherever she was, she was close. He might have mistaken her for a Jakal in his first scan, but it was clear from the depth of her emotion that she couldn't be.

Yet nothing stood upright in the house save his Pack. He looked upward once more and realized there was another floor above the third. And there, up in the farthest corner, he spied a small ball of the dimmest heat.

"Darcio, did you encounter anyone upstairs?"

"No, My Prime. I only sought the one stray you noted."

"Then this is the female I'm sensing. Lord and Lady, but she has strong emotions," he marveled as he stepped over an incapacitated Jakal.

"One emotion, My Prime. One bound to attract a man of good conscience," Darcio said suspiciously. "It's magnified just as you magnified death to the Jakals. What manner of creature can do that besides yourself?" *And even Reule shouldn't be able to do such a thing,* he thought. No man should hold death in the power of his thoughts. Reule had always been fair and just with his power, but things like this had a way of changing a man. Even a Prime.

"You're mistaken," Reule said as he moved with increasing surety out of the room. "There is no magnification. It's . . . pure." The word kept springing to his mind. He decided it suited and left it at that. Darcio didn't say anything, but Reule could feel him repressing arguments because he didn't want to contradict his Prime again. Darcio was a good man, ever his voice of caution and conscience, always advising him to consider carefully. Reule valued him beyond measure and he made certain the thought made it through to Darcio before they took off up the stairs together.

They made it to the third floor of the ramshackle building, clearly abandoned long ago. The roof had leaked and the ceiling was rotted through, as was the wooden floor they now negotiated. Reule and Darcio took care with every step as they edged toward another stairwell, this one narrow and stinking of the closed-in must and mildew surrounding them. Gypsy Jakals were always roaming the lands, scavenging and causing trouble, squatting wherever they could. This band had been around long enough to make this hovel a home. Homey enough to bolt a chair in a central parlor for the purpose of torture. It meant they'd been here for some time. Reule would never have known it if Chayne hadn't accidentally stumbled into capture during their hunting trip.

Reule tested the narrow little attic stairs and wondered how anyone could be up in the garret. Getting there seemed a dangerous task. Then again, it made its own sort of prison, which was a far more likely case considering who had occupied the house and the distressing feeling washing through him.

He made his way to the head of the small stairs, Darcio his ever-present Shadow as he pushed open a heavy, stubborn door. He instantly was confronted with a chasm of missing flooring. A wide, dangerous section had rotted out.

Reule and Darcio could see straight down to the storey they'd just left.

"You're lucky these stairs even held," Darcio muttered as Reule entered the room one careful sidestep after another. His Packmate was right. The hole in the floor came to within a mere foot of the door and stairwell.

And of course his target was all the way on the opposite side. Even though it was all one large room, he still couldn't see her. There was a crowd of crates blocking his view of her, though he could still sense her dim heat.

"I'd really like to know how she got over there," Reule said in honest curiosity. Darcio nodded his agreement as they tried to plot the best course of action.

"I should go. I'm lighter. Less chance of the floor giving way."

Good point, but Reule didn't want to relinquish the task for some reason. Her pain was so bittersweet, beautiful merely by virtue of its purity and depth. Anyone who could feel pain so deeply, logic reasoned, was used to accommodating its antithesis. Reule only hoped that pain wasn't all she *could* feel after this.

"No," he responded after a moment. "There's a strip along the wall that looks sturdy enough even for me. Since this is my folly, I might as well be the one to risk breaking my neck."

"My Prime," Darcio protested.

"It's a joke, Shadow. Take ease."

"I will once we're out of this dangerous hellhole," Darcio countered sullenly.

Reule turned away to hide a smile. Leave it to Darcio to take all the fun out of an adventure. Still, he wasn't swayed so easily. His blood rushed with adrenaline as he negotiated wet, creaking boards that were maybe days, or even minutes from rotting away completely. He tried not to touch the dank, mildewed wall running next to him as he went. Some molds in the damplands were poisonous or flesh eaters. An ominous crack sounded through the room, and Reule abruptly realized exactly how unstable the entire building was. The Jakals were insane to risk staying in such a place. If the floor inside was rotted, he could just imagine the state of the roof above them. He glanced back at Darcio and they exchanged a mutual understanding that they needed to get out as soon as possible. If nothing else, they were agreed on that.

Reule exhaled carefully when he reached the other side of the gaping hole, unwilling to relax so long as he stood on water-stained boards. He gingerly made his way over to the boxed crates and peered into the dark corner behind them.

The only thing he could see was the palest little hand. His heart skipped a beat as he realized that this was probably a child. A renewed sense of rage flooded him and he began to think of the Jakals left alive on the lower floors. When he left this property not a one of them would be left breathing, he vowed to himself fiercely. They had feasted on their very last victims.

Very carefully, Reule grabbed one of the crates and slid it a little aside. The frightening creak of the protesting floor halted him instantly.

"To hell," he muttered, planting both hands on another crate and effortlessly leaping over its four feet in height as if it were nothing. His feet hit the only clear piece of flooring available without landing on the girl. He heard Darcio curse baldly when his weight met protesting floorboards.

Reule ignored him and squatted down to better see her through the darkness. He reached for her hand as he bent forward. Her pain had become like a repetitive tune singing through him, no longer reaching extreme highs or lows. It wasn't that it weakened, only that he was adapting to the force of it.

Reule had no idea what he would find, but he certainly didn't expect to feel a second hand spearing into his hair from the darkness to grip him with surprising strength and drag him downward until his face was pressed against a baby-soft cheek that should have been warm, but was instead icy cold. A pair of lips, both rough and supple at once, rubbed over his ear as finally something warm, her breath, washed over him. The contrast gave him an involuntary chill, aided by the hoarseness of her voice when she whispered to him.

"*Sánge, bautor mo.*"

Please turn the page for an exciting sneak peek of
Kate Douglas's
HELLFIRE,
now on sale at bookstores everywhere!

now on sale at bookstores everywhere!

Ginny Jones wrapped a clean kitchen towel around her torn fingers and glared at the screeching cat she'd finally managed to shove into the carrier.

Her cousin Markus leaned over her shoulder and sighed. "Poor Tom. I sure hope he's not rabid."

"No shit, Sherlock." She glanced at the blood-soaked towel and then at Markus. "And what do you mean, poor Tom? Did you see what that cat of yours did to my hand?"

Markus shook his head, sending his long dreads flying. "I don't understand. Tom's a sweetheart. He's never even scratched anyone, much less bitten before."

"Tell that to your neighbor. She's going to need stitches in her leg, not to mention what he did to my hand. C'mon. We need to get him to the vet so they can quarantine him before animal control shows up, or they might just take him and put him down."

Markus grabbed the keys off the hook by the back door and picked up the carrier. Tom screeched, a long, low banshee wail that sent goosebumps racing along Ginny's arms and raised the tiny hairs on the back of her neck. Tom didn't sound anything like any cat she'd ever heard. Why did that screech sound so eerily familiar?

Like it was skirting with the edges of her memory?

She stared at Tom glaring back at her through the bars of the carrier, but nothing clicked. She'd never seen a cat with eyes like his. They flashed blood red. When he snarled, she was almost certain he had extra rows of teeth.

She shivered again and wrapped her arms around herself. *Beyond weird.* Everything about the stupid cat was freaking her out. Frowning, Ginny followed Markus at a safe distance through the back door to the garage and watched while he stowed the sturdy carrier in the backseat of the Camry.

Tom howled again. Ginny shook her head. "I don't like this one bit. Shouldn't we maybe put him in the trunk?"

Markus ignored her suggestion and got into the driver's seat. "Get in. No cat of mine rides in the trunk."

Ginny stared at the red-eyed cat. Tom returned her stare.

Markus glared at her. "You scared of a cat? Cripes, Ginny. Get in."

She took a deep breath. The last thing she needed was to look like a coward in front of her baby cousin. "Well, if he gets loose from the carrier, you're putting him back in—and I'm outta here. I've bled enough for the cause." Ginny slammed the door and reached for her seat belt, wondering for the hundredth time what she was doing visiting her cousins in Sedona anyway. It wasn't like they were all that close, but for some reason she'd gotten a wild hair, packed her bags, and headed to Arizona without any plans or advance notice at all.

So far, her timing sucked. She'd barely parked the rental at her aunt's house when the shit hit the fan. Old Tom, the fattest, laziest-looking cat she'd ever seen, had suddenly launched his porky butt off Aunt Betty's front porch, screaming like the devil was on his tail.

He'd practically flown over the six-foot hedge separating

Aunt Betty's house from the one next door. Every hair stood on end and he looked like a flying furball with fangs. He'd gone straight for the poor neighbor lady who was just getting out of her car with her arms loaded with groceries.

The bags had gone one way, the woman the other, but Tom latched on to her left leg and buried his teeth deep. It had taken both Markus and Ginny to pull the cat off the poor woman, and then he'd taken off, still screaming. Aunt Betty had freaked out, grabbed the two little ones, and as far as Ginny knew, she was still hiding in the bedroom with the kids.

Markus, with typical teenage thinking, had gone after the cat with a big bass net like it was a four-legged fish. Ginny'd been the one who finally cornered Tom against the fence, but he'd gotten her good with claws and teeth before she managed to shove him in the carrier and latch the damned thing.

Not quite the entrance she'd imagined on the flight from Sacramento to Phoenix. If she had to go through a course of rabies shots, she was going to kill Markus, and anyone else who gave her grief.

Like Alton. Especially Alton.

Now why in the hell would she be thinking of her friend Eddy Marks's tall, drop-dead gorgeous, egotistical jackass college buddy Alton? They'd barely met, though for some reason Ginny kept associating him with her being here in Sedona, which made no sense whatsoever.

Neither did the fact he'd kissed her the first time she saw him. For some reason, her memories of that kiss were all fuzzy, but she knew they'd locked lips, if only for a moment.

And very nice lips they were, in spite of his bossy attitude. He was a spectacular kisser. She remembered that much, but little else.

Like *why*. She couldn't recall anything leading up to the kiss, or even what happened directly after. This wasn't like her. Not at all, but confusing memories of Alton were all jumbled up with boarding a plane for Phoenix and grabbing a rental car for the drive across the desert to Sedona.

And now she was headed to the local vet's with a crazy cat, her crazier kid cousin, and a hand that was bleeding through the dish towel she'd wrapped around the scratches.

If this was a vacation, she'd definitely had better.

"Is it always this busy?" Ginny rewrapped the towel around her hand while Markus drove around the block again, looking for a parking place. All the slots at the vet's clinic were taken and there wasn't a single empty spot along the road.

Markus shook his head. "Never. Especially on a Tuesday morning."

He finally pulled into the parking lot in front of a grocery store a block away. "I'll carry the cat." He glanced at Ginny and seemed to notice the blood soaked rag for the first time. "Is that still bleeding?"

"Yes, it's still bleeding. Your sweetheart of a cat nailed me good." She got out of the car and started walking toward the clinic. Markus fell into step beside her with the carrier clutched in one hand. Tom had quit screeching, but his incessant growling and snarling was almost as bad.

Markus was big for eighteen—at least six-foot-six with broad shoulders and legs like tree trunks. As tall as she was, Ginny had to look up at him. He might not be the sharpest tack in the box, but she figured if he couldn't protect her from a stupid cat, no one could.

Though, come to think of it, she was the one bleeding, not her cousin. She was still thinking along those lines when Markus grabbed the door to the clinic and held it open for her. Ginny stepped into total pandemonium.

The small clinic reeked of sulfur, which made no sense at all. Usually vet clinics smelled like cat pee. This one was filled with crying kids, screeching animals—most of them in cages, thank goodness—and a couple of staff members who looked as if they were ready to run and hide. Ginny turned and looked at her cousin.

Markus stared wide-eyed at a large cage holding a big blue macaw. The bird spread its beak wide and screeched. It sounded just like Tom. Markus swallowed with an audible gulp. Ginny took a closer look at the macaw. Teeth. Rows and rows of teeth.

Now, she was no expert, but she'd never heard of birds with teeth. Ginny blinked and refocused, but the macaw's mouth was still filled with way too many razor-sharp teeth. A sharp yip caught her attention and she glanced down at a scrawny little Chihuahua that was, thankfully, wearing a muzzle.

More teeth. Not just sharp doggy fangs, but rows of shiny, razor-sharp teeth filled the little mutt's mouth. A lop-eared bunny in a cat carrier just like Tom's snarled and hissed and curled its lips back. More teeth. Every single animal in the clinic looked like something out of a cheap horror film, all of them snarling and screeching and trying to take bites with mouths filled with way too many rows of sharp teeth.

And just like that, her memories crashed back into her head. The big concrete bear chasing her that night back home in Evergreen, her best friend Eddy's dad, Ed Marks, and Alton—though she hadn't known him then, that tall, good-looking friend of Eddy's from college—rushing out of the darkness and attacking the impossible creature, saving her life.

She saw it like a movie on fast-forward—Alton carrying a huge sword made of glass or crystal, jabbing it into the concrete bear like the thing was made of butter. Jumping up on the creature's back, riding it like a bucking bronco, with the bear screeching and wailing.

Screeching and wailing, just like the animals here in the veterinarian's clinic.

Ginny sucked in a breath as images flowed into her mind. Alton lopping off the concrete bear's head with a powerful swing of his sword, the crystal blade flashing by in a slashing arc.

The bear crumbling, just turning into a pile of rocks and dust and sulfuric stink, like it had never been alive at all. And the smell. That horrible stench.

Just like this vet clinic in Sedona.

She remembered Alton and Ed walking her home. How could she have forgotten that night? That was the night Alton kissed her! A girl didn't forget a night like that. It made no sense at all.

Except she was remembering now. Remembering it as clearly as if it had just happened. The bear, the battle . . . Alton's lips. Oh, Lordy . . . his lips, warm and full and so sweet, pressed against hers, moving over her mouth in a whisper of sensation and seduction.

The noise, the screeching animals, the stinky veterinarian's clinic all faded away as Ginny pressed her fingertips against her lips and let the memories flow.

There'd been another night, too. She blinked as it came into focus. Just the two of them, walking arm in arm down the street to her house, standing on her front porch. She was thinking of inviting Alton in. He'd been just as bossy and arrogant as the first time they'd met, but she'd laughed with him, too, and even though they'd only met the night he'd saved her life, he was really very nice under all that bluster.

How could she forget that he'd offered to stay the night on her front porch? Offered to protect her. That was sweet, even though she didn't need any protection. Not in her little town of Evergreen on the slopes of Mount Shasta. Safest place in the world.

She remembered saying goodnight and for some reason

she'd kissed his cheek when she'd really wanted nothing more than to drag him inside and take him straight to her bedroom. Her toes actually tingled, remembering. Her womb felt heavy, her breasts full, recalling now how she'd gone in alone and closed the door. Leaned against it, thinking of Alton. Hearing his voice.

Hearing his voice? How could she have forgotten his voice in her head, that sexy whisper . . . giving her orders?

Damn it all!

Telling me to come to Sedona.

Ginny clenched her hands into fists and bit back a scream that would probably have shut up every screeching animal in the room. It was Alton's fault! Somehow he'd hypnotized her. That had to be it. He'd hypnotized her and made her forget the bear and his kiss and . . .

She growled. The macaw shut its big mouth and stared at her, but all Ginny could see was Alton. That insufferable jackass had sent her here. He'd saved her from a bear made of concrete with rows of razor-sharp teeth, a bear that couldn't have been real, and he'd sent her down here to frickin' Sedona, Arizona, where the cats and bunnies and birds had the same kind of impossible teeth.

Ginny spun around and glared at her cousin.

Markus took a step back. "What'd I do?"

"Nothing. Not a damned thing." She took a deep breath and let it out. Something very weird was going on, and Alton was involved, all the way from the tips of his sexy cowboy boots to the top of his beautiful blond head. "I have to make a phone call. You sign in. I'll be right back."

There wasn't a stitch of clothing covering her perfect body. She was tall and slim and her stylishly bobbed hair swung against her jaw with each step she took on gloriously long legs. If she hadn't been trying to kill him, Alton might have found her attractive. Instead, he wrapped both hands around the jeweled hilt of his crystal sword and swung with practiced ease.

The blade sliced cleanly through the juncture between her neck and shoulder. He watched with grim satisfaction as the mannequin's head bounced off the wall and rolled across the sidewalk. The jaws gaped wide, exposing row after row of razor-sharp teeth framed by perfectly painted pouty lips.

Alton stepped back out of the way, giving Eddy Marks plenty of space to aim the point of her crystal sword. She held DemonSlayer high, slashing through the demonic mist as it flowed through the hole in the mannequin's plastic neck.

The eerie banshee cry of the escaping demon sent shivers down Alton's spine. The screech ended abruptly the moment Eddy's sword sliced into the mist and it burst into flames. All that was left was a puff of foul-smelling smoke.

"Well done, my lady."

Eddy smiled at the sword in her hand. "Thank you, DemonSlayer." Then she sheathed her weapon and rose up on her toes to accept a kiss from her beloved Dax.

Alton couldn't help but think that Dax was one very lucky ex-demon, to find a woman like Eddy Marks, one brave enough to have gained immortality along with her own sentient sword. There weren't many women like her, not in the world he'd come from.

In fact, there were none like Eddy in the lost world of Lemuria. As far as he knew, she was just as unique to Earth.

"That was a new one," Eddy said when she finally peeled herself away from Dax. "Have you seen any more like her?" She nodded in the direction of the mannequin lying on the sidewalk.

Alton dragged his gaze away from Eddy and Dax and stared at the mannequin. "Thankfully, no, but this isn't good. It was bad enough when demons were using ceramic and stone creatures as avatars, but plastic's a new medium for them. Can you imagine the chaos they're going to cause? There's no way to get rid of all the potential hosts for the damned things."

Dax knelt down and ran his hand over the body, as if he needed to see for himself what it was made of. "What I want to know," he said, "is where the demons are coming from. All of a sudden, there's no shortage of them, either. There shouldn't be so many. Not since Alton sealed the gateway from Abyss."

Eddy shoved her bangs out of her eyes. "Maybe they've opened a new one."

Nine hells.

The three of them stared at one another. A new portal was the last thing they needed. Alton sighed. Not two weeks ago he'd been a perfectly bored resident of the lost world of Lemuria, wondering why nothing exciting ever happened. Then he'd helped two humans, a tiny will-o'-the-wisp, and a mongrel dog escape from a Lemurian prison deep within Mount Shasta, and nothing had been the same since.

Exiled from Lemuria with a price on his head, he'd joined the battle against demonkind's invasion of Earth. Not that he was complaining about all the changes in his life, but was there no end to the demon invasion?

Of course, Dax and Eddy's lives had changed just as drastically. Dax the demon had become a demon slayer, working for the good guys to halt the demonic invasion of Earth, and Eddy Marks was a newspaper reporter who had saved Dax's life without a clue what she was getting into. Alton figured she probably hadn't expected immortality, a demon lover, or a crystal sword that talked to her.

And Bumper had been just a dog. The dog barked. Alton leaned over and scratched her curly head. Bumper looked up at him, and Willow's thoughts flowed into Alton's mind.

I think that demon was the only one. Bumper and I checked.

Thank you, Willow. And Bumper.

He couldn't imagine Willow's life now, trapped inside a mongrel like Bumper. The tiny will-o'-the-wisp had been sent as Dax's companion, able to draw energy from the air to fuel his demon powers. In that last big battle on Mount Shasta when the demon ate Willow, she'd managed to transfer her consciousness into Bumper just in time. While Dax no longer needed Willow for energy, Alton knew they all needed her as part of their team. Whether she looked like a tiny fairy or a curly blond pit bull, Willow had the soul and spirit of a warrior.

Just like his other companions.

Alton carefully sheathed his sword. HellFire, the crystal sword he'd had since reaching manhood, had finally, after so many millennia, gained sentience and begun to speak. Proof that it finally considered Alton a warrior, a man of respect.

They'd all earned that respect in the final battle with the gargoyle, which explained the crystal swords Dax and Eddy now wielded as well, replicates of his own sword.

DemonFire for Dax, DemonSlayer for Eddy.

Sentient crystal swords, perfect for fighting the demon invasion that threatened to offset the balance between good and evil. Three warriors, their sentient swords, and a mongrel dog melded to the mind of a will-o'-the-wisp.

They were all that stood between a demon invasion of Earth and the unsuspecting citizens of this world.

Alton couldn't help but worry they might not be enough.

Eddy's cell phone played "Ode to Joy." She reached for the phone and turned away to take her call.

A chill raced along Alton's spine.

Eddy stared at the phone in her hand for a long, long time. Then she slowly slipped it back into her jeans pocket.

Alton and Dax were deep in conversation, and it looked like BumperWillow was right in there with them.

BumperWillow. Eddy couldn't think of one without the other. Not anymore. Thank goodness she'd been able to get things straightened out with the shelter and they'd agreed to let her adopt her foster dog, Bumper, or they'd really have been in a fix. When the gargoyle had eaten the little sprite's body and she'd slipped into the closest available host, at least she'd found one who loved and welcomed her.

The symbiosis between the brave little will-o'-the-wisp and Eddy's funky mutt couldn't have been better, though after seeing how gorgeous Willow'd been as a sprite and how silly she looked as a pit bull crossed with a blond poodle, Eddy couldn't help but wonder if Willow ever had second thoughts about her choice of borrowed body.

But that was the least of Eddy's problems. Ginny Jones's phone call had just opened up a whole new can of worms.

"Guys," Eddy said, "we've got a problem."

Alton kept his arms tightly folded across his chest. He was afraid if he didn't hold himself contained, he'd fly to pieces. Ginny was in danger, and it was his fault. All his fault, for sending her to Sedona.

He'd known there was more than one vortex in that Arizona town, but he hadn't even thought of the demons using one as a passage from Abyss to Earth's dimension. No, all he'd thought about was getting Ginny away from Mount Shasta and the demon invasion here, but this community was probably the safest one around for now, especially with the three of them keeping things under control.

He glanced at the headless mannequin lying in the alley. *Well, moderately under control.*

This was not good, but the problem in Sedona sounded

even worse. Family pets with glowing eyes and multiple rows of razor-sharp teeth? Loving animals suddenly going berserk and attacking their owners? It sure sounded like demon possession to Alton, and he knew the others agreed. Until today, they'd thought demons could only animate things of the earth—ceramic or stone, concrete or clay. Plastic was essentially more of the same, just a different material, but taking on living creatures as avatars took a lot more power, showed more intelligence.

Ginny could be in terrible danger.

BumperWillow whined. Alton looked at Dax and Eddy, and realized they were staring at him too. All three of them. What had he missed?

"Well?" Eddy slapped her hands down on her hips.

Alton blinked. "Well, what?"

She rolled her eyes. "Are you going? Is there a passage through the vortex that will get you to Sedona now so you can check on Ginny? My best friend's in danger because you sent her there."

He cringed. "I know. Yes, there's a passage, and yes, I'll go."

Eddy's sudden smile hinted at something more than mere concern for Ginny. "Be sure and pack some extra clothes," she said. "You might be gone for a while."

Eddy's dad, Ed Marks, gunned his old Jeep up the last steep stretch of dirt road. He'd offered to take Alton as far as he could up the rough flank of Mount Shasta, but they'd just about reached the end of the road. Alton knew he still had a good hike ahead of him to find the portal.

The way was steep, the ground slippery with loose rock and scree that often meant slipping back two steps for every step forward, so the ride this far was welcome. Plus, he enjoyed spending time with Ed.

It shouldn't have surprised him, how much he liked Eddy's dad, but their close friendship had been an unexpected bonus. Alton figured it was as much his need for a father figure who treated him with respect as the fact Ed was just a hell of a nice guy. His own father still hadn't accepted that he was an adult, a capable man able to make his own decisions. Ed saw Alton as a warrior, a brave companion to Dax and Eddy.

And he treated Alton like a grown man, which might have been silly under other circumstances. As an immortal, Alton was already centuries older than Ed Marks, something that didn't seem to bother Ed at all.

He wondered if his own father would ever see him as anything other than a disappointment? What would the ruling senator of the Council of Nine say if he knew his son's sword was now sentient, that Alton had proven himself as a warrior?

Fat chance of that ever happening. Now that he had a Lemurian death sentence hanging over his head for helping Dax and Eddy escape from their prison cell, Alton had to accept the fact that going back to his world inside the volcano probably wasn't going to happen.

Still, it was something to dream of—his father learning his only son had actually accomplished what no other Lemurian in recent history had done—he'd established communication with his crystal sword. Even though the story of Lemurians as warriors and demon fighters was a huge part of their history, no one alive now could actually remember anyone strong enough or brave enough to bring their sword to life.

Yet Alton's sword spoke to him. Respected him enough to communicate, sword to Lemurian.

In fact, he was the only Lemurian alive today who'd actually taken part in a battle with a weapon other than words. While his people took pride in being known as philosophers and statesmen, they'd lost their fighting edge—the very qualities that had kept their society safe for so long.

Just as they'd lost their strongest allies—their sentient, speaking crystal swords. The sword each young man received when he came of age had become nothing more than a fancy ornament.

Crystal swords had no reason to speak to men they didn't respect. Why talk to a warrior who didn't know how to fight and wasn't willing to risk his life for something of importance?

Alton had not only risked his life, he'd discovered an inner strength he hadn't known he possessed. He'd proved to both his sword and himself that he was a warrior, one willing to die for a cause he believed in—protecting the known worlds from the threat of demonkind. All of them—Eden, Earth, Atlantis, and Lemuria—were at risk from the encroaching evil of Abyss.

The danger of reaching a tipping point, of the ages-old balance of good and evil finally slipping over to the dark side, was still very real. Thank goodness the demon invasion of Earth had barely gotten under way before the Edenites recognized the threat and recruited Dax, a fallen demon, out of the void. With his borrowed human body and Willow by his side, he'd become the perfect leader in the fight against demonkind, against a demon king powerful enough and smart enough to lead the demon hordes to victory.

Gaining strength by the hour within his stone gargoyle avatar, the demon king had almost won. Dax's brave sacrifice and Eddy's strength and determination in the face of certain death had bought a temporary victory when Eddy'd courageously risked death by wielding Alton's crystal sword.

The demon king was gone, for now. But he'd be back.

Had he resurfaced in Sedona?

Alton stared at the trees they passed and thought about Dax and Eddy and the love between them that seemed to grow stronger each day. He'd be jealous if he didn't love both of them so much. Eddy was brave and true, and Dax, a man who had begun as a demon, had shown more integrity and good than anyone Alton had ever known in Lemuria. Dax and Eddy deserved the immortal love they'd found with each other.

So why did that make him think of Ginny Jones? She was nothing like Eddy Marks. Nothing at all. Ginny was mortal, her life no more than a tiny blip on his life's screen. Plus, she was stubborn and opinionated and had no respect for a woman's place—a woman's role as the helpmate to her man. Not that Eddy was anything like the Lemurian women Alton had known, either, but she was Dax's problem.

Did that make Ginny his?

The engine revved up and the Jeep's wheels spun as forward motion ceased. Alton glanced at Ed.

The older man shrugged. "This is as far as I can go, Alton. You'll have to hoof it the rest of the way." He slipped the gears into neutral but left the engine running. The trail wound upward from here, climbing through the last of the trees before it crossed areas of slippery scree, the shattered stones that littered the sides of the dormant volcano above the tree line.

Alton climbed out of the Jeep. He checked his scabbard to make certain his sword was secure, grabbed his pack, and slung it over his shoulder. "Thanks, Ed." He glanced around, orienting himself. A harmless-looking pile of rocks lay beside the road.

Harmless now, but they were the remnants of the gargoyle that had become the avatar of a powerful demon. Eddy had destroyed the avatar with her singular act of bravery, but she'd missed the demon's soul and it had escaped back to Abyss. Unfortunately, it could still return to create havoc on Earth.

Alton shook his head. "Hard to believe this is the same place where we fought the demon—and almost lost."

Ed sighed. "I'll admit, I've never been so afraid in my life. For myself, for my friends—the image of that monster twisting Dax's body and throwing him to the ground still wakes me up at night. I never thought I'd see the boy alive again." He cleared his throat, wiped a hand over his eyes. "The truth, though? Mostly, Alton, I was afraid for my daughter. Her bravery astounds me, even now."

Alton reached out and shook Ed's hand. "We don't need to worry about Eddy. She's a lot tougher than she looks."

Breaking into laughter, Ed threw the Jeep into gear. "That she is, son. Now you get. I'm worried about Ginny. She doesn't know what we went through here, so she doesn't have any idea what she's up against. You go take care of that girl." He winked, turned the Jeep, and headed down the hill.

Alton watched until the Jeep disappeared into the forest. Then he started the long hike up the hill. The mountain might be the vortex, but there were only a couple of places where he could cross into the other dimensions and access the portal that would take him to Sedona.

Or the one that led to Lemuria.

No. He couldn't think about home. He'd made his choice when he helped Dax and Eddy escape from their Lemurian prison cell. He'd walked away from everyone and everything he'd known and loved his entire life, but he'd chosen for the greater good.

He wondered if his friend Taron had had any luck at all convincing the council to join the battle against demonkind. That was Alton's only hope of ever going back home. Taron could be persuasive, but were his powers of persuasion a match for the council's stubbornness?

The sun had moved to the west by the time Alton paused in front of a mass of tumbled boulders and knew he'd reached the portal. He wrinkled his nose against the stench of sulfur.

There shouldn't be any sign of demons here, but their smell was all around him. That made no sense. He'd closed the portal to Abyss.

Unless they'd managed to open a new one.

Alton faced the lichen-covered rock, but before he stepped through, he removed his sword from his scabbard. As he wrapped his fingers around HellFire's jeweled hilt, he realized how much the sword's sentience had changed things. He no longer felt alone—not when he had HellFire beside him. Addressing the crystal blade, he asked, "Do you smell their stench as I do?"

The hilt vibrated in his hand. "I do," the sword answered. "I'm ready."

With a nod, Alton stepped through the portal, walking through what appeared to be solid rock. The dark cavern he entered glistened with the light from the various gateways leading to other dimensions: the green and turquoise that led to Atlantis, the gold and silver that would take him to Eden—and certain death should he attempt to pass into that hallowed land.

The portal glowing gold would take him home, to Lemuria, a land where he'd always been welcome. Now, were he to attempt to cross into Lemuria, he feared he faced death as surely as if he'd tried to enter Eden's sanctuary.

Facing Ginny Jones and a whole passel of demonkind sounded a lot safer.

Alton turned his back on the gateway to his home world. The one that had once led to Abyss was still sealed shut. Why, then, did he smell the sulfuric stench of demons? Where were they coming from?

He held his glowing sword high and used the light Hell-Fire cast to search along the stone walls. A small portal, tucked into a nook toward the back of the cavern, glowed with the colors of a setting sun.

Sedona. He recognized the multicolored hues of red rock

and blue skies, but swirling within the portal's depths he sensed something else.

Demonkind.

Demons had passed this way, and not so long ago. Were they somehow making their way from Abyss to Sedona, and then north through the connected vortexes to Mount Shasta? He'd have to ask Eddy and Dax about that.

After he got to Sedona.

He touched the cell phone Eddy had tucked into his pocket and wished it worked within the portals, but Eddy'd explained to him how they needed towers to carry the signal, and there certainly weren't any deep inside the volcano.

Alton took a step toward the portal, but he caught himself, pausing in midstep as a dark mist slipped through the multicolored gateway. Silently it flowed along the wall toward the portal leading to the flank of Mount Shasta.

Demon!

His sword vibrated with power. Alton swung. The crystal blade connected with the black mist and it screeched and burst into flame. Crackling and sizzling, it disappeared in a puff of smoke, leaving only the stench behind.

Alton stared at the spot where the demon had emerged. A shiver raced along his spine. This one had come directly from Sedona. His heart gave an unfamiliar lurch. Ginny was in Sedona—and so were the demons.

Demons powerful enough to take on living creatures as their personal avatars. Creatures strong enough to kill.

Holding his sword aloft, Alton stepped through the portal.

"Who'd you have to call?"

Markus's question snapped Ginny out of her convoluted thoughts. "Eddy. I called my friend Eddy Marks."

"I hope it was important." Markus backed out of the parking place he'd taken at the supermarket. Without Tom. The vet had insisted on keeping the cat for observation, which suited Ginny perfectly. Damned cat had really chewed up her hand. She peeked under the bloody towel and wished she hadn't looked.

"You were gone so long I had to take Tom into the vet by myself."

Ginny scowled at him. Her hand still hurt like the blazes and not once had Markus thanked her for risking life and limb while catching his stupid cat. "Well, Tom is your cat, cousin of mine, and I would really like to get back to the house so I can clean up the mess your *sweetheart* of a cat made of my hand."

Markus stared straight ahead. "Aren't you gonna ask me what the vet said?"

Ginny shook her head. "I figured you'd tell me if he had any idea what happened."

Markus curled up one lip and made a snorting noise. "He says they're all possessed. I knew he was into crystals and vortexes and all that New Age stuff, but I thought it was just for show. He's dead serious."

"Possessed? By what? The ghost of Christmas past?" Ginny stared out the side window as Markus drove the few blocks home. *Possessed.* It sounded totally unbelievable, but how else do you explain a cat with four rows of teeth, glowing red eyes, and a scream like a banshee on meth? A scream that sounded horribly familiar.

Since her memories of that crazy night in Evergreen had begun to resurface, Ginny'd had the sound of the bear's ear-shattering scream in her head. A scream that was nothing more than a louder version of the strange howl coming from Markus's fat old cat.

Had the bear been possessed? Had some sort of evil entity turned a concrete statue into a slavering, screaming killer? Something made it come to life. She hadn't imagined

the damned thing, though she'd thought it was just a weird
nightmare.

But all those animals at the vet's—the birds and bunnies,
cats and dogs—every last one of them had acted unnerv-
ingly similar. Screeching, trying to bite, flashing those rows
of sharp teeth, and staring out of glowing eyes.

Possession didn't sound all that crazy when you took it in
context with what they'd seen today.

With what had attacked her just a few days ago.

Markus drove the car into the driveway and pulled into
the garage. He shut off the engine and turned in his seat to
glare at her. "You're making fun of it now, Ginny Jones, but
how else do you explain all those animals? They weren't
normal. Birds don't have teeth. Rabbits don't hiss and snarl
and screech like that little bunny we saw today. Something's
making them act crazy. If they're not possessed, what's going on?"

Without waiting for an answer, Markus got out of the car
and slammed the door. Ginny sat in the front seat for a few
minutes, thinking of Tom and the other animals they'd seen
at the veterinarian's clinic, thinking of the concrete grizzly
that had attacked her.

Thinking of Eddy's friend, Alton. Why did she know he
was the reason she couldn't remember anything? Now that
she was away from him, the memories were coming back.
She recalled him saving her from the bear, walking with her,
even laughing with her.

Most of all, she remembered his kiss.

What she couldn't remember was why he'd kissed her—
or why she'd kissed him. One thing she knew for certain—he
was the only reason she'd come to Sedona.

None of this made sense, and Eddy hadn't been much
help, either. She'd merely said to hold tight, that she was
sending someone, but she wouldn't give Ginny any details
about who or why or what the hell was going on.

Muttering under her breath, Ginny rewrapped the bloody towel around her hand and followed Markus into the house.

Covering vast distances via the vortex was more disorienting than moving between dimensions, but the 1,030 miles between Mount Shasta in northern California and Bell Rock in Sedona, Arizona, took less than a minute down a dark tunnel lit only by HellFire's crystal light.

The sun was beginning to set when Alton sheathed his sword, passed through the portal, and stepped out on the rocky ground near the top of Bell Rock, one of many vortexes in and around Sedona. He stood for a moment, lost in the glory of a desert sunset and the brilliant red of the rugged, wind-shaped bluffs. The gentle breeze seemed to sing to him—a deep hum that resonated within his—

"Where the hell did he come from?"

Alton spun to his left and blinked. Row after row of men and women, most of them wearing loose robes or colorful skirts, sat cross-legged in the dirt.

Meditating?

Well, crap and nine hells. He'd materialized out of solid rock, right in the middle of a yoga class.

Straightening to his full height, Alton pressed his hands together beneath his chin and bowed his head. His waist-length blond hair, unbound, flowed over his shoulders like silk and he knew his full seven feet of height, aided a bit by his boots, made him look pretty impressive.

With any luck, his appearance alone might help him get out of here without too much trouble, considering the audience.

"I come from within." He kept his voice unnaturally deep and bowed his head once again. Then, biting back a powerful urge to laugh, he looked straight ahead and walked past the rows of stunned yoga practitioners.

Popping out of the portal in the midst of an evening meditation class hadn't been an issue the last time he was here. Of course, it had been awhile—give or take six hundred years.

Obviously, he really needed to get out more.

Alton found a well-traveled trail that took him down off the mountain and into a parking area. The light was beginning to fade and only a few cars and one old, beat-up looking bus remained. He figured the bus must be here for the group he'd surprised up on top.

Maybe he could catch a ride into town with them . . . or not. Grinning at the thought of Lemurian royalty hitching a ride on an old bus painted with rainbows and flowers, Alton set his backpack down and pulled the cell phone Eddy had given him out of his pocket.

He carefully followed the steps Eddy'd shown him, found Ginny's number, and pushed the button to connect the call. He almost shouted when Ginny answered on the second ring, but he managed to control himself.

"Is this Virginia Jones?" he asked.

There was a long silence. Long enough that Alton wondered if he'd done something wrong.

"Who's this?"

Nope. That was Ginny. "This is Alton. Eddy Marks's friend."

"How'd you get my number?"

Definitely Ginny.

"From Eddy. Ginny, I'm in Sedona. Would you be able to come get me?"

"Sedona? How the hell did you get to Sedona so fast? I just talked to Eddy a couple of hours ago, and there's no way you could have come—"

"I'm here, Ginny, and I'll explain everything once I see you. I'm in the parking lot at Bell Rock. Do you know where that is?"

"I'll be there in fifteen minutes. And you'd better have some answers for me because I've definitely got questions for you."

Before he could answer, the line went dead. Alton stared at the phone for a moment before calling one more number. Eddy's voice mail came on. He left a message and wondered where she'd gone, why she hadn't answered the phone. Then he tucked it in his pocket and leaned against a rock. Folding his arms across his chest, he waited impatiently for Ginny while the night grew dark around him.

I met my vampire lover on a Wednesday.

I almost missed my destiny that day by oversleeping, but if I had missed it, wouldn't *that* have been my destiny instead? Usually I take the bus to work, but since I was late I drove my Mini to the lot next to our building in downtown San Francisco, resigning myself to the hemorrhagic rate of three dollars every twenty minutes. At lunchtime I'd move to a cheaper lot. After parking in a half-space that could only have accommodated my elfin vehicle, I stopped to watch a sailboat glide under the Bay Bridge. Sun sparkled on the water, the boat, the bridge, and the bikini-clad woman lying on the sailboat's deck—a picture worth framing. It was the second Wednesday in October, the time when savvy tourists come to San Francisco because they know it's when we have our best weather. Since playing hooky on a sailboat was not an option, I consoled myself with the promise of lunch at an outdoor café. Little did I know it would be the last time I'd be enjoying sunlight for quite a while.

I revolved through the door of 555 Battery and waved to

Clive, the silent security guard. The elevator was packed like the Tokyo subway, so I opted to walk the three flights to my office. Letters etched into a wavy glass wall in the lobby proclaimed the owner of my labor as Hall, Fitch, and Berg, Advertising. We were also known informally as HFB (and sometimes as Heel, Fetch, and Beg due to our reputation for doing anything to acquire an account). If a jingle pops into your head spontaneously while you're cruising the supermarket aisle for soda pop or laundry detergent, it's probably ours.

The administrative assistant, Theresa, was standing outside her cubicle nibbling a fingernail. She ran to meet me, her three-inch heels clicking on the polished concrete floor.

"Oh good, Angie, you're here. The clients will be here in fifteen minutes, Lucy's still not here, and Kimberley and Les are in Dick's office waiting for *you*."

"Lucy's still not here?"

My boss, Lucy Weston, had missed the last two days of work without notifying anyone. This was out of character for her, but not unheard of at HFB. Last year, one overworked account supervisor had gone out for coffee and sent her resignation from Puerto Vallarta two weeks later. So no one had taken much time to worry about Lucy, as we were all busy trying to make her absence invisible to the clients. I had been in the office until eleven o'clock the night before, working on the Unicorn Pulp and Paper account, which was why I had overslept.

Theresa shook her head. "No, nobody's heard from her."

"So is somebody going to call the police today?"

"Mary from HR is going to do it, but she's trying to find any friends or family to call first, to see if Lucy told anyone where she was going."

I was harboring a secret hope that I'd get to do something around a client besides play stagehand for Lucy, so I had to admit to being somewhat grateful for her absence.

"Which room are we using?" I walked toward my office with Theresa following in my wake.

"Nobody told me anything," she answered. "Lucy usually arranges the rooms with me."

"What rooms are available?"

"Hammett is being used. Kerouac and Ferlinghetti are open."

"Kerouac will do. Pull down the projection screen and set up some snacks in there, okay?"

"What do you think they want to drink?"

I couldn't resist the obvious answer. "How about some fresh blood?"

Theresa laughed dutifully and veered off toward the Kerouac Room.

I made this quip because our new clients were vampires. Macabre Factor consisted of a twentysomething Goth couple who were into the vampire club scene in San Francisco. They started out creating makeup that they used on themselves; chalk-white base tinged with blue, fine-tipped red liner to outline the veins in the neck, and fake fingernails in shades of green, gray, and blue. But when they showed up with real fangs and topaz eyes friends and admirers began clamoring to buy their products. Thus a business was born, with cosmetics manufactured in Sweden, contact lenses from China, and a dentist in Los Angeles with an exclusive contract to manufacture custom fangs that attached to your canines like dental crowns.

I rushed down the hall to my office. All of the account executives have real offices, as opposed to cubicles, which makes us feel very grown up, but every door has a narrow glass window next to it so our bosses can check up on us as they walk by.

For two years Macabre Factor concentrated on selling only to their own kind through their website. But they had recently decided to expand their client base, and with many of the highest rated shows on TV this season featuring an un-dead creature of one sort or another, the market research showed that they had picked the perfect time. I wasn't sure where the capital was coming from, since Macabre Factor was a small company, but it was going to be a big launch.

This morning we were going to pitch our preliminary ideas for their campaign. Had Lucy been here this morning my job would have been to show up early and set up my computer as a backup in case Lucy's went on the fritz, fol-low along as she gave the pitch and supply any details she might have forgotten, and make sure everyone's coffee cup was full. But I had done a lot of the background work on this account, so with Lucy absent I was hoping Dick might let me manage the meeting. It occurred to me that if anything bad had happened to Lucy I was to feel awfully guilty. In fact I already did.

I threw my coat over the Aeron chair and shoved aside the pile of illustrations that I had been going over last night. The logo for Unicorn Pulp and Paper was a unicorn surfing on a ream of copy paper and we'd been choosing a personality for the new iteration. There was a classical unicorn, a chubby unicorn, a mean-looking unicorn with a drill-like horn, and an angelic unicorn whose horn resembled an upturned ice cream cone. In my dreams last night the mean unicorn had skewered the angelic unicorn like a shish kebab.

When I turned on my computer the screen was cluttered with files, just like my desk, and the floor behind my chair, so I wasn't surprised when I couldn't immediately locate Macabre Factor. But after I did a search for it and turned up empty-handed, that was when I really began to panic. I'd spent five years working as an actor before starvation drove me to the ad business and one of my biggest fears then was forgetting my lines, imagining myself staring into the foot-lights like a stroke victim. This was the ad agency equiva-lent.

I opened my e-mail and began searching through the two hundred and eighty three messages in my inbox. We'd e-mailed the Macabre Factor illustrations back and forth dozens of times between Accounts and Creative but my e-mail showed no evidence of it. At this point I started having another creeping feeling. This one was suspicion. I allowed myself to use a curse word that I was raised never to utter, but I was alone and in this case it was justified.

I might have accidentally deleted a file, I could admit to that. But I did not go through two hundred and eighty three e-mails and trash every one pertaining to Macabre Factor. No, it was clear I had been sabotaged.

Dick Partridge's office was three doors down from mine. I knocked and went in without waiting for an answer, since I was already late. As VP of Consumer Product Advertising Dick had earned a large corner office with windows facing the turning cogs of progress in buildings across the street. It wasn't a view of San Francisco Bay, but it was much nicer than my blank wall. He also had space for a round table and four chairs, which was where I found Dick, Les, and Kimberley.

"Good morning, Angie," Dick said, looking at his watch conspicuously. "I trust you have a good reason for your dilatory behavior, so let's leave it at that, shall we?"

We'd have to, since I had no idea what he was talking about.

Dick Partridge talked like he had cotton balls in his nose and a stick up his you-know-what, using the longest words he could find to express the simplest ideas. Today he'd made the unfortunate choice of wearing a pink Oxford shirt. He looked like a pimple ready to burst.

Next to him, writing industriously, was Kimberley Bennett, my fellow assistant account executive. She was also my

roommate, although we never came to work together because Kimberley kept earlier hours than I think is healthy.
Kimberley looked like Hollywood's idea of an advertising
executive: blonde hair (fake, but not so you'd know) to her
shoulders, big blue eyes, and an hourglass figure. To complete the image she wore skirts so short and heels so high
she looked like she was on stilts. The black A-line skirt I was
wearing ended sensibly at mid-calf, grazing the tops of my
black leather boots. No sense competing when the game is
fixed.

Les Banks, the graphic artist, looked up from his Black-
Berry to give me a nod and a smile. Because Les was a "creative," he was allowed a laxity of attire that would never be
tolerated in the account executives, who are known as the
"suits." Today he was wearing black jeans and a black T-shirt
adorned with a grinning skull. His buzz-cut brown hair revealed a perfectly oval head, both ears sported gold hoop
earrings, and he had a tiny rectangle of facial hair under the
lower lip, which, when I first saw it, I thought was the result
of neglectful shaving but later realized was a fashion statement. I secretly thought Les was quite good looking. In boring meetings I would sometimes fantasize about what his
half-inch long hair would feel like rubbing over my stomach.
I managed a smile for Les, despite my misery.

"What did I miss?" I tried to sound peppy.

"We just convened," said Dick. "As you are all aware, the
clients are arriving instantaneously. We probably should
have postponed, but of course nobody could have appre-
hended Lucy's absence. Speaking of which, I'm sure no one
wishes to arrogate her duties, but if she's not back by tomorrow we're going to have to discuss an emergency distribution of her clients. I've already set a meeting for ten o'clock
in the Ferlinghetti Room. Which we'll cancel if Lucy sur-
faces, as we trust she will. So, Kimberley and Angie, I guess
this will be your chance to fly solo. Are you ready?"

Kimberley jumped in before I'd even opened my mouth. "Oh, yes, Dick, the presentation is completely ready."

"Well, I would certainly like to attend, but my presence is required by a major client," Dick said. "So you three are going to handle Macabre Factor this morning."

Kimberley batted her eyelashes at Dick. "Dick, since Lucy isn't here, someone is going to have to take the lead. I'd like to volunteer. I coordinated the market research and I'm the most familiar with the account. And I've got the presentation right here on my laptop, ready to go."

Kimberley was the most familiar with the account? I cursed silently, but I couldn't really blame her. We had both been laboring in Lucy's chain gang for months; of course she would be plotting a break out as well. The only difference was that she didn't care if there was collateral damage. But there was nothing I could do without making myself look like a faker, a whiner, or a tattletale.

I looked at Les, expecting him to be claiming his free ticket to the ladies' mud wrestling show that was about to begin, but he was busy digging dirt out of his fingernail with the cap of his pen. I made a mental note to myself to stop fantasizing about him.

Dick didn't miss a beat. "I suggest you handle the presentation conjunctively. Two heads are better than one." He waved the backs of his hands at us. "Well, go ahead. Mustn't keep the clients waiting. Although since they're vampires, I suppose they are *immutable*." His arch delivery indicated a joke, so we all laughed. Kimberley grabbed her laptop and rushed out the door.

In the hall I saw Les walking in the wrong direction, to the Creative Department rather than the Kerouac Room.

"Les, aren't you coming?"

He turned around. "Listen, Angie, I'm swamped with another account. Do you think you could do this one without me?"

His expression was plaintive. I had never noticed before that his hazel eyes were flecked with dark stripes, like a cat's, but with him staring so intently at me I couldn't miss it. Most of the people in Creative were chronically behind, the mark of an artist being asked to work in a widget factory. Les, however, had never asked me for special favors. I wondered why he was starting now.

"Yes, all right, but only if you promise to keep your phone on in case they have any questions that only you can answer. Is that fair?"

"I owe you one. And Angie, please don't tell Dick I didn't show, okay?"

"Okay."

He surprised me with a brief hug before dashing down the hall.

When I arrived at the meeting Kimberley and the founders of Macabre Factor were already there, chatting amiably under a photograph of a cloud of cigarette smoke with Jack Kerouac inside it. Although I knew their legal names from the various contracts we had signed, Douglas and Marie Claire Paquin, they insisted on being called by their *noms de sang,* Suleiman and Moravia. These vampires didn't seem to be the daylight avoiding type. Even though it was nine a.m. they were as bright-eyed as game show contestants.

"Good morning, Suleiman, Moravia." I hurried to say, "I'm so sorry to be late."

"No, please, do not worry about it," Suleiman answered, as he bowed over my hand. "Theresa made us very comfortable."

Suleiman's accent was British plus something else, possibly Indian. His black hair was slicked back from his slightly receding hairline with a shiny hair gel, probably the one from their line called "Sleek." His eyes were dark and thick-lashed and his skin was olive-toned. His outfit was straight out of *Hedda Gabler*: a pinstriped cutaway frock coat, pais-ley vest, and a red silk cravat secured with a pearl tie tack. He was unusual without being over the top, and despite my better judgment I was intrigued. I also wanted to know where he bought his clothes.

Once, when Lucy had referred to the clients as "the vam-pires," Moravia had corrected her.

"We don't say 'vampires,' we refer to those *in the vampire lifestyle*."

Since then we always used the politically correct term, at least to their faces. I assumed the vampire lifestyle meant dressing in black, frequenting night clubs, listening to Goth music, and drinking Bloody Marys. Although I'd never been to a vampire club, I felt I understood something about their chosen lifestyle. Taking on an unusual persona gives you an entrée into a world that is glamorous and different from your own mundane life. You can easily recognize who belongs and who doesn't. I can't count the number of late-night, cof-fee-driven conversations I've had with other actors about how much different (and better) our world was compared to the nine-to-five one. Of course, I recanted those statements when I couldn't make my car payments, but I still under-stood that need to feel special.

"Will Lucy be joining us this morning?" Moravia's breathy voice interrupted my reverie.

Human Resources had already told us yesterday that until we had some definitive answer about Lucy's whereabouts we were to simply say Lucy was "unavoidably delayed."

"Lucy was unavoidably delayed this morning," Kimber-ley answered. "But Angie and I can't wait to show you the great concepts we've prepared for you."

Moravia nodded and leaned back in her chair, giving me a view of the tops of her breasts, perfectly round and the size

of small cantaloupes. Her cleavage could support a pencil
upright. She bore a close resemblance to Elvira, Mistress of
the Night, who appears in display ads (not ours) in liquor
stores every Halloween. Her long black hair was parted in
the middle and worn loose down her back. Her face was an
artful display of all of her company's wares, with translucent
white skin, black-rimmed eyes that could give Cleopatra a
run for her money, and juicy red lips. Moravia might have
been plain if you caught her just out of the shower, but then
you probably wouldn't be looking at her face. The two were
the perfect spokesmodels for their brand, and that was the
pitch.

Kimberley projected the first illustration, of Suleiman
and Moravia in a red Ferrari convertible driving out of a
Transylvanian-style castle on a mountain. Suleiman was
smiling at Moravia while she laughed with her head thrown
back, her hair blowing in the wind. Both were wearing sunglasses and had visible fangs. Moravia's dress was classic
Vampira, with jagged-edged sleeves, while they'd put
Suleiman in a playboy smoking jacket. The caption under
the picture read: "You're going to live forever. Make sure
you look good." Below that the words "Macabre Factor Cosmetics" dripped down the page in a spidery Gothic font.

The rest of the illustrations had the same combination of
style and campy humor: the couple at a Hollywood-style
party, toasting each other with glasses of red liquid; skiing
down a mountain dressed in bright parkas, red lips sparkling
against the snow; in the stands at the horse races, shielded
from the sun in huge hats. Kimberley ran down the campaign logistics—the magazines, the websites and blogs, the
rollout in select cosmetic and department stores—and I
helped her the same way I helped Lucy, filling in relevant details and statistics.

Finally it was over and we were silent. Now was the moment of truth.

Please turn the page for an exciting sneak peek of
Jess Haines's
HUNTED BY THE OTHERS,
now on sale at bookstores everywhere!

Long, delicate fingers caressed the stem of a wineglass, trailing upwards to catch a few small beads of condensation on the glass. Sultry eyes the color of the sky during a summer storm bored into me from across the cloth-covered table, with all of the woman's not-inconsiderable powers of compulsion behind them. I knew what she was trying to do, which didn't make it any easier to resist.

Taking a deep breath, I forced my gaze away as nonchalantly as I could to look through the bay window beside our table. Staring at the rippling black waters of a little man-made pond, dotted with reflected lights and a single white swan, beat falling into a black enchant by looking into Veronica's eyes. The bird floated, serene and oblivious, as a laughing young couple threw bits of bread at it to try to lure it closer.

Swans were pretty but vicious if you got too close. Much like my dinner companion.

She was still waiting oh-so-breathlessly for my reply. With a sigh, I dragged my attention off the sights outside and back to the mage, careful not to meet her gaze directly.

"Look, it's not that I don't need the money, but I don't kill vampires for magi. First and foremost, I'm human. I can't compete with you guys. Second, I'm a private detective, not an assassin. Not to mention that it's still illegal to kill vamps without a signed warrant."

It took every ounce of willpower I had not to look into those overbright eyes and change my mind. Hey, I hated vampires as much as the next human, but I wasn't about to go *hunt one down* like a crazy person and get myself killed. My job was scary enough without adding angry vampires to the list of stalkers trying to get a piece of my hide to make up for the grief I caused them.

"Shiarra, I'm not asking you to kill him. Just," Veronica paused, her persuasive tones trailing off into a throaty "hmm" before she continued, "just find out what he's up to. Detain him if necessary. Find the location of a little trinket for us. My coven will take care of the rest."

Her cherry lips curved in a smile more predatory than any vamp's, her pinkish tongue darting out to run suggestively along her upper lip once she noticed that was where my attention was focused. God, I hate magi.

In the back of my mind, I wondered darkly why Jenny, our receptionist-slash-bookkeeper, had set this appointment without checking with me first. Belatedly recalling that she went over the bills with my business partner on a regular basis, I realized she must have decided the need to pay our bills outweighed my likely moral outrage. Under any other circumstances, the moment I found out a potential client was an Other, I walked. Jenny knew this. She also knew that since money was so tight, I'd probably at least agree to hear the mage out.

After finding out what she wanted, though, I was starting to regret agreeing to stay through dinner.

"I know I made the news with that whole Were incident at the Embassy last month, but honestly, that was my first run-in with supernaturals. I don't have the experience or the equipment to deal with vampires."

I tried to sound reasonable, though I was afraid I was coming across more testy and frightened. This woman really put me on edge, though I tried to tell myself it was what she was asking me to do, not the aura and crackle of magic surrounding her, that did it. Maybe it had something to do with her coming on to me? Either way, I didn't like it.

"Frankly, I don't think you could pay me enough to put my life on the line against a vampire. Shouldn't you be getting a half-blood? Or another mage to deal with him?"

Little furrows appeared between those perfectly shaped brows of hers. Her hair was a lovely mahogany shade that didn't quite match the dark brown of those eyebrows, framing her delicate, oval face. I hated that she could pull the look off so effortlessly. My hopelessly curly red hair would never look as sleek and sophisticated as her artfully careless 'do. It was probably spelled to look that way.

"The Ageless would know us for our magic. That wouldn't work at all. A half-blood would kill first, ask questions later. Same with a Were." She paused, thinking. "Unless, of course, he killed them first."

I leaned back in the chair, crossing my arms over my chest. "Not really helping your cause here."

The woman started tapping her perfectly manicured nails on the table, leaning back as she eyed me anew. Something in that look told me wheels were turning and her plans were changing. Uh-oh.

"A human is our only chance. You have no taint of magic, no scent of change on you. You also now have some familiarity with, and have proven yourself capable against, supernaturals."

For a moment, Veronica's lip curled faintly in a sneer, venomous but gone almost as soon as it appeared. I would have missed it if I hadn't been staring at her lips and nose, avoiding looking directly into her eyes. Her features resumed that intent, predatory look that told me she was only barely hiding her contempt for the lowly pure-blood human, doing what she could to put me on edge. Sadly, it was working.

"As I said, we do not want him dead, just watched. You can get close without fear of injury, since he has plenty of willing donors and is known for his restraint. The worst that could happen is you being banned from his places of business."

It was my turn to tap my nails. "Aside from an abrupt, painful death, that *is* the worst thing that could happen to me. Alec Royce owns half the nightclubs and restaurants in the city. Those are the places I go to track my marks."

I glanced at my watch in an effort to give her the hint that I wasn't going to stick around much longer for this crazy talk, even if she was picking up the tab.

She gave an overly dramatic sigh, no longer hiding her annoyance. She dropped the sickly sweet tones she'd been affecting and finally put a cap on the damn aura she'd been exuding since this dinner started. No wonder the waiter hadn't come to refill our glasses in almost an hour.

"Shiarra Waynest, you forget yourself. The other half of the city belongs to The Circle, and we are more than prepared to compensate you. Fifty thousand, plus expenses, and an extra ten thousand if you find what we're looking for. Five thousand up front, and your pick of equipment from The Circle's own security vaults. We'll give you protection, and more work if you do well at this job."

I sat back, speechless. Five grand to start? My usual take only came out to two thousand, sometimes up to four if the job was tricky or somewhat dangerous. Plus equipment? Expenses? Maybe this really *was* a godsend in disguise. I wondered if she might know that I had debt up to my ears and a car payment that was killing me. Plus I think my PI license was about due for renewal, and let's not forget taxes coming just around the bend. Mental note: get Jenny a very, very nice thank-you card and a bonus.

Taking my stunned silence as a bad sign, Veronica narrowed her eyes and threw another bone on the table. "Is that too little? Fine, make it ten if you get the information, and another twenty if you find the location of the artifact."

Lifting my napkin up to my mouth to hide the fact that I couldn't snap my jaw shut, I took just a moment to close my eyes, take a breath, and remind myself that I'd be walking right into a death trap if I took this job. I thought bleakly about the stack of bills that seemed to grow larger every day. Most unsettling was the one from my landlord that had appeared in my mailbox a few days back. I hadn't quite been able to bring myself to open it yet. My cut of the deposit for this job would be enough to cover the demands of my landlord, and maybe a few of the other creditors demanding a good chunk of my income.

"Well?"

Though I couldn't help but feel I was betraying something inside myself, something important, I gave her the words she wanted to hear, however grudgingly. "I'll do it. What is it I'm looking for?"

Veronica leaned back in her chair and smiled grimly, a sly light in her eyes. I really hoped I would live long enough to regret this.